GHOST RIDER

GHOST RIDER

A Novel

B.D. James

Writers Club Press
New York Lincoln Shanghai

Ghost Rider
A Novel

Writers Club Press
an imprint of iUniverse, Inc.

For information address:
iUniverse, Inc.
2021 Pine Lake Road, Suite 100
Lincoln, NE 68512
www.iuniverse.com

Whilst the author has made every effort to trace the owners of copyright material, she will be pleased to rectify any errors or omissions in subsequent editions.

ISBN: 0-595-26534-0

Printed in the United States of America

Dedication

The Requiem theme of this novel makes it a perfect one for dedication to those friends and family members who are no longer with us:

my grandmother, Stephanie (+2002)
Anthony Burgess, Monaco (+1993)
Andrew Burgess Wilson, his son, London, England (+2002)
Bruce Walker of Channel 9, Perth, Australia (+2000)
Warren Jones, also of Perth (+2002)
Tiny (+2001)
Elio de Angelis of Rome, Italy and Cap Ferrat, France (+1986)
Leo Loudenslager, Thompson Station, USA (+1997)
Margarete Lenser (+2000)
Werner Egk, Inning, Bavaria (+1983)
Gilles Villeneuve, Berthierville, Quebec (+1982)
Ingrid Bergman, London, England (+1982)
the victims of wars and torture everywhere, including those who took their own lives

A thousand years ago
five minutes were
equal to forty ounces of fine sand
Outstare the stars: Infinite foretime and
Infinite aftertime: above your head
They close like giant wings, and you are dead.

—Vladimir Nabokov

The past is dead, and all that was good
is buried with it. And here's this thick
horrible door of the present with its
tantalizing keyhole. You can press your eye
or your ear to it, but you can't turn either
into a key.
The past goes on inside, that perpetual party,
becoming wilder and wilder, but there's no
admittance.

—Anthony Burgess

When physical exhaustion drove me at last up to
my solitary bed, I would lie awake and breathless
—as if only now living consciously through those
perilous nights in my country, where at any moment,
a company of jittery revolutionists might enter
and hustle me off to a moonlit wall. The sound of a
rapid car or a groaning truck would come as a strange
mixture of friendly life's relief and death's fearful
shadow: would that shadow pull up at my door? Were those
phantom thugs coming for me? Would they shoot me at once?
At times I thought that only by self-destruction could
I hope to cheat the relentlessly advancing assassins
who were in me, in my eardrums, in my pulse, in my skull.

—Vladimir Nabokov

Thank You:

To my husband, family and friends. Especially to my mum, for countless hours of proof-reading in small coffee shops. My grandfather, for treating me to five weeks' bed and breakfast stay on a real farm, so that this book could be written. My grandmother, who came to collect me at the train-station, sometimes in the middle of the night, after research journeys to all corners of Europe. My husband, Phil, for keeping everything in order, manuscript wise and home wise.

As ever, Anthony Burgess who taught me writing and music. Peter Churchill, host of Eurosport Europe's showjumping program, for his assistance on the showjumping courses of Europe. All the riders who kindly allowed me a glimpse behind the scenes of their world, especially Helena Weinberg, John Whitaker, Leslie McNaught, the Beerbaum brothers, Jan Tops and all the others too numerous to list. Also all the stable grooms, course builders and behind-the-scenes people who shared their insights with me. For information given: amnesty international and various torture victims rehabilitation centers, in Europe and the United States. All the refugees from Latin America and Eastern Europe, for sharing their painful experiences with me. The city of Salzburg for special access to Mozart's birth house. Paul Phillips of Brown University, Rhode Island, Department of Music, for help with the coronation concerto. David Lynch, not only for Angelo Badalamenti, but also for showing in his movies that disjointed images can make perfect sense. The Schoenberg family of rural Bavaria for allowing me to witness their pig slaughter ceremony, distasteful as it may have been. Michael and Nicole and George at TAS, for their new-age insights.

Acknowledgements:

Russian Love poem, freely adapted from Pushkin, with special thanks to A.K.

One—the traveling life

Long after her memory had wandered through dusty holes of rooms where his image still lingered like an ancient ally, she saw him again, the faintest traces of his scarlet silhouette hesitating doubtfully like the remnants of a mythological scenery. Escaping the overfilled streets that were the unfortunate result of an Europe-wide, uncontrolled immigration policy, she had fled for solace to her television, searching for intricate human interaction where none could be found.

Alone with her television, she could partake intimately in the dramas and joys of others' lives. She welcomed their little ejaculations of pure emotion, which were transported through the television screen without necessitating to offer a word of comfort or to join into someone else's laughter at times when her own emotional funds were low and perhaps she would have rather practiced dying.

The interaction with her television was entirely one-sided, shielding her from curious eyes while allowing her jump into whatever spectacle the program guide had to offer. The countless, nameless faces on screen spoke freely of their joys and woes but when they started boring her, she could change the channel without the bother of finding an appropriate word of exit and whoever had displeased her was gone, leaving her free to peep into another life.

She could choose between joy and tears, horror or delight, a nature show or a visit to a discotheque in Rome. Owing to the wonders of satellite television she could even choose the language of the people on the screen. A decision was to be made between British or American English, French, Spanish, Italian, German, and even Turkish.

On that particular day, it seemed hardly feasible that she would see him again. She was sitting in luxurious surroundings in her hotel on Lake Geneva, forming a comfortable alliance with her red-velveted, antique chair and eating the finest food room-service had on offer. Served on a platter of sterling silver, for instance, was a miniscule slice of duck liver mousse, for the price of forty dollars. Her pure-bred Pekingese, a champion show dog she had laid down in excess of four thousand dollars for, sat by her side as she flicked through the channels of the hotel's television and forked liver mousse into her mouth not too passionately. In hopeful anticipation of a slice of duck liver, the bushy beast droolingly wagged his bushy tail at her fork and said *snnnnrrrr snnnnnnrrrrrrrrrr*, in the typical snore-manner of the Pekingese breed.

As the cause of her erratic channel flicking she could offer the genuine fact that she traveled a lot and had cultivated a certain independence of soul having grown increasingly tired of new faces or voices as she listened to their endless, new life stories or told her own, in skillful narrative, to infinite ears for infinite times, over and over and over.

One day, an embitterment of affection had caused all the ears and faces and life stories to fade into one giant blur and after that she was no longer enthralled by the prospect of meeting interesting people who would listen with interest to her interesting story in order to repeat it while performing an interesting dinner conversation during an exceptionally boring evening with their own, less interesting friends. She was drained by the travel and her constantly changing surroundings that came with her work as a writer of cheap romance novels that bestsellered at airport stores, mail orders, fat-woman-frequented supermarkets and were in reality piles of bound paper filled with inky blots of nothing. The staleness and dust of her love stories might insolently crowd the library shelves, making her more money than she would ever be able to spend on optimizing her fleshy bosoms, yet the broken bones of their literary merit could not be denied. She was tired of discussing her text-chopping editors or her purified, sickly heroes, and of the great flow of letters from her fans.

In new cities, she increasingly opted for the anonymity of her television screen that never asked questions, never made mindless remarks without being instantly punished through turn-off, and was a far better friend to a weary traveler than the endless array of new faces that kept entering her life to ponder, chatter, mutter and growl without cease.

Two—murder of the Turkish peasant woman

She had just watched the ending of a kurosawaish movie on Turkish television. Although she could not understand the language, she was moved by the pictures she had seen:

> A beautiful woman, from her dress a peasant, had fought a gang of men. Driven by hunger—there could be no mistaking their motive—they had invaded her house to steal a meager piece of bread that the woman sought to save for her children.
> In the ensuing battle the children were struck down with an axe, as was their mother. The men looted the house of all food, but one suddenly changed sides and tried to defend the woman, resulting in him being struck down, too.
> The scene changes: the men have left. On the floor, we see the woman, clinching among her stiff fingers the meagre piece of bread whose upper half has been torn away and whose insides vulgarly

spill forth like the blood-drained intestine of a wounded man on the way to his own funeral. The camera moves its angle and we see the children, their little hands twitching in final death spasms. The bloodcaked-faced man who had tried to defend them drowsily drives his body to its feet.

The only one who does not move is the peasant woman. Her hair flows softly around her angelic face as the camera closes in with its greedy lens, directly into her dead, defiantly staring eyes. Like an accusing river, a trickle of blood runs slowly down her forehead, scattering timidly on either side of her finely swung nose.

She will never move again. She is dead, over a piece of bread for her children that had destined her for a funeral with square-and-pinched-faced mourners.

The credits now begin to run slowly, over her eyes and her unmoving face, as we learn the Turkish creator's, director's and actors' names of this sad story. The dead Turkish peasant's eyes keep staring, accusingly and unblinkingly, through the letters on the screen...

...into her luxurious hotel room.

The dead eyes haunt her with their stare and it does not matter that the story was not real nor that the actress who had made such cunning use of her eyes would soon be received into another character to become absorbed by another story. She knew that stories like this were happening in the world outside her hotel room, where mortuary chapels of small hot countries filled daily with scrambling mourners for scattered victims of hunger whose discolored eyes would never see again. Worse, those stories were happening not too far from where she had just shared a slice of duck liver mousse with her expensive, snoring Pekingese dog.

Three—Enter the Rider

Trying to erase the memory of the Turkish woman's eyes, she continued flicking through the channels. *Click.* A German talk show. *Click.* An Italian song contest. *Click.* A French ad for easy-spread, herb and garlic flavor cheese. *Click. Click.* Each click brought her further from the Turkish woman and she started running from her, trying to leave her behind in a maze of screens, channels and cables. She began to click faster until the frames moved by in a croaking, rapid blur and she was no longer able to distinguish languages or pictures, until...*click*...Wait a second. *Click* back. No. Not here. It must have been another channel back. *Click.* Not here either. *Click. Click.* Ah...here!...until she saw the horses.

The frantic clicking stopped, the memory of the Turkish woman faded into nothingness as she greedily absorbed the images of the majestic, noble animals. How she had once feared these parcels of concentrated power with their sheer, shiny muscles; how she had come to love them, following her first encounter with a silky nose. She still remembered their bodily solace, above carefully placed hooves, as they carried her trembling weight around the ring during her first riding lesson. The gentle beasts brought her to near ecstasy even now, as she watched their perfectly polished bodies leap over enormously-sized hurdles with an astonishing grace as could never be reasonably expected from such an imposing body mass.

She forgot about her dog, the duck liver, even about the Turkish movie and placed her hands over the left side of her chest, as remedy for the untoward malady her heart suddenly displayed when it began to joyfully dance inside her chest, venturing beyond the rider on screen whose leaping horse the camera followed with an expert eye and whose every move the presenter skilfully commented. A sheer impossibility that she could find her soul's contentment in a society like this, but with a dangerous show of force she made a fool of herself, in the privacy of her hotel room, as a strong thumping in her chest forced her to close her eyes to the leaping beast in the ring and follow her tachycardia-ing heart that scattered about, seeking *him*.

The remote control fell from her hand, thudding on the floor as she flew into the image on her screen with but one set of thought inside her pathetically misty heart,

Was he there?
  Would she find him?
  Would she see him again, sooner than she had expected, at least on her television screen?
  If he was indeed participating in this competition, had he already ridden or would he still appear?

Her waiting turned to impenetrable anxiety, at the source of which lay the regrettable fact that her heart, eagerly exploring the stable corridors, the warm-up area beyond the show ring, the rider's canteen, could sense everything but see nothing. What a nuisance that, having made acquaintance with his nobleness, it had to go in search of him. Now she could feel him near but she did not know whether her heart could be trusted with this information. So long as she allowed herself to think of him, her heart would feel him near whether he was near or far, and at the thought of him give off an odor of sweat despite a chilly season. Warmed by the image of his memory and connecting with him through the broad shadow of its desire, it would create and recreate the precise sensation of being beside him, even if he were a thousand miles away.

Did he know that she was firmly planted before her television, waiting for him? Had he any idea that, today, she would be watching him? What if he knew that her flicking finger had stopped for him?

Idiotically, her lips began to form an urgent prayer, for him to appear. She had been raised a Catholic and took prayer very seriously. Especially in situations of emergency, prayer was always a deliberate act, never a diversion and now an urgent flow of words crawled off her lips, toward a God whom she sincerely hoped to be benign and listening.

Four—Ghosts and advice

She recalled the words of Franz Liszt, written over a century ago, as an expression of tender solicitude to Marie d'Agoult. Liszt had written that all life mattered not for youth, nor pride, nor desire, but for its content of love and that a life devoid of love was overshadowed by a sadness and despair of dangerous depth, at the end of which stood certain death.

Over the years, Liszt had become one of her closest friends, highly esteemed for his silence and his one-sided friendship, where he disposed freely of his advice whenever she had need, sharing his deepest secrets without attaching the chains of friendship nor expecting her to give up her own secrets in turn. Never fearing his influence, she had come to trust Liszt and often sought him out in his writings, where he had built a bridge between their two worlds.

She had since long understood that Liszt's talent did not restrict itself to music but expanded to a profound understanding of life itself and she knew that he had been right in warning about the dangers of a life lived without the diversion of a good and solid love affair. Had she known where to reach him, she would since long contacted him to admit that she, too, had been walking in the shadow of the very same death he had written of, the kind of death looming in absence of genuine love and passion. She wanted to tell Liszt of the times she had felt death's cold embrace on her pulsating skin, his seductive stroke with a pale marble hand down her cheek, of the many times she had walked so closely with death that she had almost come to believe his promise of peace and joy beyond the grave and had almost allowed herself to take his hand and follow him into his mysterious world, recognizing only at the very last moment that only bloody fools will die for love and only bloody fools will die of sheer obstinacy, in a childish attempt to punish life for the absence of music in their hearts.

But now death's hold over her was temporarily broken; the arrival of the Rider had torn her from the tranquil sky of Liszt, Chopin,

George Sand and all the other dead writers and composers to whom she was more attached than to any living man. Suddenly there was a different interpretation of life, it was dim and cloudy no more. Because *he* was here, she would fight to remain in a world she had fervently rejected, not so long ago.

His smile had drawn her back into life, warming her cooling heart in the secure knowledge that a man as extraordinary as he was alive in her time and that greatness was not exclusively to be found among the shadow people hiding their winged thoughts between the yellowing pages of parched books, who may have preserved their lives to bridge the gap between one century and the next, but who could not deny that they had lived their time and were *gone, gone, gone,* leaving behind only their words as a reminder of the profoundest of all human tragedies, that no matter how brilliant, how deep, how beautiful or how beloved, everyone is destined for the ashes, their lives but one short glimpse on earth's back, a flea scratch perhaps, a desperate refusal to be swallowed by the ever advancing night, a final outpouring of illustrated words onto blank pages in the hope to leave behind at least one thought, an emotion, a love…and then, blackness—distributed through space and time, a soul that was here today is gone forever, lost in a land of no return that has always been the same for all the cultures and religions across the world, its destiny the insane hope for a glorious, crystally-sharp white light.

To die courageously was the best she had hoped for, or to fill the mere glimpse of matter, in the eyes of space and time, that she had been allocated with at least one noble action before she would be gone like those were gone who had walked before her. Perhaps she would be carrying with her the memory of a beautiful sunrise, an ocean wave's friendly lapping to a sandy shore…as final images of a life whose book had been closed before it was ever truly written. But there he was and all life was suddenly filled with significance, regardless how short, because he was living, breathing, walking across the same world. The Rider was a brilliant mind, an exceptional soul who, unlike her friend Liszt, was not imprisoned among the pages of a creased book but was very much alive, in the same time as she.

Five—about love at first sight

Unable to remember the color of his eyes, she clearly recalled the colors of his soul but would naturally never admit such a corruption, since *soul* had become a dirty, unlawful word in the fast-moving, fast-loving modern world she inhabited, where external values were extolled…age, looks, height, eye color, hair color…

How much money does he earn?
How does he earn his money?
Is he from a respectable family?
What kind of car does he drive and is it an expensive one?

She did not ask nor seek answers to questions of that kind. She cared little that he looked older than his years and she never wondered about his financial status, his clothes or his make of car. Straying directly beneath the masks he wore, she saw only his solid heart and intricate depth of thought. Like many wise men he wore a coat of noble solitude, not forcedly through exclusion from society, but by self-elected preference. Bypassing the words he spoke to her, she had studied his face and seen the wounds of time planted there, sharp tracks of broken dreams and shattered hopes, and memories lapping softly around his heart like muffled flutes. In his exquisitely shaped face she read that he had once known a kind of love to make sense of all life, however brief, turning fear into strength, but had stood by helplessly as it crumbled into nothingness inside his desperately grasping hands, where it died shamefully even as he sought to contain it in his breaking fists. The corpse of that love now lived beside him, sharing his bed, his home and his life, its cold ashes that had once, burning, warmed him at night now chilled him to the very bone and their lingering embers' glow had spread a shadow of hopeless apathy about his features, forcing him to accept, at last, that life was not the beautiful song he had dreamt it to be. But she also saw that long after having attended the funeral of his most cherished dreams, he kept alive a stubborn hope.

His eyes said that the fast traveling life with its cheering crowds and frequent victories had once brought him joy but was now a chore turned noisy routine. He increasingly abhorred the loneliness of ever new cities, hotel rooms and admiring crowds of strangers who patted his horse and wished to know, their sweat-soaked damp hair hanging in wisps around their eager faces, how he could ride so brilliantly. Amidst the admiration, he had withdrawn to live deep inside himself and he did not often laugh. A sad albeit perpendicular man, who had been disappointed by the great expectations he had once held, he was unable to comprehend how his life had become a mere imitation of the passionate dream he had once dreamt. Not long ago, he had still been a daring adventurer, dreaming great dreams and asking daring questions of the very source of life itself. Now he relied on false friends who, slowly and with metallic clearness, drained him of his life, causing him to all but shed his noble coat of solitude for one of helpless isolation. There, he dwelled surrounded by suddenly fragile walls that had once been of steel and turned to glass under her gentle, steadfast eyes.

Having entered without resistance, she stood in the secret chambers of his heart, boldly looking about herself, and realized that she would never march home again. He was a brother, lover, or a friend...a kindred spirit at the very least. The recognition opened before her a life of unknown possibilities, but it also caused her to retrace her steps in haste and tear herself out of his heart without a word of warning as she bolted from his secret self with the bight conviction that she should have never entered there. Far-fetchedly, she firmly believed that they would meet again, one day.

She tore herself out of the memory, back into her hotel room, with the picture of her final exit; she had his address in her pocket and his image in her heart. Now she watched him ride on her television because God had answered her prayer, understanding the great need that formed part of her devastating attachment to him. She was grateful that there was nobody to observe the infantile movements of her heart, which had been conquered by the mere sound of the Rider's speech. She still recalled every word he had ever spoken to her, and watching him she realized that she held the key in the palm of her hand to turn the ashes of his life into a flame once more.

Six—Exeunt

Her heart walks by his side in silent embrace, for the time she can still see him on the screen, calmly preparing to love him when they meet again. Emerging swiftly through the wood of lingering confusion, her fingers practice their journey down his exquisite cheek. Her mouth prepares for the first kiss on his lips, her palms rehearse the gentle journey down his back in a moment of instant mutiny. As she watches him on her screen, the promise of loving him keeps her alive, although he is not a handsome man and his best years have been given to someone else, although he has been spent in the fight for his dreams, has lost his fight and no longer cares. Still, she wonders whether he thinks of her, at times, or has forgotten the candles of her eyes without a passing thought. In his eyes, she reads that he has at last confronted the truth of man's slow march toward the grave and that he asks himself, now that time is getting short for him, whether he has taken the right road or could have turned, here or there, to walk another path. She knows that he has always explored the abyss of abominable twists and turns that life can bring and that he would like to laugh again, one day, because the longing for a happy life still burns on, brightly, inside him.

As he leaves the ring at last and the proud, brown beast beneath him moves its splendid muscles in the setting sun, the camera lingers a moment too long on his *exeunt* and she realizes that she already loves him but will never tell him. She knows that he will die alone,

one day, still imprisoned by his walls that had turned to glass for her. Perhaps then, she would tell him that she had loved him and could not go to him. But at night, she sleeps in his embrace, at night, when the dreams come...

The End

CHAPTER 2

One—not a poor man, but full of foul memories

Some lives resemble war parties and some lives resemble peace parties. In the latter, reality and dreams interweave, clasp firmly to each other and unite with a shudder to start afresh after an intolerable ending. Tired of all the staleness and dust of a war party life, she decided on a peace party because she could not let him die for nothing or end his lucent journey inside her heart, just like that. The lumpish *fine* she had foreseen was not fitting for a man desired with such urgency.

She waited until she had met him numerous times in her dreams, where she slumbered safely in his arms night after night. When he was no longer a stranger invading her through a process of narcissistic evolution but had become familiar to her as a dancer returning always to the same lover when his dance is danced, when she had imagined him naked and in dinner jacket, jeans, shirt and shoes, when she knew from her dreams the smell of his cologne his aftershave and his talc, when their love had turned into a harmony of wills where he met her joyfully each night on the nether side of her sleep, extending his arms toward her perfectly molded breasts, she sought him out again.

Despite her assumption to the contrary he proved to be rather wealthy, monies he had accumulated from his frequent victories with his horses that had turned the poverty of his childhood into a bad, distant memory. In a small, dark corner of his considerable estate, his lips found hers in the impeccable style she had, at night, often imagined. His body was superb. He drew her to his magnificent chest, kissing her shyly at first, then bolder. Her dream, that for unwillingness to relinquish its embrace had kept her in bed long after the sun had passed the sky's midst, humbly receded in view of such a glorious reality. There was a sudden sunburst inside their heads as their bodies touched in healing, aromatic warmth and life took on an entirely different meaning.

He left his wife of twenty years, a frumpy short woman, with harsh lines on her face, drawn there during long years when she had labored her husband out of poverty. Beneath his humble roots lay a hard farmer's life and the memories of short, cold nights, when he had lain in his bed shivering for lack of fire wood to heat the small room he shared with two of his five brothers and when he could not sleep for the hunger gumming his intestines to the inside of his stomach walls and had dreamt of bacon, deviled kidneys and two fried eggs as his version of paradise. His childhood had contained flour-water soups, bitter tears over a cow dying whose milk the family depended on, and the desperate uncertainty overshadowing each sunset as his mother kept laboring behind the stove and his father grew older and grayer in the fields by the day, with his back more bent as he turned the hay year by year. The bleak memories of life's harsh indifference toward the simple man had caused him to seek sanctuary on the backs of his horses from their periodic prosecution. Even today, his heart palpitated when he thought of the hell he had been living that he had only been able to extract himself from through to his brilliantly amazing talent with the horses.

By fortunate instinct, he had known that life at the top was clearer. If not happier, at least the air was cleaner, the food healthier and the living space wider. In the despair of poverty he would die, this much he knew. As a young man, his heart had often ached with the threat of an impending coronary attack, in protest over the miniscule rooms reserved for the farmer's children, his lack of privacy, and the simple minds of his own people who would never be able to understand him. At the end of the working day he read Marlowe and Seneca and they, wide-mouthed, small-eyed and gate-toothed, sought their happiness in a bottle of ale, a piece of bread, a plate of pickled cabbage and some cheese. While he spoke, alternately, of the meaning of life and of great men of letters, they spoke of bringing in the next crop and they were hardly glittering in wit.

They slaughtered a pig with unfeeling hearts, thinking only of the price its meat would bring, and he hid in his room, mortified, having witnessed the unfortunate pig's deafening screams of fear, the thuggish, bullish hitting of its forehead with an ax, the cutting open of its trembling, twitching throat, the crimson gush of blood as its screams grew thinner, the throwing of the twitching pig into the trough and, finally, the skinning of the still whimpering, living animal. He had watched with great terror when his silent father had poured big, brown buckets of boiling water over the pig as life drained from the panicked animal, to facilitate picking the bristles from its shuddering skin. The long-term effect of that scene was an irreversible estrangement from his father, to whom the pig's life had meant nothing, and his mother, who had stood by watching, without the slightest sign of pity, and had quietly begun to whip the blood that had collected in one of the large buckets reserved for that purpose. His parents came to represent a cold world where people could be caused to do terrible things for money, without regret or feeling, their lack of money already having hardened their hearts beyond repair. That kind of world scared him, all the more if it were to be lived in surrounded by poverty and rough-hearted people like his family.

The instant he looked into the pig's mortified eyes, he had understood that a life of wealth, at the very least, represented the freedom to leave the farming life and to choose his own company. Single-mindedly, he had pursued his dream of leaving the alien group of people he had been born into. He rode purposefully and with iron determination, having discovered his talent when one day he was given a gray, not too ornate, gelding from the track that, having proven itself too slow, had been destined for slaughter. He had taught himself to ride it from full-page photographs of high-jumping horses, learning how to wrap his legs around the horse's slender body and to leap with it toward a dream of his own name. His parents commented that he had chosen the wrong path but that at least he had dreamt the right dream.

He had been surviving many a hard fall on his way to the top, during hard years when the frumpy woman with the mousy hair had borne him four children and they had shared a derelict hut where she had raised their offspring on what little money they had left after his horses had eaten and he had paid for their transport to the next show. There had been times when food was so scarce that she stayed with him not out of choice, but for having become imprisoned by their very poverty, when she had not even dared dream of jewelry or of fine clothes. The hardship had worn away at the foundation of their love, causing fine cracks in their unity as his wife lost her careless laughter and became like a sister to him or a mother or a companion. One day, he no longer touched her with passion but with familiar and slightly indifferent tenderness. A barrier of unspoken words and dying emotions stood between them as his wife turned from the young girl he had once desired into a short, frumpy woman with a thick face and stocky legs. He began to look with different eyes at his fresh-faced groom, a girl of barely seventeen, not yet acquainted with life's harsh realities. She grew closer to him than anyone else because she traveled everywhere with him, helping him on his horse and becoming the one familiar face by his side to share his triumphs and his failures. Her simple mind never understood the complex webs that his thoughts wove, but at least she was there and her breasts were firm. At night, he sometimes dreamt of taking her after a horse show, in a dark corner of the stable, when everyone else was gone, but in the morning he awoke ashamed of his sinful sinning desire. As degrading as he recognized the rules and restrictions of religion to be, he had been raised a Catholic and was haunted by visions of hell and eternal damnation, as punishment for even the thought of marital infidelity. Caught between his passions and his vague dreams that he could frowningly taste in his mouth like sour meat juice, he lived and died each day.

Two—visions of the future

When at last *she* appeared, she was a flower in his barren land, where victory chased victory but had ceased to matter and his hopes had long ago been buried under the thundering, black-nailed hooves of his horses. The sun shone again in both their lives, turning them into a road that grew steadily hillier and greener as it took a definite swing toward the light. He stripped away his memories of yelling crowds and his solitude and his clammy isolation disappeared as he spoke to her, surveying his most secret thoughts until he no longer had the impression that his body wanted to sag under the stress of an unhappy past whose scars were etched into his mind.

She felt privileged that *he*, with his graying temples and his thinning hair, his fine nose and his indulgent eyes, considered *her* to be the key to his happiness. His elegance of movement was reminiscent of a Concorde Airplane gliding through the sky as his heart burst wide open allowing her to trace the serpentine saga of his life with its wonder and its violence and its flavorful desires. He needed her, like a man drifting in a wide, open sea needs his yellow life-belt. Like children, they ran hand in hand over the sandy banks of tropical islands framed by luscious palm trees and clean surf, laughingly playing beneath coconut trees. He stated that he had never been happier and the violent enemies of his past came to be laid to rest, as fellow heroes in the story of his life, whom he no longer needed because he now shared his life with her.

As often, when he drew close to a desirable woman, he began to feel humble and somewhat unworthy. Her slender body was delicious, he could not understand what she saw in him, when she could have had any other man, or what precisely his qualifications had been to awake such a fantastic passion inside her well-fleshed breasts. Her passion seared his heart with guilt because his reflection in the mirror showed him only a shadowy, little man who knew how to ride horses. Although he realized that he should not be thinking such things, he could not help wondering when her bidding for his heart would stop, and treason and treachery follow.

One day, she had explored every hidden cave of his withdrawn self and had held him in her arms for many a passionate, tender night. Behind them lay the memory of seven happy years, filled with her loving him. That day, she asked herself why she had married him and openly wept as she looked at the history of their love together, finding not one memory when he had disposed words of comfort or encouragement to her. There were only memories of *her* comforting *him* whenever his forehead had been lowered in anticipation of life's newest blow. Walking through the fields of their memories, she encountered all the times when he had told her with an appreciative glance how glad he was that she, sweet thing, understood him without words, because he was just not good at saying things and it was ever so fine that she was satisfied with his chaste kisses and understood why he never brought her roses nor told her that he loved her. That day, she recognized that all her years had been spent making him happy. One morning, she woke up beside a balding little man who never smiled and never spoke. It was the morning she left, following years of having given her love with fine generosity. As she walked out the door he snarled that he had always known she could not be trusted.

When she looked into their joint future, she saw them caught in their own apprehensions. Their love, even as it was being born, already resided in a home for the immobile cripples of their respective pasts. She knows she cannot carry him for the rest of his life and decides to foreclose on the years of happiness because of the outcome she has envisioned. She will never call him, or land his heart ashore. Putting her arms around their rough, brown bark, she whispers to the trees that she loves him and still embraces him every night. In the morning, she rubs her wet cheek and catches the image of his face at the threshold of another dawn, but they laugh and love only in her dreams...

The End.

CHAPTER 3

One—but there is hope

Following the cursory run over their joint future, she suddenly changed her mind, declining to follow her original plan, on a warm summer's night on Lake Geneva where she had set off for a little trip on a charming steamboat. Watching the sun set over the distant *Matterhorn's* snowy summit in brilliant bloody-orange colors, she became a different person as the Alps reflected its final glow and the sky changed into gradual, dual blue, leading to the kind of sublime black of night that is an intrinsic merit of Alpine nations. As the little boat's bow plowed its way through the darkish waters of the lake, she understood, as through a heavenly flush, that she had never loved except in her books. What was the use, she wearily wondered, if she kept inventing the most charming stories, where chivalrous men of great strength drew true blood as they gloriously conquered the seductress of their dreams, when in true life her years flowed into each other like an endless river as she wrote on and on, until her own words surrounded her like a grave and people she met were of interest only as possible characters for her next book. It was the lingering nature of her illness as a writer, she sighed, cursing her pen point, a sheer cross to be blessed with an intellectual heart.

That much she had learned, that time seems to stand still only in early youth, when a year is forever, but its river flows increasingly faster with advancing age and catches everyone in the end, bringing not mock-killings but certain death. It would catch the Rider, too, whose image was still clearly imprinted inside her mind. There would be feigned regret and mourning from his fans and real mourning from her. Why had she such an unhealthy appetite for him, the silver bit of his horse, his frayed leather boots? Since meeting him, she had bled her desire on every blank page that came before her, filling it with his face, his eyes and her every memory she had of him.

Following the boat trip, she had spent the next day, from ten in the morning until half past two in the afternoon, with her Swiss friend Charlotte, a handsome woman with very good hands and illuminating eyes, and then, from four to six, she spent two hours on the train, watching the countryside pass outside the windows, with its brilliant green fields and its glorious cows, but thinking only of the Rider and wondering whether he would magically appear if she were to wish for him strongly enough.

Two—cowardice at St Gall

The train pulled into the station of *Zurich Central* and she looked out her first-class window, at the people on the platform. Watching their scurrying to and fro, their urgent faces, their self-important lives, she wondered, could he have been anyone? Why not this one, over there, with a country air about him, who had a certain similarity in looks but was taller, laughed more freely and whose nose was shapelier? Why not open her train window, right now, and call him over, to offer him her unconditional love? But it could not be this one, nor that one over there, nor the handsome stranger with the German accent who now entered her compartment and informed her with a voice of liquid velvet that he was a visiting physician attending an important conference in St. Gall. It had to be the Rider, nobody else. Faces were responsible for the souls that they clothed and only his face had spoken to her.

When the train had left Zurich, a wondrous thing took place, as good a thing as she could have written in any of her prose. They had passed fields and admired lake-reflected, sun-setting spectacles over clean, little villages. Her time had been spent dreaming beautiful poetry into lush green fields outside her window, where she had meditated the Rider's face a hundred times into the setting sun. Then the compartment door opened and a young man had entered, nodding his head in greeting. Although she was rather ignorant of medical matters, she could see that he almost instantly began with the study of an electrocardiogram graph and she indulged herself by reading it also, across the space that separated them, for he had taken his place in the row of seats opposite her. He appeared masterly and when he noticed her observing his materials, he offered an explanation, that he was a cardiologist preparing for a lecture at the university of St. Gall, where he currently resided, although he worked at a hospital in Zurich.

"Ah", she replied and settled back into her chair to continue letting her eyes wander over the cultured countryside outside the window, traversing field after field with a solitary, purposeless glance, in the hope of ordering matters inside her soul.

When the cardiologist suddenly sneezed terribly, *haaaaaaatschiiii haaaatschiiiiii*, she offered a polite *bless-you*. That was when her eyes fastened on, and quickly gabbled over, the headlines of a newspaper that lay, creased and greased, by his side, the local *St Gall Morning Star*. She asked him to borrow it and spent a mere two seconds wandering up and down the columns until she had ascertained that the city was preparing for a horseshow this very weekend and that the gates would be open from Thursday morning at nine. Her watch confirmed that Thursday was tomorrow, that *he* would be riding she saw from the starter list published in the newspaper.

Her hands trembled fiercely as she wondered whether, by the power of her wishes alone, she had succeeded in bringing him to the very town her train would be entering in another 20 minutes. Her mental heaven must be of revolutionary strength, she mused, to cause the Rider to appear the moment she had imagined him. She applauded past decisions to improve herself mentally, but then discarded that thought as nonsense and, in a peculiar kind of humor, thanked the man upstairs for conspiring with her to enter into sinful shamble, breaking up a man's marriage that had by all appearances since long become devoid of expectations.

About thirty minutes later, the train pulled out of St Gall and she was still on board, much maligned, her flaming heart thumping angrily inside her chest. She had an air of inverted deliberation as she very flatly pointed out to herself that this would have been the wrong moment for meeting him again and that (*she thought this with a smile of sour affection*) a man like he was wrong for her, in any case. Staring fixedly out the window, she suddenly saw a hellish winter scene; the delicate rays of summer had disappeared on account of her having failed to act on the information in the cardiologist's newspaper. *He was wrong for her? Why was he wrong for her?* She lay the burden of proof on herself, asserting that her vision of the future could under no circumstances be expanded to include the capturing of a horse rider's heart.

In her travels, she had seen dying children of Third World Countries. She had seen men, handsomer and nobler than the Rider, mowed down in the fields of senseless wars. She had seen the tears of these men water the earth as their lives ebbed away in silent shudders reminiscent of the death spasms of a glorious butterfly caught inside a spider's web. She had seen valiant men smile their final good-byes at the sun as the blood drained from their bodies, and in their eyes, before they turned glassy and forever sightless, had stood the longing for one more day, one more hour even, of life. She knew very well that the Rider, wealthy, privileged to have grown up in a world of physical safety, living at the center of admiration from countless people around the world, had not been subjected to a sufficient taste of contrasts. Perhaps it was true that he boozed with ruff and gruff men in Italy and Spain and France, but he deserved no pity, nor her comforting arms, which were better lain around the shuddering shoulders of dying men in Colombia or Peru. If she had to love a man outside her books, a real man made of flesh and blood, then he should be a freedom fighter with passionate eyes and a glowing zeal for improving the lot of the poor. Together they could lighten the yoke of his people and under the shadow of death they could bravely fight until the crowds would grow to adore them for their passionate dedication and eventually recommend them for President of State and Country. One day, the people of his country would stop dying their senseless deaths, because of her love for whatever freedom fighter she would pick to shower her attentions on.

Let the Rider wrap the adoration of his fans around himself like a shielding coat, she thought dramatically, let him dry his tears with the purple velvet of his mantle of privilege and let her return to the arms of the Dying of far away worlds! She knew that the Rider's mild life was a sham. And yet, knowing that he was devoid of compassion for the dying children of Latin America and that his energies went not into building hospitals for the world's poor but were expended soaring on the backs of majestic beasts over hurdles that the man before him had already cleared, to determine whether he could do it faster, knowing about the futile content of his life, she still could not stop her desire for him without knowing what dawn or doom awaited her beyond the gateway to his heart.

Three—Riders and Race Drivers

Was he in reality but a 'dream, borne of a distant and forbidden desire? Now that she thought of it more clearly, she realized that he reminded her of a ghost she had once loved. That ghost had rewarded her for her courage of crossing the threshold between his world and hers with a pure love that forever after she sought to recreate with a living man. Perhaps she hoped to have rediscovered, in the Rider, the ghost who had stolen her innocence.

Enter: Memory of the Ghost

She is fifteen years old and barely that. Since the blossoming of her womanhood she has been admired by many, but allowed none to love her. Her heart is still of virgin desire, young and fresh and innocent and kind. Two days after his death, she met the ghost who was to become her first love. He had exited his young life unexpectedly and she had watched his demise, live, on her television screen, as though it were a game. Television had featured prominently in her life, even then. She had first met him during the nightly news hour, on Channel 10. He had been a rally driver, partaking in the Paris-Dakar, and his car had been catapulted high into the air, saltoed, and then had ejected him at a speed faster than the camera could follow, although it kept its eyes on him as good as possible as he flew through the air, then thudded onto the streets of a small, cobblestoned French village in the bright June afternoon sun. The fortunate little village had made a killing from tourist dollars forever after, instantly becoming a famous place of pilgrimage for rally fans from all over the world who flocked to France almost at once, eager to see the place that had claimed the life of one of their most admired drivers. She had had no interest in rally racing but channel flicking had already been an annoying habit of hers, in the days when her writing had been too poor to warrant publication and had been a mere pastime, to be engaged in when the light was too bad to read or when she impatiently awaited her new order from the library because she read between twenty and thirty books per week and required constantly new supplies.

Flicking the channels that day, she had unexpectedly come across the image of a man flying through the air without parachute, having been ejected from a green-white car. Like a smudge of fluff, she saw him tumble once or twice through the still summer's air, grotesquely silhouetted against the background of a romantic French fishing village, then he hit the cobble stone with a sickening thud and remained there in an outrageously twisted position. It had been her first time to see someone die. Sitting on her heels, she watched with near-disabling terror as the accident was repeated a second, then a third time. The third time, the camera wandered over the final segment of the race with dramatic deliberate steps, before showing the accident once more in very slow motion to give the viewers their ultimate thrill, with the camera zooming in for a close-up. Over the images came the pasty voice of the commentator, who apologized slyly that it had not been possible to get an even closer frame of the flying, dying man's face, one that could have perhaps shown the precise instant when his neck had snapped—*as we have just learned, ladies and gentlemen, from our chief reporter who is at the scene of the accident right now* (the commentator spoke from the air, seated in the helicopter, where the camera showed the entire rescue operation from above), *the neck snapped between the second and third vertebrae.* But even if showing the event had been possible, the commentator added sorrowfully, the actual *snap* could not have been heard (*our reporter has been informed by the doctors on the track that there is an audible snap as the vertebrae break*) because the microphones had regrettably as yet not reached a sufficiently advanced state of technology to transmit such a fine sound over distance.

"But there is always a next time," the host gaily announced, promising that the next rally accident would certainly not be too far away and by then, he would make certain to position his crew at a more favorable angle, to offer a more exciting instant close-up, complete with sound.

She had promptly switched the channels in disgust, but not before learning that the flying driver was still alive, albeit seriously injured, and that he had been flown by life-supporting helicopter to a hospital in the next biggest city where one would wait and see whether he was to survive the night. The faceless driver meant nothing to her and yet he meant everything because it was the first time she truly understood the fragility of life. Not until the live drama on her television had she grasped that dying was not just an old wife's tale, reserved for the bent and wrinkled at the end of their long, fulfilled lives. For the first time, she realized that young people could die, who were not yet withered. Having watched the live dying show on television, she understood that the driver was in a very real danger of changing in one night, from a living, breathing, maybe even laughing young man, into a corpse destined to lie stiffly in its narrow grave. She envisioned his hands, folded neatly over his livores-sprinkled chest, covered with shovel-fuls of stinking crumbly earth, and, a few months hence, the young driver swollen and in decay, with white fat maggots sharpening their teeth before feasting on his eyes and crawling between his fingers to peel away the pale flesh with their disgusting fish mouths, his meat falling from the bone in dark-gray strips, until ten years later a bare skeleton would remain, ready to dissolve into dust.

Following this horrifying vision of his future, she grew very afraid for him and wanted him to continue living at all costs. She hoped for him, all through a sleepless night, as she tossed and turned amidst her sweat-soaked sheets trying to construct his unknown face. *Was he brown-haired, or blond? Did he have wrinkles? A beard? Glasses? Was his hair curly or straight, his nose fine or coarse? His eyes narrow, like a rat's, or set wide apart to provide him with a noble view of the world?*

Despite her hoping, she had learnt the following afternoon through the radio, that he had died from his injuries. Her thoughts went *oh my God, oh my dear God, it is not possible, oh no* and *Lord have mercy on us.* Although she could not recall his name and had never seen his face, a black shroud of imminent danger lay itself around her, obscuring her from the warming rays of sun. Night darkened the summers of her young life from then onward. As she had been afraid for him yet in her fear been unable to save him, she grew afraid for herself. Ever since, the summers of her young life had been overshadowed by the day death had shamelessly grinned at her from the young man's eyes and had moved into her youth because she had opened her heart to the dying driver. She cried diamond tears from innocent eyes, also because she realized that one day she, too, would die and from that day, she set out to live a hundred lives. Death was a foul fault of life, she realized, and that she had better act very fast.

The next morning, his photograph was in her breakfast paper and she realized that he had not been an ugly man, although she had held on to the feeble hope that at least the beautiful were immune from dying young. But he was not the type who, sweaty and soaked-clothed, would have puked foully into smelly house corners. In fact, he looked so clean as to suggest that he never vomited and never sweated. His eyes looked haunted, though colorless on account of the black-and-white photograph, and she could tell that he had not been a happy man. She thought she would have liked to have taken him by the hand and asked the photograph why he had been sad, sadly because she knew he would never answer her. He looked back at her from the final page of his dying day, unable to understand that he was truly gone and that he would never speak to her, not now, not when she would be growing up in the years to come. *Where has he gone to*, she asked the setting sun, feeling cheated and driven by a need to be speaking to someone, but the sun in all its brilliance knew no answer. Bring him back, she implored the sun, I would have wanted to have known him and then, perhaps, his life would have been different and he would have laughed more. The sun remained silent and shining.

Four—to meet and love a ghost

The young man's face stayed imprinted in her mind when she lay down to sleep that night, burning into her soul. Sobbing with self-pity, she would have signed anything to bring him back. She could not grasp that his eyes would never see again, and especially, never see her. Whether or not he had a wife was of no concern to her. Her soul sank when she drove home to herself that he would never speak or walk again and would never shake her hand. In the days following his death, she thought of him often, intensely longing to speak to him, so it came only as a marginal surprise when he appeared two days later, as a subtle voice inside her head.

"Good afternoon," he stated politely. "It has been brought to my attention that you wished to speak to me?"

"Who was that?"

Startled, she looked around her in the lush meadow where she had lain down for her afternoon's sleep. Although his voice was soft and melodic, it frightened her because she could see nobody it might belong to. The voice seemed to come from inside her and yet from far away, some kind of telepathic phenomenon, a direct communication from another mind into hers, thought to thought, a distinct absence of word-walls that usually shaped thoughts according to their own prejudice before sending them forth.

"It is I," he replied gently. "The driver from the photograph," he added, less surely now, suddenly afraid that she did not remember him. "The one you watched die."

"But that is impossible! You are dead!"

"Regrettably so, yes," he said and she mussed the nodding of his head, the blinking of his eye, the outline of his hair against the grass. "But you have called me and so I have returned."

She nodded in stupefaction, only pretending an understanding that in reality evaded her. She had called out to him. He had returned. Of course. It was very simple. She laughed at him with a hint of insanity and could instantly sense that her laughter scared the unseen voice beside her, so she toned its coarse sound down and got herself back under full control.

"I remember you now," she told the voice, joyous that she was getting to speak to him, at last. "What was your name again?"

This was to test him, because she could not recall the driver's name and if the voice came from inside her own head, neither would he. Worse, he could be any departed man, an imposter perhaps. He obediently gave his name, his date of birth, his date and hour of death, his mother's maiden name, his children's birth dates and the maiden name of a wife who, he assured her, had never loved him. When she asked him for further credentials, he added the name of his high school, his father's address and, obviously lacking discretion totally, the date and place where he had lost his virginity. Having done all this, he stated unnecessarily, somehow thinking that this would serve to calm her jittery nerves, "it is not true what they say. We don't die when we die."

He said that he had no idea where he was, but that he was not dead, at least not dead in the sense people generally understood dead to be. A chuckle escaped her, quite against her will. His words sounded most absurd, but when she sensed his questioning anxiety, she realized that it would be best to apologize to him for having laughed at his misfortune. He accepted, and then continued speaking in a composed and orderly manner. Complaining scornfully about his condition, he regretted that he no longer had features to settle into a position of sour disdain.

"Everybody thinks me dead and gone, everybody. They have buried me and turned away from me, toward the world of the living, of which I no longer am part. They cannot hear me, or maybe they do not want to hear me, although I keep calling out to them."

He spoke with great deliberation and she wished for a face to discover the expression accompanying his words. She had been trained to speak to people with faces and the experience of the faceless, voice-only driver was rather unusual. Although she understood the driver's problem, she could also understand the unwillingness of those he had left behind, to speak to him without the benefit of a face.

"Dead people," he continued plaintively, "are of no use to the living. Unable to perform any work of value, they are no longer productive members of society. They are useless, even as lovers, having no eyes left into which to gaze with depth. Dead people are very much alone among the living."

The voice added in strictest confidence that he was very afraid of being dead and that he wanted her help. Far from being menaced by his strange request, she thought it worthy of serious consideration. She could not agree with him more about the shabby way the Dead were being treated by the Living. She, too, had no love for the theory that only productive people were people of worth, because it excluded the old, the sick and the Dead from within the ranks of modern society. After all, it was not his fault that he was dead, so suddenly, without having been granted even the courtesy of a warning. From one instant to the next he had been thrown into the uncomfortable and highly unjust loss of his body, something which had turned him from a celebrated rally driver into a much-abused dead person.

"How could I help you?" she asked, cautiously but not unwillingly. Already, she was fond of his theory about the Dead and forgotten. She told him that she was not very much taken with the modern world either and that she considered it unworthy of intelligent man, for its degradation of the individual. Although she was by no means hostile, she stated that she was still unsure whether she could help him, warning that she had no expertise or experience with dead people, or with dying in general.

"Nor do I," he assured her as the general diversion of night began around them. "This is my first time, too."

He wanted her to stay with him, he said, explaining his contrivance in his frank, earnest voice. He knew for certain that love was the most important lesson to be learned on earth and he had never loved, except with obsequious adulation his racing cars. Now he could not go on. Having spent his life with meaningless tasks, he had missed the chance to applaud someone else's soul and it seemed that, perhaps owing to his birth or his religion or his artistic temper, he had been given a final chance to love and solve his most pressing problem. There were no notices written anywhere about what had happened to him, he explained, but he assumed that he would not recover from dying unless she were to love him.

If this was drama, she could not see why there had ever been a need for Marlowe when, apparently, the disembodied Dead were all around them, seeking to call to themselves the attention of the Living and to write their final essays of sublime love.

"Very well," she answered, bemused by his glorious ideas. "But I don't know you, so how can I love you? Even in ancient love, at a time when our grandmothers were still running around in pumps, the prerequisite had to be met, which is, at the very least, *one* encounter of the lovers."

"Oh, but you will know me, you will," the voice cried dramatically. "Ours shall be a fine love, separated from any immorality or physical climax in each other's arms. We shall be all ether, spirit, art, uncontaminated by the material."

"Hm," she said.

"Just say that you will love me and all else will fall into place."

He might as well have said that he could eat glass and walk on hard nails, his credibility factor would have been no lower. Between earfuls of his grandiose plans, she suspected that there was something wrong with him, perhaps on account being newly dead. What he was proposing seemed and sounded absurd. And yet, she was entirely willing to free him from whatsoever discomfort, so long as the action brought no dishonor on herself. Above all, she was moved by his well-preserved mind and by the soft caress of his swinging voice. She tried to conjure up memories of his face, his haunted eyes and how she had watched him tumble through the air, how the race, by consent of the majority of watchers, had proceeded before his blood had dried on the French cobble-stones, how she had sat up for him all night in the hope that he would survive, how she had cried over him when he had not pulled through, despite of not knowing him. She had longed for him to cross the threshold of mortality and return for her—now he was here, albeit a ghost, but he had returned. She even understood his valid argument that he could no longer enter her world, owing to his obvious lack of material matter. Having listened to him, received and processed all his arguments, she knew that she either had to send him on his way or undertake a love, with fire and pleasure but beyond the edge of the earth, as he proposed.

Summing up her experiences with romance, she had to admit that none of the men she had met among the living had excited her much. They were mostly self-absorbed, contaminated by the poisons of money and success, always selecting audiences to show off their wealth or skills to. Having been raised in a climate of modern materialism, they were fond of fame and money, devoid of fresh ideals, and completely blind to Marlowe's eloquent considerations of the human soul. Their excuses usually turned out to be lies. Worse, they did not even believe in souls, professing to be renegade rebels living for the moment in an elevated, nationalistic, life-celebrating, materialism-celebrating frenzy. None of those men had found her approval and she doubted that they ever would. Being dead, this one at least would have time to spend with her and would not try forcing her to know as much about Wall Street as he did, or disdainfully drown her in his superior babble, stating that the art of writing was fluid stuff, since long forgotten, and useless.

"Yes," she replied firmly at last. "I would very much like to love you."

"Then close your eyes," he instructed happily, "close your eyes and see."

When she did, he gave her all his memories with one sublime, steadfast move; *his solemn face in the mirror, his self-analysis as a young man, his observant manner of dealing with his parents, his inner discontent that was relieved only behind the wheel of his car.*

They all flew into her mind and settled there in her own memory, all the years of his life, with his every hardihood of thought, his every expression, his every laughter, all his happy and sad moments, as she became observer and observed of all three decades of his short life, the collector of images and dreams from his fading existence. In the instant it had taken him to transfer his memory banks to hers, he consumed her heart with immense fire, kindling inside her a love she had never known before. She loved him because she knew him more completely than she had ever known any human being, tracing his every thought and emotion. Like a book, she read the sum total of his deepest fears, his most cherished hopes and his unfulfilled dreams, causing her to love him with a fervor she had never dreamt possible as their two souls melted into one. She felt a tenderness for him as infinite in its promise as earth had been when it lay still unformed on its first day.

Their love began long after other loves had ended, as though they had been listening to the conversation of angels and understood the language that they spoke. No words wearing solid teeth stood between them. They were stronger than the wind in their together-ness, or the mountains or the stars. His gift was not common. He gave her all the confidence of his deadness and she never felt awk-ward in her growing years, never speculating about complex cross-rhythms or counter-rhythms, like other lovers did. Not standing aloof like the other living, she in turn helped him through the adjustment of being dead, with her fresh body and her strong, young life. Her bright laughter stilled his pain over the loss of his body.

They were no dramaturges yet their love became like a composition of great art, linking them by a noble bond. They were a fine and remarkable couple, as they walked hand in hand through the streets of her growing years, one dead and one alive. Defiantly, they built a bridge between the land of the Dead and the land of the Living, protesting against a process implying, by selection of those with over those without a body, an open disapproval of the Dead. They were a memorable couple, bypassing all circumstances that should have by rights separated them.

One day, he frightened her, stating that their love would have grown withered and decayed, like a forest after a session of heavy tree-felling, had she been older or had they both been alive when meeting one another. Their love would not have been possible, he maintained, had her heart not stood at the gateway of its first bloom, because the heart oldens together with the mind. Although he had perhaps somewhat severely handled the explanation, he was right, without a doubt, when he went on to state that the heart wears masks with the years, to cover pain or disappointment, until one's world view changes and finally, nobody is ever trusted completely, without weary considerations of what the future might bring. He confessed that he, too, had been wearing masks all his life, never disclosing to anyone the ruins below his palace.

The End.

CHAPTER 4

One—otherworldly love

His theory of masks proved to be an interesting instruction in the light and shadow existence of human life. During many nights, from half past ten until four the next morning, he taught her that masks were like long black limousines hiding the faces of their unknown occupants and that, like limousines, they were rather funereal. Masks were phony, he explained with seventeenth-century graveness, adding that one should not wear a mask lest one becomes the mask and turns into what one pretends to be. Should the desire then arise, one day, to remove the mask and reveal the person below, perhaps as an emotional duty toward a lover, the task becomes one of riding against a thrusting wind, a scrunching laborious impossibility, because one has already turned into the mask. As though speaking inside a huge ghoulish fairytale, he lectured that mask-love was phony, since mask meets mask, loves mask and leaves mask, reducing the very essence of true love to an absurd rubber-and-wire romance substituting the old-fashioned melting of souls with a cheap second-hand copy. He repeatedly warned her never to wear masks in her life and to leave those not overly fond of her, rather than shape herself to their liking. As a deterrent he used himself, confessing to having been overly enthusiastic in wearing masks until his mask had become welded to his face, where it had grown thicker and stronger, but it was all a wilderness underneath there. Finally, he had been forced to live alone behind his mask and present to the world a different man, who repeated jokes at the kind of parties a rally driver was made to attend and whose admirers expanded to a sheer insufferable number but whose true self had remained hidden, in a wild-goose game behind his mask, far removed from his phony friends.

He even expressed a certain gratitude at having died, although he admittedly had been harassed by the event at first. Once the solid darkness had parted and he had grown accustomed to the vulgarity of being without a body, suddenly all intellect, he could at last exclaim *how wonderful* and come to appreciate the fact that, in death, there was no need to wear a mask or a face. He went on to speak of the respective impacts and implications of his death-ness, confessing to be almost glad to have died, before she had been overtaken by the vanities of life with its various creative emotional and social activities. Ever so glad he was, he sighingly admitted, that she was still so refreshingly young and had not yet lost herself to other people's viewpoints.

But now (*he stated this very contemplatively, careful of not appearing too harsh a critic but still wishing to point out the catastrophic impact of his demise*), death having performed its function, he wished to return to the world of the Living where they could be composing a sonnet in bed together, canto by canto chronicling the power of their loins. His happiness over his death and their meeting was replaced, out of a sudden, by a deeper sadness and a kind of longing never to be fulfilled. He was not alone in his thinking. She, too, was bewildered now. However benevolent she wished to appear, she was no longer able to appreciate the beautiful gift of his being dead. He must be given a kiss, a letter at the very least, but he had been ruthlessly slaughtered by his car, and both their fates cunningly sealed.

True, they had a most exquisite love, but while other lovers silhouetted in the sunset against the flushed sky, they were doomed to only one silhouette and to singing sentimental solos instead of beautiful duets in some kind of spirit-love. The temptation of reaching out to him became increasingly difficult for her to resist with the years but whenever she gave in to the sentimental tradition of touch, she reached into nothing.

What am I to do with this, she thought, *I have other ambitions.* In her demented youthfulness, she even arrived at the point where she wished to follow him and to live fully in his world. With harsh reprimand and great urgency, he warned her against laying hand on herself. At first, she was dejected by his disapproval, then she shrugged with accepted regret and relaxed into her love of him, a pitilessly absolute, but separated love. Her enchantment over his presence covered the lingering after-effects of her disappointment that she would never be able to boast of him to her friends who presented the various intrinsic merits of their own lovers. They had passports. They were drunk or sober. They were snot-nosed, dark-eyed, bearded or clean-shaven, they were tender or rough, but at least they were alive.

He also warned her never to speak of him to others, rightly pointing out that a love like theirs was generally only attributed to red-haired, green-eyed witches in the middle ages who, under the sufferings of great pain, had been burnt at stake for it. He vigorously urged her to remain silent, stating that he was concerned for her physical safety in case that she should blab about him. Although he admitted that witchburning, having enjoyed quite a vogue in the middle ages, had succumbed to the dreams of men and women with liberal mindsets and was no longer practiced, he was worried about the children of the children of the children of the witchhunters, who these days joined each other in the front row of Verdi's *Il Trovatore,* to approvingly watch Azucena sing her heart out before being burnt at stake. Those he was worried about, who were still wrestling with the tradition of their forefathers and with what was right and wrong. These old faithful retainers of ancient traditions considered love with a ghost to be wrong by all means, punishable by exclusion from society at the very least. He wished to spare her a life at the edge of society that would cause her to die long before her time, oppressed by sublime loneliness and the sudden emergence of hatred from people surrounding her. Being a ghost, certain finesses of human nature had evaded him and caused him to make an awful mistake in his calculations. Bidding her to remain silent about him as though she were in the midst of some kind of medieval Spanish intrigue, he had sentenced her to become an outcast among the living all the same. She dwelt partially in his world and partially in hers. Although technically not persecuted as a witch, she remained haunted by the fear of discovery, imagining in stolid detail the ensuing witchhunt he had warned her about.

Once she had watched the burial of her youth while he introduced her to the outside world under the auspices of his own wisdom, she had lead his life all over again. Exploring another life with him, she encountered his friends, lived where he had lived and became a dead man's only memory among the living.

Two—to love and to be left

Having done all this for him, forsaking her growing-up years, an accelerating pulse driven by a young heart at the prospect of meeting a first love, going-away on summer's vacation with a pimply lover and sitting hand in sweaty hand on pink-mauve cliffs with him, never experiencing in the month of August the sudden emergence of carnal sin under sage bushes lining winding roads, having had all that wonderfully nonsensical first-love *slush-slush* concealed from her and giving it all up for him without as much as a hard swallow, instead contenting herself with walking lonely mountains slopes under an overcast sky by the side of a ghostly lover, he announced one day that he was going to leave her, vaguely promising to be there at her life's end as he had been at the beginning. Seeing her drooping face, he promised to erase in the end whatever sour memories might remain, of all the stupefaction emptiness and injustice her life would bring. Then he delivered a reasonable rendering of Sir Lancelot, waved one last time and abandoned her, with the prospect of seeing him again when she was very old and very wrinkled and very dead. Once he was gone, she leant against the rocks of her favorite mountain's foothill where, surrounding her, were lush, blue flowers and the demons of her past with him.

She had grown so accustomed to his life running alongside her own that his sudden take-off did immense harm, generating the collapse of her entire universe. He had been beside her for a lifetime, suddenly he was gone, and when she called his name she encountered the echo of her seeking soul instead of his familiar voice. With his absence came a sublime coldness that was softened only by her memories of him, which she could trace as though on a travel map; here a familiar path he had led her, there shone his promise that they would meet again some day, and here, hidden amongst the disappointment, lay the secure knowledge that his leaving her had not been his own choice but because the universe had its own rules by which even ghosts had to abide.

Having lived almost her entire life in the shadow of death, she emerged from the clusters of her memories, seeking to re-enter life once more, but it was no easy task. Having been concealed for too many years, life refused to be invaded by her, who had been touched by death and brought with her the outrageous memories of a rejecting ghost. It scurried away from her like a mischievous pup, unwilling to welcome yet another pathetic story in its midst and frightening her out of her wits. With the arrogance of a haughty swan, life at last admitted her back into its chattering, dozing peoplehood, its meadows teaming with milkweed and ironweed, and its mountains that shone brilliantly in the setting sun, but only because it had to. Unable to exclude anyone not yet dead, it welcomed her as a weed on its fields but warned that there would always be a place inside her eyeing toward the grave. It blatantly advised her to seek another man, at once, with whom to kill the memory of the ghost if she wished to prevent the arrival of her own death and the question, *when will he come for me?*, to be asked before her twentieth year.

Three—modern love and ragged faces

She tried her best to love someone else but to no avail. Modern love proved a punishment not a pleasure, some dull, gray thing bearing down on her. The separation, built by the masks her prospective lovers wore, had created too large a gap as their memories of past disappointments undermined their love-ability in the present. They were either atheists or mathematicians, in either case analyzing everything, and their childish hurtful games made her temples throb with pain, although she initially braved them with infinite patience and a somewhat listless disgust. She could not understand why they still kept carrying all that baggage on their breaking backs of memories of wives and lovers long gone, exiled hopes since long turned to dust, shattered dreams clothing their souls in thorny garments designed to slay, without cause or reason, anyone approaching. All this was more in line with the American Indians, dark of eye and skin, who painted faces on everything, even on their walking sticks, and to whom faces and masks were of sufficient importance to equal them, by giving them the same name. In a commentary sense, their name for death was *without a face*. Only in death, they maintained, does the heart shed its mask, opening into the light as all masks dissolve into nothingness and all life is bathed in honesty.

Envisioning life's warning, about death coming for her in shape of a dragon spitting fire and whirling its wings, she did her best to love the living but encountered only hearts caged by fear. Once noble men, who had synchronized with the very heartbeat of life, had been changed into withered old men by too many years of malevolent isolation. Like sheep who dare not question their shepherd as he leads them at dawn across solid green fields, to terminate by the lilac birth of night at the door of a commercial slaughterhouse not a lambs wool factory, these men accepted that they would always wear masks and love others wearing masks. The marvel of it all had ceased for them. They stood watching their hopes decompose in the storms of a lonely life, but no matter, no matter, green is the color of happiness and of frustration.

The broken ones she met also, who had, each of them, composed a separate canto for the big poem of life itself. Their dreams of love, experienced or promised, still hung about them noiselessly, dreams that by all accounts were best left behind, living in a world extolling the wonders of technology and worshipping fast cars. In a materially oriented world, such dreams could prove rather detrimental when measured against the short flights masquerading as love, with their soft moans from adjacent bedrooms, their women obligingly crowding into plastic surgeons' waiting rooms to enlarge their breasts and lips, their men whose smoothly running world comes unscrewed the moment they distressedly discover that their urinal neighbor's genitals are larger and who suffer, because of this horrible, humiliating experience, a massive crash in self-esteem making the man in the mirror appear flabby, feeble and clumsy. Rising from their shame into some appalling definition of love, these men's wallet sizes, from then onward, determine the quality of their love, as soon as they learn that beautiful women travel in connection with wealthy men and that truly wealthy men, especially when their wealth is coupled with even modest fame, escape all kinds of knockings about the sizes of their objects. Years later, they are to be found flat on the floor, at the hour of their demise, when all banal motions are removed and their lonely world that had been buried under a layer of luxury disintegrates. Unable to foresee that no lie survives death, they usually plan badly for the event and, afraid of going to the devil, pathetically cry out *salva me, salva me*, but tend to encounter only a gentleman-pensioner God not caring about their size of object or rate of thrust.

Others, who had refused to relinquish their dream, turn it against the wall and have it shot, who had stubbornly kept alive the search for an image all too perfect, were no better off. They were usually speaking to themselves in underground stations or, supported by a parliamentary act of charity to the displaced, sharing their bread with mysterious strangers in the homeless shelters of big cities. They could even to be found among the wealthy, losing their peaceful sleep when finding themselves buried under the banal motions of their own society and turning to drugs or drink to escape the dreams refusing to die inside them. They were also like the weary man she had seen at the entrance to an underground station, not half the man he had once been but still handsome, although his ashen face lay in rags and his fine hands trembled as he spoke to himself.

Encountering them in her search to re-enter life, she wondered about the broken people with their disintegrating faces who had been driven into madness by their solitude. They were considered to be terrible creatures but she was always lacerated with pity at their outward show of insanity, because they were genetic variants in a society that no longer remembered love.

All these dramatic observations could not keep her from arriving at the point where she longed to touch the swollen belly of a living, breathing man rather than the fading memories of her ghostly lover. To her dismay, she found the men she approached to contemplate instant withdrawal, driven by the need to wage war fast and afraid to be without clothes before her. They far preferred hoisting themselves onto heavenly virgins and tearing into their innocent flesh while muttering of love and so on. *You think too much,* they told her, adding that their objects were fleshy weapons to be used in short bursts.

By circumstance, not choice, she came to live inside a sublime solitude that only the memory of her ghost filled, but she was save inside its cocoon. He kept her warm there, at night, with his comforting words still echoing in her mind. But all this did not change the fact that he was gone. His voice was gone. His smile was gone.

She was warmed not by his presence but by the memory of his presence, which gradually grew dimmer until it became a mere whisper. How to reconcile the throbbing in her loins with his ethereal promises? She was not as innocent as the ghost thought her to be and wanted nothing more than to say to a man *let's pass an inn along the way* to engage in a flow, not trickle, of their joint body fluids. Spending the night together can be a great picker-up, she thought without shame, but where to find the one willing to give his bare body for the purpose?

Pacing up and down inside her bedroom like an expelled puppet one day, mechanically fumbling with her luscious black curls, buttoning and unbuttoning her shirt several times, she impatiently (*she had better things to do with her life than all this detached, analyzing nonsense*) admitted to herself that she could not live in a world reigned by the continuous, pathetic search for love when love was subjected to certain acts of policy and pushed away whenever it reared its outcast head. Titled *frightening, scary, too soft, undesirable,* it had long been buried under a wall of regulations, as to when it could be shown to whom, and when it was to be murdered under the auspices of being a vulgar nuisance.

On that particular afternoon, she had dined somewhat late, sharing a mahogany corner table at the local restaurant with a friendly couple, strangers, whose incompetent half-paralyzed conversation rang all the laughing bells in her. They were a fitting example of modern love in all its cruelty. Smiling indulgently, the woman sheepishly admitted that she had met her escort for the first time just now, adding proudly that hers had been the one reply he had picked from an entire catalogue of hopefuls who had answered his ad in the local personal column. He was a man of some wealth, a true catch, she was a delicious nymph and yes, (*both smiling sheepishly now*) here they were at last.

She kept listening impolitely as he freely spoke to the woman, of a pain in his groin driving him mad, and even added that he had not slept for two nights. Grinningly, the woman replied that she would make a fine, young wife for him and then stated with ancestral feminine coyness that she was a woman with the pride of a king but the uncontrollable hunger of the seven deadly sins. The man's eyes impatiently traveled down to the woman's fleshy chest. Her smile faded momentarily, then he took her hand in hers and she smiled again, once he had looked her over and stated, kneading the fingers of her right hand in his huge paws, that she was the right one for him. His massacring of women's hearts, he sighingly admitted, had to come to an end. He was now of an age to settle down, once and for all.

"I am of royal blood," he stated grandiosely, reassuring the woman that on account of her blond hair, her long legs and her pretty hands, she had his approval and, if there were no unforeseen delays (with this, he impatiently looked between her legs), she would never want for money again, yes, there would be plenty for both of them. Then they contemplated moving to another country to start afresh, somewhere safe where people still left the doors of their houses open.

"I see you have plenty of fine eggs in your ovaries," he cried out happily, "and I can split nails and wield a hammer." He added that everything was a matter of instinct now. Being blond and long-legged, he already knew that she was right for him, especially once she stated that she was also a sportive woman, mountain-biking and windsurfing and fencing and what ever else. This she had told him as proof that she was not boring although she could cook a rather good, bloodless steak.

She had been quietly sitting beside them, not wishing to reveal his foolishness to them but wondering whether the falsehood he had spoken would ever dawn on him. She felt a strange sensation, gut-

wrenching and vaporous, whenever she looked at the man who may
have been acting the gentleman but was in reality nothing but a
ragged grinner whose stomach betrayed his habits, that he wined
and dined on beer and bread and more beer. She wanted very much
to point out that his stomach looked rather flaccid and would have
liked to criticize his street-fighterish hands for being too droopy, but
more than anything she wanted to tell the idiot that hands and hair
did not matter one inch, nor whether that poor woman went mountain-biking after an exhausting day at the office just to prove herself
to him. All that mattered was the color of her soul or what memories
had been carved into her tree of life, at what depth the lake of her
heart lay or toward what heights her thoughts aspired. She tried to
analyze his love for the blond woman and found nothing to excite
her, only the devil grinning from between the coarse man's fleshy
loins. She excused herself, leaving the couple behind without speaking another word to them. Saying anything would have been useless,
once she had understood that their love was reduced to chemical
compounds and that they would never submit to reason.

Four—the contest

Having peeped so closely into modern love affairs, she wished under
no circumstances to participate in a game judging the other by the
colors of his raincoat rather than the rival functions of his soul. Living people, in their blindness, were best left to themselves. The only
exception was the Rider, who distinguished himself from the pale
light of other men with almost prismatic malice. His soul was a true
treasure house of dazzling radiance, not unlike her ghost's, and he
was also very much alive. Blood ran through his veins, maggots had
never tasted his flesh, his eyes could see the colors of the world she
would have no need to describe. The Rider's hand would not reach
for her from the shore of a chaotic afterlife but touch her with the
warmth of a glossy orchid. She would feel a jolt of electricity run
through her body, and have no need to imagine his hands as their

hastily doffed clothes fell to the floor in a lumpy heap. Gone was the useless search for men whose personalities consisted mainly of shadows, here was a man who stood above childish small-town principles and local bylaws, but what to do with him? There were rules in love as there were in solving chess problems and she would need to love him completely if she were to do anything to his body. The passion of coupling would not be enough for him, nor a clumsy skin-rubbing driving the blood into his genitals. A bald man with a gray beard and a habit of drink would perhaps be satisfied with rolling about in crumpled bed-sheets, even one who was all pure muscle and instinct might look for nothing more, but not the Rider. He appeared to have been cast down directly from the Gods and would want another one of those afternoons, where he would touch her as though she were holy, and then another. He would want to plunge into the heart of human passions with her, but also explore her soul between acts of the bed, until his horses would come to know her well enough to whinny her a greeting when she entered their stable. He would leave nothing to the chaos of chance and would tear the mask off her face; no appeal, no support, no advice, no protection, just soul-melting love coupled with a celebration of human passion.

What if she took the wrong turn somewhere and destroyed him, to be added to his spiritualistic case history as the one who had dealt him the final, brutal blow? Would his friends point finger at her and scream *Assassination*? He was scheduled to break slowly under the sheer limitless degradation of searching for depth but encountering only the superficial in its wake, yet he refused to bow to the rules of a diabolical reality. With beowulfian valor he fought against the danger of losing his dream through sheer absentmindedness, but he walked in solitude as punishment for keeping it alive.

And the ghost? He had never blundered and had promised to wait for her at the gateway of the nether world. Could she let him go, just like that, if there was an eternity of bliss awaiting her, provided she refrained from giving herself to another man? What of eternity, if she broke her vow to him? Would her soul need to rely on the dust of its own husk? Would he find a means of killing her, and she come to pity herself at the hour of her own death? What doom awaited her if she walked away from him because a Rider whose features she could not even recall had written an entirely new plot for her life? What price would she pay, being unable to forget some stranger's eyes and voice? But today, the Rider lived firmly inside her heart, even if tomorrow she might be dead.

Opening her eyes to the new morning, she refrained from reaching into eternity, where snow began to lay heavily over the image of the driver, and found herself reaching for the fragile memory of the Rider instead. She chillingly contemplated suicide as a way out, but then realized that she could not run toward the grave to escape him. It would have been like a dream unwrapped too soon. So long as the Rider was still alive, she had to remain alive also.

That was how she came to call a contest, for them to fight each other for her affections. She would spend eternity with the man who could destroy her reason enough to make her give herself to him alone. The Rider, only with the promise of the future she had envisioned for the both of them, and the driver, with the past they had already lived together, fought with integrity. In the end, they both stood at the gateway to her heart, the boisterous ghost who had claimed her in her blossoming years, and the Rider whose singularly featureless face had not yet been formed by their joint future, and she did not know which one of them to attend because stubborn fate had caused the contest to terminate in a draw. Unable to decide between approval and rejection, she rarely wore a ribbon around her heart anymore. At first, she wondered about the sensation of the Rider's hand in hers, but then the Driver cried *where is my wife?*, meaning her, and thanked her heartily for not choosing a man of flesh and blood over him. Only sometimes did she realize she was still alive, usually when she was fast asleep.

The End.

CHAPTER 5

One—of modern men and modern women

As through study of a secret passage filled with anguish and exultation, she realized that a choice was to be made between walking down two distinct mile-long corridors stretching like crossroads on either side of her *to-be-continued* life. Her choosing was by no means the self-indulgent inner commotion of one with too much time on her hands, urging herself to choose between a living love or settling into the comfortable but mundane existence by the side of a ghost. The choice, between her past and the envisioned spread of time still lying before her, was a matter far beyond dreaming a remote dream destined never to become reality. From observations like the personal column couple, she knew that love had been reduced to disposable commercial value like brass-buttons, knickerbockers and striped stockings. The resulting isolation of the people, unequaled in any other time, had bred children who preferred computers and (constantly in volume and technology growing) televisions to conversation, and women who destroyed themselves in the attempt to balance the bearing and raising of children with a career and with plastic surgery. Women damaged by contemporary society did not dare age. They raised silver goblets at fancy parties and tortured themselves up a mountain, down a river, or jumped from high bridges with parachutes, to prove that they were sportive. They expected nothing anymore of their men, not even love, and went through great expense to prevent or minimize the appearance of wrinkles on their faces. Like police agents in disguise, they eyed the faces of their girlfriends with nasty self-satisfaction, jubilantly triumphing when they discovered someone of the same age with more lines.

Earning their own way, modern women had come to accept that they were the ones to be giving, financially and emotionally, in marriage. Since men and women had been proven, in various new age literature, to be genetically separated by a narrow-dim valley and to originate from different stars, kindness and support could not be reasonably be expected from the poor male dears. They preferred to be addressed as *your Lordship* and spent their time going golfing, applauding other players rather than their wives, some of whom thought themselves blessed and some of whom thought themselves cursed. In absence of anyone calling them to order, they rejected wife after wife for younger versions and had passed the point where they would ever return to submission, and women the point where they would ever stop feeling indebted to them.

The Rider, thin, defiant, but eating hearty meals, distinguished himself from all the other riders on the circuit like she distinguished herself from the gorgeous but apprehensive modern women. She had never been tempted to jump out of a perfectly safe airplane with a parachute strapped to her back to prove that, in addition to being intelligent and beautiful, she was also a *power woman afraid of nothing*. Indeed, she doubted greatly that it would give her joy to riot through the air at near lightening speed and she had declined a recent offer to jump, despite assurances that the most exciting stretch of her life lay directly ahead of her. Remembering her fortunate beginnings on the path of love that now had only few promenaders, when love came before calculation and mankind had not killed itself to be better, greater, younger and more beautiful than nature had intended, she remained unbent by time, as though in slow motion.

Having abandoned both men and felt nothing for a long time, she discovered that she could not live only for her career. Having known love, tasted it, felt it, she could no longer do with a cheap copy. She needed a man with whom to speak freely, not a stranger selling his services along with his own lands. Although her heart seemed to have been atrociously injured in the recent explosion with the Rider, the new arrival of a potential love could not instantly be dismissed as a bad idea. Some of her friends agreed and some disagreed that the choice to be made, for or against the Rider, was of prime importance, emotional, creative and social. She knew it was a choice between love and death and, she realized shuddering, even between life and death.

As she embraced herself through yet another nocturnal session of tired musings, she recalled that the newly dead had always appeared, ready to court her, whenever she had been trying to give herself to a living man. Newly dead, they were in search of a living woman who could feel them, hear them, and let them live what they had missed when they were still in body. She had indulged them each time and could look back on a life that had been led in the shadow of the assorted Dead, on her solitary happy times with them. The dead were easy lovers, albeit draining for their lack of life force. This was made up by the fact that their need for masks had disappeared and that conversation with the dead was always easy. They were above envy, never defected, and called her *my rose*. They were restless only when they had been murdered or wanted things uncovered and put right again, with people from their pasts searched out and given messages to. They saw a hope of having her finish their lives for them and she was in the business of completing these tasks obligingly.

Aside from their sometimes exhausting demands, the Dead were more balanced than the Living, perhaps because they inhabited a world where the material receded and the spiritual became of prime importance. The dead never surprised her by hurriedly shedding their clothes and jumping into the shower beside her roaring their favorite hymn. They were like an anonymous blind man transported by some inconceivable manner to a different estate where people he has never met are engaged in playing strange parlor games. He is forced to choose his new friends not by looks, but by their more rewarding impressions—tone of voice and touch. Like the blind man, the Dead had a distinct advantage over the Living, since looks can lie far better than sound.

Her constant dealings with the Dead had caused her to exclude the living on account of being very busy, since no cry of distress from beyond the grave had ever remained unanswered by her. Fleeing from the sunshine, she had chosen a shadow existence by the side of the Dead. Although the living were the native people of her own land, she never made an effort toward them. When they approached her, they were dissected, prepared, preserved like butterflies, and banned into the pages of her books. There, she permitted them to love her, once they had taken on the appearance of the dead and could no longer breathe warm breath, once they were made not of flesh and bone, but black ink, and could be shaped to her liking. Her books were filled with all the living breathing men of her past, who had walked proudly in the flesh, whose muscles had bulged boldly under their half-open shirts, who had sought to love her and who had been turning into disdainful pigs when she had told them good-bye. As a whole, they were not even worthy of her anger. Only of them still stuck clearly in her memory, for his country muscles and because his revenge for slaying him had been cruel, when his burial in her books had been followed by his real-life funeral.

Two—Peru's most handsome son

Having walked to his doom, he had returned to claim her life as payment. A Peruvian had conquered her, soon after her heart had been

released by the driver. Filled with nobility, he had been her first living man. Through his eyes shone the sweeping soul of Peru, perfectly
enough for her to say at once, *now is a good time to pause,* and ban
him into the pages of her latest book. There, she loved him as she
had previously only experienced love with the driver, closely connecting souls with him so that the driver's ghost stirred jealously
inside her. Caught between the two men, she finally had had no
choice but to wish the Peruvian dead. So long as he was alive and
could offer her the same depth of love as the other one, in addition
to a warm, pulsating body, he would beat the driver in the long run.
Introduced to the concept of exclusive love by the latter, she had
been taught to see life through the eyes of one man only. The trouble
was that she had already promised that kind of love to the driver,
having sworn him her eternal loyalty. With all the love stuff from the
Peruvian pouring in, her only solution was to have him die as well.
She knew that she would be restful once more if he, with his deep
Peruvian soul, were no longer alive. In this context she had wished
him dead, driven by the pathetic desire to keep herself from breaking
an already existing vow.

She had never butchered anyone before, but her wishes always had
a strong power to come true. He died, having been arrested suddenly
and unexpectedly, only a few months after she had refused to love
him. Of this she had no clear memory herself, only fermented multi-
colored fragments of images, of a time when she had been engaged
in dangerous and offensive business. She vaguely recalled that he had
been murdered in prison, where he had been tortured until he had
surrendered his final scream. She had perhaps been in a torture
chamber herself for a while, brought there by various concerned military groups, the representatives of a fine nation concerned for the
safety of their land. She did recall that, having taken a look into her
pale upturned face, they had let her go because even people like they,
caught inside their web of sensitive and self-important politics,
understood that her motive had not been political. Although they

did not understand many things in Peru, at least they understood the concept of passion.

Instead of killing her, they had banned her from Peru, ordering her to never speak of what she had seen. She never spoke again, as a matter of obedience to her would-be assassins, but also not to disappoint their trust in her. It all came down to a matter of loyalty toward those who could have killed her but let her live. In her heart grew a strange absurd love for them, borne of the gratitude that she was still alive (*what delightful people they are! They could have killed me, but they didn't, how very sweet of them!*)

The Peruvian, on the other hand, was not as forgiving of *her* transgressions as she had been of the torturers'. He took an entirely different view as his whole body burst in a manic fit. Having ascertained that she had killed him with her indifference, he had returned for her as a ghost, grimly determined to kick the bottom out from under her feet. On that perilous night, the instant of his death had been the instant he had decided on blocking her life. He wanted her to love him and he would get her to love him, whether he was dead or alive. As far as he was concerned, they were welded together by their common pain. Somehow the eyes of her mind saw him and the muscles of her mind felt him as he courted her with the powerful mechanism of sweeping verse. When she had availed her heart to him, he had performed his dreadful duty with a kind of languorous pleasure. His revenge had been to surround her until she could feel his figure burning hot against her body and then to instill his own love for his country inside her heart, and she willingly took it, until the faces of his people haunted her like a sorrowful song, even in her waking hours.

Brushing off the dust of memories of her own nation, for whom there was no more room, she understood that his true revenge had been his people, to whom she suddenly felt closely connected as if by magic. She had even imagined that she could see their faces calling out her name, beckoning her to join in what might turn out to be a dangerous game of remembrance of their one and only, all Peruvian, hero-turned-torture-victim. The Peruvians were fascinated by her willingness to toss differences aside and become, in a sense, a light in the dark darkness of their oppression. She had come to love a country where she was a stranger and would always remain a stranger. Sustained by a sense of belonging to a people not her own, all the people of Peru stood joined together in her soul as one humble family. She felt their reflection in her heart, which was in danger of shattering with their collected pains and joys. Even the aroma of yellow, brown or black meat containing cholera, and the slowly smoldering, rising smoke of roadside eating stands, smelled delicious to her. She longed to gorge herself on it, even if she might vomit afterwards and diarrhea would suck the fluids out of her body and burn fire through her bowels. Amidst all the phlegm and stomach fluids she would vomit up, grossly, through every pore and every available passage of her body, the pride would remain that being *gringo*, she had not been broken by the attempt to become Peruvian.

Three—of Gringo Imposters and Death Squads

The strange sensation she felt for Peru was not easily cast aside. She had entered a pact with a man whose mind had been made of solid materials not paper mache and Peru became something far more than the annoying mirage shimmer of a distant mirror play. Whenever her stomach settled long enough to think clearly, she felt personal pain over any Peruvian peasants dying, although they were a family that would never accept her as anything but a stranger. Whenever she cried out to them, *but I am one of you, I think and feel with you united*, they pointed out her different skin color and that she neither spoke their language with native tongue nor lived among them in the stinking, gastrointestinal-infection-ridden slums, but dwelt in the world of the white man. They cared little that she carried the memories of Peru's most handsome, long-legged son inside of her.

Her color of skin and her shabby gringo accent branded her an out-cast, regardless.

This had been his revenge for her wishing him dead, when her wish had come true and he had been cruelly slain, struggling angrily against the oncoming night as his life ebbed away. He had become careless in his political fight only (he kept maintaining, even long after he was dead) because she had not permitted him, in his living years, to undress before her. Newly dead, he had returned for her, in the name of *our* people, *our* land, commanding her to continue a struggle whose certain outcome, this much she knew, would be a horribly messy death. No sooner had she muttered "nonsense" and turned away from the absurd images inside her heart than he insisted to brighten her little dark evenings with definite proof that she had a Peruvian soul. On a blank screen that he erected in a hastily charted and somewhat shabbily constructed imaginary movie theater (being dead, he had easy access to her mind), he screened memories she would have rather forgotten:

Enter memory number 1:

She is in her dimly lit room where nobody can see her, on the floor and on her knees. In her hands she holds a simple rosary, the kind they sell for ten *Pesos* outside the church of *Santa Maria de los Angeles*. She has taken on the simple religious mind of the people of Peru and in her simple (and, to any self-respecting gringo, highly embar-rassing) faith, she dissolves in the prism of her own tears, streaming down her face as she cries out to a silent God to save "her" people. He, a God of the Latinos, knows about her lies and is not happy with her pretending to be Peruvian. She almost kills herself in the attempt to prove that her being Peruvian is not idiocy but truth.

For God, she recites images from her memory: *The devilish dying rooms. The filthy hospitals. The pale, staring eyes of a young man with a worn face, coughing blood from his half open mouth. Nurses walk by him with girlish grace, avoiding him, helplessly afraid themselves.*

There is no medicine to give him and there are so many others who are dying, too. She shows God an image of the nurses pushing the gurney with the dying man under the North window, outside which a starless stirless night rattles the windows for admission. Indifference is etched into the women's faces, as if they are not really supposed to be looking at him, but she explains to God that were the nurses to feel the pain of seeing him die, they would be breaking under its enormity.

She also shows God her happy memories, to make him see that "her" people are indeed worthy of being saved, in case that *He* should subscribe to the theory that occupants of a Third World country are somewhat inferior, and not fully worthy of being saved. No traitor of the Catholic faith, she still believed somewhat in a vengeful God and thought it safer to defend her fictitious Latin-hood with solid proof that she wished to adopt the Peruvian people, at the very least as her cousins.

> *An old woman in the market place who states that she, the gringa, would make a great president for Peru.*
> *The greatness of "her" people who overcame, with a rich desire for peace, the wounds of a long and bloody war and broke bread even with those who had brutally slain their dearest loved ones.*

She shows God everything, each night, in well-framed prayer, the noblest images and the most horrifying scenes of Peru, begging his mercy for a still starving people. God watched. God remained silent as she lay on the floor on her knees, night after night, unable to understand why "her" people had been chosen for exile and disposal. Together with other Latin American nations, some bigger, some smaller, they constituted the anguish-marked nations of "lasts" that had been promised in the bible, as reward for a dreadful life, the certain inheritance of the next kingdom, so long as they would walk without complaint through life while shivering in the rain under their broken umbrellas. The sharp truth was that they were a people that had been marked to distinguish themselves through their ability to bear hardship while smiling widely. While she wantonly made herself unhappy over the tragedy of his nation, the Peruvian had his revenge for her wishing him dead. He had killed her, even as he lay dead himself, and it mattered nothing that she still had a body when he had already slain her soul.

Like the driver who had come before him, he had isolated her from life, but he kept using her for his own ends to salvage a country where knives and machetes called the shots and even the inns smelled of death. His friends were the simple people of the streets, under attack for their poverty. They were all Peruvians, or from neighboring countries. He had hovered around her long enough to convince her that despite her wide blue eyes, she could be transformed into a Peruvian, too. To him, death was merely like going on a long vacation, the bodiless-ness problem could be solved simply, by playing some sort of child's puzzle where the black hair and tanned skin of a *gringa* could be used to build a female, Peruvian counterpart of himself. She had looked at him doubtfully at first, but then agreed to try the matter out. She and the ghost had both gone out together, invading the Peruvian people with her black curls. In the end, she belonged not to one country nor the other, because she kept trying, as one quietly insane, to claim a people as her own that was not hers. Once more, she had become an outcast among the living, as the Peruvian had become an outcast among the dead for his unwillingness to truly die. When he was through with her, the Dead of Peru were rotting in her soul and their stench fouled up her living years.

Enter memory number two:

A dream scene. She lies down to sleep. She is wearing a button-less sleeveless pajama top, nothing else. Her pillow is huge, oval, luxuriously flounced, her bed expensive and triple-sized, in a clean bedroom with brocade curtains and an exclusive, antique bedside table.

A book, by George Sand, *Histoire de ma Vie*, is open, face down, spine spent and near cracking, on her bedside table. She has just read, inside the book, of the hollow futility of revenge: *you will only be harvesting dead leaves, my friend, let it be.*

But the Peruvian has not read George Sand, she knows this when she closes her eyes to sleep and sees:

> *A scene in rural Peru, Calle Plantas des Realos. The air is still and humid. Caressing her bare skin, the setting evening sun cannot make up its mind between staying and leaving. She is in a happy mood, driving with Carlos and Rosa, her local friends, toward their house, where a delicious dinner awaits. She is especially pleased about the conchas on the menu, as she loves the small black shells with their gibberish flesh, to be eaten raw. They give her a gastrointestinal infection each time but she does not mind, the pleasure is well worth the whimpering pain that follows. They are in a white car, laughing and joking.*

Between exhaustion and drowsiness, the dream gets deeper as sleep extinguishes the last glimpses of the bedroom, diminishing the limpid life around her. Only through a distant fog is she still aware of her bed with its paltry fancies. This dream is not going to lead into a cold, dark gallery, it will be a happy one. She thinks that it is safe to dive deeper into sleep and submits control, advancing into the pink claws of the twilight world.

> *The car drives up the winding road. Palm trees line their path. Down below, she can see the horse stable where she often rents a horse to ride out into the rainforest, where butterflies blend in with the flowers and she picks coffee beans from the bushes when she passes on her horse.*
> *The car stops, suddenly.*

In her bed, she engages in some feeble whimpering as she becomes aware that the fraternal atmosphere of the dream has changed.

"Something funny here," Carlos insists, clearing his throat. They exit the car, all three of them: the driver, his wife with the long black hair, and she, who also has long black hair and, from afar, is indistinguishable from a true Latina. Her lack of stamina for the sort of truth Peru was living would reveal her to be gringa, before anything else.

Beside them is a ditch and she knows with every fiber of her jarred and tired nerves that it is filled with an inexplicable evil. She wants to howl in terror but keeps silent and follows Carlos, who advances to look over its edge. Leaving the protective trees she walks behind him in the setting sun. She can now distinguish a pair of simple brown leather sandals. A roundlet of light that has been keeping its distance comes out of nowhere to illuminate the scene.

Bodies. Hundreds of bodies. Young people. Old people. Children with sandals. She especially remembers, with a shudder that all but dislocates her shoulder blades, the children. The children's non-seeing eyes form a system of dark-pale patches as they burn themselves into her soul. They look strangely alive. That they are dead she can only tell by the stench that fills her nose now, a horrible sweetish stench mixed with a faint odor of the cold sweat of fear. There are no injuries and there is no blood, but there are flies, plenty of them, bluish-greenish vulturous flies with greedy eyes and a horrible buzzing sound beneath their wings, who have made their homes in the eyes of the unmoving peasants. They have crawled into the children's mouths as their mouths lay open for a final scream and now the eyes and the mouths of the Dead are alive with the terrible buzzing of little wings.

"What killed them?" she asks, struggling to believe the scene before her eyes. All these innocent people! There is no blood. Not a drop. Not a sign of violence. Carlos descends into the ravine, to prove that she has no reason to disbelieve anything. The flies buzz away as he nears. Bsss. Bsss. Bsss. She never forgets the tragic sound and she hates flies forever after. She watches reluctantly as Carlos

*turns a body around, an old man whose face wears an expression of
odd whimsical serenity, to reveal a tiny hole just below the jawline.*

*"Icepicks," Carlos says dryly as though scenes like this were an
everyday occurrence, and turns the old man's greenish-glittering
head to demonstrate the icepick's journey from beneath the chin, all
the way up the nose, and into the brain.*

She awakes. The memory ends with the ending of the nightmare
inside her other memory. One memory, stacked on the tarred head
of another memory, of another memory, one of many memory
stacks she harbors of the restless Dead now living inside her. After
years of aptly defined memories of green flies, of staring dead eyes, of
a people who did not want her despite her continuous suffering for
them, she became a book of broken pages on which were written the
names of people with fly-filled eyes. The pages were filled with
images of streets where rivers of blood had scarcely dried and of
dying children in the slums left to scream from the twinkling ripples
of hunger until their final breath. There were also pages filled with
memories of when she had lived among them, eating nothing but
beans and rice, *frijoles y arroz*, and *arroz y frijoles*, and never enough
of either. The Dead never closed their horrible, staring eyes. The
children could scream in three languages and came running down
the steps of her sleep, night after night.

Then the Peruvian returned, once his country was devouring her
as it had once devoured him and she felt the same destructive love in
her soul that had driven him to his grave. Now she was forced to love
him because only he could understand the turmoil inside her soul.
He returned, happily whistling because she was trapped between his
love and the memories he had given her, and extended his hand
toward her from the nether side. At last, she loved him, to escape the
yoke of carrying his wretched country all by herself and she suddenly
considered him to be a most desirable man, especially when he told
her that she had been right to find refuge from Peru in the arms of

the Dead. She carried Peru with her, wherever she went, and he approved, because he had once felt the same fire burn inside of him. The only one to break diagonally through the solitude of her hermit life, he beckoned her to follow him into the land where he now dwelled, but she knew with perfect crystallization that he meant not relief but his final act of revenge, to lead her into the country of the dead. His intensely piercing desire was hard to resist, but all she ever agreed to was a cross-dimensional prattle, similar to that with the driver. She was not afraid to hold hands with a dead man, but she lost her life force for loving him. He sapped her energy, and he wanted her soul to stay alive himself. She gave freely to him, until one day there was almost nothing left of her and she awoke spent and tired every morning. Her own life became a silent memory as she left the wintry woods of her solitude to stand in the sunshine with one who had been brutally slain. His particular image always came back to her and out of her soul shone the strength and beauty of the people of Peru, and their humility. Her new-found Peruvian-ness caused her, simultaneously, to become an exile in her own land and an exile in his land also. Gone were the days her soul had belonged only to her, before it had been annexed by his country, gone the days when she had spoken a language other than Span-ish...until, one day, she became suspicious of her bamboozled life, which had turned into a distant masonry work with its displaced love mounted in the heart of a dead man. Like a heraldic butterfly, she wanted to escape the Peruvian and his memories.

Four—a green and pleasant land

Escaping him, she had to employ several subtle combinations of pun and metaphor to accommodate the definite righteousness with which he had claimed her. She returned to the small village where she had grown up under the mature melancholy glow of majestic mountains surrounded by lush green fields. Returning, she realized that she had always searched for the fascinating facets of these mountains, whether in Western Europe and in the USA, or even in Huancayo, among the blood and bone.

Walking through them once more, post-Peru, she was reminded of the devil's portal, a favorite Peruvian death squad dumping ground, only now realizing why she had loved the miserable place. Unfazed by well-conserved memories of death screams that still hung welded into its ancient rocks, she had loved the devil's portal, although many death squad victims had been found there, with machetes still embedded in their bloody mouths. She had sat there for hours, looking out over the autumnous land below, and he had sat beside her, his mind filled with dreadfully clear visions of her as the Eva Peron of Peru, and stating proudly "this is your country now, too." At night, she had woken breathlessly, feeling suffocated by the bloody stones of the devil's portal, but by day she had returned, over and over again, not knowing why the place was special to her. The had called her "blood princess" and a monster, for not being menaced by all the misery and pain that hung welded to the place, regardless of whether dead bodies could still be seen crouching there or not. She had even made the place attractive for herself, telling herself comfortable little lies, which she truly believed, about the bodies having been killed by falling rocks not machetes. Once, she had even found a man there, still alive, his grievous face expressing agony, a sword hole in the back of his head. To please her own imagination, she had thought of the man as an innocent victim of a stone avalanche, and of herself as a rescuing hero who had arrived too late. She stood beside him as he drew his final breath, her eyes filling with tears, her twisted thoughts bemoaning the fate of the wounded man while looking in vain for the rock that supposedly had come bearing down at him.

Now the ghost of the Peruvian walked by her side, a royal captive to his memories, as she returned to her own village. He watched reluctantly as she lay herself into the knee-deep grass. There were flowers everywhere around her, and dragon flies with their wings spread. The wind sent waves of music through large, green larches. A birch tree recognized and welcomed her, asking "Where have you been so long?" and taking her into its branches where it rocked her in safety and shielded her from the dark venom of his memories. She was home, at last, and she turned to him, filled with pride that the tree remembered her name. For the first time since she had known him, loved him, killed him and been conquered by him, she was able to proudly tell him "this is my life".

Suddenly, matters changed between them. She had been jealous of him, for belonging to a country which did not want her, and to a people that had excluded her and had never ceased to call her *gringa* or to make her feel that she was white, but now she was jealous no more. Her return to the mountains of her childhood was proceeding in a most satisfactory manner as a sudden friendly breeze washed away all memories of being an outcast and he became the one to be jealous because the trees had recognized her. He was jealous of how easily she blended into the grass and that the flowers moved to stroke her face with an ever so tender touch, jealous even of the bee who approached her in greeting, hovered before her face, softly touched her elbow and then flew away into the sunshine. He was jealous of the mountain sun that sought to draw from her pores every painful memory and strange passion not her own, and he stood by helplessly as the sun healed the torn pages of her book and proceeded to erase her memories Peru. He suddenly understood why she had always fought to stay alive, although he had isolated her, tortured her with dooming images and turned her into outcast whenever she sought to enter the world of the living, be it in his country or another. The driver had been an easy enemy to conquer. He had since long departed and only the memory of his memory was still feebly alive within her when he, the gentlemanly freedom fighter of Peru, well versed in Italian and some French as well, had claimed her. He had always made sure that she would find nobody to bind her to the world and had driven her into a friendless existence outside the borders of his country, where no other man could break through the wall of ownership he had erected around her heart. But she had held on to life, with an astonishingly firm grip in her trembling fingers. Screaming, struggling, crying, she had refused to let go and to follow him, although he had conquered her dreams, even the children of her dreams, until she was surrounded by various groups of kind strangers to whom she had no real connection. Even when she was in their company, he had buried her inside a fortress of memories, inside whose walls he tortured her with his own image, until she never looked another man into the face again. Strangely, she had refused to die, even when he had become her only ally and all she had left to shield her against images that still haunted her of Peru.

But today he stood beside her as an outcast among the fields and flowers, and a stranger to the trees. He became a visitor to her world as she had been to his, and he was jealous because she had a family of trees and flowers and mountains. He revealed unexpectedly, driven by the marvelously honest material his soul was made of, that he might have never had the urge to give his life for Peru, had he been born into a likewise beauty, adding that he had never known such peace. He confessed for the first time that, having been born poor and in Peru, he had never had opportunities to examine literary masterpieces or travel to America. In his country, where murderers were tortured together with innocents in an appalling kind of indulgence, the only way to escape the terror of his land had been to love it, be willingly and gladly slain for it and cause himself to become a hero. But now he understood that his choice had been only between two roads, and none of them too marvelous. The ultimate truth was that his only choice had been to love his land or to hate his land. For people like him, unable to escape Peru for their lack of funding or their lower class birth, there was nothing else. He had chosen to love Peru, he explained to her as though answering to questions in an interview and wishing obviously to speak in sordid detail of his life, because he had seen that those who chose to hate Peru perished sooner, but without having any orchids planted in their name on the fields of glory.

The birds sang in the trees and in the mountains there was a kind of peace he had never known in his living years, which penetrated his *post-dead* soul as the flowers welcomed him. As though by miracle, both their minds were in that instant completely at rest. Peru lay hidden, far beyond the mountains and the trees, and the tangled screams of its children were drowned by the cuckoo's song in the sky above. A little way away some rabbits were playing in the sunshine. The Peruvian wanted to continue bestowing a kind of confused grief upon her, mingled with feelings of terror, but his heart was not in it any longer. The sun had touched his heart and melted it, and he let her go, having realized that she was a daughter of the mountains who had no place among the blood that still flowed in crimson rivers through his land. Relieved and released, she turned her face into the sunshine to let all his defective memories with their terrors be washed away when he, suddenly afraid that she would escape him completely, warned her with a stirring love she still felt for the people of Peru who had failed to understand her:

"Do not forget your people!"

"I will never forget *your* people (correcting him), but I will not be slain for their sake as you were slain. Your people are still dying. They were dying before you gave your life for them and they will keep dying even if I were to give mine. I shall not give up all of this (roundabout motion with her hand) for the sickening political mess of Peru. You have asked a lot of me and now I must ask something of you. I will feel much better once I find my home here, again, among the mountains and the trees."

In the valley below, where the fields ended, she saw a riding stable, in painstaking detail as if hand-painted by diligent aquarellists. She directed her moving hand at the stable and the Peruvian's attention followed her. He could have stopped her with another dose of grinding hell memories, but he stoically stuck to his promise of either letting her go or imprisoning her by her own free will. She almost wanted to embrace him, that was how sorry she was for him when she looked into the future and in a somewhat premature dream, drawn up by the diligent female mechanics of her mind, she saw the horses of the Rider (she knew their names now, and their colors, and their ages and the descriptive markings of their bandaged legs) jumping in that very stable's grounds and the Rider laying on his back beside her, amongst the flowers. She envisioned herself floating through life in dreamy peace, here among the trees, snuggled safely in the Rider's warm, pulsating, alive arms.

The Peruvian warned her, jealously, but slyly disguising his jealousy as caution: "You do not even remember what he looks like, do you? You think you are going to be sleeping with an angel but you know nothing of him. You made him all up, inside your mind."

She was annoyed by his snuff-boxing tone and tried to create an image of the Rider from her memory but the image did not come forward and remained blurred. A man on a horse. Could have been any man on any horse. No nose. No cheeks. No forehead of distinction. Somewhat limp looking. Shabbily dressed.

Triumphantly the Peruvian mocked: "Is this love? Hah! How can you build a life with someone whose face you do not even remember? (adding with almost comical self-effectuation) At least you always knew *my* face!"

He invaded her memory his own face, in all its perfect glorious detail that was nothing but good: his high forehead, his dark deep eyes with their enormous soul, his small fine ears, his chiseled profile. He poured out his full beauty into her mind, taking her breath away. She had to keep herself from looking and from reaching out to him to softly trace with her index finger the outline of his delightful lips. Her instinct was to stammer something along the lines of, "I am terribly sorry. It was as though he had cursed me. He is no good. There was nothing between us. You are the only one to make me smile."

But then she checked herself. What was this? No sooner had he let her go than he was trying to invade her well-lit life again, although he was unable to kiss her hands or massage her feet.

"No!"

She wiped his image away. "Were you alive, there would be no other. Fain would I have taken you into this paradise alongside me, but you are dead."

"So is he," the Peruvian gloated nastily while smiling an angelic smile at her. "Anyone is dead whose image you cannot conjure up inside your heart. What a sickening mess you propose to make of your life!"

"I do not remember his face but I remember the color of his soul," she exasperated. "I am sure you will understand, once you see it."

With this, she painted the colors of the Rider's soul into her memory and the Peruvian stood by, watching in awe. He could see nothing except bright colors sparkling. Even he had to admit, albeit reluctantly, that the other was indeed very much alive inside her.

The End.

CHAPTER 6

One—the poem

Walking by her side, the Peruvian followed her further into her world. She dragged him along with authority as they walked through lush green valleys, at the foothills of majestic mountains that almost came to embrace her. Her main objective was to show the Peruvian a different kind of world that existed outside the army camps of Latin America. She spoke kindly to him as she sat down on a hill bathed in sunlight. The flowers bent their heads to greet her and the sun warmed the dreadful space inside of her that was still filled with guilt for having survived at all.

"I am terribly sorry, it is all my fault," the Peruvian exclaimed suddenly. "We were two humans in a very rare, unusual situation that I should have never dragged you into. Today, I have learnt something. We will never forget being here together."

"I didn't notice the torture, anyway," she shrugged. "In fact, I am grateful to you for my Latin experience. The Latino love for God is rare in this day and age. As for the bloody mess in the torture chamber, I learned a very useful thing long ago, in school, which kept the torture from troubling me. They might as well have been burning dead leaves instead of live bodies!"

"What was it that you learned?" he asked guiltily, his guilt merging with feelings of grief.

"A poem, a very good poem. Nothing has damaged me because I recite it whenever something bad happens. It takes you to a good place, even if they burn your pale feet with hot irons."

When he prompted her, she recited for the now friendly Peruvian the first verses of the poem that spoke of all life, of all death, of all mankind, and of lost or fading memories. The poem made time stand quite still as it spoke of the gradual decline of loved ones, parents and grandparents and relatives whose faces creased daily, painfully slow and yet much too fast, hair that turned from black to gray to white and eventually disappeared, hands which grew ever more wrinkled, callused feet which could one day walk no more, old people who grew shorter and smaller and into the earth. Watching their slow dying process, accepting but never understanding the reason for a temporary kind of existence and for all life being a small and all too brief flash of light between a black and mysterious abyss on either side, a man could either turn to insanity or to poetry. The poem asked the one question modern man tried to avoid, burying himself in various important tasks and seeking his happiness in phony luxuries like fast food and fast life and fast sex, *what dawn, what death, what doom, awaits consciousness beyond the tomb?*

Her young fingers, with their suntanned skin with its youthful shine, picked a leaf off the hazelnut tree before her that was not yet heavy with seed and then she told the Peruvian the poem she had learnt, which had saved her from living through the abdominal torture in his land.

*I was the shadow of the waxwing slain by the false azure in the windowpane...*her voice danced from verse to verse as she gave her words a tune. Her inner eye stabbed her with a swift vision, of an ashen bird smashed by flight into a windowpane, a young boy's first encounter with serious death and his resulting addiction to explore the abyss beyond death, where the bird had flown. The poem followed him, from his boyhood to his sixty first year.

The silent mountains towering above them suddenly took a great interest in what she was saying and she could not help sounding pompous, even somewhat schoolmasterly, as she went on about the phantoms of the boy's youth and about him visiting his old home, which now belonged to someone else, and his memories of his parents and his aunts and his French-Canadian maid, even of his long departed daughter.

The Peruvian listened to her voice move rhythmically to and fro, over the various Cantos of Nabokov's *Pale Fire,* and he forgot all about his sadness of never being able to wear socks and trousers again. He had been a terrible dead man, a crazy dead man even, but suddenly he recouped his innate artistic merit and seemed recovered from his disease of hating her.

"How splendid!" the poor man exclaimed. *"How wonderful!"*

Although he was still clinically and actually dead, he was suddenly moved to consider that it might not be her fault. How could she have known that torture chambers existed, having been raised in the mountains, with an intellectual diet of *Pale Fire* not torture manuals?

She felt a sensation strange and odd, like a great relief, wash over her out of a sudden.

"I was perfectly innocent of your death," she dared telling him and because he replied nothing to that, she assumed that he agreed.

When she came to look around herself again, she encountered not the phantoms of *Pale Fire* but her own phantoms, of the sunny paths of her youth; the young girl she had once been, gaily galloping on her horse over a wide green field. On the horse beside her gallops her best friend whose long blond hair flows in the wind and who had grown up to become a doctor of psychology specializing in dubious behaviouristic experiments, having had to heavy-heartedly sell her horse to finance her studies.

Two—the mad castle

Her old school was not too far from where they were sitting and she decided to take the Peruvian there. Her school was a castle, which still stood. A woman had once been murdered there by a jealous lover and the woman and her dog still haunted the castle grounds at night. Now she saw the phantoms of young girls who had stayed up centuries ago, all night, in their long and silky gowns, in the hope to encounter the hissing, clicking ghost, but the woman and the dog had evaded them. The girls had not taken into account that ghosts were not in the haunting business all the time and that they sometimes took an entire century's rest before spooking again through places where they had found their undue demise. It was different with the Peruvian. He was not an official ghost with a fluent gliding path and a white flowing robe, besides, he was a foreigner, being Peruvian.

As she walked the lower path leading around the old castle, she recalled her bedroom, now reserved for another child, perhaps with the same hunger for life she had once felt and the same impeccable strength of youth already fading from her. She felt protective of the old castle, which for centuries had seen many great stories that it never told. The castle could be trusted to keep its cold stony mouth shut, always, and the secrets of those who had cried or laughed within its walls remained there forever.

She realized, there and then, the motive of the mountains for calling her home. The castle had need of her, to include her among its exciting, passionate, ancient memories. There was something strange and odd about the castle, which called everybody back who had once lived inside its walls, to ask them their stories and to bleed their memories into its cold stone. The castle did not speak in a foreign language and she had no need for an interpreter to understand its somewhat reasonable request. It surveyed the Peruvian with its oyster-colored eyes and quickly drew the memories from both of them, to mingle inside its ancient walls with memories of ill-dressed little men, of old hardened creatures with trenched faces, of plumber-like men clapping in tact to strange medieval music, of exquisite young creatures with milk and honey skin and sparkling eyes, of flaunting girls in silk and velvet dresses, of nice blondes with welcoming breasts hanging out of their open dresses, and of bellowing musicians and medieval crusaders.

In a chattering tone, the castle complimented her and the Peruvian, saying if she could only improve her Spanish and decide to part her delicate lips for him completely, it would fain welcome them as ghosts into its ancient walls, because theirs was one of the finest and noblest stories it had heard. The castle hastily went on, about them promenading its grounds every first of February with their arms round each other, conversing in rapid and (accent free! the castle emphasized accent free!) Spanish. They would be instructed how to become the most delicious nocturnes of its haunting life. With Latin America being quite in fashion now, they could make a real killing, as Latin lovers of finely composed ideals who had become the tragic victims of traitors and of misrepresenters of the revolution. The castle had a strange and nervous hunger for publicity and envisioned tours of chattering tourists, glad to pay for a bad night's sleep, traveling from far-away for the promise of seeing, sitting waiting and smoking, well-wrapped and rugged under the midnight sky outside the old back gate, not all too clearly (of this they would be forewarned) the tragic Peruvian couple telling laughing stories to each other in rapid Spanish, over the excited chatter of the ghosts of the slain peasants.

The castle made a gesture that suggested them to be a genuine catch, especially when taking into account that everything had changed: times, and places and the expectations of the people. Medieval dames in deplorable flowery frocks were a boredom for the ghost hunters of modern times. Something new was needed. A handsome, charming couple who had been slain tragically in an exotic land and who were now suspended between one world and the next, for their fervent love of a people whose ghosts thronged around them…this, the castle stated with dreaming eyes and a blinking smile, would be a ghost show to die for.

"How on earth can they care about your story if they do not even know you exist?" it exclaimed innocently enough, but using in reality negotiation tactics it had learnt from a business manual that had been left behind by a visitor. With the money earned, the castle said, affected by the revenue it foresaw, one could free oneself from the taint of shabby stones, perhaps even paint one's mediaeval, breaking exterior in a bright-softish pink (the castle explained that it had always loved the color pink, a fact which elicited contempt among its castle peers, and wearisome pitiful smiles from the ghosts living inside its walls).

The Peruvian was all for the idea, he saw it as a sure way to keep his people from dying.

"You have taken me somewhat by surprise, I haven't got all the details, but what you propose seems to be sound," he said. "I am dead, so the ghost performance should not be too much trouble."

When the castle thanked him for coming and they began to confer in scrupulous Latin American slang, she was almost terrified of their profound manner and serious tones of voice, wondering as much about the Peruvian's dubious intentions as the castle's ability to speak accent-free Peruvian-type Spanish with a darkish-crowded voice. In their world of ghosts, she had no escort to lead her back to the living and she wondered what to do when they began to speak of chains to be added as a romantic nightly burden and the castle commented, quite seriously, that the rattling of chains had always delighted the various ghost hunters of the region.

They stood under the porch for a few minutes more, talking with the castle. The Peruvian's eyes grew into small slits that stared, hypnotized, at the castle as through he had already lost his identity to the castle's magnetic message. He envisioned affinity, respect and more, for his people and their under-rated plight. The castle's eyes were very bright because, in its mind, it had already crossed the road and seen her dying. She, on the other hand, disliked the whole scene completely and seriously wondered about the castle's sanity, especially when it mentioned that it wanted to meet the ice-pick-murdered folks as well.

Three—the Russian love poem

The castle was not incompetent in the art of languages. Having learnt Russian during the second World War, when some Russian soldiers had dismounted for a quick few days of rest among its bourgeois walls, it taught the Peruvian a sad, swinging love poem that spoke of unfulfilled desire, which they were certain would cause her, through sudden, bold inspiration, to follow him. The Peruvian had tried on the unfamiliar tongue like a new coat, until he was comfortable in the raw, shuddering language with its melancholy *scurr scurr* rasping rhythm. Now he spoke to her in a luscious, highly romantic but also sad voice, with an accent impossible to anatomize:

Ya vas liubil; liubov yesho,
ticho i besnadezhno,
buit-mozhet inogda umiraja ot radosti.
V dushe moyey ugasla rewnost' nye sovsyem…

The castle translated dramatically:

I loved you,
I loved you silently and without hope,
perhaps sometimes nearly dead with joy,
and sometimes nearly dead with jealousy.
I loved you
with such tenderness and sincerity
as God may allow you to be loved some day by someone else.

"…*kak day vam Bog liubemoy buit drugim.*"

The Peruvian had used up all his Russian and he looked at her longingly and the translating castle looked at her greedily, and she had to close her eyes tight to shut out the image of the Peruvian who had recited an old Russian love poem to conquer her heart. She had a feeling of naked danger in case that she looked at him again. One more glance would cause her to take his exquisite hand and to live with him, forever happily, amongst the ancient walls of a pink castle, delighting the tourists on weekdays with haunting appearances.

"How do you feel about that?" the castle asked seductively. "You and he together, here inside my walls, saying hello every now and then to my tourists?"

In the off-season, it added, their appearances would be daily, in high season hourly, operations.

"There would be no set times, so long as you keep to the basic schedule. I am very interested in you two, indeed. What do you say?"

She shook her head with wild determination and wiped away the image of such premature a future. The castle held very strong views on the subject and this whole matter had turned into a rather delicate situation. Trying not to appear ungrateful, she said that she had considered the attractive terms the castle had to offer and had very much liked the Russian love poem (she thanked the castle for its speedy translation but could not bear to meet the eyes of the Peruvian to thank him for his recital) but that she could not justify becoming a ghost just yet. She explained to the castle that she could not return forever, and certainly not stay on as a ghost. Even in her present, living state, she could at best tarry for a little while.

The castle squinted nastily from its upper tower window and sneered at her and she had enough for one evening and wanted to cry because of the castle's solemn, questioning glance. The castle kept looking at her in a puzzled manner, not understanding why she could not stay on, even on as a living person, to serve tea from china cups to the tourists, perhaps, or to empty the tables again, brush and scrub its floors, and to ask visitors "can I do anything for you?"

She explained that the castle and the mountains and the fields were all the same, the seasons having passed them seemingly without change, but that she was different now. The events that had shaped her in the past years had been of sufficient gravity to close her way of return into her village forever. She could not come back, because life does not tarry with yesterday and does not permit erasure of the past. Walking the fields she had walked as a child, she could not undo the experiences she had had lived. Her soul had been formed and molded by strange, haggard people speaking in foreign tongues. It had been introduced to Americans and Russians and decadent pigs promising things they never kept. She had seen indifferent gringos, and been ashamed to be seen, frowning, in the company of indifferent gringos who walked through the filthy hospitals of Ayancucho, calling the people there horrible and uncultured, because the appropriate departments of their brains had been unable to carry out the order for compassion.

She did not wish to die in order to perform for the castle's tourists. Living, she explained to the rather mad castle, she could no longer be trusted to integrate into the kind of tranquil society to be found here, not after having been shaped in strange lands and now communicating in somewhat cryptic squiggles. She had smelled other countries' trees and had walked through hills with strange foliage. Her hands had touched foreign rock and her face had been warmed by a sun shining on the faces of people with dark skins and foreign cultures. She had become part of these people, of their land and their brutal hot sun which was rarely a friend. There were many scars on the once smooth surface of her heart, left there by pictures she had seen, and she was still shaken by minimal tremors of the terror she had felt there, a kind of terror that had never been experienced in the meticulous orderliness of the mountain villages.

Four—a warning from the future

Morning had turned to afternoon and the castle still listened with great interest as she explained that she had returned, seeking to sort out her confused memories and hoping for comfort among the ancient mountains. She could not bring any phantoms back to life, not the phantom of her younger self nor the phantom of her adoptive parents, who had still been un-creased when she had left, and very agile. She had tried to reach a hand from the future to the young girl she had once been, who sat laughing in the meadow, under a very kind and very un-Peruvian sun. She meant to tell her that she would return two decades later, well-traveled and weary, and she wanted to warn her to stay out of Peru, where they would only give her the hospitality of their cells, and also not to love the man with the inviting brown eyes but to let him go because that love would lead to the marching sound of brutal feet (heard, not seen, through the spyhole of a prison cell, where eager military men demonstrated to new cadets how to make disappear those who had proved useless to the land, who were roughly swept and kicked there and had every natural tooth kicked out of their martyred mouths) and to her disappearing innocence.

She meant to tell the young girl that it would hurt at first, letting him go, but that he was going to get killed anyway. She wanted to tell her that the nagging thirst for life, which she thought she must quench at all costs, would be stilled at too high a price, in loving a man like the Peruvian, and that it would be better to hold her heart rigid and turn away from him the moment she met his eyes, not when it was already too late and he would cause himself to be tortured to his death in an insane reaction to her rejection of his bloodshed-filled life. In the cool, clear light of a Peruvian winter he would die, his own tongue being handed to him on a plate before he drew his final breath. She wanted to disclose for the young girl a future she would rather not encounter, where she would return to her village spent and damaged, having traveled alone for a long long time, having loved and lost and been tortured into listlessness. She would be hoping to recoup her stolen memory, seeking phantoms of her past among the shades, only to encounter framed jaws chewing crossly when she had once again interrupted a peaceful dinner at the pub with her strange story-telling.

She would find that her memories of torture did not belong among the mountains and the cows, because they were not part of the ordered, cleanish life being lived around here. She would meet with arms folded cross-wise before guts-and-glory chests, and with work-hardened pranks with unkempt claws raising themselves in traffic-stop motion to keep from becoming even an idea in her mind and doing everything to shield themselves from her memories.

It's the security that's important, she wanted to tell the young girl, *not the adventure*. She meant to warn the young girl on the sunny field to never see with the eyes of the Dead nor rely on the advice of ghosts in books, because the ghosts and the Dead could never anchor her to the world. But she already knew that the girl would not listen. In the girl's eyes already shone the wonder of a mystery that she wished to explore. Already, she was trapped in the obsession of a poem she had barely learnt and wished to know *what dawn, what death what doom*…having become enticed, at once, by the prospect of sharing her life with the ghost of a rallye driver who lived on the other side and had stories to tell beyond her wildest dreams. She was dunk with the promise of loving without masks and she was set on a path where one day no living man would be enough for her. How could the young girl know that lack of experience was a blessing not a curse? One day, her feet would hurt like the feet of a woman ten years older and she would return to find her adoptive parents creased and bent, because they had grown old and small in her absence and now could not help her anymore. She would be all alone.

Having explained all of this to the castle, she stated that she now wanted something solid and real, something as simple as love with a living, non-freedom-fighting, non-endangering man, to be protected in his strong arms from the howling winds in her soul.

"I shall die one day," she promised the castle, "and then I shall return."

The castle gurgled cheerfully at that formidable promise, and told her not to worry. Waiting for her timely end, one could, if all else failed, sell off one's furniture to repaint one's face, which had begun to peel from having lived through terrible historical changes and famines and scorched earth. Examining her face and finding no complaint with her ordinary little wish, the castle told her that it would wait for another half century, because time meant very little to a medieval castle.

The Peruvian, still standing beside her, had listened to her every word and now he triumphed. He sang joyfully, in slightly Russian-accented Spanish (it took him some time to shed the new language again completely) "Gone, gone. They are all gone. You are alone in the world, nothing to hold you here. You have become a stranger, even in your own home. Come with me, I shall love you."

Five—the Peruvian's speech

She left the castle, not wishing to find herself paralyzed there by the desire of the Peruvian, whose mind seemed to have few tracks all leading toward the same end. Rolling up her sleeves nearly to her armpits in the warmth that greeted her outside, she closed her ears to the voice of the ghost and smiled into the sun. She walked across the hills and found herself looking straight into the blank eyes of a curiously staring cow as she finally told the Peruvian in very fluent Spanish: "*Mir* means 'world' in Russian and 'mine' in German, and this here is *my world*. I have the mountains and I have the sun and they will hold me here, where I belong."

"You will be so much closer to the mountains (he was now increasingly losing his Russian accent until only a very faint trace remained), you will feel them so much nearer, once your spirit soars across them and is released by the chains of the material. You will wish yourself on that moutaintop (the ghost pointed enthusiastically) and you shall stand there, your spirit distributed between this summit and that one over there, you shall be the grass and the cows and the flowers and the mountains, and your consciousness shall be everywhere and nowhere. You shall in the same instant stare out of the cow's curiously bulging eyes and be the bell around its neck, you shall even be the mocking bird's song overhead. To love the mountains, you need not stay alive, of this I can assure you."

The Peruvian said all that, shamelessly plagiarizing from the poem she had taught him, and also because he had learnt *Soviet negotiation tactics* from the manual in the castle. Because of his Russian tick he put the two together and to what he deemed to be a good use.

Strangely enough, without seeming to obtain any satisfaction from his observation he turned to her, stating that a life like hers was no life. What of a life that was only bearable through having people and events dissected, processed and banished inside the pages of her books?

"The Rider is a worthless man, but I love you!" he intoned seductively.

She was somewhat tending to agree with him, about the Rider not, but about her shamble of a life where she only pretended to be happy. All her *post-Peruvian* memories showed her alone with the crowd inside her head, whose discreet murmurs and subdued expressions originated from her unseen friends like Franz Liszt and other disembodied writers and composers who had made their homes inside her mind as a spiritual adventure they could later write or compose about. They all crowded into the great void that had been left, its door wide open, by her distress over the matter of Peru.

Shivering in the warm sun, she sighingly drew her shawl about her. It was a somewhat mournful sigh, because she had always regarded herself as clever for her choice of friends from the pages of great books, but now the Peruvian proposed, perhaps rightly, that her life with her clever friends had been nothing but a disguise for a living death. She had the urge to run away from it all. In a very distressed state of mind, she pictured a plan that entailed returning to the castle and flinging herself out the tower window, thinking only vaguely of the messy splash on the ground, and clearly of an almost instant reunion with the Peruvian. George Sand appeared, towering on her right-brain, logical side, where a considerable crowd of other literary figures now collected, ready for fiery or bloody entertainment as they witnessed the fight between life and death.

Sand watched the crowd cooly and spoke with confidence, savoring her cigar. "Far from it, dear friend, you are guided, not insane. Your pursuer is in error. It takes true courage to seek friends in books instead of among the useless chatter of the Living. He has great grief inside him because of the kind of captors he has been having, and now he wants to possess you. He is deprivedly insane, thinking you his beloved and waiting for you because he does not realize your death would bring him an even greater grief. You go ahead and live your own life, and don't let him tell you what to do. He might be dead, but you are alive. You want to know a lot of things, and curiosity is a characteristic of the living."

George smiled reassuringly, rocking her smile from one side of her mouth to the other and back again for special emphasis.

"Do not listen to his folly. He only wants to be moving into the castle with you, but you must live for the sake of studying the finesse of language. Tell him that you, like all writers, are a visiting card of your craft."

The crowd applauded softly, standing there with pale eyes and discretely stamping their feet as if to encourage her, and then they stood patiently, awaiting the Peruvian's response. The Peruvian frowned a little and then laughed in a rolling, rich commentary. Conscious of the crowd, he disclosed his brilliant ability to become instantly pop-

ular to whatever crowd, in whatever place. Tuning down his originally contemptuous-intended laughter, he laughed disdainfully but
not unkindly, as though he possessed special knowledge he did not
want to boast about.

"*She* is the one you must not listen to," he began hopefully and she
could hear in his voice a definite desire to reduce George Sand to a
housewife in denim trousers, with an iron in her uncomplaining,
patiently working hand. "What does *she* know of life? Her days were
not spent swimming in a sea of solitude. Her friends were not out of
books but made of flesh and blood. She had a castle, which she did
not have to die to enter, and she never had a worry for her daily
bread. She had the love of a fine and living composer. She had children. What advice could *she* possibly give to *you*, who walks devoid
of children, devoid of castles, devoid of family love, devoid even of
an *en corpus* lover…who walks through life by the side of ghosts."

"I, too, shall have a castle on day," she replied with particular ami-
ableness, also conscious of keeping on her side the good-will of the
crowd, which now grew a little impatient. "I, too, shall have children
one day, with the man I love…"

The Peruvian interrupted her hoarsely. "I *am* the man you love
and I cannot give you children anymore."

"You *were* the man I loved," she corrected him, "but you are
dead."

An image of the Rider flashed inside her head that she had not
been able to prevent from coming. The crowd obediently admired
the other's aliveness, feeling a certain insecurity and instability
because they themselves were dead, and exclaimed a respectful if
subdued *ah* that rippled through them like a soft wave. The Peruvian
saw him, too, and stepped back fearfully. He had seen the Rider's face
quite clearly, and also that he was very much alive. He had since long
known that the Dead were no contest for the living. "I, too, shall one
day find myself some flesh-and-blood friends," she concluded her

reply and nodded, slowly and sincerely, having spoken. She could believe this vision of her future.

"Hah," the Peruvian barked contemptuously. "Friends? What kind of friends would understand the pictures in your head (he briefly flashed an image of the icepick victims and she could see the small holes quite clearly, underneath their chins, and looked one second too long into their blunt, unseeing eyes before returning to the mountains beyond which their odd sobs remained)? And him (now he flashed an image of the Rider, but he was beautiful no longer. Being Dead, the Peruvian had access to considerable powers of adding visual commentary to pictures, and he made the Rider appear as though in a distorted mirror. He had indulgently drawn dull, thick lines on the horseman's fine face, and in his jealousy he had painted him a seagull nose and lecherous hungry eyes under which dark gray bags of tired skin shuddered. The Rider had a rabbit mouth and the crowd now covered their faces and held their bellies, appalled by his bitter ugliness and the fact that he had no teeth), do you honestly believe that he will love you? Good grief! How could he understand you, who were released from the killing fields of Peru, who still bears the collective pain of my people and have lived with them through their darkest years, when the skies of Lima turned red with blood and the sun's brutal heat resulted not in sun-burnt skin but in the stench of rotting flesh from the bodies of roadside death squad victims? *You* propose to love a Rider? And what will he do when the screams of my people keep you awake at night? Do you think he will understand their simplicity of mind and that the same simplicity has touched you, too? Will he understand that you would rather talk to a tree than dress up for a fancy party? His head will be in his paws when he realizes that a part of you belongs to the *Iglesia Popular* and makes you wear a rosary for 10 *pesos* around your slender neck, where he would perhaps rather see a necklace of fine pearls."

The Peruvian shook his head sadly at what he deemed to be a hopeless dream and then he continued as if by sudden bold inspiration, urged on by the kind clapping of the crowd.

"Do you suppose that he, who all his life has ridden noble horses along familiar territories, who has always slept on soft white pillows and dined in luxury, would understand why you followed me into the slums of Lima? To him, my people are aliens and my country is a miserable tragedy best kept hidden away. Will he understand that you dwelt there, in mud-floor huts, and that you knew starvation, together with my people? That you knew days when there was never enough rice or water and that you have been formed by hunger and thirst? Does he realize, do you suppose, that your body has been soiled by roaches that came at night to share your bed, and that you once loved a foreign country's most noble son and killed him when you banished him inside your books? Does he know, do you suppose, that you watched someone be tortured to death, for the sake of a bloody, blooded land? He will run from you, I tell you, he will *run!*"

Sympathizing with the handsome Peruvian's wounds, the crowd looked at her reproachfully. Somehow, she thought that it would be best to take on the fawning look of a dog which knows it has been naughty and has no specific spot to crawl to. The crowd approved when her eyes filled with tears and she looked very sorry for what she had done. She still cowered a little when the Peruvian, encouraged by the crowd's compassionate smile, continued to speak.

"What folly to think that he, with his fancy horses and his fine hotels, his stable groom and his ordered life lived around hurdles in different parts of the world, would understand a woman of your kind, (the crowd now shook its head at what it recognized to be extreme folly) a woman in whose veins flows noble blood but who has shared her bed with peasants and has broken bread with Latino peasants!"

"He, too, is of humble birth," she defended the Rider, this much she know of him. "He, too, is from peasant stock."

The crowd looked expectantly at the Peruvian, content with this new piece of information and curious whether this would make the Rider appear more tolerant, and her dream not altogether mad. The Peruvian knew to handle an insecure crowd and he smiled confidently, grimly determined to scorch the Rider's working class roots like one scorches a cancer despite great advances with antibiotics.

"He has outgrown his peasant roots at an early age," he cried out, flashing his shiny white teeth. On his face lay an expression of great triumph (several of the women in the crowd swooned and nearly fainted when he fixed his glowing quirky eyes on them. A red rose spilt on the stage, landing at his feet. The Peruvian gracefully bent his slender body to pick it up and continued speaking, with a look of provocative purity, and with the red rose firmly planted among the slender fingers of his right hand. Seductively, giving the gesture an appearance of a distracted impulse, he twisted and turned the flower among his thumb and index finger), "he never knew poverty or hunger in his grown-up years, which have not been soiled by despair as yours have been. He never fought for his life (the crowd nodded in unity, looked at her, and said "mmmhhhh"). You have made a home inside your soul for the people of Peru and I alone can understand you. Come with me, my love. You are already dead. We have both nobly given our lives to the people. One day, the children in the streets shall sing our song, playing in the coal-dust by the roadside near the *Mercado Central*. They will visit our grave in the *Cementaria General* (roughly smoothing his tousled hair with his free hand, he offered gracefully that she could share his grave in Lima) to bring us flowers. Come with me my love, come with me and be dead and happy at last. You have no place among the living. Forget the gringo horseman who has never seen people starve, who has never cared that the daily grain he feeds to his horses would keep a dozen Peruvians from starvation. He has never seen the desperate, pleading eyes of a child as life ebbs from his little body before it has fully begun. Leave him to his beasts and come with me. Come!"

He gave a gallant little bow at the end of this speech and extended deep, probing eyes toward her, followed by his rose-clad hand. In the eyes of the younger women in the crowd glimmered collective jealousy because he had invited her to be dead with him. She was somewhat unsure of herself now, wondering whether she was being ungrateful for having rejected his kind offer of becoming a ghost with him. What the Peruvian said could very well be of merit. True, she was tired of him being dead, but this alone did not disqualify him from observing simple truths. How could any man understand the killing fields inside her or the subtle thread that linked her to his homeland? How could a Rider, who had only known his horses, understand that she carried inside her the love of a martyred freedom fighter for his country, that she had almost lost her own life, alongside him, and, worse, that she would have given it gladly for a people not her own? And yet, she longed for the horseman's clean clear world, which existed far from the evil of mankind and seemed very inviting because it was free from images of dirty little men in blood-soaked bandages and had not been soiled by murder. There were no people wantonly killing other creatures. His wonderfully glowing world was full of strange customs concerning the leaping of horses, and the greatest problem at hand was the height to which a strong horse could jump. Her eyes had seen the evil that men do and his eyes had not seen, but that was an attraction not a disadvantage. She wanted to become part of a world where horses ran quickly toward hurdles, leapt over them, then walked proudly out of the ring. The smell of scorched meat had lost its attraction, it was no longer a magical smell, and now she wanted a life where she could settle into sleep safely. In Peru, she had feared everything, every human on the street had been a potential enemy or a torturer in disguise. When night came, the death squads came, making hungry, tired and frightened people vanish, sometimes releasing them as corpses, sometimes releasing them as shells with no identity and no being. She was hungry for the Rider's clean-scrubbed innocence that allowed him, even after decades, to still pursue as his highest good the riding of a horse. She would be able to explain him the night-mares which periodically came to haunt her sleep and he would understand.

"Never!" The Peruvian interrupted her glorious future vision, frowning suspiciously. "Never. Never. Never!"

He got so excited at the utterance of these words that despite being dead he was like a working organism, overcome by a clinking and sudden hiccup, which sounded somewhat like this *hiccu, hiccu hiccu.* In his fervor to keep her from leaving his land, of need and hunger where nobody was enough loved and where she would soon find herself haggard and droppingly depressed with her head hunched as if in sickness, he *hicuped* urgently and explained in very fast, earnest Spanish: "The kind of love you *hiccu* want is not of this world. He...*hiccu*...wears a...*hiccu hiccu hiccu*...mask and you wear you...*hiccu hiccu*...yours. His mask...*hiccu hiccu*...and your mask will meet...*hiccu*...and the...*hiccu hiccu hiccu*...masks of the...*hiccu* ...sum total...*hiccu*...of all your and all his disappointments and...*hiccu hiccu hiccu*...excuse me *disculpa!*"

"*No importa*", she said and politely waited for another furious row of *hiccu hiccu* before he was able to continue, "...the sum total of expectations...*hiccu* and dreams and hopes and what you think and he thinks you or he should be will...*hiccu hiccu hiccu*...meet and you will...*hiccu*..."

...she interrupted the Peruvian to advise him of a very effective technique to conquer hiccup by thinking intensely of three bald men while drinking a glass of water and holding one's breath.

"I cannot...*hiccu*...drink a glass of water," he reminded her, "I am dead. Dead people cannot drink."

"Then you must imagine drinking the water," she advised the Peruvian, "and it will work just as well."

The Peruvian obediently imagined three bald men and drinking a glass of water, which felt like liquid velvet traveling down his throat that was parched from speaking, and then his hiccup was gone and in his eyes shone a terrible crowd-winning innocence as he continued, this time without the annoying hiccus.

"It will be a love of mask meets mask, the masks of your memories, your fears, your weaknesses and strengths, your real and imagined selves. One day, the masks will be worn and tired, but the souls that are buried beneath will never have been touched. The love of the living is not for you. It is a love borne of fears, of solitude, of half truths, of minds split from the many problems which come with living in a world as this. It is not the clean kind of love you seek and know…"

The crowd listened to him admiringly, the younger women with their lips slightly parted, perhaps imagining in the privacy of their own minds a discreet encounter with the fervent speaker. Most of them were literary or musical figures who had always preferred the perfumes of spiritual principles to those of the body. Now they nodded their heads in satisfaction, too polite to blatantly tell her that the Peruvian was right, but telling her all the same with their approving eyes.

George Sand paced up and down a little and began to yawn at the other literary women in the crowd who were now only half-conscious, having succumbed to the influence of the Peruvian's genial charm. Then Sand whispered into her ear that this was not the nineteenth century after all, and that she must order her own life in accordance with her own wishes and should not give in to the pressure of having her sensations and impressions of the Rider analyzed before a largely female crowd feeling the need for intelligent sympathy with the Peruvian. Thus empowered to express herself, she thanked George Sand and in a very defiant manner wiped away the applauding crowd, banishing them back amongst the pages of their respective books or musical scores.

"Ah shut your mouth," she snapped impatiently at the Peruvian, "remembering is the real grief, not living."

She descended from the mountain, pausing now and then to pick some flowers by the side of her path, where the grass reached to her knees and she enjoyed its caressing touch on her bare skin. The Peruvian considered the mere act of picking flowers as solid proof that she was dead, solid enough that he was ready to bet on it.

"If you were alive, as you claim to be, you would have been content to look at the flowers and enjoy the mere looking at them. But no, you had to stop to slay them to take their corpses home with you and plant their dead faces, heads up, into your vase as though it were a grave. What shame and misery is there to be found in this act. By this, you prove that the Dead delight you more than the Living. Believe me, you have no place among their shabby towns. Whatever are you doing in this world, all by yourself? Come with me, I will look after you."

Six—the cinema

The Peruvian announced that he would undertake to prove how truly dead she was, by showing her an assimilation of sheer irrefutable facts. Very proud of himself for having succeeded in so thoroughly researching even the most hidden parts of her life, he promised that already *Fact Number One* would no longer enable her to continue walking as a mere impostor among the living. The facts, she learned, were to be presented in a little cinema he had constructed especially for this purpose. He pointed out, not altogether modestly, that the cinema had been erected at an amazing speed for a work of such detailed and fine craftsmanship. Inviting her with his personal magnetism to step inside, she followed him and as they entered he explained, giving his voice a seductive tone, that works of divine design like this, constructed at such speed, were a skill reserved entirely for the Dead.

"There are many places a dead man can go," he pointed out with utterly poisoning passion, indicating the great freedom that came from not being restricted to things that could be seen and touched. She snorted in response, to show him that he was offering a black dream and that being dead was the last thing she would be thinking of. He bid her to sit down and choose from any of the chairs, which all had a lining of crimson velvet. She took a chair in the fifth row, her preferred place in a cinema. She had always loved cinemas, a fact which the Peruvian probably knew, having run across all her childhood streets in his researches. He now began to speak of childhoods, saying that everybody had an unhappy childhood but that some recovered from it and some didn't and that those who did not recover had in all actuality been slain by their parents. She looked at him with faint interest, puzzled as to where he had uncovered such a load of nonsense, and wondering seriously whether there was something wrong with him aside from being dead.

The dark brocade curtain, which had been hiding the screen, opened and on the screen she saw written in black, bold letters:

FACT NUMBER 1: The subject was never meant to be born.

Next, she saw the following scene:

Cut to: EXTERIOR/DAY/PARK/SUNSHINE

A woman, her mother, young, beautiful, happily laughing. Beside her is her unknown father, also young, but serious, with a face already settled into the features of depressive tendencies. They are sitting on a park bench, holding hands. A comfortless little look passes between them. They are dressed expensively.

MOTHER (*with determination*)
We don't want it. We don't want another one.

FATHER *(nodding his head in agreement)*
Not with the two I already have from my first marriage. We need some money, time for ourselves as well.

MOTHER *(nods)*
Especially since you are still depressed over the cancer death of your first wife. What a sad tragedy!

They walk toward a dark, gray building. Camera follows. Camera zooms in on a sign over the entrance. Sign reads ABORTION CLINIC

FADE TO: INT/CLINIC/DAY

The mother and father are in the waiting room of the clinic. They sit on simple wooden benches. From inside another room we hear the screams of a woman, obviously in deep pain. The mother grows pale.

MOTHER *(fearfully, to father)*
I am afraid

FATHER *(confidently)*
Everything is going to be all right. You will be fine.

MOTHER *(panicked)*
No, it won't be. I am really afraid. You hear so much about women dying during these kind of undertakings. I'll say, let's go home. Let's have the baby. We'll find some use for it.

FATHER *(shrugging his wide shoulders)*
If you want to. Makes no difference to me either way.

CUT TO: the inside of a study room. A middle-aged man appears, dressed in a gray suit. He is very serious, obviously a scholar.

MAN:
Conclusion of fact number 1: you were not meant to be born.

Possible deduction from this fact: you were meant to be born later, in another land, most likely in Peru.

She shook her head in wonder at how illogical this final deduction had been. When he had finished his movie and the screen had gone blank once more, she asked, earnestly astonished, how one conclusion could follow from another. The Peruvian remained unperturbed and told her a fantastic story, the basis of which was a dubious theory that children destined for abortion, having already been selected for life, would have been subsequently born to another mother, in another land. Her mother had rejected her, even if her intended abortion did not take place. The Peruvian ignored the dark, suspicious look she gave him when he stated that she might have been born with a body but had been born already dead, because she had been born into a life she was not meant to lead.

"Those kind of children lead an existence somewhere between life and death," the Peruvian explained, with what he deemed to be authentic authority. He added that he had conducted considerable research into the fate of children destined for abortion and had read many books in many languages on the subject. She rubbed her cheek in wonder as he was spilling out these odd words at her, contemplating briefly whether ghost could become insane in his dying years or whether insanity was reserved for the living. The suspicion that he might have gone mad became all the grander when he moved on to the next picture on the screen and asked once again for her undivided attention.

Title (big black bold)

FACT NUMBER 2: CHILDREN DESTINED FOR ABORTION LIVE THEIR ENTIRE LIVES IN THE SHADOW OF DEATH

EXT/DAY/A MOUNTAIN SCENE

The suited gentleman appears before the background of a beautiful scenery. He explains with a solemn voice:

One of the chief characteristics of being dead is the unwillingness of the afflicted person to accept the painful severance from the Living. Death can best be diagnosed by the fact that to the dead person, nothing material is tangible. This condition is best proven in the following scenes from the subject's life, where the subject, the instant an attachment occurred to a person, place or thing, was removed by circumstances entirely outside the subject's control from said person, place or thing.

The following scenes appear in rapid succession:

Friends moving away, shortly after a friendship is formed. Work requirements making a move necessary, within months of settling into a new home. Growing up in a succession of strange homes and strange cities. Discovering new stores to shop in new cities and having them to close down or change management within months. Hiring an accountant or an attorney to have him die, of an unexpected heart attack, within weeks of meeting him. Arriving to visit friends in far away cities as someone unexpectedly dies and they attend a funeral.

NEW TITLE (Big, bold, black) **FIRST LOVE WAS A GHOST**

In fast forward, rapid succession: scenes of the race driver's demise, the beginning of a cross dimensional love affair, the ghostly driver and she walking hand in hand, one dead and the other one alive

TITLE NUMBER 4 (Big black letters) **FRIENDS THE SUBJECT MAKES ARE ALREADY DESTINED FOR DEATH**

In rapid succession, the following scenes: A friend announces: I have Aids. Another: I have cancer. Another one dies in a car crash. Another one is drowned.

FACT NUMBER 5 (big black letters) **THE SUBJECT'S CLOSEST FRIENDS ARE GHOSTS FROM BOOKS**
Scenes of her conversing, through their books, with the 19th century French Writers Circle (we recognize George Sand, Sainte-Beuve, Flaubert and de Musset, among others), with Thomas Wolfe, Stefan Zweig and Franz Liszt. The subject contrasts sharply from the others as the only one who is alive and the only one appearing in color. Everything else is black and white. The subject laughs with the others. She seems to be fully accepted by them but sticks out like a sore thumb, for being in color and alive.

FACT NUMBER 6: THE SUBJECT IS BORED BY THE LIVING AND LOVES NO LIVING BEING, EXCEPT FOR THE PEOPLE OF PERU
Rapid scenes showing her bored at dinner tables with assorted strangers, making polite conversation. She is reading while others talk. The final scene shows her walking, laughing and smiling, through the streets of Lima. A group of locals point to her behind her back, saying *gringa*. Her efforts to appear Peruvian appear rather silly.

FACT NUMBER 7: THE SUBJECT WOULD BE HAPPIEST AS A GHOST, WALKING THE STREETS OF LIMA HAND IN HAND WITH A GENUINE PERUVIAN AS A NON-MATERIAL ENTITY WHOSE COLOR OF SKIN NO LONGER MATTERS.

FACT NUMBER 8: THROUGH HER LIFE OF CONSTANT TRAVEL AND HER UNUSUAL EXPERIENCES, THE SUBJECT IS EXCLUDED FROM ANY TYPE OF ORDERED SOCIETY: SHE

**ILLUSTRATES HER SENSE OF EXCLUSION IN THE FOLLOW-
ING DREAM SHE REPORTS FROM THREE NIGHTS AGO**

CUT TO: INT/DAY/ACADEMIC ROOM
*The Academian (speaking in a very serious voice and straightening
his old fashioned tie):*

The subject and the rider are at the same horse show together. The
subject observes the Rider, introducing a young girl to his fellow riders, in perfect Spanish. The young girl shakes hands with the other
riders. The Rider introduces the young girl as being from Peru, and
currently to be training with him. The subject waits until she sees the
young girl sitting on her own, outside the stables, and approaches
her. She finds out from the young girl that she had met the Rider
when he was in Peru to play Polo. They had fallen in love and he had
taken her to Europe with him. She had no money, but she was beautiful and she was in love with him, as he was with her. He was paying
for her stay and he would help her with her riding. Subject notices
that the girl carries a halter for his horses, which he has bought, and
understand this to be a gesture of intimacy. Subject does not mention that she also has an interest in the Rider. Subject asks the young
girl about the dying people in her homeland and the young girl
begins to cry and states that she would fain help but that she is powerless. Subject tells the young girl—and this is an exact quote from
the dream—*be glad that you are out of that shit-heap country*. Subject
then states to the young girl that if it does not work out with the
Rider, she will at least have built an existence outside of that horrid
land but the Peruvian girl insists that she loves him. Subject grieves
when she sees that the girl is not prettier than she, but is younger and
she has blond hair, those being two distinct advantages in the eyes of
the Rider. Subject understands that the Rider will be loved by someone else and she returns to her desk to write another book and to
ban the Rider between its pages. **THE END**

The Academic turns and walks away.

Seven—to erase memories

Triumphantly, the Peruvian appeared, silhouetting himself breathtakingly with his strong profile against the clear canvas of the screen. He was certain that his moment had come. With his soft melodic voice, he proposed to turn her grinding hell into paradise.

"There is nothing to hold you here. Come with me, my love, come with me and be happy."

He extended his fine hand with its long, artistic fingers and fastened his deep, brown eyes on her as she sat in terrible fear, uneasily aware of being tempted to take his lovely hand to follow him. Her leg was at once seized and held strongly by her remaining reason and she tarried because she knew that the journey would lead into an absurd and gothic version of heaven. The touch his hands would be cold, his cheek would disdainfully disintegrate as she ran her hand along its soft curve and her journey would lead into a wet grave far beneath the flowers, where the sun could no longer warm her. Her bridesmaids would be maggots, clawing at her decaying throat with their paws.

Watching him cautiously, she knew that she could not follow him and that she would need to find another love fast, to keep her here. Being Peruvian, and a man, he only noticed what his eyes could see and he never realized that her heart was heavy or that her confident smile was not composed of warm water but of blood because she would never forget that in her heart she had already hummed a song titled *Don't cry for me, Peru* or that she knew that she would always love him, whether he was dead or alive, and had been wrong to run away from him and drive him to his death. She would never forget him, this she knew. They had been bonded too deeply by his bloodied land, they had fought side by side for its people, and they had died together, day by day. Many a death they had died in the six months it had taken them to kill him in captivity, before she escaped with her life and he went to his grave. But she could not tell him this and so she lifted her head wearily and tried to sing a song of independence, thanking him for the hospitality of accommodating her inside his heart, after all these years, but stating:

"That dream is nonsense. It has been proven that dreams are just dreams, nothing more. They unite the sum total of all fears, hopes, wishes with the day's images. I have dreamt also of his groom and of his horse, and I have dreamt of him and I together, in various places of the world. I have dreamt of his lips on mine (the Peruvian's handsome face twitched jealously when she mentioned this, but she had to keep going. She had to keep hurting him even if she resented herself for it), of merging our piercing desires. I have dreamt of his embrace in the shadow of a palm tree swaying softly in the tropical evening breeze. I have dreamt of such happiness for him and I as you and I would never know, a happiness devoid of blood and pain and death squads and broken limbs and tortured bones, stemming from a love without horrific images, borne of purity and lived in his simple little world. His friends may sometimes turn and shout, they may be rather rough, but at least they exude sweat smell and not blood smell. I am sorry for you and for your tragic people, for the children of your country waiting by the roadside, like sparrows, for breadcrumbs thrown by tourists, but the fates of any number of people will not change the fact that I cannot return to Peru and that all these human lives, through a vast play of chance, will be lost, whether I return there or not. As for the Rider, I know that he has been thinking of me daily, wondering whether he shall meet me again one day, wondering where I am, whom I love and whether I would love him."

She stamped her foot childishly.

"I know. I know. I *know!*"

The Peruvian sprang to his feet with such fervor that she, standing before the screen as she had been, stepped back in response and almost tore the screen, doing so. The projector dropped from her hand, for she had been meaning to show him a little film of her own to underline her words. No need now. Her purpose had been reached, the ghost was bleeding, but now the heat, the crush, the darkness of the screening room threatened to overwhelm her. She felt faint, and bitter bile rise inside her mouth, as she looked at the ghost she had loved, killed and just killed once more.

"And I am sorry for you, you prevaricating fool! There is absolutely no proof for the Rider to be thinking of you," he shouted in his rapid, dry Spanish. Goosebumps rose on the inner side of her thigh and on her lower arms as she recognized the danger of him drawing her in to love him, once more. His bright eyes were sparkling with a sheer irresistible fire but she remembered at the last moment that he was a ghost and as such he could be received in any language she chose. She did not have to hear his caressing voice, his unmistakably individually tailored way of rolling the syllables of his own language when he said *absolutamente nada*, which also happened to have been the first thing she had ever hear him say, albeit in a different context at some sort of a bizarre military demonstration where it was the way he said *absolutamente* which had made her fall in love with him, in another life that now lay buried under the memories of the different person had been then.

She was confident that she could now resist him in almost everything, but not his talk. She simply switched him to English and the Peruvian gave a brief mime of a hiccup and then continued in English, (that was much better, he spoke English with the accent of an American and she had always sought American English highly unromantic. It took much more for her to be falling in love with an American than his voice and his being dead, so she felt quite safe) "...there is absolutely no proof, whatsoever, for this primitive Rider to be thinking of anything or anybody, aside from his horses."

She wished to interrupt him and defend the Rider, but the Peruvian treated her to a performance of cumulative excited knee-slapping and was unstoppable in his fervor as he continued in a high-pitched, nasal American slang. She now decided to give his English a distinctive Texas twang that caused him to say Ma'am every so often and to draw out his vowels, the way they did in Texas. Also, she dressed him in a miserable white cowboy hat and in jeans, and cowboy boots. The hapless Peruvian never noticed the poison of her thoughts, he only saw himself speaking as he always been speaking and was not aware that she had changed him inside her mind. Being dead he was unable to predict such changes, and quite powerless to stop them.

"...to think that a man as he, a man who has built all his hopes and burnt all his dreams around the same old village square, who following his travels has always returned to the safe bosom of his own people and his own land, to think that he..."

The Peruvian had so excited himself that he had to gasp for air, that was how much he was bent on showing her that the Rider belonged to an inferior species. Gasping, his ridiculous white cowboy hat fell deeper into his forehead and he pushed it up angrily. When he did, she could see that his exquisite brown face had taken on a reddish tint. Between the freckles of his nose, a strong and angry vein grew into his forehead and began to pulsate mortifyingly fast. For a moment, she grew brutally afraid that he would perhaps succumb to a sudden heart attack, but then she remembered that he was already dead. He continued to address her, standing alone in the empty screening room, fighting for his dignity with his Texas jeans which she, to divert attention from his words, now envisioned as lacking a cord and riding themselves up to his knee. She was somewhat shuddering with guilt because he kept fighting for her love, despite her having caused his most painful death. Guilt crept up inside her like a clammy, transfiguring snake, causing her to involuntarily answer his appeal with a silent, perverse affection for the beautiful, passionate, but very dead man standing before her. Remorsefully, she allowed him to shed the Texas accent again and to throw away the stupid hat and the cowboy boots.

Pulling herself together, she was suddenly inclined to clothe him
in a most fetching pair of white pants and a blue shirt, and then his
hair fell seductively in lush, black curls around his glorious face and
he had the crisp, ironed look of a most handsome man. She even
allowed him to switch back to Spanish like he had once spoken to the
people of his own land. She wanted to stroke him when he appeared
like this before her. She still loved him, defiantly and annoyingly, and
opened her mind in a receptive manner when he rose his head
proudly and shook his fine dark hair with great passion in the soft
breeze she had created especially for that purpose because she
wished to see him, once more, in all his glory. As he spoke, he
remembered everything and so did she. He spoke with an almost
religious fervor and they remembered the blood-fields of Peru
together, their memories contained in the sound of his voice as they
both recalled the last time he had spoken with such tragic force.

Enter memory:
He speaks. "We will win the game, we will feed our people!" She
stands beside him, an extreme dose of passion in her eyes and love,
not only for him but also for all of his people, all the millions of
them, even all the *in utero* children, all the soldiers whose hearts they
were going to soften to create an united Peru, the world's first nation
where all live as brothers. In both their eyes shines a complex web of
openings, ploys and sacrifices, at the end of which stood a social not
a military dream, where no Peruvian would ever raise his hand again
against another Peruvian.

Enter memory:
Machine guns are grumbling quietly, like dogs, in the distance of
night. Palm trees create sumptuous shadow-plays and the night air
curls hotly around their naked arms. She speaks, her eyes filled with
genuine terror:

"Altruistic idealism will never kill the growling terror in this land. We can perhaps cause a few to exchange liberty for oppression, but there are others who decide what the people want. We are small and inconsiderable, mere pawns in a bigger chess game. There is something bigger, some organization behind this. They will kill us before they allow us to change this land."

The Peruvian looks at her impatiently and when she has finished, he says: "We *will* win the game. There are openings, ploys, sacrifices..."

She opens her lap top and begins to write another book, pushing the Peruvian's arm away. His eyes become piteously hollow, his voice is breaking with uncried tears (being Peruvian, crying came to him as easily as would be admitting he is queer) as he exclaims dramatically: "Very well then, I shall remember your face during the torture part of the interrogation, to keep me from screaming."

Having coughed up such bitter a memory, they folded it back into the appropriate segments of their respective minds, but when he continued speaking on a completely different subject, they remembered another untidy piece of their joint past, how he had been tortured brutally to the death for the sake of his land. Then the monster inside the Peruvian pointed out that he remembered—and this was where their memories parted—her having driven him to his demise. Had she loved him, he would have loved Peru less. He reminded her that she belonged to him, dead or alive, and that no rider would ever have her, no red-jacketed, disillusioned, tragically unfulfilled rider who had never explored the depths of human nature. She would be better off by the side of him, a man devoid of the spirit of youthful dilettantism who always strove to pierce the significant heart of everything. She could not walk by the side of a rider, who drew out a line of order by way of his show-jumping hurdles, to become trapped in mindless conversation with his friends and their well-dressed women, who would force her to reduce her past to order by way of a trifle diagram: from horse show to horse show with the same kind of riding people for whom, he could not deny, a great contempt devoured him on account of the limited world in which they moved. They were people who had never heard the simple cries which are the savage rhythms of men pulling for one country, for one land, for one freedom. He would make her understand, this the Peruvian swore as he spoke, that he, the beautiful, the passionate, the noble fighter for freedom, within her heart came first and second, and third came Peru and there was no place for anyone else.

She watched the him pour out his anger at her feet like some costly ointment and became so absorbed with his handsome manners that she permitted him to continue with his contempt of the Rider, and with his conquest of her heart.

"…to think that he would understand you, he who has never walked with unflinching gravity through the cholera-bacteria-ridden puddles of the *Mercado Central*. He would even disbelieve, being too cold-hearted to be abashed, the brutal Peruvian sun. Has he ever walked the rainforest's path to find the rotting dead, their sweet smell providing an opportunity for serious contemplation on the fact of death? He knows nothing of staring into the small, cold eyes of bony battered faces of soldiers, their machine guns pointed, with somewhat ingenious arrogance, at the middle of his head. He knows nothing of the hour of approaching death, the instant you realize that all life, like a book, has been lived, printed, and stands not to be changed, an instant arriving in Peru without warning, when death concentrates itself on one man or one woman, halting not for wet weather nor unsaid good-byes, allowing only one final moment of gratitude that you have lived at all. Does he know, your rider in his lily-white breeches on his clean white horse, the terror of night when you are trapped in a small dark house, light and telephone having failed, and by some hidden doctrine or otherwise inspired, machine gun fire echoes from the streets outside, advancing in a silent, learnt conspiracy to take your life? I do not predict much success for your advocacy of this love," the Peruvian pressured her, "with a man who knows nothing of the continuation of the story when, caged like a rabbit, you light with shaking fingers your final cigarette, the ashes burning into your skin as they fall and you welcome even the pain, knowing it may very well be the last time you feel anything. You draw the fatal smoke in deeply, burning your lungs one last time as fear takes residence inside your soul with death's advancing grip growing colder around your heart, its iron paralyzing fist promising unspeakable abominations and you wonder with a shudder whether your death, announced by the machine guns, will be heroic or monstrous. *Will you scream or show brilliant and noble courage? Will the public flock tomorrow to collect your broken body from beneath the vultures, outside the cemetery gates? Where will they bury you, how many bullet holes will there be in your torso, to be counted by men holding handkerchiefs before their mouths and noses to shield them against the smell of your putrefying body as behind their handkerchiefs they pray with cracking voices a timid little thank you to their maker that it was you, and not them, who died this time?* He knows all of this, your rider, does he?" the Peruvian contemptuously spat out the words, "and the mourning that follows when the gun-wielding men, now that you have prepared yourself to die, drawn up your own funeral and rehearsed your entry into the other side, grin at you through their near-ruined teeth, solemnly announcing, W*e can't. Not today. We are terribly tired. Not here, not this time. We will be back,* before they turn their brutal legs and drunkenly dance down your street, away from you, firing their machine guns into the air and you never know when they will come for you again."

Her eyes glazed over because her heart was already terribly crowded with images of the Rider and, in spite of all considerations, their future had in its forecast already reached symphonic length.

"Look at his world, look. They are *pets*, not men," the Peruvian exclaimed and she looked directly into the open mouth of another rider. As he jumped, his tongue jumped with him and when he had landed, he was feeding it back in. The face that went with the tongue was fresh and cleanly scrubbed, perhaps all of twenty years old. She looked again and saw fistfuls of money shoved across expensive marble tables by an expensively dressed man buying a horse for his plump, dark-haired daughter who wanted to ride. She saw the plump daughter tugging at the nose of some middle-aged riding champion who was now training her and for whom her father bought another horse. The Peruvian closed the image before she could discover whether the middle-aged champion paid the plump girl for the horse in any other manner, aside from training her. Then he showed her images, of jostling and fighting girl-wives by the side of short old men, and handsome young riders with pretty young women. Whatever way you looked at it, she could not deny that their world was an accumulation of wealth and beauty and grace.

"They will think you filthy and uncultured, despite your beauty, because you have taken an excursion outside their nice little world. They will never lay an arm around you in friendship or offer you anything but vinegar. They will soon discover that you are playing some deep game, pretending to be one of them, but that your eyes hide the image of terrible memories of events which any good rider is not to see."

She exhibited slight depression now, very definitely interested in what the Peruvian was saying. She felt even somewhat obliged to admit that he could be right. But then she remembered a fundamental matter, that one of the girl riders had also lived outside the normal lines of experience and been a survivor of a brutal war not unlike the war of Peru. She could also produce the sobbing kind of memories any war-survivor harbored.

"But she keeps them well-hidden," the Peruvian replied. "She will never commit suicide, because she is able to separate the things that are today from the things that were yesterday and today she is riding horses, with the dead of her war buried in the past. You, on the other hand, have obtained a dose of memory that will last you all your life. In her eyes shines innocence, still, and in your eyes severity and the kind of watchful care needed for survival in the slums."

The Peruvian now pointed out, making her feel very guilty, that it would be ignoble of her to continue loving the Rider, soiling his innocence with her throbbing memories. Only pretending acquiescence to the Peruvian's severe ideas, she resolved, in a secret corner of her mind, to undertake a detailed study of the burial of memories.

The End.

CHAPTER 7

One—the old composer

To deafen the cries of Peru, she undertook to study music, having read somewhere that a captive heart could be set free with good music even when the doors of its chambers stood heavily guarded. She was lucky to be beginning at once. There happened to be an unassuming, kindly ghost well versed in such matters, having once been a composer of some note. She had not wanted to bother Liszt with her request, fearing him far too advanced to teach an absolute beginner. This ghost was not from among the ranks of men of fashion and adventure, rather, he was a modest little man, who, due to his baldness, could never stand to see himself full-length and had cut the top off every mirror in her house, even the one opposite her green sofa.

It was the third month of the year when she began her studies. The ghost had been quite a genius. She asked him to kindly teach her music, explaining that she knew very little of the subject but needed music to stay alive because in her memory occurred daily disgusting outbursts of violence, arrests and executions and she was in danger of surrendering to the hopelessness of the situation. The cries of the dying Peruvian children might draw her back to Lima where she would find certain death, either in its dirty streets or by way of the remaining death squads still awaiting her there. The composer-ghost trembled under the reflections of her memories and saw at once the necessity of transporting her to another place, agreeing to instruct her in the task of composition. The vastness of the view thus obtained, he assured her, would supply her with superiority over the country of Peru and over the glorious dream-way of the Peruvian.

She complained to the composer about the Peruvian having prophesied that she would never love a living man again, turning her into a morose captive haunted by the images of his people struggling through a desperate war that had taken his life and the lives of many others. Under a serene sky performing full splendid plays of sunset, she confided that, imprisoned by walls of words from the books she wrote, her life might not be worth living at all.

"Where there is music, there is life," the composer reassured her with the wisdom of his three-something dead years. He greatly urged her not to abdicate the stage of life, which was a necessary tool for putting her in touch with the numerous adherents of music.

The composer was a peculiar man who liked playing the piano but even more, he liked turning colors into music. In his living years, he had often been collecting stones and painting pictures on them, all the while singing to himself softly the tune of a new piece he was composing. She had often tried to study, but never truly understood, the science of transforming colors to music or music to colors and he stated that he was going to teach her, at higher than college level, the respective impacts and penetrations of colors in classical music, a skill he promised would enable her to compose, anytime and any place, a symphony from the marvels of nature.

Her consciousness flickered on and off when he said this, but she was willing, more than ever, to engage in the deep process of healing. Quickly and swiftly she rose from her chair, feeling much better than she had ever felt since her escape from Peru. She opened the street door of her house to discover an alleyway stretching before her. Walking a few steps, she found it took a sharp turn to the right and then she happened upon a beach. She never questioned how the beach could be so closely located by the mountains nor why it had foreign mysterious feel of a strange land. Half-heartedly joining into his enthusiasm, she followed the composer's instructions to collect there, while listening to the sound of the surf, dozens of white clam shells that had been bleached by the sun and washed out by the ever-present sea. Considering that they were dealing with torture, his plan of collecting clam shells seemed rather futile.

"Something should happen now, something important," she complained, bending down to pick up another shell. Unfazed by her resistance, the composer explained that the shells were meant to enhance her tonal talents and urged her to reflect on the eternal presence of the sea, the polished velvet sound of the waves, and the small glimpse of life that she represented on its shores. He warned her to enjoy every instant of soft deep life, whether hers was death-padded or not, and never to give into the urge for a warm bath of physical dissolution before her time. Adding a dose of wisdom, he assured her from his own experience that darkness would come soon enough, darkness or relief, whichever way she wished to look at it, but there was only one chance to be alive, which had to be exhausted to the fullest. There would be an eternity of the universal unknown, when she would be unable to remember important things and taste what it meant to be fully dead, but there was only one glimpse of time to be alive in and this glimpse was not to be given up, not even for the sake of the Peruvian and his wooing death.

"I am afraid you are too much in a hurry with that dying business," the composer grumbled after a bit of general chatting, "You are afraid of him, his presence enrages you and so you think it might be better to let him muddle through his mad statements and give him what he came for. What a mess you've made of this whole situation. Where is your common sense? You should never have given him that opening to attempt stealing your life. You must never meet the death he so kindly invites you to, your place is here, among the living."

She adored the composer for his attempt to keep her from yielding to a burning desire of deliberately laying her life down for the Peruvian's sake. Once he had spoken his words of reason, her soul was no longer in a state of shock but seemed to be recovering from its odd instability. Although she could still recall her dramatic past with its horrible rituals, the words of the composer promised perfect safety where night, at last, might be parted by the smooth sensation of an oncoming morning. It was a luxurious promise that the horrible memories inside her would never darken the pages of her life again but be destroyed by rich music, and the Peruvian would be forced to keep his mouth shut once and for all.

"Right," she said. "I have had enough of people and voices pushing into my life." Alive with the fore-glow of her anticipated liberation and turning one sleek white shell in her hand, she no longer considered the task of collecting clam shells as something fishy. "How many shells do I need?"

The composer, speaking from long experience, replied without tarry, "One hundred and seventy five, precisely."

To her surprise, her memories of two uniformed military men, carrying her down the stairs into a Peruvian prison cell, subsided with each shell she collected. With his wary, silent face and his cryptic, angular language, the composer stood beside her, watching and commenting. Now and then he advised, "This one no, it has an uneven edge", or, "Not this one, there are too many furrows on its back."

Somehow, she realized that he was engaged in the task of saving her life. She had long become a stranger to her own family, communicating with them only once per annum and then on a superficial childish level. The last time she had come home and they had asked her how she was, she had told them "fine, fine" because she could not tell them of the Peruvian torture chambers and of ambulances, hospitals and people dying from machine gun wounds on their way home from work. With their ordered little lives, they would have at best given her the advice to get up at the same time each morning, to eat at regular hours and get to sleep before midnight as though, through leading an orderly life of discipline and hard labor, all evil could be banned. They had often insisted that all her troubles stemmed from her refusal to do precisely that and that one who slept until almost noon and wrote until the early morning hours could never come to much, it was a clear as night and day. Regarding the torture chambers, of which they knew from her telling them, in little fragments and sparing all the details, where she had been, her disciplined and stern mother had to say this, "You are now away from there and I can only advise you, my child, to never look behind you. Get yourself a proper job, where you can work during the day like ordinary folk, and everything will be well."

With all this going on, she had no choice but to find her family with people like the composer-ghost, who listened closely as she told her story and then played seemingly innocent games of shells and pebbles on the beach with her, but in reality he went underground inside her soul, burrowing his green-blue eyes beneath her memories so narrowly and deeply as to almost drive her insane and finally extracting from the deep darkness of her past a foul smelling piece of sloth resembling black velvet in its texture. The composer's find seemed to cause a momentary change of scenery as he filled the abandoned passage of her memories with Mozart and Mozart came through for her most unexpectedly.

She had seen the need for moving away from the people of her childhood and her mother's four-story house with a basement if she was ever going to leave the Peruvian behind with his dark little celebrations, but there had been a real problem with Mozart at first. The trouble was that she hated Mozart. His music uttered little whining sounds and sapped energy from her pores, as far as she was concerned. She told the composer so when he had first insisted on her to be studying Mozart, not Bach. Once she had collected the 175 shells, which had taken a long time because he had with a disdainful look discarded the broken, dark colored and unclean shells, he made her enter a store on the beach front and buy a total of 100 different coloring tubes there. The colors were four only, of different shades, red and blue mainly, but there was one gold and one white tube as well.

It was then he first started talking about Mozart and she made the offensive remark about Mozart's music resembling a pair of inhospitable soggy swimming trunks, causing the composer to clear his throat hollowly because he did not like for Mozart to be insulted. "You can't insult Mozart", he said, "not here, with me, you can't."

He seemed to understand nothing of her aversion because he thought of Mozart as a friendly and eloquent composer who had harbored inside the scarlet skies of his soul a fabulous kingdom of genius. She, on the other hand, had always considered the music of Mozart, in its audible proximity to the superficial, to be as unformed as the blind poking of time itself. At first, she had not considered herself very fortunate when the composer announced that she would be studying Mozart. She had left the store carrying a box of colors, and grumbling softly from behind the box about Mozart's prolific mediocrity. She had kept on grumbling, all the way back down the alleyway and into her house. Impatiently, she had cleared the shelves in her living room of assorted knickknacks to make space for the colors, as the composer had asked her to, all the while hoping that he would be unable to distinguish the expression of dispassionate interest in her features because the dusk had become almost dark.

He was, after all, willing to give up a section of eternity in order to free from her memories and the least she could do was to straighten up and enter the world of Mozart cleanly, even if she considered it of low-enough scale to be buried, scores and all, in a jagged deep hole. Once she paused to think about it, it did not even seem to matter anymore that Mozart had been a pale young man who had spent his life trying to find ever more success. Her face became all blotchy and wet when she thought of the marvelous fact that the composer evidently cared enough to be slowly reassembling the scattered pieces of her mind, seeking to make her whole again. He was taking the whole matter seriously and would not permit her to creep back into the cheerless domicile of her past in order to continue leading her life with a heavy heart and mistaking herself for a graveyard. Observing her sharply, the composer could not help wondering what could be so tear-provoking about having to study Mozart. She dislodged a pale long-nosed memory in response, showing her not very caring mother wearing a face of guilty disgust that clearly announced she did not care about the state of her daughter's soul. She could barely tell the ghost how glad she was over his caring before he had turned away, completely flustered, and she realized that, being British and from a very proper family where emotions were dislodged and hidden behind stony faces to be pulled down like strident blinds, a kind of family that never talked and never hugged, he was unable to cope with the exhibition of any kind of emotions. His family had been made up of silent talkers who preferred peeling onions to entering telephone boxes. They had turned him into a kindly man wearing spectacles to hide the impure vision of the ruptured shadows of his own memories and she was aware of having embarrassed him with her gratitude.

She strained to turn her attention onto the task at hand and the composer's look changed to one of rapture and reverence when he realized that he did not have to deal with her rapidly emerging emotions and that he could unclench his nervously kneading hands to concentrate on the considerations and deductions to be found in Mozart's music. She sat down on the laminated floor of her large living room, where she spread the shells before her like in rows like a silent army. This did nothing to change the fact that she still desperately tried to understand how exactly the composer might be proposing to turn colors into mouth-pieces for music. He made her stand all the color tubes in a row, first the blues, then the reds and then the gold and white, and then the paintbrush beside the paints. There was also a small plate, where, he explained, the paints were to be mixed and then there was to be a pot of water, for the brushes to be cleansed between colors and then "...the music is missing" the composer noted crossly. Although she did not quite understand what he wanted with the shells and the music and the paints, she got on her way again, riding her bicycle through cold gusts of wind, anything to silence the endless wail of suffering Peruvians. She arrived at the shopping center with her hair tangled from the wind and as she walked to a music store the composer walked beside her with an expression on his face as though they were entering a sacred place. Following his instructions, she selected some Mozart from the Compact Disc racks, since she had reluctantly learnt in recent years that a laser disc was preferable for the quality of sound than records. Buying it, she could not help wondering how she, still clinging to records and typewriters and tender love, had been outdated so soon, becoming old fashioned so young in years. She bought, compliantly and although she despised him, a copy of the *Coronation Concerto K 537* by Wolfgang Amadeus Mozart. With the self-pity of a lost Verdi traveler stumbling through the land of another composer whose music seemed to have been made to strangle, she remarked to the girl at checkout, knowing this would be overheard by the composer: "I don't understand why I should be buying this, seeing that I hate Mozart."

The checkout girl looked at her as though she were not quite sane and asked why, seeing that she hated the concerto, she would be buying it. Thereupon, she explained to the increasingly more amazed young girl—she could not be more than twenty, twenty five at the most—that there was a boisterous ghost who insisted on her listening to this particular piece but that it was an utter disgrace having to spend her good money for such nonsense.

When they arrived back at her home, which had a splendid view of the water, where the ocean's waves could be seen from her living room windows breaking on the rocks way below, the composer was still so upset that despite his being a ghost his face was red, he snapped for air and the veins bulged on his neck. Fixing his eyes on a fastidious seagull outside the window, he made it known with very British, very neatly arranged anger, that he was a great admirer of Mozart, that his inspiration had come from Mozart as a primary source, and that he could not stand hearing the world's greatest music disgraced by her.

"If you do not like Mozart, then tell me why and make a good case for it, at least," he barked at her and she could clearly see his anger blowing like a strong breeze in his normally gentle eyes, which were burning like a very bright light-bulb. She fastened her eyes on the lolling roll of the sea outside the window, determined not to be moved from her anti-Mozart position.

"His music is too light," she said, shrugging her shoulders. "He has not lived long enough. Greatness in art, whether music or litera-ture, comes from solid pain. He died with his soul unformed as it came into this world. His pains were of imaginary nature: a love scorned, petty jealousy and bickering among his peers. He never had seen a loved one die and never had to scrape around for food. His soul has not dwelled long enough inside despair, where great art, great literature and great music sleeps…"

The face of the composer settled into the expression of a recently bombed airfield. His breaths were somewhat shallower now and he seemed to be suffering from a dull pain in his temples where he was rubbing gingerly with the index and thumb of his left hand. She sought it wise to continue, before whatever diabolical force inside of him erupted and her tongue would become thick and unwilling as it submitted itself to the superiority of his advanced years and teacher's wisdom.

"Verdi, for instance, was a composer of true greatness…"

"Nonsense," the ghost snapped but he could not keep himself from listening with slowly emerging curiosity. His eyes said that he found her statements deliciously silly, seeing that the field of music was practically unknown to her.

"Verdi lost his wife and child in the same year, and very young they were, too. A loss of such magnitude can break any man. A broken man forms himself again from despair and from the depth of his despair comes great art.

"For instance, A*dio del Pasado* in *La Traviata*," she continued, eager to provide examples to him. "Did he write it for that unknown courtesan, or do you suppose he wrote it with the death of his wife in mind? I say the parchment-like shade of his pain illuminates the very bottom of the tune, seeing her life slip away before his helpless eyes...you feel the pain in the music and cry along in subtle sympathy when she gives him the locket with her photograph on her death bed. Mozart! This is not even opera, except perhaps for *Don Giovanni*! When listening to opera, we need to feel the music and be moved to the point of being drained of tears. Then, having felt all the pain and beauty, we need to laugh the kind of relief-laughter that is rewards to those who have truly suffered and survived."

The ghost was quiet now, not in an unpleasant but rather an unsure manner, perhaps not knowing what to add to such strong an argument. Despite his love of Mozart, even he had to admit—and this was a fact which could not be changed—that the master had died young, had superficially loved and had never known the heartbreak of seeing his love die. There was no denying that Mozart had not received the full measure of pain available to man and that his problems had been those of a spoilt man who had never known hunger or thirst and that his soul, albeit a genius's, had not been broken and reshaped by early trauma.

"But what of the Requiem," the composer asked hopefully, relieved to have found something divine to set against her harsh words. Even he had to admit that Mozart's operas were best suited for lighter tastes because they rarely spoke of life's most difficult journeys.

"Is Mozart's Requiem not the most moving music you have known? And what of a man young in years, sitting with hunched-up shoulders over his note-sheets, pouring out his final spiritual energy into his very last piece of music, knowing full well that he is writing his own Requiem? What great tragedy, what blaze and furor, is contained in these voices, in these notes, what heart-breaking images of a young man writing, as if by divine vision, a music of splendid colors before going on into another sphere!"

She admitted, not even reluctantly, that she loved the Mozart Requiem and that it was indeed a most delightful composition, which could be painted on the last page of any fading life without shame.

"But compare this, dear friend," she said haughtily, "with the Verdi Requiem. In Mozart, death is greeted with a light heart, in the secure knowledge of a benign paradise to be found on the other side. There is no anger nor fear, not even the momentary rejection of a cruel God cutting him down while he is still young. There is only complete acceptance and the secure belief that whatever comes on the other side is going to be glorious. Dismiss ideas of life, dismiss all hopes and dreams about to be broken, and get drunk on the glory of the coming Kingdom of Heaven! Is this fully natural?"

The composer cleared his throat once more and looked at her as though she were a marvelous humorist.

"According to my deductions…" he began, but she cut him off mid-sentence. This was an important matter to her. Through the Peruvian's presence, she had by necessity thought closely about death. In nocturnal sessions, when she could not sleep for migraines brought on by the stench of the rotting dead buried inside her mind, she had, blinded but not deafened by tears, studied the requiems of a number of composers, mostly Verdi, Faure and Mozart. She had never been moved by the image of Mozart composing on his death-bed, not for being devoid of emotional or creative compassion, but rather, for finding it astonishing that any man would welcome death as a kind God's friendly act.

Seeing that the composer had personal experience in matters of death, she asked him, straight-out: "What of your own death, when it came knocking at your door? You greeted it with pleasurable anticipation, did you?"

The composer winced when she tapped this particular memory inside him. Not having been dead for very long, he still missed the utter physical dependence permeating one's being while alive and he had to admit that she was right. When his imminent state of death had been announced to him in hospital, he had not felt a burning desire to merge with God. Rather, he had felt like snubbing God and to remain, for as long as possible, an anonymous passenger on this good, old, most picturesque earth. Gone was the half-hearted attachment he had felt to life, suddenly he clung to it with all of his temporary personality, and in looking back, being faced with the promise of having his spirit involuntarily liberated, he saw all the occasions he had had to be happy that he didn't take, all the times he had stretched himself in worry or depression, when a change of attitude would have been more becoming.

The composer had lost himself in the reflections of his own memories, completely forgetting in what context they had been brought to light. When suddenly he became aware that she was still talking, he sought it polite to close the hidden projection in his mind and turn his attention back to her to catch the last of her speech.

"...do we not all, when faced with the knowledge of our imminent demise, linger on in this world for every possible second? Do we not review our lives in one instant, reflecting on where we have gone wrong, where, here or there, a path might have been walked differently and the tones of our voices might have been changed from disdain to kindness, and from murdering someone else's dream to encouragement? Do we not, even those who were raised in the catholic faith or have turned their faces away from the church in search of a kinder, gentler God, succumb to a fear of damnation and of fire that may or may not be quenched at the precise moment of our deaths?"

Two—the Requiem

An image flashed through the old composer's mind, of his great-uncle Jack, who had brought him candy, who had a way of fondling him when nobody was around and who had fondled all through his growing-up years until he felt all mangled from having been impregnated with a guilty burden he had not shed until his death because Jack had always urged him not to talk about the subject. The past opened before the composer like a ragged door and he could not help feeling that it might be best to convey her his agreement about the inferiority of Mozart, just to cause her to stop talking before he remembered, in too much detail, with what fears of hell and eternal damnation he had gone to his death on account of uncle Jack's attentions. Under no circumstances did he wish for her to get any ideas about him having been uncomfortable with his own memories at the time of his death.

He sighed thankfully when she never noticed and, in a most amazing psychokinetic manifestation, took him into the smoothly running world her childhood. Saying "here, take this", she handed him a portable cassette player containing a recent and very good recording of Verdi's requiem. She attached a second set of headphones to the one already there and they wandered into the mountains, with him shuffling after her obediently. When they had crossed a little bridge underneath which birds of various species and voices had collected on the banks of a crystal clear small river, they turned to the right, where the dreamy smile of a flower-filled, grass-rich, brilliant green meadow awaited them. Falling fully into the arms of nature, they shrugged off all memories of civilization as the meadow and the trees swallowed them up to become part of the landscape.

"Listen," she instructed the composer they both fastened their eyes on the juniper-tree-filled mountain towering before them. She pushed the play button on the little apparatus in her hands, the mechanism gave a dry little click, then she played him the opening movements of the Verdi Requiem.

"The simple and sober description of death's arrival," she commented. Humbler composers might have preferred more sundry forms of suffocation, but in Verdi the matter was crystal clear. There was the distinct fear of things to come, of losing the precise features of one's personality in death and also a long, not very rational but desperate, attempt to resist the advancing night. Amidst the desperation lay the serious contemplation of an afterlife but it was not the blind-faith contemplation of Mozart, quietly contenting itself with the warm haze of pleasurable anticipation of a life beyond the curtain. There was true fear, voices united in grief over what was to be left behind, then the solo, of one about to die, raising itself in sometimes lawful and sometimes repulsive colors. Despite her youth, she felt the not-so-subtle warning contained inside the music that her own moment would arrive soon enough. Goosebumps arose on her skin despite the warm sun because being surrounded by the mountains, they were also surrounded by one man's desperate attempt not to die.

"It doesn't work," the composer said, speaking from experience. "It never pays to refuse to die. He should go into it, it will come anyway."

The grand Dying in Verdi's requiem was situated somewhere between hope and despair, between acceptance and a last desperate clinging to the known. Muscles relaxed in serenity, then tensed again in fear. There was a hidden projection of sin and of a dying man succumbing to panic at the prospect of shedding his body.

She chose the images rather casually, not out of laziness but because, for painting the Verdi requiem in its entirety, she would need an opera stage to play the whole scene out. Normally, this would not have been a problem as she did have an orchestra stored away inside her mind for such purposes, containing the skills and faces of people she had encountered in the past. There was a beautiful first violinist with a blond-haired mane and a defiant young face greedy for life. The first bassoonist was a fat, red-haired girl of twenty-two. The others were middle-aged men mostly, except for the women on the strings. Her proudest acquisition had been a curio from the Boston Symphony Orchestra. Having once attended rehearsals there, she had stored the man in her mind and then added him to her orchestra. He had been the first oboe player, with the ability during play to swell his face like a fish sucking on a luminous waffle. But she had only a first flutist, no second bassoonist, and the first trumpet, without which she could not conduct the *dies irae,* was on sick leave, not to mention that she had been unable to obtain Pavarotti as tenor-in-residence and that her fill-in tenor, a short little Italian with cafe-au-lait eyes and a face like a pallid gland, currently still studied at the conservatory and could not be relied upon to bring the high C without fail.

As mezzo-soprano she had wanted a Russian who had once given a most touching performance in *Il Trovatore* at the Met. The spirit of the Russian had refused to be copied and added to her orchestra, and now she had only a student, all of 19 years old, a young blonde with a big nose and an air of laziness. She disapproved strongly of the flippancy with which the Blonde treated her own talent, having in the past witnessed an intolerable scene when the Blonde had stood grinningly on stage during a performance of Dido and Aneas. The truly magnificent soprano sang the Plaint of Dido...*remember me, but forget my fate...*and to her right side, surveying the audience with an idiotic grin, had stood the blonde mezzo-soprano.

Under these circumstances she could impossibly stretch herself to a full stage performance of the Verdi Requiem. Shudderingly imagining what her peculiar mezzo-soprano would do to the Requiem, she weaned herself from this idea quickly. She had been stabbed in her fore-vision by the youthfully arrogant grin of the Blonde as she was singing *salva me, salva me*, resulting in a mix of satire and burlesque being blended into Verdi's most genial work. She sought it wiser to continue with the half-heathen technical instrument in her hands. The tortured sound the portable cassette player emitted was still far preferable to the childish energy of the mezzo. Her point had to be made right now, however wrong the images might be, however lacking in brilliance.

The composer had listened with interest as she filled him in on the trivial variants of her problems with the orchestra, perfectly understanding why there could be no stage performance. Having established this, they both turned their attention to the music once more.

"And now the *dies irae*," she pointed out.

The cows drew closer, watching them curiously. She pulled the headphones nearer the cows, with the requiem vibrating throughout her head at full volume until it seemed to grow directly out of the mountains. The cows stared in fascination at the strange human with the glossy ghost beside her, wondering, perhaps, by what blunder of nature these two had appeared in their midst, but coming slowly closer to take a better look at this curious pair.

The dying voice in the Requiem sang *salva me, salva me* with all the fear and terror of its final moments and, simultaneously, the cows were touched on their curious pink noses, one by one, with a yellow flower she had picked. The ghost giggled mildly as she ran the flower up the first (brown and white) cow's nose, then up to its eyes. She turned to the composer, saying "This is life. This very moment, belonging to nobody but the cows and ourselves. But this...(pointing to her headphones now) is to remind us that life and death stand like rival factions to either side of us. We must enjoy the moment, while we have it, not with a view of looking at snapshots and thinking: *tomorrow I will think I had a good time here.* We should be saying *I am having a good time right now,* excluding any thought of tomorrow or of taking photographs, and always remember that the insipid exterior of time belies the quality of the moment."

"*The insipid exterior of time belies the quality of the moment,*" the composer repeated, trying to pat the first cow with a lofty hand. Not used to ghosts or the like, the poor animal drew back in frenzied little jumps, tearing up its head too suddenly and receiving an electric shock from the wire fence marking the confines of its paddock. The cow ran away into the shining sun, slipping on its haunches and finally hiding behind the other cows, from where it peered at them with still interested but now also somewhat fearsome, eyes.

Sticking out his tongue at the cow with boyish merriment, the composer sat back among the grass and flowers with a morose look, then turned his attention to her.

"I would be deeply obliged if you could explain the meaning of this sentence to me," he challenged, knowing full well that she loved the play of words and sometimes strung them together for the sake of stringing, without necessarily giving them an intelligent meaning.

He had expected there to be a delay, at least until the end of the *dies irae,* but she replied at once,

"This moment, the touch of the grass, the sun, the way the clouds are arranged in solid colors above the mountains, the cow drawing back from the touch of the electric wire...all this is destined to become memory. But copying the memory from its living moment, due to a tense nervous system which always transports itself into the future, is to convey the mere rudiments of a life that is to be lived. Nothing is sacred to one who picks apart his present like irritable paper shreds destined for the waste paper basket and screams for a day in the future, when money will drop into his lap or the perfect lover arrive or the half-paralyzed shadowgrapher of his external features finally make him graceful."

The composer nodded and said, "indeed."

She had already suspected the composer of questioning her merely to avoid discussing further aspects of the Verdi requiem and she saw that she had been right when he winced as she paused the cassette at the first entrance of the mezzo soprano in the *dies irae*.

"Ah, here we have it. A very good example," she said, determined to prove him the superiority of Verdi over Mozart. "Here is what Mozart's attitude to this passage was…(she whipped out of her mind a well-worn copy of *Pale Fire*, the front cover missing, the other pages dog-eared and mangled.)" She quoted: "*…when the soul adores him who guides us through mortal life, when it distinguishes his sign at the turn of every trail, when every page of the book of one's personal fate bears his watermark, how can we doubt that he will also preserve us through all eternity?*

"This is reflected in Mozart's Requiem until the very end. We trust and we rejoice that we are about to die. And here," she said triumphantly, "is Verdi's somewhat more realistic version of departure, passage and arrival, also cumulating in a belief in providence and a Christian-style survival after death."

She switched on the tape once more and the mezzo soprano headed toward aspects of spiritual hope cast among the filth of despair.

"Do you not recall," she addressed the composer and also the few remaining cows still listening, "in *Trovatore*, the scene of Azucena waiting for her death at stake, the night before, in her cell? She cannot sleep and sees only in her mind's eye the horrific fire that is going to devour her flesh, her hair and her robe. Remember when the fear of the fire robs her of her final night's sleep, and her aria, when her son, imprisoned with her, asks her: "Mother, why aren't you sleeping?" Do you recall the images of doom coating her song? The same images you find again, right here, the very images we all, if only for a second, shall confront when it is our turn to go. In Verdi's requiem, there is fear that every sin, no matter how small, might be punished by a vengeful God and that there may be nothing but blackness on the other side of the tomb, followed, finally, by acceptance and glory in the discovery that the other side contains not hell and doom but a kind and gentle God. In Mozart, the acceptance is at once. No fear of hell or fire prior to the *Kyrie,* but an immediate welcoming of a God who has cut short a genius in the prime of a life that could have grown and suffered and learnt, and written so much more. Mozart accepts God. He does not fear him but praises him for letting him die. To hell with Mozart! His lovely requiem makes a great opera, perhaps, but when we die, we will suffer and fear like the rest."

The ghost shook his head at her ignorance.

"Very well, then, very well. Is there not one piece of Mozart you could have loved?"

"The mass in C minor, the mass in C major, both perfect in their purity," she admitted but when he asked her why, she was silent. She did not want the ghost to comment on the situation that, in all actuality, she had never studied harmony or counterpoint, could not even read notes, and judged music from emotions alone, even Verdi and Purcell.

"It has been true perhaps," the ghost answered, offering a small concession out of kindness, "that Mozart's music has always been considered as too light, even in his own time, as entertainment not worthy of deeper thought but one must..."

She cut him off abruptly, perhaps even somewhat rudely, having heard the village church bell ring four times high pitch (the quarter hours), followed by three times low-pitch (the hour). As much as she had enjoyed reproducing the image of the composer as quickly she prepared to wipe him away. He was smoking furiously because of her rudeness, but when she had explained to him that her heart ached for the Rider and she needed to return to her farmhouse to watch him ride on television, he expressed a willingness to teach her Mozart at a more convenient time.

The composer shook his head sadly once she explained that she had internalized every jumping show on the schedule of the current season from her television program and that she had saved every news-cutting on the Rider while yet trying to remember his face. She confided to the still head-shaking composer a very strange circumstance, that even when she had seen the Rider on television, the next instant his face was wiped away from her memory and replaced by the colors of his soul, which was all she ever remembered when seeking to conjure up his image.

Half-shutting his eyes against her folly, the old composer still had some trouble understanding why she would forego Mozart, Verdi and a perfectly painted summer's day for a featureless Rider, then he muttered something about the insanity of love and then he muttered "very well, let's go". Politely, in a grammatically perfect request, he pleaded with her not to wipe him away but allow him to share into the spectacle on television. He would be definitely very interested in seeing the Rider, he stated, seeing that the Rider was connected to her by a set of strange circumstances and that the colors of his soul she kept seeing might well be converted into music at a later stage (the composer smiled an excited little smile at the prospect. He had, thus far, only composed music from the colors of nature, converting mountaintops and valleys and the infinity of the ocean into symphonies or chamber orchestras, once or twice even into an opera, but he had never set to music a man's soul).

Three—the show jumping competition

They had reached the television room of the farmhouse. She sank down on the right side of a wooden bench, lining its walls, and instantly became aware of the misty luminous shapes of the Peruvian and his crowd, on the opposing, left bench. This was strange.

"I am awfully sorry," she apologized to the composer. She should have known that by permitting the elderly composer to watch the live broadcast with her, she had kept open the space between the dead and the living. The Peruvian, who now appeared in perfect crystallization, could not miss out on this opportunity, which he hoped would permit him to demonstrate, once and for all, to the sympathetic crowd that the Rider was much flabbier and much uglier than he and in general not worthy of being labeled the hero of her gradually mending heart.

At first, the composer did not even venture to sit down, but remained standing in the doorway. "I think you're crackers", he said to the other ghost, indignantly surveying the Peruvian and his crowd. They sat uttering little moans and waiting for the horse show to start on television. The Peruvian and the composer grimly stared at each other, fully aware that they were going to play around with something belonging to her remote past, one bent on depriving her of her future, one determined to win it back for her.

A hush went through the room when the first horse pirouetted into the ring and the composer sat down on her side of the bench. After an exchange of civilities there was icy silence between the right side of the bench (with her and the composer) and the left side (containing the Peruvian, who moodily fixed his eyes on the television screen, and a group of learned literary-women ghosts whose admiration for the Peruvian ran through them in twinkling ripples as each of them tried to snuggle close to him).

She explained to the composer that one would hope for the current horse in the ring to throw either its mounted rider or as many of the hurdles as possible, "…to provide less competition for our Rider."

"You go and get stuffed," one of the women shouted. The other women snorted contemptuously and the Peruvian announced that his side would clap for each hurdle the other rider cleared and rejoice as her Rider's competition got more definite.

"What's his name, anyway?" a French writer, attractive despite being dead, shouted across to her side of the bench. The literary ghosts and the Peruvian knew as little about show-jumping as she had done, prior to meeting the Rider. She shrugged her shoulders as though she hadn't heard, telling the composer that the enthusiastic clapping of the women was to be ignored, since she was unable to throw them out of her television room without throwing him out also. The composer nodded earnestly and the commentator introduced a short, fattish man with eyes like decayed windows as the one most likely to win first prize. As the commentator continued, they learned they were unexpectedly being treated to the most important competition of the year and first prize was a huge sum of money.

Once the amount of prize money had been mentioned, the Peruvian immediately turned to his crowd and was marvelously successful, clapping both palms to his face for emphasis, in convincing them of the sin of paying huge sums of money to a humble Rider when the entire population of Peruvian children could be fed with the first and second installment. To the Peruvian's delightful surprise, a tremor of reproach ran through the assembled women like a fever. They flared her a look suggesting her sense of inferiority because they had seen a vision of a modern Peru, built with the moneys of first and second prize, and turning her into a killer for her overt approval of such a waste of financial resources.

The Peruvian flashed a boyish smile at the women and a guilt-inducing one at her. She was surprised when, having seen quickly blended in pictures of the short-legged rider's Cadillac, his palace and his swimming pool, the Peruvian and his women announced that they would root for him to win. The hypocrisy of their statement amused rather than infuriated her when the composer replied nastily that *they* would hope for the short-legged one with his loud stained face to have a fall that would cause him to lie spread-eagled on the ground and castrate himself while falling. The women folded their arms before their chests in attack-defense position, staring over at them, and the exchange of comments between the two opposing benches grew quite vicious, with words like *insufficient, dirty pajama, blind, dropsical, hippopotamus, sluggish* flying back and forth.

When her Rider appeared, the women spat at the screen in disgust and instantly began to exclaim, "ugly rider, ugly horse, ugly saddle!" The Peruvian went one step further and suggested to the cute giggles of the crowd for the title "hero" to be replaced with a more appropriate one, such as "unremarkable little man". The women now roared with laughter, both to suggest that death is hilarious and that her Rider would never beat the one with the distinguished Cadillac.

"He will win", she said dreamily, shouting a great cry of affirmation into the ear of his horse before each jump, "You are the best!"

The composer nodded in agreement, supporting fully her faith in the Rider. Having listened to the commentator boast about the Cadillac rider's almost certain win, the Peruvian asked enthusiastically, "Would you like to sign a statement to this effect?"

Contracts were signed between the left side and the right side. With his shapely lips, the Peruvian instructed all of the women to bet on the Cadillac rider. Only the composer and she bet on her Rider, without the hint of a doubt.

In the end the situation was as follows, that a handful of competent riders (among them the Cadillac rider) had ridden without touching the hurdles and the ghosts, gurgling with excitement, learned that there would be a jump-off where all riders with clear rounds were to jump against one other and a very brutal time clock. The one with zero faults and the best time would win.

The composer looked weary and in need of drink, knowing full well that the Cadillac's horse was faster.

The Peruvian said gloatingly "har-har, we are not as stupid as we seem," to which the women nodded in great admiration, several of them at near swooning-point. The Peruvian pointed out that it had started to rain at whatever place this event was taking place (a foreign-sounding name none of them could pronounce), and by the time her Rider came into the ring, the ground would be bloody soft and his horse would most likely slip and fall and he would be thrown. The ugliness in his tone was deliberate. The composer, who had been brought up British-polite, was very uncomfortable with the icy atmosphere in the television room and briefly put himself in a friendly, tea-making mood. Nobody else wanted a cup of the hot liquid and his tea-making mood collapsed in a noisy-shipwreck kind of way when the first rider appeared on screen and the left side bellowed, clapped and growled with each jump he cleared. The Peruvian leant forward with a spotty voice, suggesting her support of her Rider to be futile and did she wish to change sides, it was not yet too late.

"You are terrible people", the composer addressed the Peruvian and his fans. In his very British manner, he was a little vague about defining the exact cause of the terribleness, saying only that the left side was behaving in a rather inappropriate manner that could only be termed oppression toward the right, that it was not *her* fault the Peruvian had given up his entire life to noble ideals only to have it ending in a painful, smelly mess and it was certainly not the fault of the poor Rider who by no means deserved to be titled "ghastly little man", yes, that it was very unkind to wish for the Rider's brave horse to be liquidated.

The Peruvian laughed bitterly, one of the women in the audience called the composer "poor, toothless little boy", and the bottom really fell out of things when several of the riders were disqualified through various spectacular mistakes, one of them even falling off his horse as they tried clearing the ditch together, crawling out of the water on his hands and knees and finally having to walk back to the stable along the embankment, his chilly, muddy hands dropping rain all over his reins and his horse's mouth.

They all sat like waiting for a bomb to drop as the contest came down to two men, the Cadillac rider and her Rider. The whole situation turned into a scene straight out of an American novel, where good and evil battle each other on opposing sides. On the right side of the bench was seated good-nature, blue-eyed innocence, proper British politeness and hospitality, represented by the ghost of a sixty-eight year old composer. On the left sat meanly staring women with werewolf eyes—as though they would really care about the jumping, were not for the sake of the handsome Peruvian. The composer now looked at her uncertainly (the other horse was faster, after all, the other rider ranked higher) and time stood still as she created inside her mind a little private room with simple double bunks and sound-proof walls, where she shared with the composer a fundamental matter of importance, which she assured him would guarantee the Rider's victory no matter the circumstance.

The Rider, she explained, was getting increasingly ill with self-doubt and auto-character-assassination, something she had discovered during the grand inquisitional session of his soul. This sad circumstance had made her feel obliged to help him since she was most definitely interested in his well-being. This had caused her to enter a Latino simple-faith kind of state and with the unbelievably elegant simplicity that usually moved the God of the *Iglesia Popular* to perform veritable miracles, she had asked him to mend the Rider's soul, bewailing the difficulties of his life. In no uncertain terms, she had advised God that it would be of utmost importance for the Rider to change his sliding attitude about himself, otherwise he would be self-destructing. She explained to the composer that she had sent the request to God via the straight line to heaven that had been opened by the *Iglesia Popular,* somewhere in the depths of Latin America.

The composer nodded unsurely and said "ah". Like most gringos, he did not share her simple peasant faith. "I hope this works."

She shrugged her shoulders confidently. "He needs this victory, all the more because nobody believes in it. It's not the money, it's the mending of his self-confidence."

The ghost said "ah" once more and they returned to the world of the Dead, just in time to see her Rider entering the ring. She took no notice of the parrot voices of women mimicking the Peruvian's expressions of disdain, who now threw unkind words into the room, shouting: "shabby costume", "unskilled proletarian", and—addressing his horse—"dog meat". The Peruvian was busy pawing his tie, chin, collar, forehead and ears in an attempt to make himself appear handsomer than the Rider and he pointed out to the agreeing nods of his audience that the Rider's face was coarse in comparison to his own, chiseled features.

The Rider greeted and the sound of the starting bell could be heard, at which time the ghost of a plain, pigtailed, bespectacled girl with a cheeky talkative face, who entertained a hopeless and devotional love for the Peruvian, began to roar insults at the Rider's horse, her lips spreading in a tight malicious smile. The ghosts were thereafter not very well ordered. Rather badly behaved, they called loudly and with blank cruel eyes for the horse to throw the pole at each hurdle. When, half-way round the course, her Rider was still without fault, the ghost of a heavily painted woman whose eyes also contained a deep affection for the Peruvian, proposed that one would jointly concentrate on a young featureless boy, one of the stewards there, who was positioned in the midst of the ring, not far from the last hurdle, holding on account of the rain a green and white umbrella over his pale little head. The women applauded, and the Peruvian looked at her approvingly, when she suggested a twisted little plan where one would combine the powers of one's ghostly minds to influence the boy to turn his umbrella, precisely when the Rider passed, in a way to paralyze the horse with fear.

"Let's count to twenty and then all together," the painted woman schemed and the unruly ghosts began to establish connection with the boy's mind. The composer had watched patiently but now the noise and the unfairness of the undertaking caused him to become very angry and he uncovered his own considerable talent, unleashing the full power of a Haydn Symphony into the ears of the young boy. In the next instant, the boy could be seen rubbing his ears while trying to keep his motions to a minimum to keep from disturbing the horse as it cantered past him. Amidst all the noise in his head, the boy had been unable to disentangle his thoughts and capture the shameful suggestion of the painted woman. The Peruvian pouted sulkily.

"That was a nasty trick, a very nasty trick indeed," the pigtailed woman said, glancing around the room disdainfully. "But we will win. When he (flashing an admiring look at the Peruvian) wants a thing, he goes for it. You'll see."

Arrogant-looking, the women herded together around the Peruvian.

"Courage, eh?" the Peruvian shouted at the composer. "I'll show you what true courage is!"

He pointed at the screen containing the last rider, who was the Cadillac with the decaying eyes. The composer looked anxiously about, hoping for the Peruvian God to come through. Suddenly, there was a strong storm and the Cadillac's horse crawled almost blindly against the wind, toward the first hurdle, lifting its legs with difficulty. But then the horse raised its head with an air of triumph, managed to haul itself over the jump, and galloped with neat large strides over the next hurdles, debasing the value of her Rider's round through being much bolder and faster than his horse had been.

The Peruvian began to whistle and the women planned, with proudly swelling eyes, a new addition to the Cadillac's home from the money he would win, putting a sauna in the basement. The Peruvian twitched his nostrils in rumba rhythm to show that he was having a very good time and the composer grew increasingly worried. With each hurdle the Cadillac cleared, she put herself into quite a state and she already wondered whether her Rider would understand that life is a matter of constant adjustment and readjustment and that he might win next time, provided he could preserve his ageing horse. But then the composer tested her faith, reminding her of the God of Peru, and at the very last moment, as the Cadillac's horse turned toward the final hurdle, he did this:

de da de da de de da

full power, orchestra at the noise level of a medium heart attack, he played the *Symphonie Fantastique* straight into the Cadillac horse's ear, reminding her that this action had nothing to do with fair or unfair but was a matter of bare survival for her Rider. The Cadillac's horse snorted *Bsss*, let go a small river of urine and, in a terrible state, the poor thing crashed, slipped and sliced into the hurdle, taking all the poles with it and nearly unseating the Cadillac. The composer and she beamed, feeling very proud of themselves and of their Rider, who had just snatched the most important Grand Prize of the entire season.

The Peruvian jumped up from his chair, screaming, "This is the limit", the women muttered "Sabotage", and the composer smiled a smile of cold, scientific triumph at the left side of the bench. She remarked, quite happily, that it was high time to face reality, that her Rider was simply the best.

Now the Rider appeared on television beside the commentator, explaining his operations in the ring and wearing a charming little smile. The sound of his voice lit a small fire inside her and within a few moments the coals inside her heart burst into flames as she gushed "Isn't he adorable?"

She greatly regretted that he would celebrate his triumph alone because she was still surrounded by the Peruvian. The noble freedom fighter had great trouble keeping his women in bounds, who now joined each other in queues to kiss him comfortingly on his smooth handsome cheek. One of them suggested that the victory of the Rider had been a perverted one because somehow the hurdles had been lowered for him. Then the chattering ghosts began to disappear from her mind and she was alone with the Peruvian and the composer.

The picture of the Rider had since long faded from the screen. She very much wanted to know whether it was still raining there, where he was going now and who he was going with. The Peruvian caught her thoughts and suggested that the Rider would, no doubt, be celebrating throughout the night with the 22-year old bombshell Blonde he was currently training, but she replied angrily that he was only training her. With his usual candor, the Peruvian said that it was her turn to face reality and that no man would merely be training a girl like the Blonde. With her half-dead soul, she would never hold up beside the young girl, the Peruvian said, but only to cushion his shocks. Having never seen her Rider close up as in the interview following the victory, he could not deny that the Rider was indeed a most adorable and charming man. The Peruvian could see this, although he was fundamentally not homosexual and although his natural conclusion was to wonder whether the Rider really wished to die.

Now that it had become impossible to discredit the Rider any longer for his looks, riding skills or horse, all three of which had proven quite superior in quality, he thrust into several different openings. Talking in connection with the very happy smile she wore on her face and her remark to the composer that she was very proud of her Rider, his rapid Spanish words, spoken in a thick-ish kind of voice as though blood were stirred into them, were intended to ruin her laughter and cause her to feel ashamed at her sense of irresponsibility. "In Peru, the children are dying for lack of medicine, and she is happy because the Rider has jumped higher than anyone else. What does it matter whether he jumps higher than the others, when the children are dying?"

The only reaction he achieved was her smile broadening to near cracking point and the composer muttering that there was always a certain madness to be found in love (the Peruvian cringed at the word).

In fact, she had almost arrived at depression point over her urgent need to see the Rider again, but she told the Peruvian nothing of the sort, only that he was "…right in saying that it is of no importance, in the grand scheme of life, whether he jumps faster around the course than anyone else. Naturally, he is playing a rich man's game to be occupying his mind with such follies when the children of Lima occupy their minds with the search for food. But…"

The Peruvian's neck-arteries looked dangerously distended, his face had swelled to wine color and his stomach began to throb like an engine when she continued.

"…for whatever reason, it is important to him to jump higher and faster than the others. If it makes him happy to jump quickly around the ring, then I will be happy for him when he achieves his goal. If it made him happy to paint a tree, or to milk a cow or to raise a calf, then I would be happy for this also. It matters nothing to me whether he jumps faster than the others, slower or not at all, but if he finds his satisfaction there, so be it."

She beamed at the Peruvian, who stood helplessly and trying to smile, but then his anger overflowed. From contempt-dripping lips, he spilled out: "Shouldn't he find his happiness, rather, in feeding the children of Peru?"

"With the money he has won today, he could build a cancer clinic," she replied cordially, fully agreeing with the Peruvian that a clinic was desperately needed.

"But he won't," the Peruvian exasperated, his contempt giving his Spanish a terrible tinge as the lights went on all over his face and his whole body joined into the second exclamation, "but he *won't!*" (with solid emphasis suggesting great injustice and a great reproach bathing there in the dark amber lake of his serious voice)

"Shut up, shut up, shut *up,*" cried she when the Peruvian's reproach had been repeated. She felt very guilty that her soul still shook with happiness over the Rider's victory and tried to get herself back into position as the responsible Mother of Peru, even making an earnest attempt to recoil her happiness, but then she connected, in an instant and fine close-up, with the Rider's soul. She saw the aromatic satisfaction that had spread there on account of his victory. There were suddenly all warm, soft colors there, causing her to almost cry with joy and gratitude that he had won and that the dark suspicious shade around his soul was gone.

The End.

CHAPTER 8

One—colors in music

When the Peruvian had finally disappeared, her shoes had been kicked off in the heat of discussion and her face was still flushed. She turned to the composer and stated, quite definitely, that she wished nothing more to do with the Peruvian and his wretched country. Everything had to go, everything. She begged the composer to teach her the vast mechanics of opera and allow her to set music against the screaming children, to prevent her return to a country she was certain would devour her, with its self-righteous smile of pride and power, claiming that it had only killed, at last, what it had righteously owned all along.

"Very well then," the ghost said and told her that he would begin teaching her, "...but only on condition that your final judgment on Mozart is to be reserved until a full analysis of his music has been conducted, of a piece I see fit."

Mozart had evidently played a big part in his life and she felt that there was no choice but to agree to his terms. If they delayed any longer, the news of her death might come through before he had a chance to teach her anything. Were she to lynch Mozart, it seemed reasonable enough to get to know him first. The ghost caused her to enter into her CD player the *Coronation Concerto K537* and to shut her eyes while listening.

She closed her eyes. The music started and the composer sang along: "*de dedutdada dade dedum, de dedutdada dada dedum, de di dit ditdada da dadamdadadam da, de da dut da ba now dut da da dut da da da da da, di da da dut di da ba, da di da ba da da da bum...*"

He turned off the CD player and asked, "What do you see?"

"See?"

"The colors! There are colors in Mozart's music," he insisted.

"Nonsense, there are no colors in music," she replied.

"Very well," he replied crossly, "just one more matter lies at hand, in this case."

He called up from his mind, as a ghost this was no problem for him, Beethoven's 6th Symphony, the *Pastorale*, second movement. "Close your eyes," he instructed once again. She closed her eyes. She listened. *To we to we towetowe to we.* He stopped the piece and asked her to open her eyes again.

"What do you hear?"

"Flute, clarinet, oboe," she said.

"These are the instruments."

"Yes," she replied unnecessarily.

"Again! This time, I don't want the instruments," the ghost instructed. "The instruments are what you hear. What do you see? I am only interested in what you see."

She closed her eyes again. *To we to we towetowetowe to we.* On the inside of her eyelids appeared a cuckoo. Then trees. Sunshine. Green fields. Mountains in the background. Snow.

"Very good." The ghost was pleased. He fast-forwarded the music.

"Dark clouds," she said uncertainly. "Why would there be dark clouds in the sky? I still see blue. Now increasingly darker."

"You are doing well," the ghost complimented her. He stopped the music, explaining: "this was the scene of the thunderstorm."

"Oh," she said, for lack of something better to say. She was uncomfortable with the fact that she had not studied the piece before and very obviously had not known the description of its movements. The ghost did not mind her beethovean ignorance, seeing he regarded Beethoven as a necessary evil who had been too popular for his own good. In his opinion, popularity in music, especially classical music, did not equate quality of sound or depth.

"But his symphonies are marvelous," she defended Beethoven, wisely withholding the most vital part of information how Beethoven and she had first met, through a most brutal, ridiculously popular movie where his 9th symphony had served to underscore scenes of a rape, a brutal beating and a man jumping out of the window to commit suicide. The composer had hated that movie with the same fervor she had loved it. She thought it better not to tell him that she had set out to listen to Beethoven only after he had provided the soundtrack to one of her favorite movies. To her credit, she had liked what she had heard and Beethoven and she, although not intimately befriended, had formed a somewhat continuous acquaintanceship, extending to his Emperor Concerto but excluding the operas.

The ghost interrupted her train of thought and demanded absolute attention. "Now back to Mozart," he commanded and re-started the music.

Da, dadadadadadda, dadadadadadaddda, dadadad dadaddadummum. She listened. He instructed her to close her eyes. She saw the recent ugly scene with the Peruvian and the Rider and knew that, should she do nothing to undermine the Peruvian's continuing presence in her life, her future would degenerate, characterized by a sickly fear of the phantom and causing her to remain dead for the rest of her life because the Peruvian liked dancing with her. She was pretty sure that, through some obscure intuition, she could succeed to draw colors out of Mozart's music. Anything to ban the dark, disturbing thoughts ruining her future with the Rider. She strained until her brain hung flaccid and the outlines of her rapidly firing synapses could be recognized even by the Peruvian. She had the distinct sensation that her brain was smoking, being weighed down under the colossal task of drawing colors out of a music she considered to be extraordinarily barren. The composer felt satisfied by the emerging smoke, seeing it as proof that she was making an honest attempt, at least. He stopped the music once more, rewinding it, deciding to help her further in what he considered to be a fit of majestic generosity.

For the next few hours, she moved between helpless rage and implacably sweet mirth of knowledge as her brutish opinion of Mozart was destroyed by the serene security found among the colors of his music. Once the first subtle strands of blue and red had appeared through the instruments, the colors began forming themselves. At first, she had uninterestedly dabbled with the paints and the shells but her students' bad manners disappeared once she had learnt to relate the score to the colors, turning the composer's schoolmasterly rebukes into overt approval. When 175 hand-painted shells finally lay before her, each containing a separate movement of the concerto, she had learnt to pick up any one of the painted shells delicately between thumb and index finger to identify the colors on its back and match them to the corresponding notes in the concerto (for instance, white bottom, midnight blue top: flute under cellos and violas). This prompted her to associate a romantic and noble glamour with the Coronation Concerto. The colors gradually had driven home to her the genius of Mozart as she had learnt to look under the glitter and rattle of his squeaking violins. Eventually, her previous opinion of him crashed completely and she understood that Mozart's music was far more than a harmless enjoyment characterized by penurious scherzos mingling with discords.

Two—a soul like a Haydn orchestra

Sitting on the floor of her bedroom, she had taken it all in. Once her opinion of Mozart's music had shifted, from considering it a lump of pain to understanding its divinity, the composer suggested they call in the Peruvian to measure her new-found skill against his ghastly, depressing country. They lay in wait excitedly, wondering whether they had succeeded in improving the movements of her memory. Slowly, the Peruvian took shape directly before of the shelf where they crouched to await his arrival. His image gradually became clearer as he bridged space and time with the desire for another opportunity to turn her life into an anti-matter. This time, he had left his lynch-mob of women behind. Licking his lips, he flashed a striking smile at her, formidable in its simplicity. Despite all her good intentions, she found herself to be no longer completely anti-Peruvian. She even wondered whether her heart had been crippled for life by him and began to feel that the thing with Mozart might very well amount to a matter of injustice and deception. If everything went well, Mozart was going to bring death to him, when his only crime had been the desire to sing love duets with her. There might be a compromise found between assassinating and marrying him. Guilt-ridden, she turned to him with a welcoming smile, embracing the murder in his eyes.

The Peruvian had recovered from the detrimental experience of the Rider's victory and had succeeded, once more, in reducing the horseman to a dull, fading image while impregnating his own reflection among the shadows and the lights inside her heart. She reached towards him under the incubus of remorse and he cheekily used his genius to cross over, into the melting avenues of her heart that still led toward the Rider.

Dipping and re-dipping into her memory banks, he recreated the scene of the Rider's victory. Then he showed her a small country lane, plastered completely with the money the Rider had won. The

Peruvian dealt out his judgment in a diabolical manner when now appeared the Rider, walking down the lane and carelessly stepping on the bills beneath his feet. The Rider was dressed expensively and wastefully. His shirts, socks and trouser pockets were stuffed with pound-bills and silver coins but he engaged in a greedy howling for more money. She had just been able to see that the Rider had thick, abnormally hairy arms before the Peruvian changed the scenery and another image appeared, of children dying in the Lima *hospital general*. Driven to the limits of exasperation, they begged for medicine to save their little lives. Blood-soaked sheets were tightly wrapped around the emaciated body of one boy recovering, or trying to recover, from a series of deep gashing stab wounds. Superimposed, the Rider walked above the image, clothed completely in money and stuffing his face until his money-shirt was soaked with the remains of champagne, lobster brains dripping from a broken carcass and turtle-egg soup.

"That boy is of no consequence anyway. A Peruvian peasant, no more," the Rider could be heard muttering. Standing above the head of the blood-soaked child, he swore at the inconvenience of the image and wrung champagne from his trousers, prior to wiping his face with a soiled but by all appearances very expensive handkerchief. The bloodied boy stretched his little hands toward the hot ceiling of the hospital and directly into the path of the Rider who burped and rudely walked past the little brown arms, muttering: "Riders have no interest in Peruvian peasantry," before continuing down the money lane. In the hospital room below, the boy died from a combination of profound hunger and septic infection caused by lack of penicillin. Nobody even noticed him dying, except the old man in the neighboring bed who made the dead boy's clothes and shoes disappear under his own bed in a bundle.

Very humbled now, she came to see that the difference between rich and poor was grossly unfair and that those who did not denounce injustice were as guilty as the rich ignoring it. The Peruvian beamed with self-satisfaction. Increasingly confident now, he added other images of their contrasting worlds:

Enter the Rider, walking through the grounds of his considerable estate with an expression on his face stating that he was only concerned with himself and his horses. Enter image of a worried Peruvian peasant woman who, having learnt of her husband's death by paramilitary unit firing squad, searches in her bombed-out soul for a reason to go on, wailing in Spanish: "...and now I've got nothing. Nothing. Nothing...*Ya tengo nada. Nada. Nada...*"

The woman's *nada* reverberated inside her soul, threatening to erase the Rider there, but the composer took the strained expression on her face and her drooping, quivering lower lip as an invitation to end the Peruvian's specifically diabolical performance. His protective instinct awakened, he felt a distinct craving to twist and tear the noble freedom fighter's testicles. Then, being a very prudent and very British man who had learnt never to surrender to a manic fit, he patted her thrice on the shoulder and—having obtained her momentary attention—placed a shell into her hand.

The pain inside her was great, the Peruvian had transported her back to Peru with a vengeance, and all she had was a shell to have her sanity restored. She took a hard, long look at the shell, gloom curling about her like tobacco smoke because she had earnestly hoped for an improvement of relations with the Peruvian following the Rider's victory and had not anticipated that he would return to destroy her. She turned the shell in her hand, feeling its rough edges and tracing the red *zig zag* line above the turquoise background, then turning it over to contemplate the hawked white line over its crimson bottom. There was a sudden burst of loud music in her ear and the shell played Mozart, second movement, *Coronation Concerto,* as colors danced inside her head and the Peruvian faded in a helpless rage, his voice drowned out by cellos and flutes. The tragic images of his country dissolved under the red roof of the violins and the ragged blue of the base. When the music stopped, all that remained of the Peruvian was a distant memory. She raised her head to look out the window at an admirable sunset in a most unusual combination of soft colors. The composer saw it too and stated that one must not lose out on this very wondrous performance in the sky, which seemed to be the occurrence of that rare phenomenon when a symphony was painted on the firmament. The composer exclaimed excitedly: "Come, let us go outside. There is a symphony in the sky that we should look at."

Although she would have liked to have read music books for some time, refusing his offer would have filled her with guilt, seeing that he had placed the saving shell in her hand. After all, it was an evening with something to celebrate, not only the Rider's astonishing victory but also the Peruvian succumbing to the colors of Mozart's *Coronation Concerto*. A curving stairway spread before her, into her new life, which she, with near disastrous fervor, hoped would be containing the highly adorable, very handsome Rider. Outside, an image of sublime beauty presented itself, inviting to be banned on canvas by the observing eye of a painter.

They had now reached the birch tree at the beginning of the field stretching behind the farmhouse. From the wooden bench beneath the tree, they intended to watch the poetry hanging in the sky. The sky was beyond rapture and reverence, it was a palazzo of colors, a mysterious eruption into the very heart of life. Orange in the most delightful variants, light yellow over light-blue fading, deepest red, violet, a curious natural blue, an inexplicable pink…every hardship was forgotten as the colors embraced her. Life emerged from hiding as if by supernatural force and time stood still as the day seemed to become arrested in the process of its own fading.

The colors were by no means a small gift. There was something very familiar about them. They seemed to spring forth from a semi-transparent memory she had not wholly forgotten but when she reached for it, she reached for the inaccessible. She had the distinct sensation of standing in shallow water for as far as the eye could reach, with the memory she sought buried beneath. The composer exclaimed: "Freedom. Absolutely clear freedom!" and began to hum the music going with the colors. Sharp chords for the entire orchestra, set inside wide spaces of silence. Recapitulation of heavy horns, a noble tune of strings over it.

"Haydn," the composer remarked, recognizing the tune he had hummed. "Haydn has these ceremonial colors seeking to preserve the past."

He went on to explain that Haydn and Mozart were distinguished by the fact that Haydn had been homeless and hungry in his youth and knew the merciless struggle for survival all too well, something that had always caused him to be somewhat angrily insecure and unsettled, despite being well-padded in his own genius. Pointing to the clouds in the sky, silver velvet clouds, and the marble-arteried sun slowly sinking into the distant mountains, the composer explained:

"Mozart is giddy, light. What you see is what you get. No connotations. No hidden sanctuary. On the surface, Haydn is light as Mozart, but somewhat sober. Underneath it all, a volcano boils ready to erupt, where we encounter anger, fear, ebony and arctic seas all mixed into one. The reassuring smile of the strings belies their fate. The surface of Haydn is hardly scratched by superficially listening to his music, which seems like an empty emerald case but hides a jealous and angry man perpetually engaged in breaking a peace treaty with himself. In dealing with Haydn, one must never restrict oneself to the audible."

Pointing to the various cloudlets in the sky, the composer taught her to translate the instruments of a Haydn orchestra into their powerful colors.

"Life is the important thing," the composer suddenly exclaimed, and also that her future stretched before her like a bottle still to be opened. In the same instant, she recognized the colors in the sky as the same colors she had seen in the Rider's soul and she realized that, by way of an inexplicable miracle of the mind, the Rider had somehow succeeded to illustrate her sunset with the beautiful variants of his essence.

"A soul like a Haydn orchestra," the composer, who had overheard her thoughts, said in a tone identifying him to be a humble admirer of the spectacle in the sky, and of the Rider's soul.

The End.

CHAPTER 9

One—the picture

When she saw the Rider again, the phenomenal sunset of his soul had become a foggy memory. However dull the information she harbored about him, she had not wanted to evict the horseman completely from her heart and was grateful for their next encounter. Browsing through the rather unattractive book section of her local department store she had opened a horse-riding book.

The thought of shopping gave her no joy, she would have rather washed gray, muddy shells on the beach with the composer, but it was a necessary evil. To make matters worse, the store was large enough to bring about physical exhaustion with its many sections, most of which were without any distinction. Anything could be bought there, from stockings to candybars, from fine clothes to animals, Hi-fi systems and books. Modern man liked for all his goods to be kept together. Breathless from the brutal pace of his life, he sought convenience in every aspect. Life might have been full of great people who had been damaged by its pace, but the clownish sadness on the faces of the other customers in the store, their dropping mouths and mask-like features, made it very hard for her to be in their presence. The inventing of department stores had not only damaged formerly charming city faces but also given rise to people wishing to encounter sympathy, coffee-shops, telephone calls and striped underwear all under the same roof, at a very reasonable price.

Gone were the days when one could walk into a small store with kind windows, to be attended by sweet bespectacled men looking after one's needs with friendly smiles. Going into a department store was more like going into the woods at midnight, since the very act of shopping had become a strange mixture of fearful and dazzling impulses, where solitary customers searched, by themselves, inside giant stores for what they needed.

Little old women could be seen arching their backs, to obtain a roll of string from a top shelf hidden behind a lower shelf stacked between two other shelves. Owing to idiotic personnel saving policies, over-worked and suspicious-looking shop-assistants were prone to flee whenever they found themselves being stalked by a helpless customer. As a result, only very few and very brave shoppers dared asking for help anymore. They scurried about confused rather than embarrass themselves asking anyone for anything. Askers were immediately surveyed by cherry-cold, only marginally cordial faces with guilt-inducing eyes shaming the culprit unable to find his own way through the store. The unfortunate stammering customer, having asked with a jittery groan where one might find little lose latches, for instance, was stared at like an evil hallucination and then marched off in direction of the latches as his guide painted a humoring-nastily-smiling expression on his face, suggesting to other store-keepers that the asker, by all accounts innocent but by now usually stuttering an apology, was inept at social functions and basic matters of intelligence.

Most customers merely said, "all right, all right, I'll go find it myself", too tired to object to being treated as though the favor were on the side of the store for taking their money in exchange for its goods. The dreadful situation, where modern man was subjected to traumatic shopping experiences without a gleam of comfort, continued with no end in sight, but it was such a store she had found herself entering.

Strangely unsettled by the Rider's fading image in her memory, she had been searching for news of him, very much hoping to find at least a book or two about him, seeing that he was one of the best in his field. But these days, the few books still being read by modern man, working himself to near self-destruction point and having little time to read, were very basic, with their contents geared toward the fearfully dull tastes of the masses. She found nothing about him, although she had only recently read in a horse-riding magazine (she had taken up reading of these type of magazines) a very tightly written advertisement, by a little girl seeking all published materials about the Ghost Rider (she had named him so because she sometimes awoke with the touch of his hand still imprinted in hers but he was never truly there. He was thus, like the Peruvian and the composer, a distinct presence without body and hence a ghost). The ad had named a fair number of materials that had been published on him and she had learnt that books and videos existed about him.

Rather than telephone the Rider, she remained intimidated by the Peruvian's assertion that he would never love a survivor of Latin American torture chambers, nor she love a Rider without destroying the world-removed innocence he needed to keep on riding. After all, what could she hope to achieve for a man with a soul like a Haydn orchestra, when her own soul played morose pieces like Vaughan Williams' *Job's answer to God* and the colors of her own sunset were various shades of gray created by rain-clouds in danger of sudden liquefaction?

To protect the Rider from her not so humble passion, she was intent on seeking everything that had been written about him and know him only through distant spasms of silent lightning, without having to make an instant decision whether to meet him again. She had not yet decided whether he would continue to exist merely as a fond notion inside her head, or whether she would see him again. If so, whether she should wear a mask...and...*what would he do when the mask cracked*? She understood, from the sunset message he had sent, that matters could not continue as they had in the past. If she wished for another encounter with him, she would need to show her true face not a mask, but first she would need to decide whether she still existed now the torturers had left their mark on her. Until then, searching out his picture in book sections (flanked, to the east, by a fat woman and, to the west, by a shabby little man) was far less complicated.

She had been leafing through some horse-riding magazines and found a photo of his winning horse, him on top. The story beneath spoke of his glorious victory over the Cadillac rider, stating him to be the world's best, ranked much higher than the Cadillac could ever hope to climb. He was dressed in smart riding gear and looking very good there on his horse, in his red jacket. She was glad for him and, although not yet entitled to be, she was also proud of him. The only thing she regretted was that the photo was of his horse and did not show his face as close up as she would have liked.

The sad fact was, the Peruvian had been right with his dark prediction. Although the colors of the Rider's soul remained clearly imprinted in her heart, shining brightly enough she could have composed a symphony from them (and thought of this in passing, too. After all, Berlioz had composed the *Symphony Fantastique* to gain the heart of his beloved. But then she realized that it was now just a matter of claiming his love or recoiling from him), she could not recall his precise features and so she wanted to see his face again, but anonymously. The photograph not having turned out to her satisfaction, she dragged her listless feet past the shabby man, muttering "excuse me, pardon me" and went on to another table, with a sign that read GRAND SALE, where she found a picture book designed to teach riding to young girls.

The situation then began to unfold as follows: she started to leaf through the book, containing color photographs of stone-faced, square-shouldered riders enforcing strict discipline from their trembling horses. Supposedly, the photographs were an inspiration for young girls to ride like that one day. That precise wish was written all over the face of a little girl who stood beside her and, leafing trough a copy of the same book, and had removed her hair-band in her excitement of studying the photographs. She wondered whether the misty dreams of the girl would one day become reality and the inner court of her heart reserve a marble-flagged gallery in the name of a still-to-be-anointed rider. She had been watching the girl for a while, looking over her shoulder, then she turned her attention back to her own book. To her delight, the little girl had tended to tarry at inappropriate segments, omitting a fair number of pages while leafing through the book. One of the previously unseen pages contained his photograph. There he was, unmistakably, but some ten years younger. The photograph showed the most handsome man she had ever seen and she closed the book in shock, then opened it again. She checked his name and double checked it, unable to believe the sensual man in the photograph, who in no way lacked behind the Peruvian for beauty, to be truly him. Although she could not recall his face in detail, she did recall that he had not been a handsome man. Rather, his face had been the corpse of his younger years, a mere funeral shroud of his former self. She could not help wondering how he had buried such a face in ten short years. *What doom had befallen him*, she asked his photograph, *what wounds had time etched into his face? Why seemed he now so much older than his years? Had it been an unhappy love or the loss of someone he held dear? What hopes had gone unfulfilled, when he seemed to have reached so many? Why did he walk in solitude, why had he chosen this route?*

The picture was silent as its living pendant and she brutally realized that she was not going to get this glorious man, and be envied by every woman, but was going to be taking on his wrecked self. If she went through with her plan, she was going to get a man who had given life his best shot, and been utterly disappointed, and whose soul only performed Haydn symphonies in the sunset anymore when he had won a horse show. Doubtlessly, his best years were behind him, spent by another woman's side. She was going to get a man behind whose back they talked, despite his recent victory, only waiting for him to fall and to take his place. He was a mere shell of his former self, who had given up on life outside the riding ring and whose fire had been given to others while she was going to get the ashes.

Two—memories of glory and memories of destruction

He was no longer at the top but she had no choice except loving him. Yet there remained the disturbing fact of his twenty years with another woman, some of which, at least, must have been happy. Against this she had to set ten years of memories with the Peruvian, the last five of which he had been a ghost.

He had memories of glorious days at the Olympic games and she had memories of prisons. He had memories of jumping horses and she had memories of dying children. He had memories of being with the world's most celebrated and she had memories of living among the world's most despised. He had memories of luxurious hotel rooms and she had memories of roaches crawling over her bed at night, in the slums of Lima. He had memories of having to watch his weight, with all these great buffets they had at the hotels, and she had memories of fighting for her life in the slums where there was never enough food or water. Never enough. Never enough. She had memories of looking death in the face and he had memories of looking glory in the face.

His days were spent riding his horses and her days were spent silencing the scream of Peru. He had lived in his own country all his life, where he had roots and a big family, and she had lived in many countries and had no country to call her own. Her roots were in her books and her family the characters she created. He had children and she had none. She would never be the only one he loved, there would always be his children he loved more. They were his own flesh, but she would have only him and her books.

Her books were her children, but they did everything to make her happy, filling their pages with frog trees, oversized ardors, lakeside cafes and lavender villas at her command. His children would perhaps do just the opposite, controlling his moods and standing in the way of their happiness. When they behaved badly toward him, he would brood, and he would be happy when they were kind to him. This glorious, middle-aged athlete was somebody's father and would be receiving letters written by fresh-faced young creatures, addressed to *Daddy*. Their life would never be just the two of them. She would come second in his affections, always, with his children taking first place whom he looked in the face to see another woman's features.

He would come into their encounter with glorious memories of family and children and thousands of admirers. And she? With Peru standing like a shadow behind her, with memories of torture chambers, with her still smoldering hatred for her captors, with the ghosts of a composer who taught colors in music and a Peruvian freedom fighter who sincerely wished her dead, with the constant call of a country he had never heard of, for her to return and die there in its deadly embrace. *What chance could there ever be for them?*

Having taken his clue, the Peruvian appeared, gloating with self-satisfaction as he looked over her shoulder at the Rider's photograph in the book. He had tried reaching her by telephone, he said, but had been advised that the Dead were forbidden from accessing such forms of communication. Now he stated how pleased he was that the opportunity had arisen to speak to her once more. First, he remarked on her exquisite beauty and then performed a slight bow, promising to have only her best interests at heart. Looking pityingly at the photograph of the Rider, he remarked how sad that the Rider's handsome face was merely a transparent pseudonym for another greedy, self-centered, rough-hearted and calculating gringo.

"You will never love a gringo again, you will never live in gringo society again," he prophesied dramatically.

"What do they understand of human suffering and overcoming hardship? Seeking adventures in their dreary lives, they might partake in vacations to third world countries, to get a dose of true suffering while living in a mud-hut as part of a package-tour adventure trip or trudging up steep mountain lanes to reach the broken people of a foreign land. Then they return to gringolandia, their heads filled with romantic notions and stone steps of unfinished houses they are going to build there, but they never risk their own lives or lose their lives. They never enter torture chambers, except as observers of useless human rights pressure groups, and they never forsake their own homes or their own future. You have, and doing so you have abandoned your gringo-ship to become part of the people of Peru. Only there can you live with the memories you carry. Having been tortured like a Peruvian, you must now be strong like a Peruvian, and only Peru can teach you this."

She nodded unsurely. Images of the warm welcome she had always encountered in Peru blended with memories of empty gringo palms and empty gringo hearts. She took a brief excursion into the future where there were two distinct roads, the gringo road with its lonely lives and its suicides and its isolated people driven quite insane by their survival fight, and along the opposite lane stretched life in Peru with its high-level hospitality and its radiant belief that life held promise even in the depths of abject poverty. In the Peruvian lane, she could see people singing and dancing and embracing each other, ignoring the rain-clouds above their heads. In the gringo lane were depressed and arrogant white people who had nearly worked themselves to death during their long climbs to the top and who considered those with less money to be inferior. Already, she could see that gringo life was not for her but she also reminded the Peruvian that she been exiled from Peru, had even been threatened with death if she were to return there. There were people in Peru, she jogged his memory, whose plan had been that, finding readjustment to her own world a psychological impossibility because life in *gringolandia* would near murder her with solitude and isolation, she would return to Peru to be shot on sight.

The Peruvian ignored her final statement completely. "What's the matter?" he asked plaintively. "Don't you like me?" Then he softly sang the national hymn of Peru, snatched the key to her heart and put it in his jacket pocket.

Three—to be Peruvian

Having surveyed the photo-face of the Rider once more, the Peruvian dismissed his rival as a *gringo lampshade with landscapes*—an expression he had picked up in his living years, from an American art dealer who had been visiting Peru, that he somehow assumed to be a delicate and complex insult and was proud to be using for anyone he did not hold in high esteem. Then he replied: "To be Peruvian, you have to be courageous like a Peruvian and you must return there. There is not to be any more funny business with the gringos."

He threw in the story of a Peruvian poet, who had once written of the restless dead of his country now living inside her soul also. Puffing with the effort of consulting this already wrinkled part of Peru's past, the Peruvian told a story of the poet having lived in Europe for many years as an exile but finally shunning the chance for augmentation of his wealth and returning to Peru, torn up by the longing for his own homeland. While it was true that he had been killed there and had been found with blood still trickling down his loins, wearing cheap brown suit crimson-stained from the moisture seeping out of his chest, "…at least he died courageously," the Peruvian romanticized, "like any good Peruvian should die." (the last statement was accompanied by his seductive beastly face wearing an expression splendidly inviting such a noble death).

"Nonsense. He died begging for his life," she reminded him dryly for she knew the poet's story well, from newspaper accounts all over the world.

"He died begging until his very last breath to be let go and unhooking in his final moments the heart-shaped desire he had carried for Peru, while regretting bitterly that he had chosen death in Peru over life in Europe."

The Peruvian averted his eyes and smiled at nothing, admitting that she had caught him in what he considered to be a relatively harmless lie. All this, he maintained, did nothing to cloud his original intention, that he had only her best interests at heart, was utterly neutral and had not been lying because her death would prove profitable for him or because he wished to mark her with the nostalgia of their passion. He was very adept at cooking the sweet-sour sauce of a lie within another lie but she realized at once that the story with the poet had been concocted in the hope of leading her back to Peru, and into his arms. Still, she had to admit that he was right in some aspects at least. The truth was she had landed in the midst of a very strange group of people and would hardly be able to live with the Rider in his own society, sitting on hard benches and wearing white slacks and a black sweater, removing her coat in the sunshine or opening her umbrella in the rain as she talked of horses with people who had never lived outside the confines of their highly promoted riding competitions. She would be an outsider among them, regarded with highest suspicion.

Things did not look much better when she tried imaging the Rider living in Peru with her. The corresponding image showed…

> …the two of them together, living in a fine home in a fine colonia. Their house had all the luxuries: running water, hot and cold, a fridge filled with food, enough drinking water, a proper bed, book shelves and a bathroom filled with imported perfumes and soaps.

Their house was surrounded by considerable walls with barbed wire tops. They were living a sizable step removed from the people of the streets, betraying her ideals, the Rider with ease and she less so, by ignoring the fundamental troubles of Peru's poor.

She saw herself…

…eating as poor Peruvians would never be eating, then snuggling contentedly in the Rider's arms at night while becoming afflicted with the callous gringo disease of never looking downwards at the grief-stricken men and women in the slums, denasalised from crying. The Rider would be more than ready to have her cry on his shoulder over the loss of her ideals, he was a kind and understanding man. He would be saying "there, there" and offer her another piece of imported Swiss chocolate, explaining that being married to a man like him, she had to be prepared to stand on the other side of the fence separating the rich from the poor in Peru, and hadn't she known that he stemmed from a country where poverty was considered a disgrace?

Abandoning her noble visions, frowning and dissatisfied, she would come to understand the fundamental differences between Peruvian society and the Rider's society. In the streets of Peru, the value of a man was measured by the size of his courage. Poverty meant nothing in a country where everyone was poor, excepting the foreigners and a few wealthy families whose wealth was usually a by-product of a passionate night between an American man and a Peruvian woman, with marriage having resulted and empires having been built.

She looked hungrily still at the photograph of the Rider, but vowed to clear matters up concerning her life with him, because the Rider would never live among the Poor in Peru.

He would be part of the ruling class and frequent exclusive country clubs. On account of his immense riding successes, he would become someone very important in Peru. Perhaps, one never knew, he would even be recruited to train the yet non-existent Peruvian

Olympic show-jumping squad. Very wealthy landowners would be showing their gratitude by importing expensive horses for him, bought from the finest stables of Europe. The Rider would be seen, patting the horses and training rich little lads in the art of jumping over parti-colored hurdles. All the while, the Peruvian people would starve in the slums, choking on their beans and rice, while their children still died, screaming out for medicine to save them, but the Rider's horses would eat the finest grain and he would get that bloody big bonus once the Peruvian team qualified itself for the next Olympics. He would swiftly grin at her, pocketing the money, and ask whether she wanted a little red sports car. Also, he would learn Spanish and then his children would turn against her, for having taken their father to a far-away land.

All these images suggested there to be no chance for them together. Peru had already devoured her and was only waiting to claim what was its due. Even the woman who had headed her torture squad had said so when she had ordered her to put on a pair of sandals and find her own way out, releasing her from the prison, but never from Peru.

She knew that she could stay on for another 30 years in the comforting arms of civilization, to love white-horsed gringos in orange nylon-jackets, but in the end, Peru would win. She could even envision the unfortunate Rider giving up everything on supposition that she loved him, only to become another victim of Peru and filling its endless hunger for the lives of kind and noble men. She could see his blood unite with hers to feed the ugly crimson rivers that still flowed lazily down the streets of the *mercados,* yes, she could see him die for her, only because she had been unable to stop bidding for his heart. She could not stand the image of herself as the Rider's prospective widow and thought it wiser to leave things as they were, vowing to drain her heart of its desire in order to ensure the unfortunate man's survival.

The Peruvian nodded a satisfied little nod, grateful that she had finally seen reason. After all, the Rider operated under his own name. He would never survive in a police-military state, where major and minor powers collected detrimental information and survival depended on finding the perfect cover for oneself.

Four—the palm tree

With feigned remoteness, she was about to close the book on him when the composer appeared, his neck hairs standing on end, and warned her against giving in to this misguiding image of her future. After all, she had Mozart and Purcell and had been trained in setting their music against the call of Peru. To please the composer, she played the part of good little music student, but whenever her ear tuned into the music of Latin America or when she saw her favorite Latino singers interviewed on television, she felt herself transformed into a proud Peruvian female, with a kind of beauty that did not stem from make-up or fine clothes but from a soul strengthened through constant suffering.

The composer frowned but the Peruvian grinned, understanding precisely what she was talking about. To the composer, she explained that she wanted to break away, forgetting that they had scarred her in their torture chambers, and very much wanted to stop loving the Peruvian people but that she loved them like the Rider loved his children. Also, she loved Peru and could not leave it behind like some burly, vulgar acquaintance. Even the secret police there already knew that she would return one day. "Patriotism is a funny business, you see," she explained.

The poor Rider looked on helplessly, from the page of his book, at the exchange that would determine his future. The Peruvian began to smile again, like a recently unburdened vessel, and the composer hung on her lips, moving rapidly enough to suggest she had been trained out of some manual to explain her purpose on earth. Earnestly, she stated to be proud of not yet having succumbed to insanity. She flashed the Peruvian a grateful little smile when adding that the force keeping her at earth's center was not a gringo type of strength. The Peruvian flashed a smile back at her and history shrieked then settled, the galaxies wheeled, and in her mind appeared a disturbing image of self-important gringos who always created masks to deny their true identity and who had nervous breakdowns when their marriages failed or they ran out of money. The image of solitary gringos needing years of therapy made her hide her face behind her hands and cringe, causing her to think benignly of Peru where feelings of weakness were a luxury, not well tolerated among the peasants, and nobody had time for nervous breakdowns while brave people soldiered on with their heads held high and their pain buried somewhere beneath their faith and pride. Unlike the gringos, Peruvians were brave enough keep living without therapy even when seeing their sisters killed, their fathers decapitated, their homes raided and their children abducted to be added to the long list of the mysterious Missing.

"That's not the point, liking or not liking gringo society," the composer barked but she had become very adept at conveying messages to the two ghosts and firmly kept her stance.

She wagged her finger in his face. "Don't you try that on me. You are staying here for a bit and then you'll return to your comfortable eternity! You won't be the one dealing with the outcome of this battle."

The Rider remained an outsider in their little exchanges. Alive, he could not participate since he was restricted to the slower communication mode of words. Ignoring her insults, the composer brained with her despair, challenging her to find success stories of torture survivors who had integrated into a safe country. "We've got to climb through all the memories," he said, unwilling to surrender her to the Peruvian. "It is going to be a long climb, but we'll find something, for sure."

The ghosts traveled along her train of thought as she drew up images of torture victims, lying dead among empty gin-and-whiskey bottles in Holland, Germany and the USA. There were images of torture survivors throwing the electric switch on themselves and torture survivors walking between two lines, of actual and remembered worlds, until they could walk no more and surrendered their lives to an overdose of heroin, being found by the drug squad with sticky froth coming out of their dead mouths. The images aroused genuine pity in the composer and genuine triumph in the Peruvian.

"Come with me, I am going to get you out of this kind of world," the Peruvian invited. "I know what you like and what you don't like."

"You are not going to get out of here," the composer countered. "Your are going to keep going, that's what you are doing."

Finally, an image appeared of a Peruvian journalist she had once been working with, who kept behaving as through there had never been a war although he had been tortured also. Faced with a never-ending night, he had somehow been able to act as though standing at the edge of dawn and now considered war to be a childish game best forgotten. Now that he was in safety, he lived successfully in gringo-landia, adapting very well to working with the gringos, despite never having had therapy for his post-torture adjustment. With true Latino survival instinct, he had commenced the process of forgetting false doctrines, rebuilding himself according to the criteria needed to live in a benevolent, peaceful country.

The composer forgot about his piano and his music for a moment and exclaimed, "There we are. I told you it wouldn't be long. That's wonderful", then prompted her to look for symbols of strength inside herself also. To please him, she drew a striking image:

> *Far from the bustle and vanities of the world, the sun rises over a clearing once filled with palm-trees. In the background, mountains can be seen and a perfectly calm sea. There are palm-tree stumps everywhere. In their midst, like a grateful mongrel, a lone palm sways in the wind among the stumps. It looks rested and confident, despite a rapidly advancing group of men with axes in their hands and thoughts of tree-murder on their faces. She sees herself standing*

*up to the men with the axes, embracing the palm with both hands
to protect it. Pain flows like scalding water as they attempt to prey
her arms loose from its bark, but she holds on.*

The composer remarked: "Nice photography. What a great little
piano trio this scene could be converted into", and assigned the bassoon to the lonely palm tree, just as the Peruvian recognized in the
tree-image his own worst fear, that she was not yet willing to surrender into an emotionally, creatively and socially barren life and, no
matter how many brave trees had been felled in Peru, she remained
grimly determined to rebuilt her forest from the last tree left alive.
He saw that it was necessary to hate the Rider again, and very
quickly, because the Rider's appearance in her life had been like the
ostentatious highlight of a sensational series of traffic violations,
against rules he had established to keep her heart in check and lead it
toward his country. The guileful Rider had led her to believe in life
again and fight for her very last tree.

Five—of torture-victim-aid centers

She returned from her excursion to the palm tree land, proud of the
Latino strength inside her. Like the Peruvian people, she could still
sing and dance and love in the face of evil, and defend the palm-tree
against axe-wielding men. She knew full well that the Rider did not
have the same kind of strength. He had not had a taste of Latino ways
through accelerating pulse and sweaty embrace with a native son or
daughter. She calculated aloud for the ghosts (who were still listening, the composer with an automatic interest in her affairs, the Peruvian wearing his heart on his sleeve and with his eyes suggesting that
perhaps they could rent an abandoned cabin somewhere, at 2 000
meters above sea level, take the Rider there, kick him in the shin with
a malicious smile and then leave him there) the number of years the
Rider had lived in gringo society already.

"He never had had a chance to prevent himself from becoming gringo. He is gringo through and through and has gringo problems!" The Peruvian gloated with the slick satisfaction of someone who is on top. "Only someone who has walked with death can ever hope to be fully alive!"

He might as well have torn her upper clothes off and cracked a horse-whip across her bare back. Hurting her physically would have been less cruel than driving home the nature of her pointless love for the Rider. Angry with herself for not having blasted him away, she discarded images of the Rider and began to see more of the brave Peruvian journalist. Returning to his country on vacation, one day, he had sat down with his torturers and in a civilized and cordial manner they had been drinking tea together. They had even shaken hands and tried analyzing how such horror could have occurred in their land in the first place. She wished one day to shed the remains of her gringo-hood and also return, to the torturess, and to shake Her hand in a great gesture of forgiveness. Maybe she would thank Her for letting her live, even for the pain and the inner growth that had resulted from being made to bear it. After all, She was not a bad woman per se. She had promised to let her go and she had kept her promise and given her the key to freedom. It had been a vicious kind of freedom, but freedom all the same. Perhaps she would also let Her in on her personal after-effects of the military disaster in Peru, the countless times she had, under the influence of sudden hysteria, sought help in various centers catering to the rehabilitation of torture victims. Their goals, of minding broken survivors from various wars finding themselves constantly walking in a state of half-waking from a half-dream-half-nightmare, were rarely ever achieved, but it is the thought that counts.

Her own experiences had created the wish to share with sympathetic ears the ever stranger occurrences inside her mind, where everything seemed to fall apart when nightfall reminded her of the dark streets of the *Colonia de los pobres*, where the death squads came with the fading day and she had not dared close her eyes until the break of dawn. She wished to tell the torturess, one day, of the times she had tried to seek help for this fuliginous movement inside her head. Nervously punching her right fist into the palm of her left, she had wished for nothing more but emphasizing questions that would permit her thick tongue to move about, speaking of her terrible secret before the last tree of her sanity would be felled, too. She had only encountered a kind of gringo understanding that always came coupled with not having enough time or interest, even with a swift recoiling movement, the moment they discovered she was damaged from a war they could not relate to.

Meeting with the torturess, she'd open Her eyes to her immoral doings that could not be excused even with the best catholic gestures. She would refer to several pages of notes to relate the times she had investigated torture victims aid centers, fully wishing to talk once the polished lamps in the eyes of the counselors had smiled kindly at her. They would usually say things like: "Now, now, we won't do you any harm. What is it? Won't you talk to us?"

But she had always understood that she had no right to be turning herself into a client. There was always someone else, worse off than her. With an annual budget of twelve thousand dollars, there were never enough resources to deal with the after-effects of Third World post-traumatic need and she had always smiled back kindly at the counselors and said nothing, thus producing free places for other survivors. Having surveyed the faces of broken women and men in the waiting rooms who looked like disaffected ghosts and could no longer smile, having investigated stories of multiple rapes of women who had subsequently given in to the diabolical forces left inside them by their rapists and begun slashing themselves or splitting their own backs with an axe, having absorbed the broken words and meaningless syllables spilling out of listless mouths, she had learnt to be grateful that she had a strong Latino soul, at least.

The others were from Bosnia, Egypt or Iran. They had been beaten with horsewhips, stock-whips and nine-tailed cats. Some had stout short stumps instead of arms. Their arms had been twisted like corkscrews as they writhed in agony, until they had been twisted all the way off. They had been made to walk, blindly and trembling, over broken bottles with their bare feet. They had been hit with boards, whips and sticks. Some of them had been raped, the men too, their buttocks cracked wide open by the stiff prick of an uniformed military man with a second one standing by panting, and shouting "harder, harder" until the poor rape victim had been laying on the floor in a heap, all bleeding and bloody. Some had more than eighty stitches on their backs because a military man, with the joy of the sadist, had whipped them as hard as he liked. Their free wills had been broken. Unlike her, they had not been taught, in the hills of Peru, the need for absolute survival of body, mind and spirit, no matter the terrors that befell them. She had always walked out of these aid centers keeping her mouth shut. Compared to the problems of the others, it seemed of little consequence that the ghost of a Peruvian freedom fighter had once given a grave answer to a grave question (*are you dead?*) before taking up residence inside her mind.

She would tell the torturess of her return to the gringo world, all the while harboring a deep fear of speaking about her past because gringo people considered it treason to speak of what they termed "heavy things". In *gringolandia*, it was all a matter of putting one's personal message inside a sealed capsule, forgetting the identities of members of terrorist organizations in far-away lands. Gringos wanted someone funny who could scratch his armpit in imitation of a gorilla, healthy in body and mind, with superficial or at least gringo-acceptable thoughts, who subscribed to gringo quick-quick relationships that had become somewhat like slave markets. Naturally, she fitted none of these criteria. After a while, she no longer wanted to eat or sleep. She longed to return to Peru, where lives were shorter but people did not die from the worms of depression because the were never permitted to walk without their masks beneath which they were shivering from cold on account of their locked-away emotions. In the torture chamber, she had learnt at least one valid lesson—this she was also going to tell her torturess when she met her again—that a life cut short but lived fully was far preferable than hiding one's soul for eighty years in the gringo world.

Six—Purcell to the rescue

The Peruvian gave the impression of understanding her perfectly, looked at her with love and said "come". His velvet voice made her temples throb with desire for him. But now the composer intervened. He started flooding her with the extravagant trumpet of the Overture 5 of Purcell's *Fairy Queen,* reminding her that Purcell had also survived some rather terrible nightmares, where he had been looking into the pale faces of his neighbors who had succumbed to the plague, which had angrily ravaged his entire country. He had been younger than she when all of this happened and the experience had flooded him with beautiful music, not desires for death and destruction. The old composer took another stab at changing her destiny when he suggested she peel off her drab past with the vision of a canoe breaking out of a grotto where she had hidden herself, and to paddle without backward glance into the welcoming open sea. He warned her sternly against listening to the broken rhythm of her heart. Rather, she was to turn a new leaf with her right hand and stir the canoe with the left.

"You must believe in enjoying life, that's all," he said, huffing and puffing thoughtfully. "Go for style and fun. If not here, then you could live in Dublin, London, Hull or Paris. You may say what you like, but corruption is rife in Peru. It is not a good place to be."

At first, she had wanted to reply something unkind about him not having any personal experience of Peru and being unqualified to judge it. Then she smiled and bit her lower lip. He was right, there was nothing more to be said about it. She had walked the streets of Peru long enough with freedom fighters and with military men.

Technically still loony, she began redirecting her life, not at all certain whether it was worth mentioning a trivial variant, about the Peruvian now singing in a broken-accented voice the *Fairy Queen* plaint, containing the words *I shall never see you again*. All hope had not left her. Experience had embittered her heart against the gringos, but not including the Rider. In general, she kept holding on to the view that he could very well become a fellow poet to write the remaining cantos of her life, although a secret would always stand between them on account of the Peruvian; an entire passage of her life she would never tell him about. He himself talked very little, so he probably would not mind. How pleasant it would be to live happily with him if he could accept her past.

In her imagination, she beheld herself paddling toward the horizon with the canoe, only briefly wondering about the occurrence of hurricanes. Her rapidly beating heart and the vision made her feel keenly that she still sought the Rider, with a frightening enough fervor to render her ill with stomach pains and sleepless nights. Following elaborate excavations of partially demolished desires, whose presence she had always suspected, she found herself in the midst of an immutable fable of fate. The Peruvian had been a lover walking along some dark road. The Rider not. He was still full of elegant gallantries, although he was essentially alone and his face looked older. She was not going to forsake him for the contented leer of Peru. Sometimes, she caught a glimpse of him on television. His gaiety seemed to have left him. In his weary face, she saw that, like her, he was in need of a more pleasant destiny and that his life was no longer a life for him: from town to town, from land to land, as he rode in Italy and he rode in Canada and Spain and France. There was the urgent need to make him feel less weary of life, she saw this at once...

...and bought the book, still torn—in a strange and supernatural game—between the call of Peru and the urge to bring the Rider home.

The End.

CHAPTER 10

One—of writers and writing

For the sake of intellectual argument, she toyed with an idea of writing an actual book about the Rider and their supposed life together, but that did not mean it was all true. Urged on by very good-looking hopes that the Peruvian might be conquered, she thought it a splendid idea to rely on the power of her pen in battling him. Vaguely and pensively, the angle of her future could be changed, and the book would be well received by her readers, this she knew with full faith in their loyalty. They would not refuse to believe in her. Although the outcome of the story with the Rider did not depend on their faith in her, their loving community sustained her with a sense of perfection which, she hoped, would lead to her passionate acceptance by the Rider. She was not famous like he, with his shirt and breeches, but she did have a steady following of admirers who could hardly wait for her new books and delighted in the cunningly crafted love stories she kept churning out. She was only one voice among many voices on the romance-literature market, but her readers kept her well fed, from one book to the next and protected her from the sad fate of other modern-day writers who scrawled glorious hymns to beauty, sitting on plain green toilet seats in cheap hotel rooms, ravaged by disease and their broken faith into a gentle Jesus who had not come through for them. They were permanently hungry and permanently had nothing to eat except for some cookies and crisps. They had never learnt that no virtue was to be found in suffering and that it was far better to write trash and be rich than craft fine poetry and be poor. Their hopes of wealth and abundance were transformed into despair, once they found out that painting stunning prose got them nowhere. Sooner or later, they all arrived at the point of succumbing to the necessity of wasting their precious time with mundane tasks not worthy of great artists, merely to buy themselves enough food and shelter to stay alive. They usually lived in flats above poor-looking shops, surviving on ginger beer and ginger ale and steak and kidney pies eaten and drunk at make-shift wooden tables. They soon grew weary and their urges to write great poetry turned into curses, as their expectations changed from eternal life to eternal damnation. By the time they surrendered their wretched spirits, usually by age twenty-five, they were strong and authoritative examples of failed lives.

Long gone were the good old days of Marie d'Agoult, when poets and writers of merit had been generously supported by patrons of the arts with an appetite for literary beauty. Wealthy men and women, whose own minds were barren of precious emotions capable of painting their souls on paper, had protected talented writers then and had treated them like holy relics. No more. These days, writers did not have the greatest time at playing their game. Their profession had become a gloomy business, reeking of stiff-kneed anger and depression, and writers had divided themselves into sections, according to their merit. The so-called fast-food writer usually had a two-penny engine for brains, the kind of guy to think nothing of condoning murder in his writing and plough-driving his pen across the page while considering the words spilling out as having nothing of a personal connection to himself. He was a revolting kind of writer who saw it as his purpose to invent and amuse, but he was also a writer who lived comfortably, in a society no longer ready for intellectual argument.

Then existed the natural writer whose faith in great literature was kept alive, so long as he had hands to write it and eyes to correct it and a heart to feel it, but he was a poor sod, forever starving in little back rooms and keeping himself alive on the feeble hope that a winking light might, one day, descend from heaven and bless his life. The so-called labyrinth writer lived his life somewhere in the groins of heaven, and outside the stinking hole of sea rats. He was sometimes nearly falling into the fire, sometimes sweating coldly, sometimes succumbing to near-madness while reflecting on his destination of becoming worm food, but he remained untouched by the heartbreak of cruelly quelled hopes because he had never grown even a single day of hope.

Worst off were the old-fashioned genius-writers, who, as in Marlowe's time, insisted on patiently waiting for fires to start up inside them and chew languidly at their souls, causing their pen to guide itself to paper. They could not afford living a life of glorious excesses, the kind of life reserved for the fast-food writers who had typewriters in place of higher cerebral centers and who, devoid of imagination, wrote quickly, angrily, and with dollar signs printed into their hardened eyes. A standing joke among fast-food writers went that by the end of time, there would be but one segment of writers left who had learned enough from life, the genius-writers who believed and wrote on to the point of destroying themselves, their clothes hanging in rags about their emaciated frames. The fast-food writers thought this very funny, having long understood that true literature could pass for dog waste in this day and age and that any good writer had to take note of the many elements of the crowd making up his readership and those elements happened to be calling out for murder mysteries and worse.

Two—Zweig's house

She had been lucky enough to escape cramming into any of these categories. Having noticed, early on in the game, that categorizing herself was a kind of murder, she had been spared from a life of wrist-cutting, wiping up her own vomit in smoky bars and other characteristics of a modern writer's life, but she had not been saved by wealthy male admirers whose rabid eyes lit up with greedy little flames when they offered her to live with them, be royally rich and do nothing all day, except write. Her rescue had come about by an inflammation of the spirit through her unseen friends, the ghosts of long-dead writers, only too willing to accompany new talents wait-ing to emerge. Bored with being dead, they gave their advice freely to anyone who still had hands to write, dishing out inspiration and ideas to young hopefuls awaiting their entrance into the literary world.

Ignoring the stigma of exorcism and heresy, she had allowed their strong arms to support her. Sometimes she had even had to fight off their excess of ideas with great difficulty, having somehow created a situation where she had become a receiving vessel for kindly grin-ning literary figures whose spirits swirled about a the bottom of her teacup every morning.

Clasping a tea-cup with ragged edges between her hands one morning, she had been looking for messages at its bottom, new-age bred as she was, and almost fainted when, reading the tea leaves, she had discovered all these writers who had left their ideas behind when it had been their turn to go. Looking into their rich, rolling eyes she had learnt the astonishing fact that they had jointly created memory banks any new writer could tap into for advice. They had explained to her that a writer's lot was solitude but there was a great way out, preventing any writer of merit from dying under the shivers of seclu-sion. Solitude could be shattered by the ghost of any other writer, being broken thus, yet remain intact.

I am above such things, she had initially thought. In her opinion, the new age jumble was full of teachings of things that did not even exist. New-agers earnestly chanted under park trees everywhere, attempting to control the movements of life but in all actuality only trying to adjust their so-called wisdom to their momentary moods. All that babble, about divine order and living to one's highest senses, met with as little enthusiasm from her as did the notion that humans were all threads, to be woven into the same garment of life. Tea-leaf reading fell into the same category, she considered it to be a mere playing at wisdom. If she had wrapped the crevices of her brain around that particular would-be science, it had only been to please an otherwise fine and charming friend. She had declined her friend's offer to come and meditate with her, for a week in rural Surrey at a retreat established by the followers of a handsome and wealthy Indian guru, but to make up for it, she had promised to let her teach her how to read tea-leaves at least.

Her mind became active when, following that cup of tea, she had learnt that her *I-am-but-a-poor-poet* days were behind her and that she could choose from among the ghosts a handful of close confidants to advise and accompany her. She had poured herself another cup and stiffened, her face about to crack, wondering what might await her at the bottom this time. Hurrying through the tea in fear, she got there and the same swirling ghosts informed her that this proposition was only made to the most talented young writers and that she had been luckier than most, for having been chosen. They added that it would be perfectly acceptable to consider this unfolding of events as mere madness, but that she had to relax her teacup-gripping hands and make her choice. She took a stand in favor of the ghosts, having come to consider that she had perhaps been too detached from modern society and should give tea-leaves a fair go.

Empowered by her decision, she had read first the translations, then the original works, of many French writers, delighting in the state of health of their minds. As her mentors she had chosen catching, joyous spirits like a defiant woman writer with a man's name, George Sand, whom she referred to as George and with whom she shared many common characteristics, among them fatherless-ness (George's father had died, falling off his horse, when she was four), a rejecting mother (George had been raised by her grandmother) and a late start into the writing life at age 27. Even some of George's writings seemed to be addressed to her, especially one penned for *anonymous*, to be born a century later. In this piece, Sand had accurately predicted the post-Peruvian state of her soul, and also her useless plum-hunger for revenge, seemingly having suffered through all the pangs and thrills of her precise situation. Sand had made critical remarks about the principle of revenge and had likened the mere concept to harvesting dead leaves. She had taken comfort from George's words, stating her to be far nobler than selling out to unbecoming thoughts. The idea struck her that George had perhaps seen things in a different and more accurate way and thereafter she abandoned her desire for crude slaughter of the torturess, a bloody little ceremony she had already planned in horrifying detail inside her mind.

Not surprisingly, her writer friends came almost exclusively from George's circle, including her lover, de Musset. None of them had been miserable writers writing in a mixed tone of shame and defiance and none of them had taken their own lives. They had never pathetically slaved to prove their own merit nor ever gone to sleep without supper or even missed out on knowing what a meat meal was. They had not been pathetically discovered only decades after their lonely deaths. Nor would she. She had kept up with her friends and her writing life had never been rough.

In her early writing days, she had spent much time in the house of Stefan Zweig on the *Kapuzinermountain* towering over the charming Austrian city of Salzburg. Being Austrian, Zweig had remained standing at the edge until she had invited him to join the group on account of his connection to Sand's friend Balzac. His was a fine and noble house with words bubbling out of its windows. It harbored the insane but endearing notion that it was somehow part of eternity itself. The pretty yellow house thought itself as being level with the writers. It had truly succumbed to madness and was now reveling in it, constantly seeking to prove to anyone interested that despite being uninhabited it was not dead, like other empty houses, but in fact, owing to the efforts to the Salzburg Historical Preservation Society, was stronger than ever in body and active of mind. The garden surrounding it was large enough for her to lose herself inside while walking about as the house smiled chubbily at her from its sandpaper eyes.

The house she had named Haslet on account of its red-golden hair. Over the years, they had spent much time together. Although her breath usuallly came fast and shallow by the time she reached the top of the *Kapuziner* Mountain where it resided, her heart always gave a little joyous leap when she saw its front steps in the distance. The climb made her pant, but she enjoyed its quiet, secluded location and its delicate thoughts which, in greeting, always bubbled toward her like fountain water until her eyes were bright, her cheeks shone healthily and she shook her uncombed hair in the sunlight.

In Haslet's world, nothing but the song of the birds could be heard, blessedly flying about in the trees above. A primordial innocence prevailed, shattered only by ancient stone figures depicting the cross stations of Jesus and lining the path, from the old city walls to the house. The crucifixion scene even came complete with a stone Jesus on his cross of wood, his features composed in serene silence, fixing his dying eyes on Haslet's front porch. To the figure's right and left hung the two thieves on crosses of their own and the stone figure of his crying mother cowered by his feet. It was even said that doers of evil became cognisant of their sins here, changing their lives from damned to saved, after only a few moments spent beneath the crucifixion scene on the mountain. Legend had it that a soldierly man had once laughingly crushed his sword there at the feet of Jesus, having recognized that he had been drawn into evil by imposed military doctrines that had suddenly turned into deadweight on his shoulders.

Haslet spoke an entirely different language to Jesus Christ hanging wisely on his cross and waiting to save whatsoever sinners were drawn to the *Kapuzinermountain*, but through the glimmering of its windowed eyes, the house had with great pride succeeded in communicating that James Joyce had once sat on its steps and that his spirit still visited on occasion, each time making profuse apologies for being too busy in the ghost world to visit more often. She had sat on the stone steps by the crucifixion scene, squinting and waiting for the hall-door to open slowly and for Joyce's spirit to appear. Some minutes passed. Nothing happened. She kept squinting but Joyce did not show. Breathing uneasily, Haslet had stared grimly before itself. It had very much wanted to impress her with the broad figure of Joyce and did not wish to be thought of as a mere has-been house, once fashionable with high society and now discarded. With a calm historian's voice, she had informed Haslet that she believed its story about Joyce, Joyce's presence in the house being well-documented in various writings, and that she needed no personal experience to accept its claims. That was the end of it all and thereafter Haslet always told her, with details, many fascinating stories, some of which she knew to be true and some she suspected had been made up.

During a post-Peru visit to Zweig's house, she had been sitting underneath the stone figures of the crucifixion scene, feeling that she had already joined the ranks of the damned and more than ready for repentance. The stone figures were not interested in discussing why holiness in others made so many people sick, but they willingly agreed to provide her shade while the city of Salzburg smoldered in the heat below. She looked across to Haslet's garden, and then further, over the generous *Salzburg Land*, and then to the far-away mountains, musing that Salzburg could hardly be a city filled with ordinary people. Joyce had insisted that they had great feeling for the Irish there and by all accounts, people there had to speak her language also. Haslet shared its mountain with an abbey of the *Kapuzinermonks*, so named because they delighted in wearing little hoods, which, in German, were known as *Kapuzen*.

Raising her head, she saw a monk, dressed humbly in simple brown garb. Picture-perfect and looking like a positive saint, he advanced toward her, up the stone steps, in direction of the crucifixion scene. His outline silhouetted against the house and his eyes displayed no amazement when he saw her sitting underneath the stone Jesus. He merely paused momentarily and puffed thoughtfully, then made a catholic gesture with his hand. If God's holy care for his highest creation had drawn another sinner here, so be it. Reality arranged itself so that the monk was suddenly a thousand years old and also just one day. It seemed that the moment meant nothing. The mountains, the house, the stones, the monk and the writer would perhaps always be on this same spot, frozen in this very picture frame, although the name of the monk would change and the name of the writer, like Zweig had sat there before her and a different monk had been walking up the same steps, some hundred years earlier.

The pious man and the writing woman faced each other across a thin furrow of time, which seemed to displace entire centuries as a second spread into eternity, freezing the scene involving Zweig's house, the outlandish monk and the stony Jesus. There was no Peru, no hand-holding with a murdered Peruvian freedom fighter, and no poor Peruvian people anymore. There was no death, no life and no memories, only the instant, the only instant, which would perhaps be repeated a hundred years hence as it had been repeated a hundred years ago. The moment kept to a narrow path unfazed by memories. Zweig's old tree shaded her today like it had once shaded him. Although his house was not hers and she was not even permitted to rent it, his ghost still lived there, inviting her into his world and into his peace. He saw to it that she wrote in luxurious surroundings, even at the beginning of her career when her books had not yet made her enough money to live a comfortable life. He shared it all with her, his mountain, his tree and his house, even picturesque monks heaving up the mountain now and again, in exchange for her working hard at her next novel. Whenever she had written enough to please him, he took her down the mountain and into the streets of Salzburg, his beloved town.

Three—Excursion into Salzburg

Since they had much to talk about, she took great pleasure in their walks together. Zweig had once stood at the exact cross-section of life where she stood now, seeking solace in solitude. Zweig explained that whenever he had had enough of being alone, he had descended from the mountain to aimlessly walk through the city streets below. He pointed out that no city in the world existed more animate than Salzburg, and no city had been born in all the history of men building cities that knew better to embrace a writer. He claimed that Salzburg was alive with the memories of great writers and great composers and if she listened closely to its streets, they would tell her all their stories. Rome might have God and Cesar and Jesus Christ, but Salzburg had Mozart and Haslet.

She did not dare tell Zweig about the Rider who now formed himself in positive images inside her mind. Like a sweet golden wine, a vision appeared: the Rider and she, seated on Haslet's front porch, their breaths barely sufficient to sustain the sky-boat of their new love. There was apparently an entire wing in the mansion of her mind that had remained unknown to her, for the next image showed the Rider and her studying history in the city veins of Salzburg, and walking with joined hands. Obviously, they were not disturbed in their togetherness by the difficulties usually experienced in the early stages of a relationship, when secret little pieces of information crudely take shape inside each other's hearts where they thud, sweep or slide in like a wave and then recoil, in a last minute refusal to lift the mask, its owner having succumbed to the notion that one's very survival depended on wearing it. The Rider and she had seemingly been together for a long time. She could see in the vision, which grew dimmer and smaller now, that they both walked without plotting the next move, or pretending and imposing. She had wanted to find out more about this parallel life of hers that was obviously being lived without her knowledge, fascinated by the fact that in a strange, inaccessible land, the current carried the Rider and her, not their own oars. She wondered whether they were perhaps already married and lived in Salzburg, and also what had become of the jealous Peruvian and if he knew anything of their life. But the image had already folded inside her mind and only Zweig remained, who, looking at her with eyes that expected her to be speaking very good sense, asked with earnest interest what she was working on.

Guilt scalding her like hot liquid on account of her lie, she vaguely replied, "A collection of inspirations and memories gathered in travels."

"Very good." Zweig appeared pleased, which caused her to squint at him with aching eyes, the poor dear, for trusting her so willingly, "I have done the same, and so has Victor Hugo. You are in very good company, indeed."

But then he looked inside her soul—as a ghost, this was no problem for him. Just when she thought she could no longer bear him watching and would scream at any moment, he stated that he had seen her to be an exile, living far from the country she called her home, and she realized, gratefully, that he had not discovered the Rider and their supposed secret life together.

He said: "I can see that there is a land that hurts inside your soul, which keeps calling out to you, nourishing the roots you have left behind there. Every street seems to lead you back there and every morning you awake a stranger, here in Europe."

She nodded, her ears nozzing under the chomp and honey drip of Zweig's voice, and asked how he knew. He replied that he had recognized that distinct shade of pain, which stemmed from being an exile. Then he told her of his escape from Salzburg, of leaving behind Haslet and the *Kapuzinermountain*, speaking with eloquence of his lonely times in America where he had been wandering the streets looking for a sign of recognition in the faces of the people there and finding none. He told her of the ice-cold hearts he had encountered in London and how he had always carried Halset inside his heart wherever he went, until one day he had ended up in Brazil, where he had taken his own life, unable to bear his longing for Salzburg any longer.

"You, too, are a stranger in every country but one, a distant unknown country you cannot return to. You have cried many tears at leaving it behind and now you have to keep moving, restless in your travels taking you here or there."

She nodded, thinking what a clever chap he was. He pointed out that he had titled his biography *Life of a restless one* and offered she might do so also. Then they spoke of the French writers, whom he had also loved and whose biographies he had even written. He mentioned Balzac, Sainte-Beuve and he was delighted when she took her cue to tell him about a little-known story, written by Balzac in his youth, and asked whether he had read it, too.

"…It was a story titled *Le Vicaire des Ardennes*," she began, "a strange but beautiful story of a priest who had…"

"…fallen in love with a fair maiden," Zweig continued. "He kept his priesthood from her and the knowledge killed her, for she knew in secret. When he was, at last, free from the church, having broken his priesthood vows, she was on her death-bed, telling him that the secret…"

"…he had kept from her had killed her and that she had known all along," she finished his sentence.

"And wasn't it great how the story started off," she went on, "with Balzac walking through a graveyard where he encounters a dying man writing down his life story, a noble man. When his mother comes to collect him to die at home with her, Balzac steals the story and edits it and this is the story we are reading…"

Zweig pointed out that walking through graveyards can be of great benefit to the living, not only because dying men might be found there whose story could be interesting to write down.

"Also, to remind us of the passage of time. Ranting and raving in rhyme, we writers tend to forget the years growing into each other. Before we know it, a decade has passed as we give birth to more books, and then, one day, our time is over and we have not lived, except in our own stories."

They were sitting in a small Salzburg coffee shop, in the old city, where she ate a piece of *Sachertorte* she washed down with strong, brown Austrian coffee. Zweig regretted being unable to join in the feast, complaining that in death, all food and drink became bland, and he even remarked that he longed for smelling the smell of freshly-brewed coffee. Together, they watched the to and fro about them. Zweig sighed and shook his head sadly at the changes he saw. He explained, pronouncing his words carefully on account of his vivid annoyance, that no glass-fronted shops had been filling charming little arches in his time. He added bitterly that the view across the *Judengasse* had not been straight into the polished lobby of a money-exchange bank.

Falling into melancholy, he took her through his own memories, saying, "I have something here which may amuse you".

Suddenly they were transported into Zweig's time, and still sitting at the same table but surrounded by comfortably laughing people now, out of whose pockets gleamed half-written cantos and sonnets. Looking from the cafe into the streets, nothing could be seen any-more of harried-faced people who had been all cramped together in the lobby of some bank. Now there were sillily giggling girls melting hearts with handsome men, seemingly free of obligations, walking through cobble-stoned alleys and thrusting papers at each other of symphonies in progress.

Sighingly, Zweig took them back to the present. The past, he said, was an old friend living in the same house but the door to its quarters was closed forever. Memories alone could not be trusted, the Austrian warned, they had a tendency to transport one into the arms of a heaven that perhaps never existed.

"Sometimes a little time-warp is useful", he said, "to visit the past and accept that one's engagement together has ended, waving to it from afar across the threshold."

He told her that he had once been sitting for hours in that cafe, watching people go by, but she wondered whether one could write anything in the knowledge that the good old days were irrevocably gone. What sense did it make to still be sitting anywhere, drinking anything, when everything had changed and would continue changing? She had not consented to going away and leaving her home in Peru. Modern gringo life did not become her and the old gringo life, where people were still listening to one another, was gone for good. She had shelter and food in *gringolandia*, but it was a hard life.

Zweig insisted it would be a bad idea for her to let this fact set her back in any manner. Writing, he said, was a type of art connected with learning the language of the streets and it was important for any writer to practice becoming part of his own age.

Trying to put the idea of absorbing modern man to good use, they watched the tourists pass by: the fat American, whose wife patted his arm maternally as they walked past. The serious Germans looking like moving statues. The group of young Japanese with their excited claims of *um* and *ah* and their countless cameras. The stoic Finnish one with his wooden leg. Few people smiled and even fewer appeared to be balanced within themselves. There were many couples who seemingly had long ceased talking to each other and obviously subscribed to the theory that it didn't really matter whom you marry, so long as you marry, it's the marrying itself that counts. They saw people wildly waving to one another as they took photographs they would soon ban into their photo albums, never to be looked at again.

There were husbands and wives and children, whose names were Linda, or Diana or Benjamin, and who did not feel the pulse of the city at all, merely walking over its surface, vaguely shaking its hand but never entering its soul.

"Where does the poetry lie?" she asked Zweig. "There is no prose in the steady beating of walking feet upon cobble stone. Their lives are of a different make and purpose to ours, that's for sure."

He said that he wasn't going to give her back Peru, a free and safe Peru, nor was he going to put an end to the squabble for money that contemporary man engaged in, but he could help her to explore another life, one that may not be wholly undesirable. It was all a matter of looking closely at the crowds, in search for kind open-hearted people.

At long last, they noticed a woman smiling. Zweig remarked that the smile made her very beautiful, enough so that the other women, walking aimlessly and briskly, faded into nothing because this one had a face that was not unreasonably and unbearably tired. Staring at her openly, they wondered what kind of life she might be leading, to smile like that. The woman caught her looking, smiled in a friendly manner from her sturdy young face and gave her a little wave. Having been caught staring so openly, her heart leapt in embarrassment and she cursed softly because she had been the only one to be caught. Being dead, Zweig did not have to account for his own part in the staring session. At first, she thought it an injustice but then considered the injustice weighed into perfect balance by the fact that Zweig was forced to sit before a most delicious piece of *Sachertorte* like an amputated marionette. With her back against the wall, she flashed an embarrassed little smile, accompanied by hand wave, across to the woman, and after this humiliating situation she felt ill-timid and the waving and staring stopped.

Zweig treated the whole situation as through it were some kind of joke, muttering "to hell with reason" and that she had no need to explain herself or to wipe her hands on her faded jeans in embarrassment.

They continued drinking their coffee, or rather, she drank and Zweig justly watched, finding out that there was a fair amount of disadvantages that came with being dead.

Four—of Mozart and Strauss

When she was done with her coffee, they wandered through the cobble stones of the *Judengasse* across to the old market square, which was boiling with activity this time of day. There were stalls that sold eggs and chickens, and stalls selling jingling little cow bells as souvenirs. Stopping near the egg stall, they observed an elderly British man, answering to the name of Sir Michael (they found this out when his much younger wife called out to him) who, having failed to tie his shoe laces properly, nearly tripped when one of his shoes came off. He put it on again, dancing on one leg, to the bemused looks of his wife. When the shoe was back on Sir Michael's foot, they walked on, into the *Getreidegasse,* where tourists could be overheard talking about their holidays. The tourists' justification for stopping was a brand-new *McDonald's* that stood in the line of old shops as something definitely not natural, selling cut-up corpses of cows in the form of blood-dripping hamburgers. They didn't stop there, but kept walking, to Mozart's birth house.

The house she liked at once, more so than the music, because it was yellow like Haslet and did not emit the congealed chill of the other houses in the same street. Zweig told her that Mozart had been composing inside his head there, long ago, that inside that house he had felt the first subtle tugs of love and that its stone steps were still warm with his memory. Imagination is a funny thing, he said, asking her to bend down to touch the steps and see if she could feel anything. To make Zweig happy, and also to make up for him not having tasted the coffee, she bent down, feeling rather silly, and felt a faint stirring of Mozart there. Through the stones, she told Mozart a nasty little thing, that she did not like his music much but wished him well in any case.

Never having noticed the cackle of old oboes in the master's music himself, Zweig grumbled a little when he heard her speak like this. On account of the face he made, and also because she did not want him to be complaining, she saw to it that the subject was changed and they spoke of colors in music and how to draw music out of mountains.

She was a very slick talker and soon Zweig had forgotten all about her having insulted Mozart. They slowly ascended up the *Kapuzinermountain* again, where she promised to be teaching him a thing or two about music.

At the top of the mountain, she got her breath back slowly. There was still enough light as they sat down, looking out over Salzburg, for her to show him the zig zag outline of the Alps and to instruct: "try humming the tune of the mountains!"

He had no idea what to do and looked at her as though she had committed blasphemy by suggesting that music could be hummed from the outline of mountains. He was certain that nature could not be changed into notes.

"*Alpensynfonie*," she countered, flashing him a superior glance that suggested him to be the one committing blasphemy.

Caught in his own ignorance, Zweig groaned.

"Ah, yes, that one, mountain ascent turned into a symphony."

Adapting a feeble tone, he chiefly meant to indicate that he should have known, but had forgotten, that particular composition. He almost whispered, guiltily: "Starting with black night, then sunrise, the ascent, the alms, the visions..."

Zweig had a special affection for the last movement, perhaps on account of its title, because he was a vision also. Complaining about ghosts being usually ignored for their invisibility, he appeared pleased that Strauss had also encountered them and, instead of running from them on assumption of diabolical interference, had incorporated them into his symphony. To his own surprise, Zweig discovered that he was far better versed in music than he had known. Initially too petrified to move his lips when she had suggested for him to hum the tune of the mountains, he suddenly recalled the 12th movement of the *Alpensynfonie* and hummed, alternately, the part of the strings, the horns and the winds.

Then he exclaimed, as though he had just discovered some new laws, "You can indeed turn mountains into music!"

He switched key from A-minor to F-major all by himself, and fixed his eyes on the mountains as through a whole new world were stretching before him. The window of his unknown musical talents opened wide and he no longer felt like an intruder in the wrong room as she directed him: "Up, down. Now up again. Semi-tone. Crotchet. Semi again. High C. Down to D. Hold D. Quarter A..."

Having already forgotten what he had said before, he exclaimed: "I always knew there was music in the mountains!" and, clicking his fingers in a gesture of triumph: "Sometimes one has to die to truly learn!"

He looked positively monogamous, married only to the music he created, which sounded like the woman of his dreams. He began to hum in three different voices, horns, trumpets and strings, breathing deeply and evenly to keep the rhythm. Pointing to the pale white line of an airplane tracing its way across the sky above them, she enthused, "the flute, quickly, a flute". Zweig added a fourth voice, tracing the outline of the plane as it first curved, then disappeared, and he had created a symphony of his very own. He asked excitedly:

"write it down, write it down", and now decided that he wished to become a composer, and what a blessing it was to be dead and have so much time for the discovery of dormant talents. But she rocked his boat at once, explaining that a dream was never the same as turning it into reality. Even if he were to compose some works of true marvel, and she were to write them all down for him and even to publish them, the world had become too fast-paced to appreciate classical music anymore. She pointed out that classical CDs sold in the United States for one dollar and ninety-nine cents because nobody wanted them anymore, and that they could hardly expect for his own compositions to be doing any better than the likes of Beethoven. Zweig could ill contain his disappointment, at modern age having developed in a direction so far removed from the arts, and asked her why she bothered composing music of her own then, drawing it out of the mountains and skies, if nobody wished to listen to it in any case.

"To grow the soul, nothing else," she replied. "All we ever have is the moment. When I look at the mountains and see the music in them, my soul grows wings and becomes one with nature, by drawing out its symphonies. Sometimes, there are operas and choruses as well," she added, and that there was no need to write any of the music down, since man's need to preserve everything as though it could actually fall off the earth was a futile need, at whose base lay the immense fear of acknowledging that the moment could never be captured or preserved, not in photographs, nor in music or literature. There was just one thing to be done with the moment. It had to be lived and then let go, all else was a cheap and unsatisfactory copy.

Then they spoke to each other in plainer language and composed and discarded many more symphonies, which they drew out of the mountains, sometimes roaring crescendos, sometimes B-minors that spoke of things that used to be and issued a stern warning against meddling in the past.

At day's end, she reluctantly left Zweig when the sun set in rusty crimson over the mountains of Salzburg. She promised him to return soon, so they could sit outside his yellow house, where his old weeping willow would shade them and they could celebrate the new friendship they had formed. Zweig bellowed an affectionate good-bye and returned inside Haslet, making glove-finger smoothing movements with his right hand over his left.

Five—the Rider's story

She returned to the land of the Living, where she finished writing the story of the Rider and, having finished it, she gave it to her publisher. Although she had been afraid that it would not sell, having been written in rhymeless language, the publisher loved it, asked her who the mysterious Rider was and whether she had fallen in love at all. At first, she would not give out his name and even thought of confabulating a little, but then she grew bolder. Deciding to dedicate the book to him, she asked that a copy be sent to him. Since she was publishing under a male name, as George had advised her to do, she knew that he would not recognize her as the author and she even asked for him to be sent an invitation to the book launch, where he would be courted by some of the most important people in contemporary romance literature.

...then she awoke and in an instant, Zweig was gone and the book launch and the Rider. She had not even had time to find out whether he had decided to come to the launch.

Inspired by de Musset's words, that there is never enough time in life and that she must not tarry, she decided to do this instead: she wrote a short story about him and then took it with her, pretending to have some business at the next show he rode.

There, she walked up to him: "Might you be good enough to look at a story for me, which I have written after the last show. I do not know horses well and I wish to make sure that the information I have is accurate. I am in need of an expert opinion and I would be especially interested in knowing whether you would change the ending."

He replied that he would be happy to help and took her story and shyly disappeared with it. He had not said much, and if he was glad to be seeing her again, he did not show it. Instead, he nodded thoughtfully, with a serious frown, taking his part as her literary advisor very seriously. When he left, he promised to read the story by the following day's end. Serious as he was, he expected to read a serious story about horses and because he did not look for it, he never saw her wildly beating heart. As she watched him walk away, she was overcome with a strange fear of her own boldness and wondered what he would be saying to all of this.

She kept looking at her watch, and thinking: "this time tomorrow, the whole world will have changed."

Realizing that, she blushed, suddenly had enough of thinking about a tomorrow that might change her entire future, and only barely contained a wholesome urge to run after him and to tear the story out of his hands, which she suddenly became convinced was nothing but a passionate cliche buried underneath the golden glitter of bad prose.

But de Musset urged her on, saying: "There is no time. There is no time. Feel. Feel now, before it is too late." De Musset kept flashing images at her of pure power, containing allegiances and meltings of hearts. "What is all this waiting for?" he challenged angrily and went on to state that she had lived her life as though shut away inside a nunnery, hidden behind all these books, and that it was high time she awoke since she still had a lot to learn about life. De Musset having convinced her that her decision had been an entirely sane one, she was at last at peace and waited for the Rider's reaction.

The next day, she did not see him coming. She was deeply engrossed in conversation with another rider, pretending to be interested in his lame horses and his fledging riding career, after all she had gone there under the auspices of researching a story, which, in a way, was true.

When the Rider came up behind her, he startled her none too little as he suddenly said: "About the story you wanted me to analyze for you...I have done as you have asked. Could you perhaps come with me, so we might have a word."

She had then found herself following him. Behind the riders' canteen, he took her hand slowly and deliberately then kissed her gently on her luscious mouth. In the background, the crowd could be heard howling admiration at another rider's clear round but they only saw each other. There was nothing fumbling or unhandy about the way he touched her. Then he promised her the life of a popular princess because he had been deeply moved by her words. Stating that it was high time for his love life to be uncorked, he asked her that instant to marry him, and he said never mind the Peruvian and never mind his own children, their love would be the gateway to a clean, delicious life, stronger than any obstacles standing in their way. They would be together, all was going to be well. There was a glow of a wall-less love inside his eyes and she saw that he was very willing to take off all his masks. The miraculous, often explained away with algebra in the modern age, resurrected itself in tiny tendrils of humor and affection between them.

They traveled to the next few shows together before he retired at the height of his glory and they moved to Peru where they opened a hospital for the poor, who no longer died in pain but were all cured through medicine bought from his prize monies. His children loved both of them and even came to Peru, to help them out with the hospital construction. The Rider learned very quickly to speak good fluent Spanish and became somewhat like the Peruvian in his idealism to better the lot of the poor. Only, he was alive, the Peruvian remained dead and she awoke beside the Rider's smiling face each morning while the Peruvian coldly surveyed them from the back of her mind and kept spitting fire and dragons because she had escaped him.

They were surprised and delighted to discover a bliss they had thought themselves too old and too weak to encounter anymore. There was no sweaty body mass, no tearing hands, no delirious vigil, no endless repetitions of ill-furnished words, no morganatic ceremonies or barely comforting rituals, of insufficient affection and over-urgent need. They were simply happy together, feeling no need to clothe their nakedness. Sometimes, he would still ride and she would still write, but usually, they merely enjoyed being together, knowing that they had found a kind of love that could not be disturbed.

...then she awoke once more, trembling and impotent, as she found herself making the rough passage from a dream within a dream, into a gradually increasingly dimmer room, and realized that the song of Peru had drowned the call of the Rider.

The End.

CHAPTER 11

One—the finer art of torture

Awaking from the showering warmth of her dream of Zweig and the Rider, she had found it advisable to carry her memories back into the mountains, digesting the images from her sleep as she walked out into the quiet summer's night. All busily researching her past, she had found out that the basis of torture is the instilling of a new ultimate reality inside the torturee, who suddenly finds himself walking through chill streets feeling, *I am this, but I am also this*. Out of a sudden speaking another language, having once been eloquent but now stammering, he tries finding himself again, not always with success, digging under non-divine memories of piss and shit. Having his nails ripped out with pliers generally teaches him something as he, caught and crushed in the torture machinery, tries to reinvent himself, post torture-chamber release. Latin American countries have a clear enough image of families, enabling a torture victim to return to mothers and sisters sitting with their hands folded at the dinner table, chewing kindly and offering him another *tortilla con queso* together with a form of common recognition from their eyes, on the bottom of which the torture victim may discover a glimmer of his old self.

For gringo torture victims voluntarily throwing themselves into the arms of repressive governments, the post-torture situation is not as clear-cut, she thought sighingly. Gringo society turned as differently from Latino society as other planets turn. The Peruvian had taught her that the characteristic disjointedness and egoism of the gringos creates a society that diminishes man with its unlistening money-hungry faces and its terrible purity, a society that was by no means geared toward harboring any torture victim, of whatever nationality, with whatever memories. The opposites between gringo and Latino would be reconciled in heaven, no sooner.

Finding herself lost in a society where Jesus Christ was not needed like he was needed in Peru, a kind of second-hand faith had driven her to the mountains after her release. Chain-smokingly making a chimney of herself and needing miracles more than ever, she had searched her heart for a place to return to. The only home she could think of had been a mountain village, where she had been left by her mother in the care of her grandparents shortly after birth. That charming small village, full of rivers flowing freely through its veins, was a witness to the remains of her living spirit. There, her grandparents had cared for her while their beautiful daughter traveled around the world, following her urgent desire to leave the poverty of her parents behind her and to spend with both hands all the money she had been able to acquire through marriage with a wealthy man. There, she had grown up until Peru had called her, at age 15, when a lurking Peruvian freedom fighter had disguised himself as adorable. She hoped that, walking through the fields, she would succeed in resurrecting her memory that had been murdered in Peru where, in the torture chambers, great attention is paid to the torture itself but also to breaking the tortured one completely. Indeed, those who had trained and erected the torture squads of Peru had made sure to know their stuff and had even enlisted the help of the foremost torture experts in the world, who had erected classrooms where, without timorousness, they had taught *Torture 101* to their eager students.

In the classrooms, there had been talk of all souls being equal in God's eyes, but that some souls needed to be cleansed before they could enter the kingdom of God. They had to be washed with pain until the expulsion of sweat and crapulous vomiting from their trembling bodies turned them from unworthy beings into noble beings worthy of crying out *Hoc est corpus meumto* as they surrendered the be-shitten things that were their bodies. In a torture chamber, the body of the one to be cleansed was to be rejected without apologies and the psyche inside it was to be torn up, and remodeled from something non-eternal into something divine, destroying every devil's seed therein. The earnest student was instructed in the most important principles of torture, which are still on file in important Government archives and which can be seen and studied by foreign governments in need of persuasive tactics to correct errant and revolutionary elements in their lands. Peruvian studies of heaven lay in these documents of torture methods, which connoted a distant world for the gringos and which stated the following:

> *The fear of physical pain and death is often worse than the actual event. Most people's ability to withstand physical pain is much greater than they would expect of themselves.*
>
> *The ultimate, and most effective, form of torture is not the application of physical torture or physical termination of the subject, but threatening and terrorizing the subject constantly with fear of pain and termination. Depriving the subject of its memory, through complete personality breakdown, can be easiest achieved by determining a person close to the subject and imprisoning both, the subject and the other, over a period of no less than six months but not exceeding eight months (after such time, the capacity for ultimate pain has been reached and numbness sets in. The subject feels nothing and the torture is in vain, which would be a great tragedy, considering the manpower to be expanded during such efforts).*

While depriving both persons of their freedoms and all forms of communication with each other and the outside world, it is advisable to torture to death, slowly and with maximum amount of pain infliction, the other person. The person to be broken is to be forced to watch the entire process.

For even greater effectiveness, it is advisable to cause first person, in regular intervals of, perhaps, a month of so, to believe that he or she will be allowed to save the second one, perhaps through a change of personality, of opinion or of politics, and to allocate to said person a „kind" officer who appears under the auspices of wanting to help both of them, and to have said officer only at the very ending, and just before the other one is killed, and only after the first person's hope has been raised once again, appear as the one who ultimately executed the killing order.

Prior to releasing the torture victim that has been marked for survival, it is also advisable to use certain guilt-inducing tactics, suggesting that what has happened was the victim's own fault. To this end, phrases are to be spoken by surname-lacking, uniformed men or women (It is important that the victim never be informed of the true identity of its torturers, to protect against the putting into action of what has been termed post-traumatic revenge fantasies) such as: "You left me no choice but..." "Had you spoken sooner, then..." "It is nothing personal, but what can I do if you..."

They had never pulled at her hair or dragged her bare feet across the rough edges of broken bottles. They had never hung her from her breasts on big hooks or forced her to drink her own urine. They had never touched her where they had touched other women but the memories of her time with them lay intolerably heavy upon her soul all the same. They had broken something inside her during months of terror, when a silent short one, whose breath always smelled of wine and bread and garlic, had imprisoned her inside a dark, hot stinking chamber and she had gnawed at the bars in desperation, stripped naked and of all human dignity. She had become an easy victim and had been chosen to be made into an example of what happens to overeager foreigners when they sing the song of Peru. Six months of blindfolds, of not fastening her eyes on the sun, six months when they had killed him slowly while her bloody hands had slipped from the bars of her prison as they made her listen to his every scream. Six months, when they only took the blindfold off long enough to let her see his roughly handled body. Before it all ended for him, he had smiled a final good-bye at her and his bloodied nose had done nothing to douse the magic of his handsomer self that she still remembered. In his final moments, he stated that he had just had a remarkable vision of the fall of the military empire, then he thrust out his palms against the men with the machine guns and she had gasped in terror-stricken awe as they had ordered him to lie down at her feet. It was then she had sworn her eternal love to him and also her continuing fight for a free and proud Peru.

The eyes of the man with the machine gun had been very cold when he pulled the trigger but the Peruvian had laughed at death, which in its glum way wished to keep things very serious. A split-second before the machine gun spat his arterial blood across the bare floor, the Peruvian had smiled up at her, with the great pleasure of dying for love. Death did not like to be laughed at and neither did the military man, but the Peruvian was laughing all the same because she had sworn to keep fighting for his people. When at last the Peruvian's laughter had exhausted itself in a river of arterial blood, death took on a very un-comic face. Staring at the gently flowing blood from the Peruvian, she found that something inside of her was breaking until she had begged them for death, screaming: "Cut me, bleed me, deal me the same red ace you have just dealt him."

But then appeared a woman with eyes like twinkling jewels, whom they called Lady something or other on account of her having studied in America for many years, and who had been in charge of the entire operation. The woman had been very polite, which had frightened her even more. Smiling down at her, the lady had stepped daintily over the bloody mass on the floor that had been the Peruvian and murmured that she believed in long engagements. Sharpening her appetite for more on the terror she saw reflected in her prisoner's eyes, the lady had spat heavily at the still bleeding heap of the Peruvian's remains on the floor. Then she had addressed her, saying "for good or worse, you are a person of considerable magnetism." It would be interesting to observe, from now on, the road ahead of her, when—the lady said, her eyes now glimmering in a very pleased little way—she would be released into the bosom of her family. Everyone in Peru's most feared little torture chamber knew by now that she had no family and this last remark had been intended by way of a torture-academy-taught farewell, aimed to thwart any desire to continue living. The Lady and the machine-gunned, green-uniformed men had all understood that letting her live was the crueler punishment. Her memories of the horrors of Peru would be shivering into fragments, to become first a fading, then a faded past. By then she would live in perfect physical safety, amidst people who had only ever known safety. The terror would become an image from long ago but she would be stuck inside her past, where armies were still on collective march and the minds of peasants were being fashioned to the enjoyment of the oligarchy. Caught there, she would be alone for a very long time, living among people who did not understand anything about Peru.

Two—post-traumatic management

Not having studied psychology nor knowing anything about the impacts of post traumatic stress, she would wonder what kind of a world was beginning to crack open inside her mind and why she always felt terrorized while people around her attended summer balls and spoke, with their wine-gripping hands and their authoritative tongues, in Greek or Latin or other languages of the old world that they proudly boasted to have studied at the Ivy Leagues in their younger years. She would soon find herself searching every face, looking for the Peruvian, haunted by his eyes and by his screams. He, too, would slip into the past, where he would be sharing a house with other faded memories. Then she would change, unnoticeably first, then bolder, until one day she would belong to no country, no people and no man. She would try running away from Peru, feverishly attempting to counteract the machine-gunned men's reproach that she must not exist. With her broken and exiled self, she would, politely and quietly, try to adjust to a world where she would not fit for a hundred years and become friendless and nation-less, alone with her inquisitive mind, her pain and her memories, also, because "...and what have you been doing these past few years?", asked politely at fancy parties, was not a question to be answered with the very unreasonable sentence "I watched someone be tortured to death, how about you?"

"Oh really? How interesting. What was it like?"

Carefully poisoned memories, flooding hopes and terrors into her mind like a stiff-standing prick. Sinful distress, and the pink froth of sweet goodness from the woman who had asked the question.

"Never mind. I can see your mind is too busy. Let me tell you, then. My husband and I took this delightful little cruise last year, when we were invited by Jane and Dick, you know, Dick the senator. His yacht cost almost three million dollars, can you imagine."

Coquettish giggle from the painted mouth, while in her own mind things and thoughts juggled about, seeking to arrange themselves with an empty formula: *Mediterranean cruise, lobster buffet, torture chamber, lake of blood, three million dollars...*

Her brain usually tired from polite little exchanges like this and she saw sadly that she didn't have muscle enough to fight the grinning princess in purple standing before her who now spoke of an Italian hunk she had encountered in Sardinia. She choked on a crust of her own past, coughed at the purple woman and muttered "Excuse me" and that she needed to gurgle with water now but did everything not to appear uncaring about the story of the hunk and the Sardinian yacht club in Porto Cervo, where the Monaco princess had been seen sunbathing some months ago.

The Lady had foreseen such scenes and also that she would be very much alone in the end. The day would come when nothing, not even a dream, would stand between her and Peru, and she would return there, "...one day, we only have to wait for" the lady had laughed "...she will return to this graveyard of a country, to take her own life."

Planning her final coup, the grinning Lady had poisoned her out of pure maliciousness. She had let her go, a *gringa* who had entered Peru as a foreigner but who had only known Peru for the last few years and had been stripped of her gringo-ness in its torture chambers, becoming all Peruvian to survive. Instead of stabbing or bludgeoning her, the Lady had released her in the realistic hope that this would drive her into suicide because she no longer ate the same food or spoke the same language as the gringos. The Lady had been certain that she would be killed, one way or the other, and had returned her to the sunshine, back into a civilized world where police forces were not made up of criminals and where torture chambers existed only on television. Prior to opening the prison doors, the Lady had stated with a wide grin that she was bored today and that she felt a strong desire to lose herself in luxurious abandon by playing a little game: three months after her release an execution commando, made up of men with undifferentiated, impersonal eyes, would be sent to find her. With a kind of liquid benevolence, the Lady explained that the men would search for her all over the world, but that her three months advance would enable her to avoid the dissolution of her earthly body. This sly move was equal to a slow stoning death, causing her upon release to sever all ties with friends and to introduce herself to new acquaintances without a surname. In the end, she moved monthly, becoming both a hermit and a gypsy and living with great urgency beneath a coat of solitude.

Three—the village and the mountains

Walking among the people of her village now, she had become an
outcast among them, whose senses had all their lives been flushed
with the voluptuous images of the mountains, who had known only
the hard work of their farms and who had never left. Their astonished faces creased whenever she spoke of foreign lands and the only
ones to greet her warmly were the trees extending kind branches to
embrace her, and the grass, which reaffirmed the glory of life with its
lush green. The Lady had never foreseen that her spirit might be
reformed by walking through the fields. They were not the same
fields as found in other lands or even other villages. What distinguished them was the smell of the air, the gentle vibration of the
bees' buzzing in her ears, the tender touch of the grass beneath her
bare feet, the welcome song of the trees…the fact that this very tree,
here, had been one she had climbed as a young child and that that
one, over there, bore the memory of her gay years where she had
once dreamt in its shade. Only these trees, this grass, these fields,
harbored the memory of who she had been, before Peru. Only they
carried the memory of her impatient, youthful spirit that had once
arched high towards the green-blue sky, with a sense of urgency to
conquer the world outside her village. They could not be replaced
with a different field, tree, or sky. The majestic mountains, who had
lived for an eternity and who would live for centuries hence, recognized and greeted her with their snowy smile, accompanied by the
birds' chorus in the trees, which the little creatures sang for her
return as they rasped out *welcome bacckkkk welllcomm backk*. There
was the soft sound of cowbells, accompanied by the birds' song and
announcing that the memories she still carried could be conquered
and a new life was possible, even for her.

There was music in the mountains, like she had taught Stefan
Zweig and had discovered herself. When night fell, she was called
outside by Zweig, who said "Come and see, there is a symphony in
the sky! What a night this is." Zweig had learned fast and there was

indeed in the sky a symphony, F major, as the clouds turned from blood-orange to a twinned-tender, pinkish shine. The church-tower outlined warmly in the setting sun before the reddish mountains, its bell's chime speaking quarterly of the endless passage of time and relentlessly warning against her premature dissolution and suggesting she go out into the world and keep living. The church's warning was perfectly sober. Looking at the silhouetted church before of the mountains, she understood that life in her village had stood still while she was gone and that the church was also warning her against the crawling passage of time that causes people to yawn themselves from one year to the next.

The moon had risen and set on the warning of the little church and she found herself in the midst of a perfectly sober afternoon of the following day, having made an earnest attempt to sleep off the sourness of the previous night's dream. The Rider was still very much on her mind, and the Peruvian, who said "such a brute" and offered to marry her if only she would agree to be dead with him.

Before her, in the lush green grass, appeared a small, turquoise-colored beetle with golden wings that somehow looked tired and a little drunk. This caused her to gingerly pluck it from its blade of grass. The little beetle took boldly to her small hand and did not mind the slight curve of her right index finger indicating a strong bout of arthritis waiting to emerge, a reminder of her having been made to sleep in mud-floored damp dungeons in the highlands of Peru. Fueled by a strange enthusiasm and flapping its wings in a little misfired flying start, the beetle proceeded to climb over her hand, not caring that the hand had once been tortured in another land. The tiny turquoise creature kept on walking through the road-works on her hand's back, climbed the mountain of her index finger, then made for the steep summit of the middle one, then down the ravine to the neighboring finger-tip. Then, all wound up, it jumped across to the little finger. *And now?* The beetle seemed to be panting from its climbing efforts and looked uncertain what to do next. She offered it her thumb, to transport it back to the grass, but the beetle had apparently been instructed "never accept a lift from a strange finger" and she felt a little deflated when it followed the call of the blue skies overhead, spread its little turquoise wings and took off, from the summit of her baby finger, toward the honey-colored clouds above.

After an afternoon of reflecting on her wrongs, real and imagined, and wondering whether her future was still waiting to emerge or whether she was, for the rest of her life, condemned to live in a room full of mirrors in order to drown the call of Peru, the church-bell chimed a sharp and dangerous warning. An entire day had passed but she looked as tired as she had twenty-four hours ago and her mind was still filled with the useless jumble of unordered thoughts. Death would advance unnoticed, after many such days had been joined together, the church warned in a strong voice. Or, she could choose to live her days in inconceivable richness. Then, the moment when the light seemed to dip, she would be taking with her an array of good memories and be spared the pathetic little voice that speaks inside anyone ashamed to die. Faced with the winter of its life, it still asks "when is my spring coming?" and "when shall I cease to be sing" even as his mouth turns to dust. She felt a little ashamed of her tired-ness, knowing very well that she had never sung any of the wilder, unsubmissive hymns life had written into the heavens. There was only one song inside her heart, full of the dreadful loss of final inno-cence, but the church said that the moment must be seized and that there was time enough to be weary and tired and destroyed when one was dead. Then she seemed to be taken over by some outside force, which said that the music of the heavens was full of flutes and living rainbows and that its song still had to be sung.

Like some image of ancient royalty a woman appeared on the road below, dressed in a robe made of rare cloth, the traditional costume of her village. In the setting sun the streets of the little village were flowing in gold. She glided down the hill to join the little religious procession of which the woman was head. Her village was a very catholic village and although some of the villagers were very unkind to strangers, the reciting of the rosary was taken very seriously, even among this community of gringos. Her old grandmother suddenly appeared, dancing across the garden of the church, to join the procession and be walking beside her. She found it strange that her grandmother should be coming up from the city to join her. Here was her home, her own school, but her grandparents had made their home in the anonymous city long ago. Although the grandmother never really knew her, not since she had left the village long ago, she now came to walk beside her. She found the gloomy presence about herself lifted by the slow walk through wet grass and sweet-smelling earth, already wondering whether she had perhaps been too impatient in wishing to instantly destroy the bond linking her to Peru's poor. Contemplating this while in the act of banning dark thoughts, she understood that she could not undo the past she had already lived. She saw this, by way of an image of a wedding ring flying off her left ring finger, symbolizing that she had been married to the people of this village only through her own mind's cruel blasphemy because this was no more her village than Peru was her country. Even in the midst of the religious ceremonies that accompanied the procession, she saw that she had to be grateful to be received with the warm but distant kindness reserved for strangers. Should she attempt to lay claim to the village as her home again, she was certain she would encounter a bout of divine anger, even from the village priest, and he and villagers would destroy her hopes to be called *our village's child* in a brief, wholesome massacre. She realized that if she were to keep on living, she would be making her choice between assorted strangers amongst whom some might be evil and some might be good, and assorted countries where she would never belong. Only the mountains called her "child" and only the trees acknowledged that she belonged to them, but they would never join her when she wished to roar with laughter. She walked with the village women who were beautifully dressed in their traditional costumes, but would never be one of them. Their faces had the freshness of country life and the lines of their faces spoke of a life lived in the comfort of their own surroundings and of never having known hunger or torture. The sunset procession was moving along, as were the religious songs the women sang with their clear soprano voices, but she could not help a sensation of slight annoyance brought on by the fact that the old village priest did not address his parishioners in Spanish. She neither prayed nor spoke in another language anymore. When the priest came closer and recognized her from decades ago, she saw that his once black hair had turned to white, and his walk had become uneasy and slow. He walked heavily, with a cane now, and there were new lines on his face, deeper than she had recalled, which made her wonder whether there was any truth to the statement that the bodies of anyone over the age of forty were only the corpses of a life already lived, who carried like a burden the memories of time which had passed too soon.

The lines on the aging priest's face spoke of man's temporary existence but, despite this, she recognized him. He never asked her about the life she had lived in all the years she had been gone or about her past, which followed her like a shadow that could not be shaken. She saw that he lived a dimension removed from her. He had sought to cheat the passage of time by staying all these years in the same little village, repeating the same rituals, with the same church-bells ringing him into dawn each morning. He was going to live the same life, year after year, and he was going to listen to the same church-bells each morning, noon and night. Living thus, he had not noticed that the regular ringing of the church-bells had dangerously accumulated the passage of time. Now he considered it atrocious that time had passed, despite its obvious standstill, and he had greeted the first signs of age with an angry exclamation of...*what the hell*. She regarded the priest's trembling hands with a kind of joyous satisfaction, considering it very just that, although each of his years could have been the year before, having been marked by the same tasks, the same mountains, the same trees, he had been unable to escape the passage of time anymore than she with her constantly changing environments and her expulsion from the community of man.

With a nasty little smile, she saw that time's endless river was as devoid of mercy and compassion as it always had been, that it was still unwilling to spare, here or there, a specially deserving one and had caught the old priest, too, as it was catching her and was going to catch the Rider also. Trim women would turn into soft-muscled old dears, their age would become a tough enemy one day, when recalling their younger years brought only pain to decaying minds. She realized that there was a price to be paid for life, and time was the one collecting it. The price was constant change and the need to rearrange oneself, the change being independent of any changes of environment. A man could sit for one year under a tree or on a chair, doing nothing, and he would change because something happens inside him with the passage of time, a change that cannot be touched or explained, but a tangible real change which could be neither controlled nor grasped, less obvious, perhaps, than the change she had undergone when she had passed from the dark dungeon of the torture chamber into the bright sun of freedom and into her shattered life before returning to the lush green fields of home. In both cases, the end result was the same. Bones that today seem too solid for quick oblivion are tomorrow swallowed up by the tough enemy called time, hungry as quicksand, eating everything in its way.

She walked in the procession, beside the old priest with his crane, and thought only of Peru. While the farmers prayed with earnest farmer faith and open hearts for their crops to turn out next year, she stood beside them, but not alone. Behind her gathered the unseen masses of Peru, with their broken faces and their ghostly children whose bellies were distended from a constant diet of rice and beans. All the phantoms of her chosen country hand-claspingly appeared, an accusing yet patiently suffering front, on the streets of her small village where they belonged not except through her presence. They prayed, through her voice, for brotherhood among them, for an end to the death squads and for the bloody rivers of Peru to dry out at last. In this instant, she understood that time's swift passage had caught her, too. She had once thought that she would stay young forever, but now understood that the faces she had seen, the foreign lands she had traveled and the memories she had returned with had turned her into an old woman. She looked with envy at the fresh faces of young country girls with their uncreased necks, their clear, fresh eyes, their unformed souls still waiting for the stonemason of time to shape them, their hearts filled with expectation, and envied their peaceful lives and the years which still lay ahead of them, all the clean, white pages in the yet unwritten books of their lives.

A farmer's wife standing beside her was only a few years older than she, but had deeper lines and her hands spoke decades of hard labor. Her husband stood silent and serious at her side, and her children, whom she had raised by herself, all six of them. Without complaint, she had cooked for them and cleaned the house, bearing more children after each encounter with her husband. Among the debts and pregnancies, she had helped the cows and horses bear their children, too, bringing countless foals and calves into the world. Now she was a hard-featured woman in her late thirties and her husband was strong and solid like a tree trunk, a very dependable man who never cluttered up her yard with his problems and rarely spoke, but sometimes he had a fair amount of brandy in his stomach. Looking at the farmer and the clever wife beside him, whose clacking lips were cooing out a most delightful soprano, she found herself disturbed by the image of him parting his wife with his callused fingers and she wondered whether the wife had ever known the touch of tenderness. *Was their love-making an obscenity? The crude scratching away of his barely workable tool between her legs after a day's hard labor? Had this hard working man learned nothing of his craft and was their love-making a poor, barefoot beggar before the mansion of romance?* Their very survival depended on the production of children but they were not romantic and tender like the poor Peruvians who also produced many children, but under the constant flooding of romance and tender touches. Gringo hard-workers seemed somehow like the wrong poets in the wrong season, categorizing, plotting and calculating their every move, in true gringo manner drawing warmth not from each other but from the image of being uncomplaining workers who must persist in living a life of labor and in the concept of a marriage that brings people together for the sake of the eternal obligation of hard work, producing as many children as they are able during their short lives. Gringo souls were alien to her, a sort of living grave with their insistence in the tragedy of the life of the common man. The farmer now openly spat into his handkerchief and then wiped his mouth, fragments of saliva flying to his right and left. He didn't know Belli and he had never stopped eating to contemplate with great, dark eyes whether man was indeed born into evil. This was perhaps on account that his eyes were green, not dark, but also because inside them she saw the memory of lifting countless beer jugs with both hands, of listening to bawdy jokes in the little village pub, of countless mares' nostrils widening in the disquiet which came before their first birth. She wondered how God could have made the farmer and his wife so differently from herself and, with a sudden flash of envy, she understood the simple beauty of people who could accept that man was born to work, was to die working, and between these two events was to build a new generation from his loins that would continue the work after their parents were laid to earth. She wondered also about the cows in their stables who accepted, with their big, bulging eyes and with the same uncomplaining manner as their owners, that they were born as milk-machines, to be sold like machines at market, to people capable of judging them according to their capacity to be milked, who even accepted that the day their udders collapsed after year-long service, having become useless in a using society, they would be converted to tough-chewing beefsteak and on account of their age be fed to the dogs because humans only ate veal anymore. She envied the cows and their farmers for their stoic acceptance of their lives whose second page looked like the first, who never wept *poor me* and never had any great ambitions to discover the elegant purities of existence. She also wanted to be a farmer's wife who never asked nor wanted anything more than what was at hand. She envied their noble silence where no questions and exploring inquisitive thoughts drove them to the brink of insanity, their quiet lives and their quiet deaths, because they had never known the dungeons of Peru but would always know their mountains and their trees.

Fixing her gaze on the ancient mountains that towered not too far away, looking like people in their own right with their sunlit faces and their fogged hats, she thought them to be proud stone creatures who took in a breath of snow and spat out a violent storm, who sang happily under the bright raw costumes of the rain and stirred many a writer's or composer's creative itch when crying lazy tears of sluggish mud slides. They lounged in the distance, with grace and promises of magic, and they would be there, long after she was gone. Already, she knew that she would not go without complaint, like the farmer, when it was her turn to die. In great anguish, she would wish to live longer, write more, walk the fields with her old dressing gown wrapped around her. She would ask for another day of sunshine, another season of rain, and call "blasphemy" into the face of her steadily advancing victorious death, looking like an intellectual tramp with her brain flashing music and light from its fading synapses and shaking itself against the voice which announced that the end of the sun and the fields and the music had come. It would never occur to her that, perhaps, she had been expecting too much of life or that she should have kept her time free of "urgent" appointments and television serial shows. Perhaps she would run into the mountains and tie herself to them, although she would have considerable doubts whether such action would shield her against the ever advancing hymns of the nether side. The mountains would not care whether she went quietly into the night or with great struggle, nor what the cause of her death might be. They would be expecting winter, perhaps, or the early rays of spring, remarking to each other that this was very seasonable weather. The mountains would be there, as they had been there when the last generation had lived and died, as they would be there for the generation after her.

Four—time and change

As she wondered about the possible ways of continuing anything with the knowledge of such a finite life, she came to remember a man by the name of John Francis Shade who had never been alive, except in the minds of an author and his readers. He had been banished onto the pages of a book to live there forever, but had refused to remain there, taking on a life of his own and frequently appearing in other people's books through befriending characters that did not stem from his own creator's mind. Shade had had very considerable doubts over whether he wished to die or not. Somehow, he had achieved the remarkable feat of staying alive despite of having been born dead. His creator's book had begun with Shade newly dead. Therefore he had never been alive, not even in his own book, but had somehow created his own life from the words he had been given. For a long time now, Shade had been re-creating himself inside the books of others, writing himself onto countless pages of writing strangers everywhere in the world, befriending many wondrous characters there. He had even walked into some of her own books, where he had created himself as the closest friend of one of her serialization heroes, ensuring that he would—in as much as copyright

laws and other such nonsense permitted—stay alive for eleven con-
secutive books and enter the minds of a great number of people he
had not previously reached.

Shade had greeted politely when appearing suddenly on the 54th
page of her last novel, stating, "You must forgive this late intrusion",
and she thought it was a good sign for her to be meeting him at last.

"Would you care for some tea?" she had offered, knowing that
Shade was British and also because of the late hour he might be in
need of some hot comforting liquid. Shade had blushed like a girl
because he was not used to anybody worrying about his comforts
anymore but then he had declined because he wished to proceed
immediately with the task of entering her story, provided she were
kind enough to permit. He had been all the while assuring her that
he was completely sound of mind and body. "You shan't be disappointed," he promised in a crackling voice that drew itself prettily
across the naked page in front of her.

After this, Shade had taken the book in his stride, making all the
arrangements. He had engaged in some positively sacrilegious mis-
chief at first, for instance lecturing the students of her novel's university in needle-point and childbearing. She could only suppose what
his motives had been, perhaps he had gotten bored with the intellectual existence his creator had expected him to lead. But then Shade
had turned into the admirable fighter she understood, who found
his own way even among life's most hopelessly charted course, when
he had lectured a fourth-year class of *Advanced Living 523* on the art
of booking hotel rooms of immortality in their living years.

"We often have to fight against time, with the odds seeming hopeless," Shade had addressed the fresh young faces in the auditorium,
"but nothing is more foolish than the belief that either pleading or
wrestling with time, only because the prospect of death seems a little
frightening, can bring the forces of life back on your side."

Shade said that the issue of death tended to be over-dramatized by
the living and that a little preparation could turn the matter into a

rather pleasant experience. He spoke of God and the devil, of Jesus and Bhudda, of Krishna and all the others, but then said that the only sure-fire way to assure immortality was inside of books, due to the cosmic condition that, so long as one was thought of by the living, one was not truly dead.

Shade coughed with conviction. "You may think this to be a foolish belief," he said, looking into the bluish-green eyes of a tremendously attractive girl in the front row, "but I have collected considerable evidence...

(the projection of a graph appeared on a hastily rolled down screen in front of the blackboard. Shade pointed with his upraised hands to various scientific signs and algebraic formulas. The girl in the front row quite charmingly flashed him an encouraging little smile. Shade blushed and began fumbling unhandily with the screen, giving the impression that it was a matter of arranging bones not graphs. The girl smiled again. A hard smile.

Shade muttered boldly, "...it is important what kind of dreams one's female students engage in..." and rather unkindly asked the awkwardly blushing girl to come forward under the curious regards of her fellow-students. She smiled a desperate smile as she confessed to the students and to Shade that she had been greatly unhappy, and had even considered taking her own life, because of her secret unrequited love for a certain John Francis Shade, distinguished professor of life. John Francis stood frozen in a gibber of happiness, about to draw her into his arms to plant an encouraging kiss on her inviting young lips as a fitting end to such an inviting little confession, but then a horrible thing happened: the charming little image disappeared and he found himself in a dead end street on which stood a sign that read *Welcome to Reality*.

Poor Shade had already been rubbing his hands, in anticipation of the festive night that lay ahead but now appeared the ghastly emblem of old women, the only creatures who preferred the dead grin of dentures to flashing teeth. He found it fitting to arrange himself with reality and to close the bright landscape which had momentarily opened before him, shutting it tight behind a double-bolted steel door before he turned back to the class. Nothing in his eyes—even when they found themselves, forced as if by some strange power, drawn back into the colorful sparkle in the eyes of the girl in the front row—spoke of the scene he had just returned from)

"…that the only way to ensure being thought of by the living after one's demise and to reach the minds of those one has never known, is to stay alive inside the pages of books that they will read, discuss and think about…"

The young people said "ah", understanding that having one's name appear on the page of a book after death was a symbol of great social stability.

"…and then perhaps they will have pity on you and they will converse with you for a while. Having read about your thoughts, they will perhaps discuss with you the meaning of an ever changing life."

What was so delightful about being in books, Shade added, was that one could always create a different reality by entering the minds of other writers and causing them to rewrite one's character in the most charming little colors.

Five—the wisdom of cows

Shade's appearance in her book had been a long time ago but now she remembered his words, standing face to face with the ancient mountains, and she understood him even better, especially his original astonishment over man's failure to question his finite existence. She regarded the cows who lazed about happily in the field, a faithful expression of idyllic country life. When she looked at the little Pekingese dog who was still with her, she saw in the canine's and the cows' eyes that the lucky beasts knew only the life they lived today. They were perfectly capable of laying in the sun, enjoying its warm rays, not caring if tomorrow they would still be alive. From the blank eyes of the peacefully chewing brown and white cows she learned that nothing mattered much in life. It all appeared futile now, and childish to spend so much of her time resenting the fact that life was finite when that time could be better used for the process of living. Seemingly, it was enough simply to be alive, to feel the wind upon her weary face or to hear the song of the birds in the trees. Sometimes, it was enough just to be alive.

Into her new-found thoughts of serenity burst the scream of Peru and she distinctly understood that sometimes deafness is a blessing. She hated to be torn open and raw by the stern reminder of the Peruvian's ghost and she did as she had been taught by the composer: Closing her eyes, she remembered the colors and the music. When she opened her eyes again, Haydnean horns played in the blue sky above. There was now a symphony all around her, which it drowned out the children of Peru begging for food in their meek voices. Their pleas grew louder and she turned up the horns until the children screamed no more. When the voices of the children had subsided she turned off the music and walked toward the churchyard with its village cemetery. In a little village like this, the residents were baptized in their church, confirmed in their church, prayed there all their lives, buried their loved ones there, and eventually found their own graves there. When she entered the graveyard, the Peruvian gloated and said with an air of triumph, "See! You are drawn to death. Life has failed to satisfy you, after all."

She focused on his blurry image and stated very definitely that she always associated cemeteries with life, despite the chattering dead calling out their warning the passing visitor, "Feel now, do it now, be happy now, it may be too late when the morrow comes."

The Peruvian peered closely into her mind and saw a flashing image of the Rider. Using most expressible gestures of his fine hands, he spoke until she cowered before him, apologetic and humble.

"He will never love you," he insisted. "He will love a gringo woman with gringo values. His world, with its traditional views of

what matters in life, is not a world making any sense to you and I.
But it is his world. Let him be. Let him ride."

The Peruvian warned her, once more, against getting involved
with the Rider and she felt sick and weary as she begun to taste her
future with the Rider escaping her.

"But I will love him," she said feebly.

The Peruvian's slender index finger traveled up the right side of
his mouth as he sighed: "Gringo society destroys the soul with anger
and shame." His fine nostrils widening, he added: "Gringo nature
aspires to the pure life of the soul, but it is lying and ugly and malevolent. You will not un-write the book of his past or erase the anonymous others who have shaped him."

Questioning the Peruvian's traditional views of gringo society was
something she would have very much wanted to do, but she hastily
abandoned the thought when he slammed his disquietening eyes
into hers and said "that would be very discourteous." After all the
trouble he was taking, trying to preserve her from a future leading to
her ruin, she could at last see that it would be polite to allow him to
continue on and on.

"You will not love a man like him, your worlds are too different,"
the handsome ghost droned into her ear. She subdued her desire to
roughly cast him aside and instead concentrated on the vision of the
Rider.

"...*no importa que el esta caminando solo...*" the voice thwarted
her vision, pissing all over the garden of her happiness, "...no matter
that he walks alone, you will never live in the same house with him.
You will never break through his walls. With his gringo-self-impor-
tant manner, he will run from everything you seek to share with him.
Leave him be. Come walk with me, hand in hand, through the streets
of Lima."

Definite extension now, toward her, of a slender brown hand
promising goodness and true love. She stiffened.

"...*vamos a caminar juntos, tu y yo...*"

At least he spoke Spanish, perhaps this fact alone qualified his proposition for serious consideration? Eternal life, eternal damnation, could scarcely harm her if she refused to believe in the big blackness and kept her eyes fastened firmly on the sight of heaven. Could it?

"Let us walk among our own people, who love and understand us. Leave the gringos be, with their infantile fears and their lopsided values, their sadness and their solitude. It is only faith you lack. Walk with me and hear the children's laughter..."

...she strained her ears and fought hard against the children's screams.

"...it is only faith you lack," the Peruvian repeated as though it were her fault somehow that she heard the children screaming and not laughing. She extended herself to the very edge of humanely possible reason, until she had no more imagination and thought there was no more use in suffering.

Six—conquered by a skinned little boy

The Rider, his soul all pure with nothing of sin or judgment in it, painted himself on the sky before her.

The Peruvian, snorting now, held the skin of a murdered child in his hands. "It is all horror, all hell. There is no blessedness in Lima. This man (pointing at the Rider) does not care about the children of Peru. He has no love for humanity inside his soul."

The skin was dripping blood now, slowly and deliberately. The Peruvian stood silently, great-eyed and ebony-locked, his face all gold and shadow in the setting sun. "I will show you what has inspired the rider. You will not love him then," he exclaimed, waving the skin with great ferocity. "He has traveled in the realms of gold."

She closed her eyes wearily, not wishing to look the ghost in the face anymore, nor to see the dramatized effect of the flapping skin, not even wishing to answer any more questions or to see the rider again, only to be told by the Peruvian what kind of an evil person he was and what greedy fantasies had inspired him to ride.

The Peruvian had a twisted picture of the gringos, never having weaned himself from the raw shuddering bones of the civil war's dead and never having liked the unhealthy appearance of skinned little boys outside his door. His resentment had been well-preserved, against all gringos, dead or alive, sick or healthy, and the blood-spilling, uglily flapping skin had never been forgotten. In his eyes, the Rider, owing to his fundamental gringo-ness, was as guilty as everyone else.

Speaking, and moving the skin in his left hand, back and forth between his thumb and forefinger, the Peruvian looked at her angrily. "He has seen nothing. He knows nothing about the war!" she defended the Rider.

"He is *gringo*," the Peruvian accused, waving the skin dangerously close to her face, close enough for her to catch a whiff of its sweetly putrefied stench and to make out distinct pecking holes where vultures had nibbled on the back and thighs of the skin. "Gringo men are born evil!"

She had aspirations to tell the Peruvian that his mind was very evidently and very clearly sick. But then he threw the skin aside rudely and she saw that the red from his hands had disappeared. He flashed brief looks of hurt at her, which caused her at once to separate her imagined life with the Rider from reality. The Peruvian happily rejoiced and said that his period of mourning was over for now. The Rider seemed genuinely distressed, but the skin of the little boy saw to it that she wanted nothing more to do with him and that their future together remained in its grave. Too exhausted now to separate the real from the imagined, she welcomed the Peruvian children who appeared in her ear again. This time she could hear them cry out with joy, their wounds of war forgotten, their innocence born anew in the morning sun. This was an altogether acceptable picture and the Peruvian appeared beside the children, smiling in triumph and consolation.

"Share into the simple pleasures of building an *alfumbra* for the *semana santa* with us," the Peruvian invited seductively, "leave that gringo horseman to his world that is not of our making. Let him live there, let him die there, and let me take you home."

She closed her eyes and heard the children laughing in the streets of Lima, where fame meant nothing and money even less and greatness was born from the glimmering ashes of the broken dreams of a people to whom love was more than just a word, who still shared their meager meals with strangers in the market place. She took a final look at the vision of her Rider and saw that he rode a horse named sorrow. She understood that his face was the result of having lived a gringo life because gringos were rich and unhappy as their ultimate life's goal. She patted his horse on its steaming neck, asking it to bring him home safely every day, however long his remaining existence on earth still stretched. The horse snorted through its snub flat nose and disappeared into the distance, carrying the Rider on its back. She wondered whether there was some truth to the saying that love doesn't die and whether she might continue loving him, even though he was leaving.

Casting a final look over the fields of her village, she sat in silence under the mountains for a long time. The Peruvian stood by, admiring her with his silent eyes, and she now saw that he had the kind of classical beauty that survived even the cooling of skin in death.

"I am leaving tomorrow," she told the Peruvian, asking forgiveness for her rude and foolish love for another man. The Peruvian's whole complexion lit up from the pale shine of death. He savored her words and replied, not being a very gracious winner, that he had always told her the rider was hollow-eyed, wrinkled, sharp-chinned, rotten-toothed, rude, foolish, untaught, lavatory-eared, gouty-legged, stooped-backed...

"ENOUGH, ENOUGH!" she screamed and closed her ears. He would have to learn, she told the Peruvian, looking him square in the face as never before, to control his infantile outbursts of jealousy.

"Why?" the Peruvian wanted to know.

"Because it is unkind," she told the open-mouthed ghost, perhaps more roughly than she had intended.

The Peruvian sulked handsomely and fought hard within himself to keep from uttering further insults about the Rider. And she? The earth, her heart, her imagination, all melted into one as she prepared for her flight to Peru, knowing that the Rider would not come with her and that she would never see him again. She felt better after this decision, although the appetite for his love had not yet faded in her heart. But the Peruvian had been right, it was futile to hope for the Rider to see a beauty beyond the material. The gap between their respective worlds was too large, separating them by their culture and their riding and their writing.

She would have to start all over again, alone in Peru. Every category of her life would need to be re-invented. The Rider's stanzas would be erased from the new, and much shorter, poem of her life. She wished to say, but dared not on account of the Peruvian, that the Rider had been no ordinary soul. This new turn in her life would thud and sweep him away. They would live their separate lives on opposing continents and his memory would gradually grow thinner and smaller until she would think of him only when a Haydn symphony played in the skies above South America. At last, she would sing the song of Peru.

The End.

CHAPTER 12

One—a fine residential home

She was old now and her hands were wrinkled. Small brown spots looked discourteous there, shapeless and monstrous, as they courted her withering skin. Contemplating her hands, she wondered why she had not yet outgrown her memories as her skin had outgrown her mind. She could still recall her first walks taken in the sunshine, and also the day she had returned to the mountains rather than succumb to the ills of a mutated and diseased civilization. Joyfully shivering, she could even remember jumping and running without impaction of weakness, before her body had become cruelly slow and her bones heavy and her fingers bent with arthritis. There was water in her lungs now and her head had recently begun to tremble from side to side at all hours of day. She had desire to be done with the living world and yet not die, although she knew that there was no medical cure for the decay of old age. It had never seemed as though she were aging and she could not understand why she felt so brutally young when she had since long had to stop taking much for granted. Her inner youth became a condescending prison where her fine consciousness lived, all chained up, inside an unpalatable body for which even she felt impulses of pity on account of its frailty. She was not yet prepared to die and was proud that she had held out against the cry of Peru, but sometimes she wondered whether the old people in Peru died happier. They had not grown as old as she but at least they died answering to no one and giving up their lives in the committed fight against a proclaimed enemy.

She lived in exile in disguise now, dwelling among fools and answering to sluggish fat-assed care assistants called Megan or Jane. She was 82 and residing in an orderly Retirement Village in coastal England. Her impulse had been to go to Europe to take refuge near Rye, where she felt almost like a native because Henry James' memory still prevailed greatly there. Although she had spent the better part of her life reading Sand, she had, early on, made up her mind to refuse discounting James. Shrugging off disapproving looks from her tutors, she had plunged into James' delicious prose, covertly or overtly, depending on the situation at hand. Although England was very crowded, James' enthusiasm for the charming, cobblestoned Rye had eventually driven her to the idea of spending her old age there. His personal accent was still everywhere, whether in remote little courtyards or in pubs filled with drunken, floorward cursing men. His home, now a museum, still gave an impression of his energy, especially the dog cemetery he had lovingly constructed like a holy place at the far right corner of his properly tended garden. James' photographs framed the walls of every room and his manuscripts and letters lay strewn on desks everywhere, presenting him to his English admirers.

Perhaps one might be even able to contact his ghost, she mused. There was definitely something very strong about Rye to do with James but she was through with ghosts and, in any event, she doubted that James, with his remarkable mechanics of words, was the kind of disembodied ghost to eagerly reach out to the Living. In his literature, he had discussed difficult questions and his imprint had been left on Rye, that was his answer to it all.

Rye was a good town for escaping the kind of fate she had been living. There, she even reconciled herself to Western culture once more, in the juncture tea room where she had sometimes been sitting lost in her own thoughts and sometimes had learnt from the proprietor, who had traveled all across the seas and now managed the establishment, the differences between Kenyan and Indian tea.

Now she resided in an old Manor House that seemed stately but served only butter-less bread and cabbage and fish to its residents. For three thousand dollars a month she had been given a small room with a chipped and fragile bathroom. She had paid too much for this, but no matter, it was Rye. Old horny former sailors spat into their hands in the Manor library, bragging to each other of days long gone and drinking hot chocolate from ceramic mugs. The old sailors' boasts rang loudly with hammering voices through what had been kindly termed a Residential Home, but she heard hardly a word of what they were saying. While those who could not longer see even with bespectacled eyes awaited, behind closed doors, the arrival of their final visitor who would draw no passage money when he came to take them, and mumbled a few bad prayers to prepare themselves, she still sat at her desk, spinning words into books.

Once, she had emerged from her room to negotiate with the staff for the rights of these fools of residents who kept eating tranquilizers like candy, believing them to be sleeping aids. She had kicked up quite a stink, a care assistant had even spat at her as though she wanted to instigate a war, some of the oldies looked at her with eyes of indifference, but in the end the *Temazepam* had disappeared from the nightly menu of pill cocktails and the carousel-like stumbling and falling of the residents subsided. Victoriously, she had returned to her room, asking herself why she was there in the first place but knowing that she had to stay if she was going to live near Rye because society had no use for the needful slow old hag she had become. Following the *Temezepam* episode, she remained watchful of the goings-on inside the home, uncurtaining her windows at dawn to catch a brief glance of the courtyard, but otherwise she stayed aloof.

The nurses looked in on her in the mornings, their unkind faces radiating an irritating self-satisfaction, to change her bedsheets. In the evenings, they came again, to feed her and to clean her tiny room, but they never smiled. When they spoke to her, they spoke as though to a small child or someone not quite sane. *There you go, good girl, well done, what a fine mind you still have.* Usually, she did not even answer them.

She was not sightless like the others, yet the idiots kept asking her to turn up her eyes so they could probe them with medical instruments to determine whether there was need of preparing her for a cataract operation. When she had enough of their hot breath fouling up her nostrils as they leant over her, she threw them out.

The other residents were rather ordinary, having lived their lives in waters that were clear not murky. Yet some had an airy quality about them. An old lady upstairs staunchly protested when her husband succumbed to cancer of the stomach and she kept his decaying body locked inside her room until the whole Manor began to stink. When they finally broke down the door to remove the greenish-bluish thing that resembled chunks of butcher's meat rather than an old man's remains, his wife delivered a loud performance, where she screamed that she had come here to die, and flung herself out the window in a bloody public show that ended in a big *splash* on the pavement outside *her* window, from where she had a special post of spectation.

The warped goings-on in the home almost reformed her to the point of returning to Peru to attend her own hanging and butchering, but then the raw nature of a torture death, glorious as it might be, put her off again. She realized now that the Peruvian was some kind of monster, bent on having her killed. Although she still did not know whether to love or hate him, she decided that Rye interested her more than giving in to the Peruvian's desire of seeing her butchered with her entails wrapped around her neck. Her books kept selling, although she still wrote like a college kid, bad enough to give any decent writer a solid chill. There was a street named after her now, but the people who walked along her street or read her books never asked whether perhaps she wanted to be visited and nobody talked to her anymore. The oldies at the home she could not speak to. If they did not fling themselves out windows or defended ballooning corpses, they were either senile or they had since long given up on life. Not she. As he had sworn, the Peruvian was still by her side, waiting for an opportune moment to reach out his hand and take her into his world where, he assured her, no one would continue to harass her, but he could not prevent her realization that she had not been touched by a man since he had died when she was only twenty-eight, or that she had lived by the side of his ghost for the past fifty-seven years. The Peruvian was glad for her to be inside the Home, because the gap-grinned or entirely toothless men were no contest for him even though he was without body. She had finally begun to wonder about the Peruvian's malice, at long last considering that he might be mentally unsound for wanting her tortured, measure by measure, as he had been.

The mortifying atmosphere of a fading, faded life crept upon her with each sunrise that greeted her old age. She was overtaken by a seductive impulse to put the past before her once more, when she received a warning voice inside her head threatening her with excommunication from life if she kept trying to roll it backwards. The voice proclaimed even the desolate throbbing of an intellectual, yet beating heart to be an insufficient justification for overthrowing the things which are today and bringing back yesterday. Her valiant heart had caused her to thrust herself futureward and continue with her life, which, undeniably, had become a sad, old lady's business because she had not married. Even at her age, she would still have married the Rider who kept riding his horses inside her memories like a sovereign king who had never been thrown off his throne.

Two—the old publisher

She was puttering about in the communal room of the serene retirement home, where modern society stored its useless members. Today, there was a new woman there, who had recently arrived from London. The woman had once been a publisher of note and they began to talking to each other, seeing that one had been a writer and the other one a publisher and that the publisher had a *Master of Arts* in literature and knew Henry James. That was why she told the woman her story, and because there was nobody else left to tell it to.

"...and there was never another, after the Peruvian?" the publisher asked with watchful interest, pinning *her* to the ground with her inquisitive stare, her white hair framing her still pretty face. She chewed her lower lip and dared not look at herself in the oversize mirror at the far wall. She had always been persistently beautiful and knew that now she would see white, where once lush black curls had framed her face, perhaps with no traces left of the strong-chinned beauty she had been who had survived the torture chambers and had first chastised and then chained the cry of Peru with the aid of Mozart and of Purcell. She had not returned there. Residing alone within her Latin soul among the gringos, she had never become *gringo* again, turning herself into a conscious impostor who had acted and danced like a *gringo*, at least on the surface she had done so, making general *gringo* remarks on life, but her soul had always belonged to Peru.

But now the other woman had asked her, and she had a sudden impulse to tell her the whole story, in some 30 seconds, although she had initially replied, "look, I cannot talk on this subject".

But then it all came back and she had to speak. She no longer cared whether she was right or wrong, she had to tell someone and so she told the old publisher. The past was dead and gone, in any event.

"There was another one," she said truthfully, turning the shadows of her past into account. "I met him only once but I loved him even so. Wanting him, I shall probably go to my grave, where he just now lies, of this I am certain."

The woman asked her to explain and she told her the story of the Rider, how she had not contacted him, after all.

"But he might still be alive," the other woman suggested with a dusty voice.

"And if he were, what matter," she replied, shaking her head sadly. "What matter, now that I am old and my beauty has departed, together with my life-force? I cannot run and I cannot sing and I cannot even cry! I am just tired now and needing of some rest. What would he be doing with me?"

"And he would, I believe, be 93," the other woman pointed out, "and dare I say that he would perhaps be somewhat wrinkled himself, the dear gentleman, and probably he is not jumping them horses anymore." She spoke like that because she was an American from the deep South, half black, with a cheery disposition, having married a London publisher 50 years earlier and moved to England.

They sat in their rocking chairs, one wearing a striped red, the other a blue dress and the publisher urged her to stand atop the staircase of her memories no more, prompting the faded woman she had become to speak freely of the Rider who had cantered through her dreams for half a century but who had been kept from her heart by Peru and by a phantom lover whom she had once murdered.

"I wished not to damage him with my memories," she sighingly told the other woman, "nor with the hatred that kept consuming me for the tortureress who had set me free but had robbed me of my friends and my home. For decades I have wandered through the slums of my heart, watching the sordid lives of its inhabitants, afraid that he might posses an intuitive instrument to register the perverse enmity still living there. Examining the depths of my commonplace hate, I finally found a simple truth, after decades. Conquering your enemy with slowly expanding love is the only way to survive. To do otherwise is to destroy only yourself.

"And so, one day, I murdered the hatred inside my heart and searched out the woman who had ordered me slowly put to death. Looking at her closely for the first time, I saw in her a most marketable goodness she had possessed as a young girl. Then I saw her growing up and ordering her life according to her surrounds. The torturess' eyes told a sad, undignified story, how having grown up in a society of violence, she had to become violent herself in order to be totally autonomous.

"She lived abroad by then, having been exiled herself. Thinking me long dead, she was surprised by my presence and asked why I had not succumbed to the memories she had instilled inside my mind, laying hand on myself, and why Peru in all these years had not succeeded in calling me back there to crush me with its deadly embrace. In our meeting, soul-stirring but frugal, we discussed outrage and injustice and also the benefit of her country. I thanked her for her kindness in letting me live and we embraced as she stated that she would fain reform but could not help what she had become. She reminded me of Abigail in *Nabucco* (she briefly had to interrupt herself to explain Verdi to her new friend, who was not as well versed in the arts as she was. She told of the song of Abigail, whose evil deeds hid a soft heart, but who, like the torturer, had been hardened by circumstance) when she apologized for killing the Peruvian yet saw no sin inside her action. She stated that she had always killed men, women and even *in utero* children, but assured me that it had been nothing personal, a political decision, nothing more. Concealing her nervous anxieties under a coat of indifference, she stated that the landscape of Peruvian politics had changed, through killing him and banishing me, and offered that we could become friends provided I stated my willingness to accept that what has happened has happened, that a new Peru had been formed including neither him nor me, and that I was willing to have both of us defamed to its people.

"I said that I was willing to forget the terrors of the past, yet I confessed that he still came for me after all these years, beckoning me to follow him, claiming that I righteously should have been killed together with him. I told her that he still urged me to return to Peru but that I would from now on turn away, for her sake and for my own sake, to live a peaceful life at last. She proposed to show me mercy and with one machete stroke bring me peace. Having vindicated her superiority, she kindly offered to undo her decision of letting me live.

"*Your death has been slow enough. It has lasted long enough. It's a wonder you are not already dead. Let me know the time, the place, and I shall send them for you to end it all.*"

"I commented nothing. Perhaps she had only wanted to relieve herself of the fact that every moment I still had experiences and sensations of pain was a moment when she was still a torturer, although she now lived in exile and wished to be forgotten. I shook my head, saying that I had already promenaded too many miles through the roads of life again, following release from her dungeons. She listened to everything, seemed to understand everything, even seeming to feel the distant need for sympathy.

"*I was only 28, then,*" I told her, *and today I am sixty-five. All these years, life has been lived to the limits of my strength, surrounded by whole-hearted egoists who never cared about my past, exiled, appealing in silence to unseen faces of hazily recalled torturers to show mercy when there was none. The song of the birds and the shining of the sun and the green of the grass beneath my feet never looked, never felt the same again. Defiantly present, the ghost of the Peruvian you had murdered always walked by my side, claiming my love and my life when I had no fitness for the task of resisting him and no fitness to love another man. I never smiled again without his reproach ringing in my ears over forgetting his people, whom he called our people.*

"The torturess did not ask for forgiveness, rebelliously holding on to her political righteousness. She had been raised to kill the enemy for the sake of her country and I had become the enemy. She thought nothing of crossing herself beneath the image of Jesus, alongside more simple souls, to ask him for his blessing when she was about to rid Peru of another subversive element. Her prayers were so cunningly lined and interwoven with moral deception that she believed herself to be doing the will of God when she had killed the Peruvian and tortured me. We had become less than human because her spirit had been lulled, by years of propaganda, to see in us only flesh fit for the executioner, not people with souls exhibiting great depth of thought and feeling.

"Through her eyes, I saw the vilest abominations of her mind, and also that she was not yet prepared to humanize, in her original stupidity, the man she had murdered, who had been an artist of great depth and intellect and who had thrown himself into the fangs of the torturers as a classical punishment for his rejecting lover. To her, that heroic, fabulous man remained a monstrous abomination of Peru who had not understood the importance of organized slaughter of those refusing to subscribe to the brilliant theory that all communist elements had to be erased with ice-picks and other instruments of correction. In his refusal to join the governmental slaughter, the Peruvian, although a military man, had lost her entire esteem and had been reduced to a malfunctioning part of machinery in the greater construction of a state that could only function if everyone subscribed to the notion that subversive elements were to be, publicly or secretly whichever way, removed in bulk, with much blood and circumstance and sometimes to the sounds of beautiful music, when the chiefs of command deemed this artistic extra to be desirable.

"That instant, all hatred left me that had previously lived inside me like a dark growling dog, emerging from time to time to bite and be thrown back with sticks and stones only to come out again. A thread of blackness had lain all around me for years when I could not laugh, put there by the memory of a military woman who had sought to murder me for no personal reason, simply because he had loved me. All the hatred left me then because I saw that the torturess was—loudly openly, and outside all self-control—coarsely insane."

The other woman nodded gravely, fraternally embracing her and remarking with true publisher instinct that her story would have made a great book, with its men and women under the influence of various passions, its hate and blood and war and desperation, its torturers who relied on clowns to sing to them, its raw love and its customary violence.

Disillusioning forces penetrated her old age as she realized that the other woman, too, could think only of money and how good the story would sell of a *gringa* who had descended to the depths of evil when she had dared love a handsome stranger from a feverishly conflicted country, with corrupted images of doom etched into its city streets, a country whose darker elements were at the least provocation ready for bloodshed. But no matter her cause for interest, no man nor woman nor child had listened to the story yet and she had great trouble keeping her tongue in bounds as with a fever-fit of confidence it unleashed itself for the first time after the shocks of killings seen in Peru had driven her inwards into a shamefully isolating silence. She spoke of having greatly suffered from re-entry into civilization with its superficial problems, how she had no contact with her colleagues, hardly spoke to her agents and rarely accepted dinner invitations, had barely even been alive until she had met the Rider and knew that she was still alive in view of the spectacle her heart made of itself when she had looked into his eyes.

"I could not have loved that Rider despite my wanting to. How can one love if there is hate still inside the heart? This morally unscathed man needed not the hatred of my past nor the holes in my future that the tortureress had had built for me. He needed not my hermit's life nor hear the screams of murdered children, nor see through my eyes a world that would soil him with memories not his own. He was better off playing blind games in his passionless marriage. Is it not true that man generally prefers a mediocre love with no flavor of the heroic, accepting a grave mix of feelings that he must disentangle in secrecy to filter out comradeship, coupled with good or bad relations in bed? A safe kind of love of a somewhat binding nature, not bottomless, more like two people holding and pulling at either end of a rope, and perhaps it expects nothing of seeing into each other's souls, but at least nobody gets killed.

"I said to myself, mayhap he is happy with his wife, as happy as any man in this world can be. What matter that their souls do not touch, what matter his reluctance to debate? I wished not be impolitely curious of his personal affairs, breaking through his outward self-control beneath which his desires soared that he all lived out inside his mind, without moving hand or foot. Be it enough that I knew him, in complete understanding. Be that enough."

"What utter, complete nonsense," the other woman snapped and got to her feet with considerable effort, leaning heavily on her crutch because her lower right leg had gone to sleep. The old publisher had once been beautiful and been courted by many men. She had lived well, in the center of life, and now she was old and looked out daily into the garden of the retirement home. The garden had become her life and the trees her closest friends. Indeed, she could sometimes be observed talking to the trees; but it mattered not. She was kind and she still had a lingering beauty and she did not long for death like the others, so she was her friend worthy of being listened to.

"I have never heard quite as many excuses for not loving someone", the publisher barked, "and never quite as inventive ones, I must say. It is definitely time for a new strategy. You will find him now and you will call him. Let opportunity dart forward boldly, it might be your last one."

"If he is still alive, that is."

"If he is still alive."

Three—in search of the Rider

Having reached an agreement, they became embroiled in the matter of searching for the Rider. That business started soon after her 83rd birthday, at the end of January. They sat up late, yawning, unraveling the Rider's path, sifting through old news cuttings, casting out questions in riders' circles and stating that someone who had been foolish in love needed to make contact with him. Six weeks later (it taken them this long to find him) they sat at a small wooden table outside the back porch, by the swimming pool under the birch trees. A mild spring sun shone, cleansing her of superstition and speculation. Birds sang in the trees overhead, reminding her of her younger days when she had run to their song through the fields of her small village, making her curse having given her youth so freely to Peru. Why had she not claimed it back after they had released her, stating "I cannot be thus committed. I am still a student!" Why, for so many years, had she allowed them to clothe her in black memories and had not simply sung with the birds and run with the deer, outrunning her memories and leaving all the Peruvian people behind the mountains, which, in their majestic greatness, would have shielded her willingly?

But here she sat, an old women who had come to understand that there was never an excuse not to bring about a change, even in the final seconds of life. So she decided, at long last, to put her name to a story she had never published and should have sent him long ago.

She had a small box, blue-white, her secret box. Bending slowly on account of her creaking bones, she took it from under her chair. In that box she kept all important memorabilia of her life and she opened the box as the other woman looked on. There was some tail hair of her first pony, darkish-brown horse hair that had to be handled carefully so as not to disintegrate upon touch. It was more than seventy years ago that the pony had been sold and she had cut its hair. There was a photo of her dog and a photo of her grandparents with their kind old faces smiling at her through the lens. She was well settled in the Home now, but she still recalled the day that photo had been taken, having taken it herself. Beside the bitter tasting *Never Again*, which flashed through her mind loudly, soared the comfort of a happy memory. She brushed aside certificates of Honor and even some literary prizes she had won and then more certificates. She had kept those, not knowing why, perhaps that on her gravestone they could put that she had been a writer of some note. She had kept the certificates but never photos they had taken of her together with important people. She had been too Peruvian all her life to subscribe to gringo versions of boasting, preferring to boast, like the Latin Americans, of the depth and frequency of her prayers.

Then, at last, she found the story. Its paper had yellowed and as she unfolded it, it cracked on the upper right corner, the words *television* and *population explosion* coming lose like fragments of a crackled, shedding skin. She had to pick them off of the floor and search inside her box for a roll of cellar tape to glue them back together again. The other woman said "carefully" as she unfolded the paper once more. With the story lay a folded, well preserved photo of the Rider, the same photograph she had stolen from the bookstore, when she had torn it out of the book instructing young girls how to become jumping amazons. Then, she had already known that it would become her favorite photo of him and that she had to have it, feeling entitled to tear it out because, after all, she loved him.

"Here, that's him."

The publisher admiringly absorbed the photograph of the usurping competitor. "How beautiful he is, such fine cheekbones, such a noble nose, such eyes of wisdom."

"You should have heard him talk," she responded fan-admiringly, conjuring up the tone of his voice, the way he chose his words, carefully stringing them together like pearls. She confided to the publisher that she would not remember his face, were it not for the photograph, but that she had always been able to recall his exact tone of voice.

Next, the other woman read the story and when she came to the story's end she said *lovely* and that it would have been a great success and asked why she had never published it. She replied that she had not wanted him to read it and that, once published, there would have been no guarantee to keep it from him. The two women, both of them well versed in words, took out their notepads and a pen, that the old publisher always carried with her, who now cried dramatically "success lies in preparation".

Four—it is said and done

…and they drafted a note for the Rider to go with the story they were going to send him. The Rider had since long given up his profession for being too loud. He was now a joyous convert to ecological living, having decided that nature could give him things the horse shows couldn't. He no longer sang bawdy drinking songs in dark pubs and had taken up puffin-watching instead. Aged 93, he was still of stout courage and traveled annually to Pembrokeshire to observe the puffins beak-fencing, colonizing and invading each others' burrows. His horses had been released in the paddocks, where they chewed grass and had also taken up puffin-watching. A puffin with a broken wing, which their master had rescued from Pembrokeshire, grew stronger by the day, in a specially-built puffin-run by the side of their field. This the old women had learnt from a special puffin-issue of *National Geographic,* and also that the Rider was no longer married because his wife had died.

Blushing deeply, she wrote him in her clear handwriting, her letters leaning slightly to the right like soldiers braving a considerable storm, *you probably should have received this long ago. Would you care to change the ending? If you are still mobile, I am at the Seven Acres home in Fairview, in room number 101, where I shall be waiting for you.*

Then they folded, with their trembling hands for trembling the hands were from the old age which had entered their bones, carefully and neatly, the story and the note into a crisp white envelope they had especially chosen for its silky lining, because they wished for him to see that she was old but still very much a lady.

Perhaps there would be, at the very least, one good day's love coming out of all this. They asked a nurse for three stamps, having decided that it would be better to have three of them because the letter was bulky, with its 15 pages of short story and its neatly written note in blue ink that she had signed her own name to with one determined stroke. And then the two women, one leaning heavily upon the other, one with gray hair and one with white, waddled slowly and with great effort, *sluump sluuuuuush slummmp* to the mailbox at the end of the hallway…

…where they sent the sealed letter on its journey, at long last.

Epilog

"Sign!

"No!

The woman handed her a swan feather dipped in ink.

"I am no traitor and I cannot sign my name to this."

"You are a soldier of the cause, we know what you have truly done. Sign."

She remained silent.

"You had better brace yourself," the woman barked.

She released a sourly smile at the woman that she knew she would bitterly pay for.

"I am to go into Europe, it is England I am going to."

She closed her eyes, prayed a final prayer and then returned to the residential home, where she was now firmly established with the Rider. As they cut her bowels out, everything turned black as hell and she realized that she had never made it past her 28th year, having written her final prose inside her head, in her prison cell, where she lay spent and moaning on the floor. She still saw that they threw her bowels on a pile with the Peruvian's, whose bloody corpse had already started to smell. She shrugged and did not even scream because she was lolling comfortably, in Eastern Sussex, in an armchair with the Rider. They shouted at her in ugly, vindictive tones, calling her a wretch and worse, and then they started drinking cheap wine as her heart beat its final beat, long after her memory had wandered through dusty holes of rooms...

THE END

Glossary

Alpensinfonie *(An alpine Symphony) by Richard Strauss*

Completed in 1915, this last of Strauss' tone poems (known correctly as "An Alpine Symphony," or "Eine Alpensinfonie") traces the ascent and descent, in the course of a single day, of a glacier-capped peak. Along the way, in travelogue style, we taste the sights and sounds of gloomy forest, high altitude meadow (with sheep), waterfall. We get lost in thickets, mists rise, the sun obscures, a thunderstorm soaks. There are 22 sections in all, each with their own musically pictographic ingenuities. The most inspired ingenuity may be right at the beginning, where Strauss depicts the veil of "Night" by having the orchestra sustain a soft cluster (the entire scale) at once. Through this the low trombones emerge, intoning an angular chordal block—the dark mountain looming. Connoisseurs will await their favorite moments. Among this listener's is "The Summit." When that point is reached, rather than immediate epic splendor, the composer first resorts to a lone solo oboe against cushioning strings; we are in the clear blue ether, and it's very quiet up there. Only then does the magnificence of the moment dawn in full orchestral gush. Strauss uses a massive orchestra for his purposes, including a barrage of off-stage brass, quadruple woodwinds (with heckelphone), a couple of tubas, a percussion section (with cowbells, and thunder and wind machines) and organ.

Ayacucho

City in southern Peru, capital of Ayacucho Department. It is an agricultural, manufacturing, and educational center. The National University of San Cristóbal de Huamanga (1677) is here. The city was founded by the Spanish conquistador Francisco Pizarro in 1539. Near Ayacucho on December 9, 1824, the last Spanish army to set foot on the continent was defeated by the combined forces of Peru and Colombia. The city was called Huamanga until 1825. Population (1998 estimate) 118,960.

Balzac, Honore de (original name Honore Balssa) 1799–1850

French journalist and writer, one of the creators of realism in literature. Balzac's huge production of novels and short stories are collected under the name *La Comédie humaine*, which originated from Dante's *The Divine Comedy*. Before his breakthrough as an author, Balzac wrote without success several plays and novels under different pseudonyms. Balzac was born in Tours. His father, Bernard François Balzac, had risen to the middle class, and married the daughter of his Parisian superior, Anne-Charlotte-Laure Sallambier; 31 years his junior. Bernard François Balzac had worked as a state prosecutor in Paris but was transferred to Tours because of his royalistic opinions during the French Revolution. In 1814 the family moved back to Paris. Balzac spent the first four years of life in foster care, not so uncommon practice in France even in the 20th century. During his school years Balzac was an ordinary pupil. He studied at the Collège de Vendôme and the Sorbonne, and then worked in law offices. In 1819, when his family moved for financial reasons to the small town of Villeparisis, Balzac announced that he wanted to be a writer. He returned to Paris and was installed in a shabby room at 9 rue Lediguiéres, near the Bibliothéque de l'Arsenal. A few years later he described the place in LA PEAU DE CHARGIN (1931), a fantastic tale owing much to E.T.A. Hoffmann (1776–1822). Balzac's first work was CROMWELL. By 1822 Balzac had produced several novels under pseudonyms, but he was ignored as a writer. Against his family's hopes, Balzac continued his career in literature, believing that the simplest road to success was writing. Unfortunately, he also tried his skills in business. Balzac ran a publishing company and the bought a printing house, which did not have much to print. When these commercial activities failed, Balzac was left with a heavy burden of debt. It plagued him to the end of his career. After the period of failures, Balzac was 29 years old, and his efforts had been fruitless. Accepting the hospitality of General de Pommereul, he spent a short time at their home in Fougères in Brittany in search of a local color for his new novel. In 1829 appeared LA DERNIER CHOUAN (later called LES CHOUANS), a historical work in the manner of Sir Walter Scott, which he published under his own name. Gradually Balzac began to gain notice as an author. Between the years 1830 and 1832 he published six novelettes titled SCÈNES DE LA VIE PRIVÉE. His father had died in 1829. When Balzac's mother miraculously recoverd from an illness, he started to study the works of Jacob Boehme, Swedenborg and followed Anton Mesmer's lectures about 'animal magnetism' at Sorbonne. These influences are seen in LA PEAU DE CHARGIN (1831). In 1833 Balzac conceived the idea of linking together his old novels so that they would comprehend the whole society in a series of books. This plan led to 90 novels and novellas, which included eventually more than 2,000 characters. Balzac's huge and ambitious plan drew a picture of the customs, atmosphere, and habits of the bourgeois France. Balzac got down to the work with great energy, but also found time to pile up huge debts and fail in hopeless financial operations. In his books Balzac covered a world from Paris to Provinces. The primarly landscape is Paris, with its old aristocracy, new financial wealth, middle-class trade, demi-monde, professionals, servants, young intellectuals, clerks, criminals...In this social mosaic Balzac had recurrent characters, such as Eugène Rastignac, who came from an impoverished provincial family to Paris, mixed with the nobility, pursued wealth, had many mistresses, gambled, and was a successful politician. Henry de Marsay appeared in twenty-five different novels. There are many anecdotes about Balzac's relationship to his characters, who also lived in the author's imagination outside the novels. Balzac worked often in Saché, near Tours, although a great part of his work was done in Paris. From 1828–36 he lived at 1 rue Cassini, near the Observatory, on the edge of the city. In 1847 he moved to the Rue Fortunée. Energetically Balzac used to write 14 to 16 hours daily, drinking large amounts of specially blended Parisian coffee. After supper he slept some hours, woke up at midnight and wrote until morning. Despite his devotion to writing, he had time for affairs and he enjoyed life. It is told that Balzac once devoured first 100 oysters, and then 12 lamb chops with vegetables and fruits. Close to his heart was Mme de Berny, who was much older, and whose death was a deep blow to the author. Balzac lived mostly in his villa in Sèvres during his later years. Among his friends was Eveline Hanska, a rich Polish lady, with whom he had corresponded for more than 15 years, and who had posed as a model for some of his feminine portraits (Mme Hulot in LA COUSINE BETTE, 1847). In October 1848 Balzac travelled to Ukraine. Mme Hanska's husband had died in 1841 and Balzac could now stay with her a longer time. His health had already broken down, but they were married in March 1850. Balzac returned with her to Paris, where he died on August 18, 1850. **For further reading**: *Balzac*, ed. by Michael Tilby (1995); *Balzac: A Life* by Graham Robb (1994); *Critical Essays on Honore de Balzac* by Martin Kanes (1990); *Honore de Balzac* by Theophile Gautier (1989, paparback); *Honore de Balzac: Old Goriot* by David Bellos (1988); *Balzac and the Drama of Perspective* by Joan Dargan (1985); *Balzac and the French Revolution* by Ronnie Butler (1983); *Balzac, James, and the Realistic Novel* by William W. Stowe (1983); *Balzac's Comedy of Words* by Martin Kanes (1978); *Evolution of Balzac's 'Commedie Humaine'* by E. Preston Dargan (1942); *Balzac* by E.R. Curtius (1933)—**See also**: Stefan Zweig,

Isaiah Berlin, Andre Maurois *Prometheus: The Life of Balzac*—**Note:** television film about Balzac's life (1999), starring Gérard Depardieu as the author, Jeanne Moreau as Balzac's mother, and Fanny Ardant as Eveline Hanska.—**Museums:** *Musée Balzac,* Château de Saché, 37190 Saché, Indre et Loire—a sixteenth century castle, devoted to the author who lived there between 1829 and 1837; *La maison de Balzac,* 47 rue Raynourd, Chaillot Quarter—Balzac lived there for seven years.—**Suom:** Kirjailijalta on myös ilmestynyt suomeksi teos *Perijätär,* suom. Koskenniemi (1913)

Beethoven

Pronunciation: 'bA-"tO-v&n
Function: *biographical name*
Ludwig van 1770–1827 German composer; often viewed as greatest composer; developed forms of symphony, quartet, sonata, etc. to new heights; inspired Romantics although himself a classicist; known especially for symphonies, piano concertos, piano sonatas, string quartets, opera Fidelio, etc.
- Bee·tho·ve·nian /"bA-"tO-'vE-ny&n/ adjective

Beowulf

Pronunciation: 'bA-&-"wulf
Function: *noun*
: a legendary Geatish warrior and hero of the Old English poem Beowulf

Berlioz

Pronunciation: 'ber-lE-"Oz
Function: *biographical name*

Hector 1803–1869 in full Louis-Hector Berlioz French composer; first French Romantic composer; composed **Symphonie fantastique (1830–31)**, choral work Requiem (1837), etc.
- Ber.li.oz.ian /"ber-lE-'O-zE-&n/ adjective

Burgess

Pronunciation: 'b&r-j&s
Function: *biographical name*
Anthony 1917–1993 British writer; wrote novels A Clockwork Orange (1962), Earthly Powers (1980), etc.; also produced critical studies, film scripts, musical compositions

Chopin

Pronunciation: 'shO-"pan, -"pan
Function: biographical name
Frédéric François 1810–1849 Polish pianist & composer; composed mainly for piano emotionally expressive pieces; composed polonaises, mazurkas, nocturnes, études, sonatas, ballades, scherzos, etc.

Colombia

Pronunciation: k&-'l&m-bE-& also -'lOm-
Usage: geographical name
country NW S. America bordering on Caribbean Sea & Pacific Ocean capital Bogotá area 439,735 square miles (1,138,914 square kilometers), population 26,525,670

Coronation Concerto (Piano Concerto No 26—K537) *by W.A. Mozart*

Key: D Major **Orch.:** Solo / 1 Fl., 2 Ob., 2 Bsn. / 2 Hrn., 2 Tpt. / Timp. / Str.

Approx.: 32 Min. **Composed:** February 24, 1788 **Autograph:** Heineman Foundation, New York.

If one wished to learn everything there is to know about Mozart, but could only study a single type of composition, the best choice would be the piano concerto. In this one area, Mozart produced twenty-seven pieces, more piano concerti than any other important composer. Additionally, the concerti span his entire career. The first was written when he was only eleven; the last appeared less than a year before his death. Considering the entire range of these works shows how Mozart's style developed, and it shows how the Classical style as a whole came into being, for his earliest piano concerti are close adaptations of Baroque sonatas, whereas his final few works in the genre hint at the passion and power that would become popular at the turn of the century. As Mozart and his concerti matured, so did music history reach a new stage of development. Mozart's fascination with the piano concerto parallels Europe's interest in the piano itself. In the composer's early years, pianos were still regarded as new inventions. Harpsichords, which had been the stars of the Baroque era, were as yet highly regarded. Gradually, though, the greater power and versatility of the piano gave it precedence over its predecessor. A growing demand arose for compositions suited to this new keyboard instrument, and a fine pianist (Mozart was acclaimed as one of the best) could earn a good living playing concerti for appreciative audiences, especially if one could do so in Vienna, where appetites for new piano concerti seemed insatiable. For this reason, Mozart abandoned his native Salzburg. He settled in the imperial capital in the summer of 1781. In the decade that remained of his life, he would produce seventeen piano concerti, many of which now number among the masterpieces of the repertoire. The twenty-sixth of Mozart's twenty-seven piano concerti was completed in February of 1788. Many of his previous concerti also originated in late winter, for the composer was in the habit of presenting a concert series during each Lenten season, when the closure of the dramatic theatres led to increased concert attendance. However, there is no evidence that such a concert series was presented in 1788, for by this time, Viennese audiences had lost their taste for Mozart and he was having difficulty garnering an audience. Thus, it may be that the new concerto did not reach the public until April of 1789, when Mozart performed it during a concert appearance in Dresden. The concerto's nickname, "Coronation," is of still later origin. In the fall of 1790, Mozart visited Frankfurt-am-Main to attend the coronation festivities for Leopold II, with whom he hoped to obtain a lucrative royal appointment, the sort of post that had eluded him in Vienna. Yet he would be sorely disappointed. His concert, featuring this concerto, as well as the Concerto no. 19 and one of his symphonies, was poorly attended, and the desired imperial post did not materialize. Mozart had no other option but to return to Vienna almost empty-handed. He would live for only another fourteen months.

D'Agoult, Marie

née Marie-Catherine-Sophie de Flavigny; married name the Comtesse d'Agoult; pen name Daniel Stern; born on December 31, 1805, at Frankfurt-on-Main; died March 5, 1876, in Paris. Writing under the pen name Daniel Stern, Marie d'Agoult was a frequent contributor to the French liberal opposition press of the 1840s. Her three volume *Histoire de la Révolution de 1848* remains her best-known work, and is still considered by many historians to be a balanced and accurate contemporary treatment of events in France. The daughter of Comte Alexandre-Victor de Flavigny, an intransigent French emigré, and Marie-Elisabeth Bethmann, a wealthy German banker's daughter, Marie d'Agoult spent her early years in Germany. After the Bourbon Restoration her family resettled in France and d'Agoult completed her education at the *Sacré-Coeur* convent. In 1827 she was married to the Comte Charles d'Agoult. In the waning years of the Restoration, the young Comtesse d'Agoult became a leading Parisian hostess. She was not happy in her arranged marriage, but she found spiritual and intellectual sustenance in the religious teachings of the Abbé de Lammenais and in the company of a new generation of Romantic artists (Hugo, Vigny, Lamartine, Chopin, and Rossini, among others). In 1833 d'Agoult met and fell in love with the Hungarian composer and virtuoso pianist Franz Liszt. Rather than carry on a discreet affair, d'Agoult deserted her husband and lived openly as Liszt's mistress. She was ostracized by the polite society of the Faubourg-Saint-Germain for making a spectacle of her infidelity, but she avenged herself by entertaining an intellectual and artistic aristocracy of painters, writers, musicians and political thinkers at the various residences she and Liszt shared. D'Agoult and Liszt's union produced three children, but Liszt's protracted absences and well-publicized philandering brought an end to the affair in 1844. At this time d'Agoult began a serious career as a journalist, under the guidance of Emile de Girardin, editor of the liberal journal *La Presse*. She introduced the French reading public to a variety of foreign authors, including Ralph Waldo Emerson, Georg Herwegh, and Bettina von Arnim, and she drafted political commentary based on regular attendance at parliamentary debates. In 1846 she published *Nelida*, a thinly-veiled fictional account of her affair with Liszt. *Nelida* was a *success*, but d'Agoult recognized that her talents lay more in analysis and commentary. Her journalism earned her considerable respect, and her *Essai sur la liberté*, published in 1847, was well received, winning the praise of numerous critics (including Sainte-Beuve), and establishing her as a feminist thinker in the mold of Mary Wollstonecraft and Madame de Stael. She continued to write newspaper reports on the political scene, establishing herself as a staunch supporter of the fledgling republic in the face of conservative reaction. D'Agoult published the three volumes of her *Histoire de la Révolution de 1848* in the years 1850 to 1853. Based on eye-witness reports, painstaking investigation, and personal involvement in the unfolding drama of 1848, this historical work was intended as a dispassionate and impartial account. Having spent long hours observing the national assembly at work, d'Agoult focused largely on Parisian political personalities, but she also provided detailed, carefully researched descriptions of the demonstrations and street battles that helped to shape governmental policy and public opinion. Her incisive portraits of political leaders, and her reasoned analysis of the social factors influencing the outcome of the revolution, would have a profound impact on many subsequent treatments of 1848. Despite personal tragedy, including the deaths of two of her children, d'Agoult continued to be involved in politics after Louis-Napoleon's *coup d'état*. She continued to write, notably for the *Revue Germanique*, a journal dedicated to promoting friendly Franco-German relations. At the time of her death in 1876, she had been preparing her memoirs for publication. They were published posthumously as *Mes Souvenirs, 1806–1833* (1877) and *Mémoires, 1833–1854*. Unlike her more colorful countrywoman George Sand, d'Agoult has received surprisingly little attention from historians. Best known through her personal association with Liszt, and as the mother of Cosima Wagner, her own writings and political influence have been left in virtual oblivion in recent years. *Kathleen M. Nilan* **Further reading:** Marie d'Agoult *Au Printemps des Dieux: Correspondence inedite de la Comtesse Marie d'Agoult et du poète Georges Herwegh, 1843–1867*. Marcel Herwegh ed. Paris: Gallimard, 1929. Marie d'Agoult *Esquisses morales et politiques* Paris: Pagnerre, 1849. Marie d'Agoult *Essai sur la liberté Paris: Librairie d'Amyot, 1847. Marie d'Agoult. Histoire de la R,volution de 1848*. 3 vols. Paris: G. Sandre, 1850–1853. Marie d'Agoult *Memoires, 1833–1854* Daniel Ollivier (ed.) Paris: Calmann-Levy, 1883. Marie d'Agoult *Mes souvenirs, 1806–1833*. Paris: Calmann-Levy, 1877. Marie d'Agoult *Nelida*. Brussels: Meline, Cans et Compagnie, 1846. Haldane, Charlotte. *The Galley Slaves of Love: The Story of Marie d'Agoult and Franz Liszt*. London: Harvill Press, 1957. Monod, Marie Octave. *Daniel Stern, Comtesse d'Agoult: De La Restauration à la IIIe Ré'publique*. Paris: Plon, 1937. Rabine, Leslie. "Feminist Writers in French Romanticism" *Studies in Romanticism*

XVI (Fall 1977): 491–507. Vier, Jacques. *La Comtesse d'Agoult et son temps.* 5 vols. Paris: A. Colin, 1955–62

Fauré

Pronunciation: fo-'rA
Function: *biographical name*
Gabriel-Urbain 1845–1924 French composer; composed nocturnes, barcaroles, impromptus for piano, chamber music, incidental music for plays

Flaubert

Pronunciation: flO-'ber
Function: biographical name
Gustave 1821–1880 French novelist; pioneer and master of realist style of French literature; tried but acquitted on charges of immorality for Madame Bovary (1857); also wrote La Tentation de Saint Antoine (1874), L'Education sentimentalo (1869), etc.
- Flau·ber·tian /-'b&r-sh&n, -'ber-tE-&n/ adjective

Ghost

Pronunciation: 'gOst
Function: *noun*
Etymology: Middle English gost, gast, from Old English gAst; akin to Old High German geist spirit, Sanskrit heda anger
Date: before 12th century
1 : the seat of life or intelligence : SOUL <give up the ghost>
2 : a disembodied soul; especially : the soul of a dead person believed to be an inhabitant of the unseen world or to appear to the living in bodily likeness
3 : SPIRIT, DEMON
4 a : a faint shadowy trace <a ghost of a smile> b : the least bit <not a ghost of a chance>

5 : a false image in a photographic negative or on a television screen caused especially by reflection
6 : one who ghostwrites
7 : a red blood cell that has lost its hemoglobin
- ghost·like /-"lIk/ adjective
- ghosty /'gO-stE/ adjective

Gringo

The most likely source of 'gringo' is the Spanish word 'gringo' itself, which means 'foreigner' or 'unintelligible gibberish.' The root of 'gringo,' in turn, is thought to have been 'griego,' Spanish for 'Greek,' often applied as slang to any foreigner.

Haydn

Pronunciation: 'hI-d&n
Function: *biographical name*
(Franz) Joseph 1732–1809 Austrian composer; regarded as first great master of symphony and quartet, composed 106 symphonies, 79 quartets, 54 piano sonatas, etc

Huancayo

City in central Peru, capital of Junín Department, in the eastern Andes Mountains, at an elevation of about 3350 m (about 11,000 ft). Located in a fertile grain-growing basin of the Mantaro Valley, Huancayo is a major commercial and transportation center. The city is known for its weekly fairs, where Native Americans from the surrounding areas sell food and handicrafts. It is the site of a cathedral and the National University of Central Peru (1962). Population (1998 estimate) 305,039.

Hugo

Pronunciation: 'hyü-(")gO, 'yü-
Function: *biographical name*
Victor-Marie 1802–1885 French poet, novelist, & dramatist; leader of the Romantic movement in France; author of novels Notre-Dame de Paris, Les Misérables, satirical poems Les Châtiments, etc.
- Hu·go·esque /"hyü-(")gO-'esk, "yü-/ adjective

Il Trovatore

Opera by Giuseppe Verdi

Librettist: Salvatore Cammarano Based on *El Trovador* a play by Antonio Garcia Gutiérrez. <u>Cast of Characters:</u> **Leonora,** *Soprano,* Lady-in-waiting at an Aragonese court **Inez,** *Soprano,* her companion **Azucena,** *Mezzo-Soprano,* Gypsy woman **Manrico,** T*enor,* Troubadour, officer in the service of the Count of Biscay **Ruiz,** *Tenor,* his aide **Count di Luna,** *Baritone,* Aragonese nobleman **Ferrando,** *Bass,* Captain of Aragonese Palace guard *Soldiers, Gypsies, guardsmen, messengers, jailers, nuns and palace attendants.* <u>Setting</u> Fifteenth century Spain. <u>Premiere:</u> 19th January 1853; Teatro Apollo, Rome. <u>Plot:</u> It seems the old Count di Luna, dead for sometime, had two sons almost the same age. An old Gypsy, Azucena's mother, had been discovered in the room with one of the sons. The child's health began to fail and it was believed she had bewitched the child. She was caught and burned at the stake. Azucena, the old Gypsy's daughter, witnessed these events and swore vengeance. One evening, she kidnapped the baby her mother had "cursed" and hurried to the scene of the execution. She was about to throw the baby into the flames when over come with emotions, she tossed her own child into the flames. She told no one her secret and instead raised the boy herself—Manrico. Manrico is in love with Leonora whom is also coveted by Count di Luna. The two fight over her until the Count gains the upper hand by imprisoning Azucena and Manrico. He orders

Manrico be-headed and learns only too late that Manrico is his long-believed dead brother. <u>Memorable sections of music:</u>*Tacea la notte* Trio: *Di geloso amor sprezzato* Anvil Chorus *Mal Reggendo Il balen del suo sorriso Giorni poveri vivea Ah, sì, ben mio, Di quella pira, Ai nostri monti*

James, Henry (1843–1916)

American-born writer, gifted with talents in literature, psychology, and philosophy. James wrote 20 novels, 112 stories, 12 plays and a number of literary criticism. His models were Dickens, Balzac, and Hawthorne. Henry James was born in New York City into a wealthy family. His father, Henry James Sr, was one of the best-known intellectuals in mid-nineteenth-century America, whose friends included Thoreau, Emerson and Hawthorne. James made little money from his novels. In his youth James traveled back and forth between Europe and America. He studied with tutors in Geneva, London, Paris, Bologna and Bonn At the age of nineteen he briefly attended Harvard Law School, but was more interested in literature than studying law. James published his first short story, 'A Tragedy of Errors' two years later, and then devoted himself to literature. In 1866–69 and 1871–72 he was contributor to the *Nation* and *Atlantic Monthly*. After living in Paris, where James was contributor to the New York *Tribune,* he moved to England, living first in London and then in Rye, Sussex. During his first years in Europe James wrote novels that portrayed Americans living abroad. In 1905 James visited America for the first time in twenty-five years, and wrote 'Jolly Corner'. It was based on his observations of New York, but also a nightmare of a man, who is haunted by a *doppelgänger*. Between 1906 and 1910 James revised many of his tales and novels for the New York edition of his complete works. His autobiography, A SMALL BOY AND OTHERS (1913) was continued in NOTES OF A SON AND BROTHER (1914). The third volume, THE MIDDLE YEARS, appeared posthumously in 1917. The outbreak of World War I was a shock for James and in 1915 he became a British citizen as a loyalty to his adopted country and in protest against the US's refusal to enter the war. James suffered a stroke on December 2, 1915. He expected to die and exclaimed: "So this is it at last, the distinguished thing!" James died three months later in Rye on February 28, 1916. Although James is best-known for his novels, his essays are now attracting audience outside scholarly connoisseurs. James's most famous tales include 'The Turn of the Screw', which was first published serially in *Collier's Weekly*. The short story is written mostly in the form of a journal, kept by a governess, who works on a lonely estate in England. She tries to save her two young charges, Flora and Miles, from the demonic influence of the apparitions of two former servants in the household, steward Peter Quint and the previous governess Miss Jessel. Her employer, the children's uncle, has given strict orders not to bother him with any of the details of their education. The children evade the questions about the ghosts but she certain is that the children see them. When she tries to exorcize their influence, Miles dies in her arms. The story inspired later a debate over the question of the 'reality' of the ghosts, were her visions only hallucinations. **For further reading:** *The Method of Henry James* by J.W. Beach (1918); *The Art of Fiction* by Percy Lubbock (1921); *The Pilgrimage of Henry James* by V.W. Brooks (1925); *The James Family*, ed. by F.O. Matthiessen (1947); *The Triple Thinkers* by Edmund Wilson (1948); *The Great Tradition* by by F.R. Leavis (1948); *Henry James* by F.W. Dupee (1951); *The Image of Europe in Henry James* by C. Wegelin (1958); *The Expense of Vision* by by L. Holand (1964); *Henry James* by Leon Edel (1953–72, 5 vols.); *Theory of Fiction* by James E. Miller (1972); *James the Critic* by Vivien Jones (1984); *The Wordsworth Book of Literary Anecdotes* by Robert Hendrickson (1990); *A Companion to Henry James Studies*, ed. by Daniel Mark Fogel (1993); *A Private Life of Henry James* by Lyndall Gordon (1999); *Henry James and Modern Moral Life* by Robert B. Pippin (2001)

Job—a masque for dancing (1930)—*composition by Vaughan Williams*

A Masque is usually a combination of dance, song and speech, and RVW choose to subtitle this as a Masque because he felt it was a better description than ballet. A major score, strangely neglected, the work foreshadows the bristling Symphony No. 4. Vaughan Williams based this ballet on William Blake's illustrations for the Book of Job and on a scenario derived from them by the great Blake scholar Geoffrey Keynes. I know of no other music that conjures up the complex, mystical, and deeply humane worlds of William Blake as this work does from the opening bars. The ballet is symphonic in scope and method and yet depicts the narrative as well.

Joyce

Pronunciation: 'jois
Function: *biographical name*
James Augustine 1882–1941 Irish writer; developed techniques of interior monologue and stream-of-consciousness narrative in Portrait of the Artist as a Young Man (1916), Ulysses (1922), Finnegans Wake (1939), etc.
   -   Joyc·ean /'joi-sE-&n/ adjective

Kurosawa

Pronunciation: "kur-&-'sau-&
Function: *biographical name*
Akira 1910–1998 Japanese filmmaker; regarded as greatest of all Japanese filmmakers; developed innovative style in Rashomon (1950), The Seven Samurai (1954), Ran (1985), etc.

Lancelot

Pronunciation: 'lan(t)-s&-"lät, 'län(t)-, -s(&-)l&t
Function: noun
: a knight of the Round Table and lover of Queen Guinevere

Latin America

Usage: geographical name
1 Spanish America & Brazil
2 all of the Americas S of the U.S.
- Latin-American adjective
- Latin American noun

Liszt

Pronunciation: 'list
Function: *biographical name*
Franz 1811–1886 Hungarian pianist & composer; revolutionized technique of piano playing; as composer invented the symphonic poem and the method of transformation of themes
- Liszt.ian /'lis-tE-&n/ adjective

Marlowe

Pronunciation: 'mär-"lO
Function: *biographical name*
Christopher 1564–1593 English dramatist; first dramatist to discover vigor and variety of blank verse; works include Doctor Faustus, Edward II, The Jew of Malta
- Mar·lo·vi·an /mär-'lO-vE-&n, -vy&n/ adjective

Mozart

Pronunciation: 'mOt-"särt
Function: *biographical name*

Wolfgang Amadeus 1756–1791 Austrian composer; composed over 600 works in virtually every form, a body of work unexcelled in diversity; works include operas The Marriage of Figaro, Don Giovanni, The Magic Flute, etc.
- Mo·zart·ean or Mo·zart·ian /mOt-'sär-tE-&n/ adjective

Mozart's Birth House

Date founded: 1880
seen immediately upon entering the Altstadt through the narrow opening located between Market Steg and Staats Brücke.
Getreidegasse 9 A-5020 Salzburg Telephone: +43 (662) 844 313 Telefax: +43 (662) 840 693
Media: Photos. Scores/libretti/music. Memorabilia.
Special Collections Music instruments
Wolfgang Amadeus Mozart (1756–1791), composer

Musset, Alfred de (1810–1857)

French Romantic poet and playwright, remembered for his poetry. A love affair with the novelist George Sand between the years 1833 and 1835 inspired some of Musset's finest lyrics. Much influenced by Shakespeare and Schiller, Alfred de Musset wrote the first modern dramas in the French language. Alfred de Musset was born in Paris. Both of his parents were descended from distinguished families, and his father had written several historical and travel works. Musset entered the Collège Henry IV and graduated with honors in 1827. After hesitating between many professions, Musset abandoned medicine because of his distaste of the dissecting room, and studied painting for six months in the Louvre. Musset began his career as a poet and dramatist in 1828 with the publication of a ballad called 'A Dream'. His first collection of poems, CONTES D'ESPAGNE ET D'ITALIE, appeared in 1829. The work won the approval of Victor Hugo who accepted him in his Romantic literary circle *Cénacle*. Musset's following works showed the influence of Lord Byron. In

1830, at the invitation of the director of the Théâtre de l'Odeon, Musset wrote LA NUIT VÉNETIENNE, the first of his plays to be produced. After the humiliating failure on the stage, Musset refused to allow his other plays than historical tragedies and comedies to be performed. It partly liberated him from the thoughts of "technique"—he did not care whether the plays made an effect or no. Theatre, on the other hand, was for writers a good means to reach their audience. A theatre ticked was not so expensive than a book. Musset's relatively well-made books which cost only 3.50 francs still did not reach a public of petits-bourgeois, craftsmen, or workers, who earned little more than 4 francs per day. In 1833 Musset met George Sand, and started an intense relationship with her. His auto-biographical work, LA CONFESSION D'UN ENFANT DU SIÈCLE (1835), is a fictionalized account of the affair, and reflects the *mal du siècle*, the disillusioned moral atmosphere in the period of strife between liberals and monarchists. "Everything that was no longer exists; everything that is to be does not yet exists," Musset once said. In 1834 Musset visited Venice with Sand, and they both became dangerously ill. Sand fell in love with her physician, and Musset returned alone to France. This stormy year inspired his plays ON NE BADINE PAS AVEC L'AMOUR and LORENZACCIO, which is sometimes considered his finest drama. Musset became engaged to Aimée d'Alton in 1837. The relationship faded within a year and was followed by brief affairs. His health began to fail and after 1840s Musset's literary production as a dramatist diminished. In 1845 he was named a Chevalier of the Legion of Honor, and from the late 1840s his plays started to enjoy success on the French stage. Musset's later works include the patriotic song 'Le Rhin Allemand', and the popular comedy IL FAUT QU'UNE PORTE SOIT OUVERTE OU FERMÉE (1845). Musset was elected to the French Academy in 1852. In the same year he entered into a love affair with Louise Colet, the former mistress of Gustave Flaubert. For the last two years of his life, Musset was confined to his apartment near the Comédie-Française.

His heart ailment, an unusual vascular malfunction that became known to scientist as the Musset symptom, was aggravated by drinking. He died in Paris on May 2, 1857. Nowadays Musset's popularity is second only to Racine and Moliere. Musset had a profound grasp of the psychology of love and his portraits of women were multidimensional. Many of the titles for his works were taken from proverbs popular at the time. **For further reading**: *Documents littéraire* by E. Zola (1881); *Les amants de Venise* by Ch. Maurras (1902); *Life of Alfred de Musset* by A. Barine (1906); *Un grand amour romantique: George Sand et Alfred de Musset* by A. Feugère (1927); *Le romantisme de Musset* by P. Gastinel (1933); *La vie privée de Musset* by A. Villiers (1939); *Musset: L'homme et l'oeuvre* by P. van Teighem (1945); *Alfred: The Passionate Life of Alfred de Musset* by C. Haldane (1961); *Etude historique et critique du théâtre de Musset* by M. Vantore (1962); *Vues sur le théâtre de Musset* by A. Lebois (1966); *The Dramatic Art of Musset* by H.S. Gochberg (1967); *Vie de Musset ou l'amour de la mort* by M. Toesca (1970), *A Stage for Poets* by C. Affron (1971); *The Poetry of Alfred De Musset: Styles and Genres* by Lloyd Bishop (1987); *Musset Et Shakespeare: Etude Analystique De L'Influence De Shakespeare Sur Le Theatre D'Alfred De Musset* by Rex A. Barrell (1988); *Paradigm and Parody: Images of Creativity in French Romanticism—Vigny, Hugo, Balzac, Gautier, Musset* by Henry F. Majewski (1989); *L'Esprit. Stylistique du mot d'esprit dans le Theatre de Musset* by Jean-Jacques Didier (1992); *The Romantic Art of Confession: De Quincey, Musset, Sand, Lamb, Hogg, Fremy, Soulie, Janin* by Susan M. Levin (1998)

Na·bo·kov

Pronunciation: n&-'bo-k&f
Function: *biographical name*

Vladimir Vladimirovich 1899–1977 American (Russian-born) novelist & poet; known for novels Lolita (1955), Pnin (1957), Pale Fire (1962), Ada (1969), etc., and for earlier poems
- Na·bo·ko·vi·an /"na-b&-'kO-vE-&n/ adjective

Pale Fire

Novel in English by Vladimir Nabokov, published in 1962. It consists of a long poem and a commentary on it by an insane pedant. This brilliant parody of literary scholarship is also an experimental synthesis of Nabokov's talents for both poetry and prose. It extends and completes his mastery of unorthodox structure. *Pale Fire* is one of the most singular and unusual novels ever published; no synopsis could hope to suggest its ingenious layers of meaning. The core of the novel is a poem of 999 lines entitled *Pale Fire*, by American poet John Francis Shade. Collateral to Shade's poem are a Foreword, Commentary, and Index compiled by the pompous and pedantic scholar Charles Kinbote. Kinbote, an unabashedly solipsistic émigré from Zembla, 'a distant northern land,' has a personal and distinctive interpretation of *Pale Fire* the poem, which makes *Pale Fire* the novel a comical and inventive piece of fiction and one of Nabokov's most treasured works. Named as one of the 100 best English-language novels of the century, as chosen by the editorial board of the Modern Library.

Pekingese

Variant(s): or Pe·kin·ese /"pE-k&-'nEz, -'nEs; -ki[ng]-'Ez, -'Es/
Function: *noun*
Inflected Form(s): plural Pekingese or Pekinese
Date: 1849
1 a : the Chinese dialect of Beijing b : a native or resident of Beijing
2 : any of a Chinese breed of small short-legged dogs with a broad flat face and a profuse long soft coat

Pembroke

Pronunciation: 'pem-"bruk, US also-"brOk
Variant(s): or Pem·broke·shire /-"shir, -sh&r/
Usage: *geographical name*
former county SW Wales capital Haverfordwest

Peru

Pronunciation: p&-'rü, pA-
Usage: *geographical name*
country W S. America; a republic capital Lima area 496,222 square
miles (1,285,215 square kilometers), population 22,916,000

post-traumatic stress disorder

Function: *noun*
Date: 1980
: a psychological reaction occurring after a highly stressing event that
is usually characterized by depression, anxiety, flashbacks, recurrent
nightmares, and avoidance of reminders of the event—called also
post-traumatic stress syndrome

Puffin

Pronunciation: 'p&-f&n
Function: *noun*
Etymology: Middle English pophyn
Date: 14th century
: any of several seabirds (genera Fratercula and Lunda) having a
short neck and a deep grooved parti-colored laterally compressed
bill

Purcell

Pronunciation: 'p&r-s&l, (")p&r-'sel
Function: *biographical name*
Henry circa 1659–1695 English composer; composed for every public event of Charles II, incidental music for 43 plays, chamber music, operas Dido and Aeneas, etc.

Pushkin

Pronunciation: 'push-k&n
Function: *biographical name*
Aleksandr Sergeyevich 1799–1837 Russian poet; introduced Romanticism and the Byronic hero into Russian literature
- Push·kin·ian /push-'ki-nE-&n/ adjective

requiem

Pronunciation: 're-kwE-&m also 'rA- or 'rE-
Function: *noun*
Etymology: Middle English, from Latin (first word of the introit of the requiem mass), accusative of requies rest, from re-+quies quiet, rest—more at WHILE
Date: 14th century
1 : a mass for the dead
2 a : a solemn chant (as a dirge) for the repose of the dead b : something that resembles such a solemn chant
3 a : a musical setting of the mass for the dead b : a musical composition in honor of the dead

Sainte-Beuve

Pronunciation: sant-b[oe]v; sAnt-'b&(r)v, s&nt-
Function: *biographical name*

Charles-Augustin 1804–1869 French critic & author; considered leading literary critic of his time; best known for Port-Royal, a history of the Cistercian abbey of Port-Royal

Sand, George (1804–1876) *Pseudonym of Amandine-Aurore-Lucile Dupin*

French Romantic writer, noted for her numerous love affairs with such prominent figures as Prosper Merimée, Alfred de Musset (1833–34), Frédéric Chopin, (1838–47), Alexandre Manceau (1849–65). She was befriended with the painter Eugène Delacroix (1798–1863) and Alexander Herzen and Francois-Rene de Chateaubriand were also inspired by her work. Widespread critical attention accompanied the publication of most of Sand's works. Her works influenced among others Fedor Dostoevskii, Lev Tolstoi, Gustave Flaubert, and Marcel Proust. In 1842, the English critic George Henry Lewes wrote that Sand was "the most remarkable writer of the present century."

> **"We cannot tear out a single page of our life, but we can throw the whole book in the fire."** (from *Mauprat*, 1837)

George Sand was born in Paris and brought up in the country home of her grandmother. She received education at Nohant, her grandmother's estate, and at Couvent des Anglaises, Paris (1817–20). In 1822 she married the baron Casimir Dudevant, to whom she bore one son, Maurice, and one daughter, Solange. She inherited Nohant in 1821, but because of her unhappy marriage, she left her family in 1831 and returned to Paris. In 1831 Sand started to write for *Le Figaro*. She contributed to the *Revue des Deux Mondes* (1832–41) and *La République* (1848), and was a coeditor of *Revue Indépendante* (1841). During these years she made acquaintance with several poets, artists, philosophers, and politicians, and wrote in a few weeks with her lover Jules Sandeau a novel, ROSE ET BLANCHE, under the pseudonym Jules Sand. Her second novel *Indiana* (1832) was written by herself and gained an immediate fame. It was followed by VALENTINE (1832), and LÉLIA (1833). After reading Indiana the poet Alfrted de Musset wrote an admiring letter to Sand which marked the beginning of their passionate affair. At the age of 33 she started an affair with Chopin. Their stormy relationship ended in 1847. In her early works Sand's writings show the influence of the writers with whom she was associated. In the 1830s several artists responded to the call of the Comte de Saint-Simon of cure the evils of the new industrial society, among them Franz Listz and Sand who became friends, not lovers. On a personal level, Michel de Bourges, who preached revolution, was more important. After de Bourges came Pierre Leroux, who was against property and supported the equality of women, and wanted to rehabilitate Satan. From the 1840s Sand found her own voice in novels, which had roots in her child-hood's peasant milieu. For the rest of her life, Sand was committed to ideal of Socialism, which her friend Flaubert rejected in their dis-pute. After the 1848 revolution in France failed, Sand settled disap-pointed at Nohant. During her career she played an important role in the evolution of the novel. In her novels Sand questioned the sex-ual identity and gender destinies in fiction. In her autobiography, HISTOIRE DE MA VIE, Sand displaces conventional distinctions separating male from female, fact from fiction, and public from pri-vate life. She also wrote memoirs, short stories, essays and fairy tales. Sand died on June 8, 1876. **For further reading**: *Family Romances: George Sand's Early Novels* by Kathryn J. Crecelius (1987); *George Sand: A Brave Man, the Most Womanly Woman* by Donna Dickenson (1988); *George Sand* by David Powell (1990); *Le Personnage sandien: Constantes et varitations* by Anna Szabo (1991); *George Sand: Writing for Her Life* by Isabelle Hoog Naginski (1991); *Poétiques de la parabole* by Michèle Hecquet (1992); *George Sand and Idealism* by Naomi Schor (1993); *Romantic Vision* by Robert Godwin-Jones (1995); *George Sand et l'écriture du roman* by Jeanne Goldin (1996);

De l'être en lettres by Anne McCall Saint-Saëns (1996); *George Sand* by Nicole Mozet (1997)—**See also**: *Lélia ou la vie de George Sand* by André Maurois (1952)—**Note**: Diane Kurys's film *Enfants du siècle* (1999), starring Juliette Binoche and Benoît Magimel, depicted the love affair of Alfred de Musset and George Sand. Also: Impromptu, a movie starring Hugh Grant and Judy Davies, tells the story of Sand's life.

Salzburg [zälts'boork]

province (1991 pop. 482,365), c.2,760 sq mi (7,150 sq km), W central Austria, bordering Germany in the north and northwest. It is a predominately mountainous region, with parts of the Hohe Tauern Mts. and Salzburg Alps, and is drained by the Salzach River. There are famous salt deposits that have long been worked, as well as gold, copper, and iron mines. Precious stones are also found there. A scenic area, it is noted for its numerous Alpine resorts and spas. Manufactures include clothing, leather, textiles, beer, wood products, paper, and musical organs. Cattle and horses are raised. Kaprun dam, on the Salzach high in the mountains, includes one of the largest hydroelectric facilities in Europe. The province's capital and chief city is **Salzburg**. (1991 pop. 143,978), an industrial, commercial, and tourist center and a transportation hub. Picturesquely situated on both banks of the Salzach River, the city is bounded by two steep hills, the Capuzinerberg (left bank) and the Mönchsberg, on the southern tip of which is the 11th-century fortress of Hohensalzburg (right bank). Originally inhabited by Celts, the territory was conquered by the Romans and became part of the province of Noricum. After the fall of the Roman Empire, its history followed that of the city of Salzburg. An ancient Celtic settlement, and later a Roman trading center named Juvavum, the town developed in the early 8th cent. around the late 7th-century monastery of St. Peter. By c.798 Salzburg was the seat of an archbishopric, and for almost 1,000 years it was the residence of the autocratic archbishops of Salzburg, the leading ecclesiastics of the German-speaking world. They became princes of the Holy Roman Empire in 1278 and wielded their power with extreme intolerance. In the late 15th cent. the Jews were expelled, and in 1731–32 some 30,000 Protestants migrated to Prussia after a period of severe persecution. Secularized in 1802, Salzburg was transferred to Bavaria by the Peace of Schönbrunn (1809). The Congress of Vienna (1814–15) returned it to Austria.

Shade, John Francis (1898–1959)

Poet-character in Nabokov's novel *Pale Fire*. A 999 line poem in heroic couplets, divided into 4 cantos, was composed—according to Nabokov's fiction—by John Francis Shade, an obsessively methodical man, during the last 20 days of his life. From the introduction by Nabokov: "Pale Fire, a poem in heroic couplets, of nine hundred ninety-nine lines, divided into four cantos, was composed by John Francis Shade (born July 5, 1898, died July 21, 1959) during the last twenty days of his life, at his residence in New Wye, Appalachia, U.S.A.. A methodical man, John Shade usually copied out his daily quota of completed lines at midnight but even if he recopied them again later, as I suspect he sometimes did, he marked his card or cards not with the date of his final adjustments, but with that of his Corrected Draft or first Fair Copy. I mean, he preserved the date of actual creation rather than that of second or third thoughts."

show jumping

Function: *noun*
Date: 1929
: the competitive riding of horses one at a time over a set course of obstacles in which the winner is judged according to ability and speed
- show jumper noun

South America

Usage: *geographical name*
continent of the western hemisphere lying between the Atlantic &
Pacific oceans SE of N. America & chiefly S of the equator area
6,880,706 square miles (17,821,029 square kilometers)
- South American adjective or noun

Strauss

Function: *biographical name*
Ri.chard \'ri-"kärt, -"[k]ärt\ 1864–1949 German composer; regarded
as leader of the New Romantic school; composed operas Der Rosen-
kavalier, Ariadne auf Naxos, etc., tone poems Also sprach Zarathus-
tra, Ein Heldenleben, etc.
- Strauss·ian /'strau-sE-&n, 'shtrau-/ adjective

Tachycardia

Pronunciation: "ta-ki-'kär-dE-&
Function: *noun*
Etymology: New Latin
Date: 1889
: relatively rapid heart action whether physiological (as after exer-
cise) or pathological—

torture

Pronunciation: 'tor-ch&r
Function: *noun*
Etymology: French, from Late Latin tortura, from Latin tortus, past
participle of torquEre to twist; probably akin to Old High German
drAhsil turner, Greek atraktos spindle
1 a : anguish of body or mind : AGONY b : something that causes
agony or pain

2 : the infliction of intense pain (as from burning, crushing, or wounding) to punish, coerce, or afford sadistic pleasure
3 : distortion or overrefinement of a meaning or an argument : STRAINING

to torture

Function: transitive verb
Date: 1588
Inflected Form(s): tor.tured; tor.tur.ing /'torch-ri[ng], 'tor-ch&-/
1 : to cause intense suffering to : TORMENT
2 : to punish or coerce by inflicting excruciating pain
3 : to twist or wrench out of shape : DISTORT, WARP
synonym see AFFLICT
- tor.tur.er /'tor-ch&r-&r/ noun

Verdi

Pronunciation: 'ver-dE
Function: *biographical name*
Giuseppe Fortunio Francesco 1813–1901 Italian composer; credited, along with Richard Wagner, with developing opera into fully integrated art form (dramma per musica); noted for masterpieces Otello, Falstaff, Aïda, La traviata, etc.
- Ver·di·an /-&n/ adjective

Williams, Ralph Vaughan (1872–1958)

Williams was an outstanding 20th-century composer, and one of a handful of British composers whose achievement ranks equal in genius with that of Henry Purcell. Drawing on the rich treasury of national folk song and dance, he created a uniquely English style that is also universal in its range of appeal. Many of his most popular works in the Stainer & Bell catalogue reflect this lifelong interest in the music of the people. The **Five English Folk Songs** for SATB chorus, for example, and the **Six Studies in English Folk Song**, have been firmly established in the repertoire of singers and instrumentalists for many years. Another favourite, the **Fantasia on Christmas Carols**, derived from his reforming work as editor of the *English Hymnal*. In both the **A Sea Symphony** and **A London Symphony**, the folk song essense is transformed into visionary, transcendental statements of a kind also found in **Toward the Unknown Region**, for chorus and orchestra, and the **Five Mystical Songs**, for solo baritone, chorus and orchestra.

Zweig, Stefan (1881–1942)

Stefan Zweig was born in Vienna on 28th November 1881. He published his first book of poems "Silver Strings" while he was still a student in 1901. His first storybook came in 1904 "The Love of Erika Ewald", and in 1907 his first drama, "Tersites". With his "Four Stories from the Land of Children" and "First Experience" in 1911 he was first introduced to a larger readership. Being considered unfit for military duty during the first world war he was posted to the war archives, until he was able to go to Zurich as an anti-war correspondent writing for the "New Free Press". From 1919 to 1934 he lived in Salzburg, where he wrote most of his famous biographies, stories and essays—"Marie Antoinette", "Master Builders", "Amok". Stefan Zweig chose to live in Salzburg because it was both an ideal place to start his travels, and because his secluded house afforded him the peace he needed to work. The "Stefan Zweig Villa" saw many prominent guests over the years: Thomas Mann, Hugo von Hofmannsthal, Arthur Schnitzler, James Joyce, George Wells, Carl Zuckmayr, Franz Werfel and Hermann Bahr were but a handful of Zweig's intellectual friends. During his time in Salzburg, the pacifist author mostly wrote biographies, which were then translated into many languages (e.g. "Marie Antoinette", 1932) and biographical essays (e.g. "Three Masters", 1920) which made him world famous. In 1934 he retreated to London and then to Bath. History as a Mirror of Time elucidates wide ranging essays: "Triumph and Tragedy of Erasmus of Rotter-dam" and "Castellio vs Calvin or A Consciensce vs Violence" were written there in 1935 und1936 and on academic journeys to Zurich and Paris. Increasingly unsettled he first went to New York for a few months, and in August 1941 he moved to Petropolis near Rio de Jan-eiro, Brazil. He completed his autobiography, "The World of Yester-day", and the "Schachnovelle". Balzacs biograpy remained a fragment in 1942 as he and his wife, Lotte, took their own lives "of our own free will and sound of mind". From 1919 to 1937 the "Pasching Cha-teau" at Kapuzinerberg 5 was the home of Stefan Zweig. The Zweig memorial next to the Kapuziner monastery in Salzburg was erected in 1983.

The Requiem of Guiseppe Verdi (Source unknown)

History:

The Requiem Mass, written for Alessandro Manzoni (1785–1873), was first performed at the Church of San Marco, Milan on 22nd May 1874, one year to the day after Manzoni's death) with Verdi himself conducting. Three days later it was performed at La Scala, again under the baton of Verdi. Verdi was a great admirer of Manzoni but he met him only once, when Clarina Maffei took him to meet Manzoni at his home in Milan in 1868. Awestruck, Verdi wrote to her afterwards: 'What can I say to you about Manzoni? How can I describe the extraordinary, indefinable sensation the presence of that Saint, as you call him, produced in me? I would have knelt in front of him, if one could adore a man. They say that we must not do that, although on the altar we worship many [saints] who have neither Manzoni's gifts nor his virtues...When you see him, kiss his hand for me and tell him about all my reverence.' Manzoni's novel *'I promessi sposi'* (The Betrothed) was Verdi's favourite piece of Italian literature. Set in 17th century Lombardy under Spanish rule, he had first read it in his teens, shortly after its publication in 1827. Brahms examined the score of the Requiem and declared that "This is the work of a genius". In the years following its premiere, Verdi himself took the Requiem on a tour of Europe, to great acclaim. The 'Liber Scriptus', originally written as a choral fugue, was turned into a solo for mezzo-soprano in 1875. And—this is where the requiem becomes operatic—music discarded from Verdi's acclaimed opera *Don Carlos* (tenor-bass duet following the death of Posa) before its Paris premiere was used in the Lacrymosa bass solo. The text of the Requiem follows that of the normal mass, except for the parts called *"Gloria"* and *"Credo"*, which are extracted, and the adding of the *"Dies irae"* ('Day of wrath'), which isn't normally included in the catholic mass. Verdi used an orchestra with four bassoons and four trumpets, three flutes and an ophicleide for the brass bass, quite modest by comparison with the monster forces of Wagner and Bruckner. But it provided him with all the grandeur he needed. Also, of course, are the chorus, and four solists—soprano, mezzo-soprano, tenor, and bass.

The Requiem:

Requiem Aeternam

Kyrie eleison
Dies Irae—this part is composed of nine sections.
Offertorio
Sanctus

Agnus Dei
Lux aeterna
Libera me

MESSA DA REQUIEM

for soprano, mezzo-soprano, tenor, bass, chorus and orchestra

The movements:

REQUIEM and **KYRIE** (chorus, soloists)

The requiem begins with a murmur of muted cellos only just within the threshold of audibility. From this evolves a large paragraph of twenty-seven bars for chorus and muted strings, *'Dona eis, Domine'*. The motive played by the strings above the Chorus will be used further on in the Requiem. A brief episode in F major (*'Te decet hymnus'*) allows the chorus to show its paces in flights of imitative *a cappella* counterpoint. The muted, quiet music of the beginning returns.

The *Kyrie* brings an increase of motion in the orchestra. It also serves as a sort of major-key complement to what has gone before: Over a descending pattern of cello and bassoon, the four soloists successively "launch their rockets". The sense of a continually widening vista is conveyed partly by the contrary motion between voice and orchestra, partly by an adroit combination of pitch and tonality in the soloists' entries. Then the orchestral movement breaks into semiquavers—the soloists and chorus are now on equal terms, both forcefully thrust forward. Behind the harmonic shiftings, with their varying pace, the orchestra establishes, after a while, a two-bar tramp; The music thrusts forward into D minor urged by 'fatal' rat-tat-tats from the timpani. At the climax the music breaks off. A few chords follow, like faltering questions, answered in turn by a melting, but not cloying cadence in A major. A coda re-assumes the previous material in much the same sense, doubt and anxiety being quelled by a still richer cadential phrase. A harmonic epigram (F-B flat-E-A), typical of the mature works of Verdi, brings the movement to its hushed close.

Latin	English
Requiem aeternam dona eis, Domine, et lux perpetua luceat eis. Te decet hymnus, Deus, in Sion, et tibi reddetur votum in Jerusalem; Exaudi orationem meam, ad te omnis caro veniet. Requiem aeternam dona eis, Domine, et lux perpetua luceat eis.	Eternal rest grant them, O lord, and let perpetual light shine upon them. A hymn becometh Thee, o god, in Sion, and a vow shall be paid to Thee in Jerusalem; o hear my prayer. all flesh shall come to Thee. Eternal rest grant them, o Lord, and let perpetual light shine upon them.
Kyrie eleison, Christe eleison, Kyrie eleison.	Lord have mercy on us, Christ have mercy on us, Lord have mercy on us

2. DIES IRAE

Dies irae (chorus)
Tuba mirum (chorus, bass)
Liber scriptus (mezzo-soprano, chorus)
Quid sum miser (soprano, mezzo-soprano, tenor)
Rex tremendae (soloists, chorus)
Recordare (soprano, mezzo-soprano)
Ingemisco (tenor)
Confutatis (bass, chorus)
Lacrymosa (soloists, chorus)

The 'Dies irae' is the most complicated part of Verdi's Requiem. It comprises nine sections, which verdi composed without a break, as one continuous flow of music, and yet each section has its own melodic ideas, and exists seperately as a musical piece.

Dies irae

The 'Dies irae' bursts with a volcanic force, intensified by the tonal non sequitur (A major—G minor). Four tutti thunderclaps, later separated by powerful blows on the bass drum (its skin tightened so as to give a hard, dry sound), open the piece. The whole section is conceived as an unearthly storm: Rapid scales in contrary motion, peremptory calls to attention on the brass, and a chromatic choral line collapsing into slow triplets—all create the feeling of a catastrophe.

An answering phrase in D minor (*Solvet saeclum in favilla*) brings a certain balance with its rhythmic symmetry, but it too soon dissolves into new stormy ideas based on the thundering beginning.

A musical motive appearing here for the first time, and sung by the Chorus, '*Dies irae, dies illa*', shall recur again throughout the '*Dies irae*' part, the 'Dies-Irae-theme'. Verdi used this theme to bind the whole part together, and by the time it appears at the end of the Requiem, it already achieves a certain '*Leitmotiv*' strength. The origin of this noisy-musical-idea is, in fact, generated from the soft string motive which hovered above the Chorus in the beginning of the Requiem, the same chorus which now sings '*Day of wrath*', then sung '*Give them eternal peace*'.

Latin	English
Dies irae, dies illa	Day of wrath and doom impending,
solvet saeclum in favilla	David's word with Sibyl's blending
teste David cum Sybilla	Heaven and earth in ashes ending
Dies irae, dies illa	Day of wrath and doom impending
Quantus tremor est futurus,	Oh, what fear man's bosom rendeth
quando Judex est venturus	When from heaven the judge descendeth
cuncta stricte discussurus.	On whose sentence all dependeth.

Tuba Mirum

The orchestra and chorus are mute. Nothing is heard but the trumpet. The trumpet sounds as a single note played softly. To suggest the approach from a vast distance Verdi makes use of four extra trumpets behind the scenes. The trumpet calls grow increasingly stronger. Verdi keeps to the dark ambience of A flat minor throughout and generates this entire passage from one cell, expanding the semi-quavers into triplets where appropriate. When the long-awaited tonic chord is reached full brass, bassoons and timpani weigh in, giving the music an almost thematic substance. The bass soloist rejoins with '*Tuba mirum spargens sonum*' over full orchestral chord to which chromatically descending strings give the feeling of a universe falling apart. The Chorus echo his words while the air resounds with brass fanfares.

Latin	_English_
Tuba mirum spargens sonum **per sepulchra regionum,** **coget omnes ante thronum**	**Wondrous sound the trumpet flingeth,** **Through earth's espulchres it ringeth,** **All before the throne it bringeth.**
Mors stupebit et natura, **cum resurget creatura,** **judicanti responsura.**	**Death is struck and nature quacking,** **All creation is awaking,** **To its Judge an answer making**

Liber scriptus

The '*Liber scriptum*' was originally set as a choral fugue. However, in the spring of 1875 Verdi decided to turn that into a solo for his mezzo-soprano, Maria Waldmann. He did not include it in the Paris performances of that year, chiefly because, as he told the singer: "The public's first impressions are always terrible, and even should this piece make its effect, people would say, 'It was better as it was before". The mezzo-soprano solo had to wait until mid-may 1875, and the London-audience was the first to hear it. It is a superb example of declamatory melody articulated in three massive periods each following the tercet design of the poem. *'Liber scriptus proferetur'*—is a typical example of late Verdian, three-limbed melody. The first two phrases are identical, both featuring the rising fifth like a finger raised in warning, followed by a menacing death-figure on the timpani. The third phrase is equal in length to the other two combined yet it evolves so freely that all sense of regularity is obliterated. *'Judex ergo cum sedebit'* is an expanded counterpart of the first period, introduced by a blazing brass chord in the major—the searching-light gaze of the Supreme judge from whom nothing is hid.

Latin	*English*
Liber scriptus proferetur,	Lo! the book exactly worded,
in quo totum continetur,	Wherein all hath been recorded,
unde mundus judicetur.	Thence shall judgement be awarded.
Judex ergo cum sedebit,	When the Judge his seat attaineth,
quidquid latet apparebit,	And each hidden deed arraigneth,
nil inultum remanebit.	Nothing unavenged remaineth.

Quid sum miser

In the *'quid sum miser'* attention is turned on the individual sinner. It is a trio for soprano, mezzo-soprano, and tenor. Two clarinetes and a bassoon open the musical discourse with a cadential figure, like an idiogram of grief that recurs like a refrain. As often with Verdi, it does not reveal its full identity at the outset. Not till the third occurrence does it acquire the F sharp that gives it its unique poignancy. So too with the intervening vocal entries. The mezzo soprano's first phrase, a setting of the first line of the tercet, is brought to a cadence after four bars. When she resumes it to the remaining two lines, it flowers into something like a theme. Next, the tenor takes it up the other two voices joining in, to produce a still longer variant. A third and final period begins an unaccompanied trio, in the relative major, but like the preceding two returns inexorably to the same cadential phrase of clarinets and bassoon. In this way, a tentative opening has solidified into a species of bar-form with refrain. Another binding element is the purling bassoon pattern which forms the instrumental bass throughout. The coda alternates major and minor with a sweetness worthy of Schubert; but the sense of consolation is precarious, and the soloists are left repeating one by one the three questions on rising levels of pitch. This section ends suspended like a question, which is answered brutally in the next one.

Latin	English
Quid sum miser tunc dicturus?	**What shall I, frail man, be pleading?**
Quem partonum rogaturus,	**Who for me be interceding,**
cum vix justus sit serucus?	**When the just are mercy needing?**

Rex tremendae

The 'Rex tremendae' begins with a brutal answer to the previous section: A descending arpeggio from the chorus basses, backed by the lower instruments in unison and a tremolando of upper strings. Tenors repeat the words in a subdued mutter. But the suppliants will not be silenced. The bass launches a contrasting idea ('Salva me fons pietatis'), featuring the rising sixth with its association with the concept of love. The two themes, Rex tremendae and Salva me, engage in conflict. At first the soloists' phrases are isolated each in a different key, linked only by the soprano's cries of 'Salva me'; subsequently they join together, one answering the other. Finally, just when it seems that the battle is lost, a fragmented statement of the bass idea('Salva me fons pietatis') rises like a cloud of incense from the chorus basses to culminate in a cadential variant over rich and mellow harmonies. Verdi had a way of using male choruses enhanced with brass to strengthen certain dramatic moments. The chorus usually expressed wrath at such moments. 'Maledizione' means 'a curse'. One example is Verdi's opera 'La forza del destino', where the chorus invokes a curse on anyone nearing a certain sacred cave.

Latin	English
Rex tremendae majestatis,	King of majesty tremendous,
qui salvanos salvas gratias,	Who dost free salvation send us,
Salva me, fons pietatis.	Fount of pity, then befriend us.

Recordare

The '*Recordare*' is a duet for soprano and mezzo-soprano. The two women discourse gently on a swaying 4/4 melody, announced by the mezzo-soprano over a velvet cushion of sustaining horns, flute and clarinet and a murmur of lower strings. Only a dotted figure in the upper woodwind remains to remind us of the soprano's insistent '*salva me*' from the preceding prayer. There are two episodes, neither of which depart very far from the main theme, and a tranquil coda, with some imaginative two-part writing for the voices.

Latin	English
Recordare, Jesu pie,	Think, kind Jesu, my salvation
quod sum causa tuae viae;	Caused thy woundrous incarnation;
ne me perdas illa die.	Leave me not to reprobation.
Quaerens me sedisti lassus,	Faint and wary thou has sought me,
redemisti crucem passus;	on the cross of suffering bought me,
tantus labor non sit cassuc.	Shall such grace be vainly brought me?
Juste Judex ultionis,	Righteous Judge, for sin's pollution,
donum fac remissionis,	Grant thy gift of absolution,
ante diem rationis.	Ere that day of retribution.

Ingemisco

The Tenor begins '*Ingemisco*' with an arioso suggesting helpless groaning, but he takes heart with the beginning of the movement proper, ('*Qui Mariam absolvisti*')—a rare case in Verdi of a compressed sonata design with two distinct themes, in tonic and dominant respectively. The reason for this becomes clear when we reach the second of them ('*Inter oves locum praesta*'). The oboe and tenor throw the gentle second theme back and forth. It gives a remarkably direct evocation of a shepherd piping to his flock on a mountainside. If the oboe suggests the pipe the shimmering violins rarified atmosphere, the dominant tonality serves to enhance the sense of height. Clearly, an orthodox reprise would ruin the effect. Instead there is a mere orchestral reminiscence beneath the tenor's closing lines, which in turn dovetails neatly into a cadence from the first theme, a duet for the two women, a tenor 'aria'.

Latin	English
Ingemisco tanquam reus;	Guilty now I pour my moaning,
culpa rubet vultus meus;	All my shame with anguish owning;
supplicanti parce, Deus.	Spare, o God, Thy suppliant groaning.
Qui Mariam absolvisti,	Through the sinful woman shriven,
et latronem exaudisti,	Through the dying thief forgiven,
mihi quoque spem dedisti.	thou to me a hope hast given.
Preces meae non sunt dignae,	Worthless are my prayers and sighing,
sed tu, bonus, fac benigne,	Yet, good Lord, in grace complying,
ne perenni cremer igne.	Rescue me from fires undying.
Inter oves locum praesta,	With Thy favoured sheep o place me,
et ab hoedis me sequestra,	Not among the goats abase me,
statuens in parte dextra.	But to Thy right hand upraise me.

Confutatis

In the *'Confutatis maledictis'* the bass soloist stands for both priest and suppliant, so embracing the two poles of sternness and entreaty on which the movement rests. Two themes alternate. The first epitomizes the internal conflict. Beginning *'Con forza'* ('powerfully') it consigns the accursed to their doom with octave leaps and abrupt orchestral gestures; then softens into a plea to be called among the blessed. The second theme (*'Oro supplex et acclinis'*) is purely lyrical, moving on a typical Verdian axis of C sharp minor-E minor and coming meltingly to rest in E major. But what first strikes the academically-minded listener is the blatant chain of parallel fifths with which it opens. Tovey, one of the most important of the Verdi biographers, took this to be a way of indicating total abjection, as though in an excess of humility the bass had forgotten the first rules of musical grammar. But the same device occurs in the Consecration scene of Verdi's opera *Aida*. More probably Verdi was aiming in both cases at an antique organum-like solemnity that antedates the rules of part-writing. The conflict continues, using elements of both themes. Than the second theme (*'Oro supplex et acclinis'*) returns unaltered save for a prolongation of the final bars. A codetta moves away towards E minor; but the bass's last note is covered by a final irruption of the *'Dies-irae-theme'*, leaping out, as it were, from behind a harmonic corner.

It is only a partial reprise; for before it manages even half the way for a full repetition it has already swung towards the region of B flat minor, approaching the next section with Wagnerian foreboding.

Latin	*English*
Confutatis maledictis,	When the wicked are confounded,
flammis acribus addictis,	Doomed to flames of woe
voca me cum benedictis.	unbounded,
Oro supplex et acclinis,	Call me, with Thy saints sorrounded.
cor contritum quasi cinis	Low I kneel, with heart submission,
gere curam mei finis.	See, like ashes my contrition,
	Help me in my last condition.

Lacrymosa

The tune of the '*Lacrymosa*' has its origins in a discarded duet for tenor and bass with male chorus from the opera *Don Carlos*, following the death of Posa. With its sombre scoring and disposition of voices and its B flat minor tonality, it is one of the most moving operatic laments ever written, which is why, now that modern research has enabled its reconstruction, several recent revivals of the opera have restored it. By comparison, the '*Lacrymosa*' is simpler in outline and more complex in detail. Just as Verdi had concluded

Aida with a slow cabaletta of the utmost plainness and regularity, so he rounds off this most wide ranging and tempestuous prayer of the *Requiem* with a movement whose main theme forms a period of thirty-two bars with a phrase pattern A-A-B-A With each successive phrase the tapestry becomes richer, embellished with counterpoint and an abundance of lamenting figures entrusted to voices as well as instruments. The last cadence is interrupted so as to lead into a twelve-bar coda, in the course of which the theme is broken down over a descending bass then rises to a climax taking the solo soprano over a high B flat. But this is not the end. A new pleading melody in G flat is sung by the four soloists, *'Pie Jesu, Domine, dona eis requiem'*. It is the palest shaft of light, soon to vanish as fragments of the opening melody treated in imitation take over the rest of the movement; but somehow the darkness has been softened. For the final bars, Verdi makes telling use of the full orchestra hushed, including bass drum. The *'Amen'* yields a cadence unknown to ecclesiastical rules: a chord of G major, swelling and dying answered by orchestra alone with one of B flat.

Latin	**English**
Lacrymosa dies illa,	Ah, that day of tears and mourning!
qua resurget ex favilla,	From the dust of earth returning,
judicandus homo reus.	Man for judgement must prepare him;
Huic ergo parce Deus.	Spare, o god, in mercy spare him.
Pie Jesu, Domine,	Lord, all pitying, Jesu blest,
dona eis requiem.	Grant them Thine eternal rest.
Amen.	Amen.

3. OFFERTORIO (soloists)

A short introduction opens the *offertorio*: a rising figure in the cellos answered softly by woodwind. A brief motive of great significance is introduced by the strings and the tenor and Mezzo-soprano answer it. The *offertorio* proper begins with the bass taking this motive and developing it into a flowing melody. The tenor and mezzo soon join and in the ensuing terzet respond briefly to every utterance of the bass. The fear from the Pains of hell, *De poenis inferni,* is composed as a continuation of this flow of music. The terzet ends suddenly, with the soprano's entrance. She sings a high note which completes the last chord of the terzet—a chord that is no longer there—in a beautiful transition typical of the late Verdi—All is quiet while the soprano hovers alone in mid-space. A single violin begins playing the terzet melody, floating around the single tone of the soprano's. Then both, soprano and violin, shift a semi-tone downward. Only then does the soprano begin to sing, with what to many seemed one of the few absolutely operatic touches in the requiem, the *Signifer Sanctus Michael.* The other soloists join in and finish the melody with a peaceful cadence. A rising phrase from the bass leads to *Quam Olim Abrahae.* The *Quam Olim Abrahae* is usually set as a fugue. Verdi follows that tradition half-heartedly and the fugue soon proves to be only a short fugato. This dies out quickly and in the following ambiance of shimmering *ppp* strings the tenor begins to sing the 'hostias'. It is a noble melody, the tenor standing out almost ritually, offering the sacrifice. The bass repeats him and then the other soloists join in, in a minor-key mid-section, remembering the dead. The tenor resumes the 'hostias' melody. The *Quam olim abrahae* fugato returns, and ends more fiercly this time, with a stress on *Promisisti*—'Thou didst promise'. A coda ends the *Offertorio,* with all four soloists singing the main melody which served a terzet at the beginning, tutti, and then throwing parts of it gently among them. Then only the strings remain. The melody, which took life from the strings' brief motive at the beginning, is gone back to that motive, shimmering as when it started, and brief. In silence all ends.

Latin	English
Domine Jesu christe, rex gloriae, libera animas omnium fidelium defunctorum de poenis inferni et de profundo lacu. Libera eas de ore leonis, ne absorbeat eas tartarus, ne cadant in obscurum, sed signifer sanctus Michael repraesentet eas in lucem sanctam. Quam olim Abrahae promisisti et semini ejus.	Lord Jesus christ, king of glory, deliver the souls of all the faithful departed from the pains of hell, and from the deep pit. Deliver them from the lion's mouth, lest hell swallow them up, lest they fall into darkness; and let the standard bearer, St. Michael, bring them into the holy light. Which Thou didst promise of old to Abraham and his seed.
Hostias et preces tibi, Domine, laudis offerimus. Tu suscipe pro animabus illis, quarum hodie memoriam facimus fac eas, Domine, de morte transire ad vitam. Quam olim Abrahae promisisti et semini ejus. Libera animas omnium fidelium defunctorum de poenis iferni. Fac eas, de morte transire ad vita.	We offer Thee, o lord, a sacrifice of praise and prayer; Accept them on behalf of the souls we commemorate this day. And let them, o lord. pass from death to life. Which thou didst promise of old to Abraham and his seed. Deliver the souls of the faithful from the pains of hell. Let them pass from death to life.

4. SANCTUS (double chorus)

The shortest part in the whole requiem, Verdi's sanctus is, as one
novelist described it, 'A dance of the children of light'. Apart from a
powerful beginning, all is gaiety and laughter here. The main theme
is almost a dance tune and when the more lyrical mid-section arrives
(to the words 'Pleni sunt coeli') it is only the Chorus that takes a
calmer stride. The strings and woodwind continue to hop around
like children mad with joy. Soon the Chorus returns to its previous
manner, and in a chromatic blaze of brass serving as the fastest coda
ever the whole Sanctus is over.

Latin	English
Sanctus, sanctus, sanctus	Holy, holy, holy,
Dominus deus sabaoth.	Lord of hosts,
Pleni sunt coeli	heaven and earth
et terra gloria tua.	are full of thy glory.
Hosanna in excelsis.	Hosanna in the highest!
Benedictus qui venit	Blessed is he that cometh
in nomine Domini.	in the name of the Lord.
Pleni sunt coeli	Heaven and earth
et terra gloria tua.	are full of thy glory.
Hosanna in excelsis.	Hosanna in the highest.

5. AGNUS DEI (soprano, mezzo-soprano, chorus)

Soprano and Mezzo-soprano begin singing *Agnus dei* in octaves, without accompaniment from the orchestra. The Chorus repeats their melody. Then both women sing the same theme again, but now in a minor key, with orchestral accompaniment. The chorus again repeats but in a major key. The soprano and mezzo sing again the same melody in major, now accompanied by flutes alone which lead to an answer from the chorus in major, *Dona eis*, with strings hovering magnificently from above. The chorus then repeats *dona eis* twice answered by the women—throwing a sudden shadow over the music's peaceful ambiance, but the soprano and mezzo quickly interpret it in a major key and the *Agnus dei* ends peacefully.

Latin	English
Agnus dei,	Lamb of god,
qui tollis peccata mundi,	who takest away the sins of the
dona eis requiem.	world,
	Grant them rest.
Dona eis requiem sempiternam.	Grant them eternal rest.

6. LUX AETERNA (mezzo-soprano, tenor, bass)

The 'Lux aeterna' begins with the mezzo singing above the light tremolo strings, shifting keys uneasily and creating a feeling of peace combined with just a touch of doubt. When the mezzo finishes singing the bass enters with *Requiem aeternam*—in minor key, with dark accompaniment from the orcherstra. The tenor and mezzo try to answer calmly to this but he bursts on them again with *Requiem aeternam*. Soon all three soloists join in unaccompanied terzet, *et lux perpetua luceat eis* ending in major. Then the bass returns to the *Requiem aeternam*, with even fiercer accompaniment from the orchestra. The mezzo escapes from this with a fluttering *arioso*, like a soul escaping from the fear of death. The bass repeats her melody and all three soloists join in to end the melody peacefully, stressing repeatedly *In aeternum*. Again, they become an unaccompanied terzet, in *Cum sanctic tuis* and *Quia pius est*. A short coda ends this part, with the soprano floating in with *Lux aeterna* from above, while bass and tenor answer from below, darkly, like a soul floating in the light, above those who mourn the dead. The orchestra repeats this combination of contrasting elements, and brings the *Lux aeterna* to its end quietly.

Latin	English
Lux aeterna luceat eis, Domine, cum sanctis tuis in aeternum, quia pius es. Requiem aeternam dona eis, Domine, et lux perpetua luceat eis.	Let eternal light shine upon them, O lord, with Thy saints for ever, for Thou art merciful. Eternal rest grant them, O lord, and let perpetual light shine upon them.

7. LIBERA ME (soprano, chorus)

This is probably the most complicated part of the Requiem. Whoever heard all other parts of this piece will get immediate grasp of the psychological and musical references made here. It is all immensely sophisticated—and crystal clear: The solo soprano beginning *Libera me* with an almost personal supplication and continuing *Dum venerit* with an absolutely personal fear and the Chorus praying in the background create the most operatic scene in the Requiem. Then one gets a sudden appearance of the whole Opening scene of the *Dies irae*, with the Chorus descending ominously in the much longer than before text of *Calamitatis et miseria, dies magna et amara valde.* The soprano cries amidst this storm, and is swallowed in it. The storm soon subsides into terrible silence. and then…'**Requiem**'. The opening bars of the very beginning return, this time *a cappella*', The chorus supplying its own accompaniment, the soprano soaring beautifully above it with the same theme the strings played back then. The 'a cappella' chorus develops the theme into a complicated musical canvas, giving new interpretations to every musical idea that appeared in the beginning bars of the Requiem, until it ends quietly with both chorus and soprano intoning 'Requiem' twice in a beautiful cadence. Into this peace the soprano bursts again with *Libera me.* Her melodic line falls quickly, as if swooning. Here begins the fugato that ends the Requiem. Mezzo-sopranos, Sopranos, Tenors and basses enter one after the other to join in this choral fugato, rythmic and sweeping, soon joined by the soprano-soloist pleading still above them.

The fugato slowly subsides and the Requiem draws to its end, peacefully, with the Chorus quietly intoning *Libera me* while the soprano prays the same words, isolated and to herself. Then Chorus and soprano together repeat twice *Libera me*, at last united and not contrasting. Thus ends the Requiem.

Latin

Libera me, Domine, de morte aeterna,
in die illa tremenda,
quando coeli movendi sunt et terra.

Dum venerit judicare saeculum per ignem.
Tremens factus sum ego, et timeo,
dum discussio venerit atque ven-
tura ira.

Dies illa, dies irae, calamitatis et misariae,
dies magna et amara valde.

Requiem aeternam dona eis, Domine
et lux perpetua luceat eis.

English

Deliver me, o Lord from everlasting death
on that dreadful day,
when the heavens and the earth shall be moved.

When thou shalt come to judge the world by fire.
I quake with fear and I tremble,
awaiting the day of account and the wrath to come.

That day, the day of anger,
of calamity, of misery,
that great day and most bitter.

Eternal rest grant them, o lord,
and let perpetual light shine upon them.

Mozart Requiem

By Toniann Scime, with permission

The Requiem Mass, K. 626, is one of the last of Wolfgang Amadeus Mozart's catalogued pieces. In July of 1791, Mozart had already been commissioned to collaborate on *Die Zauberflöte* with, his good friend Emanuel Schikaneder. According to the New Grove Mozart, this commission reportedly gave Mozart much pleasure; he enjoyed collaborating with Shikaneder, and Mozart's frequent letters to his wife Constanze reveal a happy frame of mind, full of affection and teasing banter concerning his pupil and family friend, Franz Süssmayr. It was during this time that Mozart was approached by a mysterious stranger clad in grey and asked to compose a requiem, all in the utmost secrecy. This "stranger' has been identified as Count von Walsegg zu Stuppach, an amateur musician who wanted to pass this work off as his own. According to Ivor Keys, this was "an innocent diversion' of the Count's, a parlor trick where, in his home, the Count would pass out parts of anonymous music to hired professional performers. Guests would then have to guess the composer, and some were courteous enough to suggest the Count. But Count Stuppach's motives are in truth unknown.

Mozart began working on the *Requiem* immediately., but *Die Zauberflöte*, another opera, a concerto, and a cantata kept him busy. His letters from this period continue to be high-spirited and enthusiastic. However, he took seriously ill at the end of November, 1791, and was treated by two leading Viennese doctors, Closset and Sallaba. Mozart's wife, Constanze, and her younger sister Sophie nursed him back to health slowly. On December 3, he seemed greatly improved and the next day a few of his friends gathered to sing over with him parts of the unfinished *Requiem*. But just before one AM, on December 5, 1791, Wolfgang Amadeus Mozart died.

Peter Shaffer's play and subsequent movie, *Amadeus*, have perpetuated quite a few myths surrounding Mozart's death and the *Requiem* in particular. In the film, Court Composer Antonio Salieri is credited with commissioning the Mass from Mozart, dressed in a costume that he had once seen Wolfgang's by then-dead father Leopold wear. Salieri allows his hatred and jealousy to overcome his love of God and takes advantage of Mozart's illness to drive him to his death—but not before Mozart has completed most of the Mass. Salieri's plans are thwarted when Constanze snatches the unfinished *Requiem* away from his clutches. The success of this Academy Award—winning movie has unfortunately validated these myths to the point that they are taken as truth by laymen. In reality, Salieri was simply a contemporary of Mozart's, and reportedly enjoyed his work hugely (Keys).

Another myth hints that Count Stuppach secretly had Mozart poisoned, but this is highly improbable. Mozart was at first diagnosed as having died from "severe miliary fever". On the medical authority of his two Viennese doctors, Closset and Sallaba, it was decided that he had in fact died of "rheumatische Enzfindungsfieber ", rheumatic inflammatory fever. His health had not recently been good, and although a young man when he died at the age of thirty-six, this fever seems perfectly consistent with the symptoms recorded (swelling limbs, high fever, paralyzing pains in the joints, and severe head-aches) and Mozart's medical history. One previous supposition of the cause of death, uraernia following a lengthy spell of kidney dis-ease, however, might make for an explanation of the hallucinations Mozart suffered during his last days, Furthermore, this might explain the somewhat abnormal attitude Mozart had towards the *Requiem*; he was, by some reports, obsessed with it.

Mozart had completed certain parts of the *Requiem* before his death; the whole *Introitus* (though without actually writing out the instru-mental parts of the *Kyrie*), and the vocal parts, bass, and leading instrumental parts of the *Dies Irae* up until its final section, the *Lac-rimosa*, which was there (incomplete) only to the eighth bar. He also wrote out the vocal parts, bass, and some of the violin for the *Dom-ine Jesu* and the *Hostias*. The rest was left unfinished.

When Wolfgang Amadeus died, his widow Constanze was fearful of losing the commission for the *Requiem*; only fifty ducats had origi-nally been advanced. She first turned the score over to one Joseph Eybler, who had attended Mozart assiduously during his illness and for whom Mozart had written a recommendation for the post of Kappellmeister. Eybler began by completing the orchestration of the *Dies Irae*, quite respectably, but stopped at the *Confutatis*; at this point, he would have needed to begin "composing" where Mozart left off.

The *Requiem* was then completed by Franz Süssmayr. Süssmayr had helped Mozart on several operas; for example, he prepared a rehearsal score for *Die Zauberflote*, and was clearly qualified for the task. Why Mozart's widow Constanze did not choose him for the completion in the first place is completely left open to conjecture; many musical scholars have guessed and created rather bizarre sto-ries about the relationship between Constanze and Süssmayr. The two had long been friends; Wolfgang had left Constanze in Süssmayr's care at Baden while he was working on *Die Zauberflote*. Scholar Dieter Schickling has suggested (among other things) that Süssmayr may have been the father of Franz Xavier Wolfgang Mozart, Constanze's youngest son, who was born around this time. This accusation is heartily rebutted, however, by another Mozartean scholar, Joseph Heinz Eibl. These soap-opera sagas aside, a far more important question concerns how far Süssmayr truly knew Mozart's intentions for the rest of the Mass.

The Abbe Maximillian Stadler was called in by Constanze to put Mozart's manuscripts into order after his death. Thirty-five years later Stadler made two important statements concerning this matter in his "Defence of the Authenticity of Mozart's *Requiem*". (Vienna, 1826): 'The widow told me that there were some few leaves of music found on Mozart's writing desk after his death which she had given to Herr Süssmayr. She did not know what they contained, nor what use Süssmayr made of them. "...and Süssmayr did not have much more to do [in the completion than most composers leave to their copyists.' The first claim of Stadler's is likely; the second, very unlikely.

Additionally, Constanze's younger sister, Sophie, was in 1825 quoted (Nissen, 1825) by saying that "Süssmaier was there at Mozart's bed-side, and the famous *Requiem* lay on the bed-cover, and Mozart was explaining to him how he ought to finish it after his death." So the picture painted by Shaffer in *Amadeus* has some basis in the truth: instead of the jealous, almost demonic Salieri working through the night as Mozart grew closer and closer to death, there was in fact simply the devoted student Süssmayr.

Still, this question of the authenticity of the current completed *Requiem* Mass is somewhat undecided and must remain so, since no other information exists on the matter. Thus it will simply remain a subjective decision made on the part of each scholar as to how truly "Mozart" the *Sanctus, Benedictus,* and *Agnus Dei* are.

The *Requiem* Mass begins with the *Introitus,* and basset-horns as the treble line, sober and dignified, and violins underneath palpitating in a manner that conveys utter hopelessness; the chorus chants "unto Thee shall all flesh come' with an almost Handelian flavor. The climax of this piece, however, moves on to more passionate, chromatic tones. In the *Kyrie,* this passion continues and we are rushed forward to our doom, chanting "Christ have mercy". This chorus continues with what Keys calls "frightening intensity" through the *Dies Irae,* held for a moment at the trombone solo of *Tuba Mirum*; the florid trombone solo acting as the voice of human pleading on judgment day. These alternations flavor much of the *Rex Tremendae* and the *Recordae*; the *Rex Tremendae* is an intense cry of eternal suffering, while the *Recordae* has once more a more human sound, almost wistful and containing some hope in its pleas. The *Confutatis* encapsulates this alternating form, the tenors and basses sing of eternity and severity, while the light lilting sopranos and altos respond with some breath of hope. Under all, the strings are at times jarring and then sweet. The *Lacrimosa,* containing the last notes Mozart ever wrote, begins with haunting strings and vocal lines, ending in a dazzling crescendo "Amen".

The *Domine Jesu* resembles the *Kyrie* in the sense that one feels one is being catapulted forward into final judgment, with no time for further repentance. The *Hostias* has a slower, more contemplative mood, and the *Sanctus* promptly returns us once more to a chordal, Handelian mood, all fire and brimstone. Fittingly, the *Benedictus* finally gives a more forgiving and comforting message to the listener and sinner, imparting God's forgiveness. Its tone is somber and yet without pain or suffering. The vocal lines and orchestration themselves sound at peace—even celebratory in the final fugal section. The *Agnus Dei* serves in this Mass as a reminder of our everlasting devotion and duty to God, combining hellfire, suffering, pleading, Handelian fugal melodies, and finally, triumph.

Requiem in D Minor, K. 626
Wolfgang Amadeus Mozart
1756–1791

Requiem

Requiem aeternam dona eis, Domine,
et lux perpetua luceat eis, te decet hymnus,
Deus in Sion, et tibi reddetur votum in Jerusalem;
exaudi orationem meam, ad te omnis caro veniet.
Requiem aeternam dona eis, Domine,
et lux perpetua luceat eis.
Kyrie eleison, Christe eleison, Kyrie eleison.

Dies Irae

Dies irae, dies illa
solvet saeclum in favilla,
teste David cum Sybilla.
Quantus tremor est futurus,
quando judex est venturus,
cuncta stricte discussurus.

Tuba Mirum

Tuba mirum spargens sonum
per sepulchra regionum,

coget omnes ante thronum.
Mors stupebit et natura,
cum resurget creatura,
judicanti responsura.
Liber scriptus proferetur,
in quo totum continetur,
unde mundus judicetur.
Judex ergo cum sedebit,
quidquid latet apparebit,
nil inultum remanebit.
Quid sum miser tunc dicturus?
quem patronum rogaturus,
cum vix justus sit securus?

Rex Tremendae

Rex tremandae maiestatis,
qui salvandos salvas gratis,
salva me, fons pietatis.

Recordare

Recordare Jesu pie,
quod sum causa tuae viae,
ne me perdas illa die.
Quaerens me sedisti lassus,
redemisti crucem passus;
tantus labor non sit cassus.
Juste judex ultionis,
donum fac remissionis

ante diem rationis.
Ingemisco tanquam reus,
culpa rubet vultus meus;
supplicanti parce Deus.
Qui Mariam absolvisti,
et latronem exaudisti,
mihi quoque spem dedisti.
Preces meae non sum dignae,
sed tu, bonus, fac benigne,
ne perenni cremer igne.
Inter oves locum praesta,
et ab hoedis me sequestra,
statuens in parte dextra.

Confutatis

Confutatis maledictis,
flammis acribus addictis,
voca me cum benedictis.
Oro supplex et acclinis,
cor contritum quasi cinis,
gere curam mei finis.

Lacrimosa

Lacrimosa dies illa,
qua resurget ex favilla
judicandus homo reus.
Huic ergo parce Deus,
pie Jesu Domine, dona eis requiem! Amen!

Domine Jesu

Domine Jesu Christe! Rex gloriae!
Libera animas omnium fidelium defunctorum
de poenis inferni et de profundo lacu!
Libera eas de ore leonis,
ne absorbeat eas Tartarus,
ne cadant in obscurum:
sed signifer sanctus Michael
repraesentet eas in lucem sanctam,
quam olim Abrahae promisisti, et semini ejus.

Hostias

Hostias et preces tibi, Domine, laudis offerimus.
Tu suscipe pro animabus illis,
quarum hodie memoriam facimus:
fac eas, Domine, de morte transire ad vitam,
quam olim Abrahae promisisti, et semini ejus.

Sanctus

Sanctus, sanctus, sanctus Dominus Deus Sabaoth!
pleni sunt caeli et terra gloria tua.
Osanna in excelsis.

Benedictus

Benedictus, qui venit in nomine Domini.
Osanna in excelsis.

Agnus Dei

Agnus Dei, qui tollis peccata mundi,
dona eis requiem.
Agnus Dei, qui tollis peccata mundi,
dona eis requiem sempiternam.
Lux aeterna luceat eis, Domine,
cum sanctis tuis in aeternum, quia pius es.
Requiem aeternam dona eis, Domine,
et lux perpetua luceat eis.

**Ho Honoré de Balzac (1799–1850)—Original name Honoré Balssa
noré de Balzac (1799–1850)—Original name Honoré Balssa**

0-595-26534-0

Printed in the United Kingdom
by Lightning Source UK Ltd.
101980UKS00001B/240